ALSO BY NICK MAY

Megabelt

Minutemen

MOLECRICKET

a novel

N<small>ICK</small> M<small>AY</small>

ISBN13: 978-1-63199-615-3
Library of Congress Control Number: 2014954560

Eucatastrophe Press
P. O. Box 841
Gonzalez, FL 32560

An Imprint of Energion Publications

eucatastrophepress.com

1

Man born of woman is of few days and full of trouble. Our farm, which spanned a great stretch of County Road 1 northwest to Indian River, was in disarray, and I reckoned since it was tended to by men, it must have also shared his fate. My fate. One I had grown slowly more accustomed to since my blighted day of birth, twelve years before. All my friends were born in war; made to greet an earth that moaned and groaned and grit its teeth. We were all just waiting around to see which way God was going to take us—whether it be by famine or by sword—while in the meantime, we worshipped him.

We were probably doing something closer to playing God than worshipping him when my older brother, Aaron, and I went on that killing spree. But in our defense, we were also trying to protect ourselves from what those creatures would inevitably become. Aaron said those caterpillars were going to turn into mole crickets right fast if we didn't kill them quick. He said the fields would be in for the hell beating of a lifetime before long. Now, I wasn't too keen on the evolutions of insects and what turned into what as much as he was. Aaron had gone to Miss Melba's science class at the Indian River School about once a week since he turned eleven or twelve, and I figured he had come to know as much as she did by then. Regardless, I had seen the hell a mole cricket could wreak on a field left undefended, and it wasn't pretty.

We reasoned that if we didn't get those caterpillars slaughtered before Easter, the horses weren't going to have shit to eat or make for the rest of springtime. We would have to move them to the hay reserves before school let out. We would be out of luck before Thanksgiving, and the horses would be dead by Christmas. Aaron and I thus decided to fashion up a handsome mess of leaf boats; a dang armada of right fine ships to carry the slaughtered carcasses of those caterpillars down the ditch that ran along County Road 1. Hell of a somber sight that was, but we had to do it. Then before you knew it, there we were, sitting on top of dead leaves on top of sand however many weeks after we had done the deed, and there wasn't a single horse or head of bovine left in the entire county (save for on our farm). Everywhere we went, it was like Aaron and I had called down the plagues of the Exodus on Indian River, by the way folks looked at us. No one had ever seen anything like what happened. For every caterpillar we killed, damned if there weren't ten mole crickets that popped up in its place, and all I heard from all those angered souls in all those cold sweat dreams was "Thanks for nothin', Moses Cotton ..."

Of course, it wasn't a thing at all if not the rash attempt of a couple boys to flex their misguided belief in their own situational omnipotence, but God is not mocked, and we worshipped him with all the more sincerity after that.

"A wicked people, destined for wicked tidin's," Pastor Obis would say, slamming his great ape hand down on his Word like a brimstone gavel calling a case in the courts of Hell. He was more than intent on the reason for our plight being the sinful indulgences of someone (or everyone), without ever implicating his own parish. That warm blanket of ignorance cast over our family and others during those regular encounters was enough to keep suspicions elsewhere. I even warmed up to it myself sometimes and felt glorious and treacherous all at once. Anonymity was a pitched tent on a perilous slope. Aaron didn't seem to care much either way. He thought Obis was horse shit.

Aaron's god was the god of indifference. His pastor and parish—brooding solitude. He wasn't devoid of his own pleasures, though. And he paid real dear for them from time to time. Aaron would go run off at night every now and again for a bit of fun with his cohorts (the few of them that were too young to die in the jungle), and they would get to wandering up the road, drinking and throwing dice. Well, he would get his fill of that and come back just before the sun would come up, drunker than hell and smelling like a latrine. Momma would be waiting real patient for him right there on the porch. She would have been sitting there since the witching hour, intent on reaching that euphoric rage, induced by the look on his face when he would come stumbling up the red clay drive to see her sitting there in the moonlight like a black banshee queen. It always started with a beating. It ended in fable.

I never heard as much as a peep from Aaron about what occurred after Momma would drag him off—both of them pissed as snakes—into the woods of the back pasture. I only knew as far as I could imagine about what went on out there, but thanks to Momma's own bit of ongoing ghastly folklore, there wasn't anything too hard to believe. One story she told on occasion still creeped the bejesus out of me. There was a narrow corridor, strewn in length with pine needles, and ages deep. It started in the young tree line at the base of the back pasture and drove a darkening spike, straight and true, all the way into the planted trees of the mill lands and beyond. To a place where eyes could no longer tell its integrity but could assume it must carry on that way for years into some other realm or untouched civilization.

Neither of us was man enough to go and venture too far down it after learning where Momma claimed it led. Momma had employed this device early on, saying a man lived deep in the woods at the end of the path; a man of terrible power who would judge our sins and hand out punishment with ruthless and unbiased appointment. Aaron would return from those late nights and early mornings looking red as a dog's dick and far too docile. I would eye him down and he would pretend not to see me. He would never tell me where they had gone to, but I had my bets.

Far as The Man in the Woods, I had hoped he was just a metaphor for penitence. Maybe he was something like Daddy's gargoyle; this old chewed up monster doll that looked like he would fit right nice way up a mile high on one of those Nazi churches across the sea. Daddy kept it sitting eye-level on the front pasture gatepost to remind the brothers and sisters to close up the fence behind them. It worked, and so did The Man in the Woods, but my brother was born bent on subversion, so it didn't much matter how authentic Aaron thought (or knew) he was. If The Man in the Woods was real, Aaron had met Him.

When Aaron and I were lucky enough to stray our minds from those proper nightmare yarns that Momma liked to spin, we were farming. That was most recently representative for making preparations to put a roof on the new barn, the front end of which was catty-cornered to our tin-roofed house, and faced south to County Road 1. Our house shared the same view facing west as the road cut a diagonal border between our farm and ten or so other houses tip-toeing into Indian River, bringing our front pasture to a sharp point all those acres out. Though the great and mighty structure of the new barn was without a cover, Daddy hadn't been reluctant to fill it prematurely with the remaining horses of those who were in good standing with their debts. Truth be told, Aaron and I figured he was just anxious to make good use of the space. I liked to imagine the man, Noah, acting in a similar way with his creatures years before his vessel was completed, shuffling about, aiming desperately to position rhinos and penguins inside unfinished stall spaces with only one or two sides, just to get a picture of how it should look. Sometimes, if I squinted my eyes tight as I could while still leaving enough space to see, I could almost picture we were building an ark of our own out there in front of the house.

The walls of the barn itself had been raised some years before. I was five or so, which seemed to be long enough ago to turn those once freshly hewn and cured pine panels to a neglected shade of sun-sapped gray. It was an image, when held against the multicolor, striped canvas backdrop of the old barn just to its right and rear, that testified of its own adventitiously spurned youth. The old barn had gone its entire lifespan without the requisite manual labor of an applied tin roof. For some reason, the austerity of the ancient edifice was broken only by a stretched canvas roof with ranks of faded color. I had inquired of Daddy why it looked so queer and he swore not to know, claiming it was there since before him, but it was most certainly the reason he, alas, decided to build the new one. Now a good half-decade older, that pale, roofless structure of the new barn had—by overzealous adoption—become the town square of our farm, and by extension, the center of Indian River itself.

On any given day, one could easily expect to find an array of miscellaneous townsfolk milling about the property, doing business they might just as well perform elsewhere, but instead preferred to do on the farm. All manner of enterprise would present itself; from trading produce, buying and selling horses, land and automotive parts, borrowing Daddy's tools to repair a saddle or sharing outside gossip with the brothers and sisters (who never seemed to complain, given their exclusive lack of social intercourse).

"Marlin's taken to fillin' his store with more of them bewitched sundries, the way he did durin' the drought."

"Prophet's name! That man's draggin' us all to hell!"

"Potions and demonic heirlooms. Filth!"

There would be an audible hum and buzz of conversation amongst the unfinished barn and lands as early as six in the morning, when familiar trucks would come gargling up the red clay drive past the main gate, which was always left open and, as a result, had become permanently overgrown with foliage and weathered to an end that made its extended arm an indefinite fixture, welcoming patrons both warmly and hospitably for all time.

At least once a month, a couple of poor souls would come traversing through the gate to perform a type of rather non-conventional trade; a trade of spirit. We were nothing close to Catholic, but Pastor Obis (who had moved onto the farm ten years ago with his daughter, Sarah, after becoming a widow man), seemed to do a great deal of pardoning people of their various transgressions. They would come across the threshold of that unlikely parsonage just the same as any other sad patron in need of maintenance or good news or companionship, while unknowingly seeking absolution. And they often found it at Obis' camp, just beyond the faded rainbow of the old barn, where he and his sweet daughter originally dwelt alone.

Over the years, those souls would stumble onto the farm, sometimes having heard a preacher lived there; sometimes knowing nothing at all. They would descend on that place—always in twos—as haplessly as downy flake, innocently devoid of any knowledge of their own depravity. But in as oft an instance as any actual flakes or shake of snow had ever befallen that farm since the beginning of the world (which was never since I'd had eyes to see it), and in as common a case as any of that cold manna had ever seen fit to stick to our afflicted piece of earth, so was the number of those compelled to stay.

The Lord had seen fit to bring us eight, not including Daddy, Momma, Aaron or me. I wasn't privy to know exactly what it was that stayed their interest in our farm, or our God, but, according to Obis, Daddy and Momma, they were our brothers and sisters, and we weren't to treat them any different. I hadn't ever expressed it to anyone at all, but it always puzzled me a spell that Daddy's natural disposition hadn't ever quite matched his implicit standard of benevolence. In damn near all other realms of his life

7

and practices, to the utmost of his being, every bit of his person painted him a man of little patience, especially with the likes of beggars and heathens. Yet for all his pedantic inclinations, there could be found within him—in the most unexpected of all times—an unabashed charity for such people.

Most recently it had been Mattie and Kenzie. They were kin to each other; twin brother and sister in their twenty-somethings. They had come to the farm, flaming red-haired orphans with a propensity for labor. Despite their apparent differences, it was right hard to tell them apart from a good ways off. They were both hearty creatures, and one was definitely weightier than the next, but you couldn't ever quite tell which. They were often more reserved than the rest of the brothers and sisters but commanded a startling efficiency between the two of 'em.

Just prior to that had come Ms. Dottie and Walter. Both of which were somewhere between eighty-five and ninety, if I had to wager. They weren't at all kin to one another but were both elderly and arrived in tandem, which sometimes gave the impression that they were either relative or nuptial. The truth was, however, that they weren't even friends. Dottie, a seasoned but cold woman, often spent untold hours sitting beside the dinner table in our house with Momma and whoever, spinning bitter words about Walter and claiming him to be a fool. On top of that, she never missed a chance to say how loose Sarah Obis was, neither.

"Just look at the way she parades that harlot's body of hers in front of the men; with her breasts proud and her legs unfurled. By the Prophet, it's a wonder they don't use her to hold train cars together on the River Line," she would say while doing a crossword, looking mild as ever and twice as sweet with her blue hats, her Sunday dresses, and her powder-soft wrinkles.

Walter might have been the complete and polar contradiction of the woman and her assertions of him. A thin, bald man and hard of hearing, he spent the better part of his days outdoors, patiently moving his seat in mid-sentence to be as close to Pastor Obis as possible. He was given to desperate attempts at holding conversations despite his near deafness. His words came loudly from a collapsed and toothless void that opened and closed furiously behind a thick curtain of coarse white hair, which, with every stuttered word, would rise and fall like the pistons of a speeding automobile.

Before them, it was Mamie. The only one to arrive on her own, Ms. Mamie was rounding forty-five in a fashion that made her look twenty years more. She was a robust woman and her hair was characteristic of a plain blonde Palomino tail, ponied in the back with a kerchief tied above, the way one might describe a Mennonite or someone from Amish country. She had devout faith in two things; God and Momma. She never left Momma's side since the start of her impressively static residency there on our farm. It reminded me of myself and how I had become with Aaron. Maybe that's why Mamie had always seen fit to curb my behavior before Momma ever could; cause she knew we were near about the same in emotional constitution, and because she knew Momma.

Second to come along were the cousins, Bill and Silas. They were discovered one night while having a spit just down the road. Daddy had heard cussing and carrying on so loud it woke him from sleep, which was a dang champion accomplishment. At first he suspected it might be Aaron. When it turned out to be the thick-built, fuzzy-headed, near-midget Bill and his younger, taller, and more awkwardly handsome cousin, Silas, Daddy attempted everything he could to get them to quit it. Turned out they were arguing about where to look for work. They were supposedly the sole supporters of their laid up set of mutual grandparents. Anyways, Daddy saw fit to bring them on the farm just to get them to quit hollering and carrying on. I often wondered if Bill and Silas weren't just a couple confidence men who got lucky on us with a well-rehearsed act. Didn't much matter to Daddy. He didn't pay them shit, and they were strong as a team of pissed oxen. They never spoke once more about their grandparents though.

The first to come and make their home amongst us, as I previously said, were Pastor and Sarah Obis. Pastor, who was easy half a hundred if he was five, was of course, a devout Wesleyan creature, mild in manner with a stern disposition and the large but well-manicured body of a right portly man. His black hair, which levied the sides of his prominent bald head, was wet-combed at the start of each day, and his glasses, two yellowed circles perched low on his nose bridge, were more decorative than serving in any practical way. A widowed man, he had known Daddy since boyhood.

His daughter, Sarah, was often saved for last in conversation, just as a sweet drink is savored slowly after hard labor and a good meal. She was the capstone of every man's daily toil. The rising steam from warm earth after heavy rain. She was never a day over eighteen, dark-complected and handsome in the face. Her body, horselike; long and muscular. Her chocolate mane fell from her head and poured over her square shoulders in every direction. Her breasts stood suspended and round, newly filled, in young skin—like clouds collecting rain but not yet pouring. They were immense, nearly ripened; desperate to be picked but still green and likely sour. She spoke not with her mouth, but with her eyes; black and green, like oil on the surface of dark water. All any man knew of her was desire, for none had breached the embattled walls of her truest soul. None dared approach the citadel of her father, lest they be killed with arrows.

The truth was, just as a woman under siege will eventually break, so a man's full retreat can often fail to thwart the advance of many lines. In the case of Aaron and Sarah Obis, I had witnessed the unthinkable on a daily basis. Aaron didn't give a whore's wages about girls then. I would watch how the two of them interacted with one another. She would come up on him as he worked and tap him real kind on the shoulder. He would barely turn enough to signal he wasn't interested, then she would march off into the pasture embarrassed as hell. And rightly so. Sarah Obis wasn't used to hearing "no" from men; especially ones that were younger than she. Boy, was she sweet on him, though. Even still.

As soon as Bill and Silas showed up, Pastor Obis had asked Daddy for his blessing to build a habitation on our land for others who might also come wandering. The modest camp he had previously prepared for himself and Sarah wasn't anything but a fancy lean-to set amidst several clothes lines and a small fire. It was an embarrassing establishment, even for farmers, and it wouldn't fit anyone else comfortably. So in yet another of Daddy's unforeseen spells of philanthropy, he agreed and even offered to help.

Together they fashioned up something at the top of the back pasture that looked like a hanger for midget planes. That was where they all lived together; the brothers and sisters. It was a simple accommodation, from what I had seen of the inside. There weren't any real walls save for the two half moons at the front and rear, and a third wall that fell lazily across them in a half-orbital fashion. It was a long building with rows and rows of bunk beds and a simple floor made from shipping pallets. Daddy had procured the design from the Army or Navy or whatever branch he had been a part of. Apparently he had stayed in something like one before his discharge. As for the building, we had just taken to calling it "the bunker".

Our own dwelling was nothing, save for an off-grade, ranch-style wooden structure boasting one level, a half-collapsed roof, and no shade given from nearby trees to protect it or us from the sun's spite (it did at least have four square walls). Daddy had thought more than once about having it bricked, especially after coastal storms paid hell to its framework, leaving it leaning two or three inches further over each time. But he never did more than talk about his intentions. To this day, a stranger might find himself wandering along County Road 1 and spy our ransacked house from beyond the gate, taking note of its unwavering proclivity for the ground and feel the sudden conviction, as any man should, to rush up and brace the cornerstone with all the might in his back, meaning to valiantly save the lives of those inside.

I reckon Daddy figured since the whole world was in shambles, there wasn't anybody who was gonna hold him accountable for fixing up his own ill-fated patch of it. I supposed he rationalized it every time he caught a crumpled picture of those Nazi towns way across the sea, all blowed to hell from a war twenty years old. He figured the world was intent on rebuilding faraway lands and starting new wars; not tending to Gulf towns or ending old ones. War wasn't something that touched us a great deal, so the folks of Indian River liked to imagine it was something one could simply elect to ignore. Our family, however, feared war itself would engender the revelation of our own foolishness someday by taking Aaron as fuel for its prodigious engine, so I watched him like a hot stove when I wasn't in his pocket.

"Prophet's name, ain't you got no fuggin' friends?" he would ask me sometimes. And I would do my best to leave him be, especially after cursing me so audaciously. I knew enough to figure boys his age occasionally needed to be left to their thoughts; to contemplate darker things like work and women and war.

Momma didn't agree with conscription, but Daddy always said work was work and dead was dead no matter how you use one to get to the other. In my opinion, Uncle Sam was the same kind of being as The Man in the Woods or the gate gargoyle (as far as the question of his existence went). Aaron played on indifference, acting as if he would move out as fast as a herd of Turks in a cloud of camel shit if he had to, but he hadn't ever tried to enlist early, neither. Not as far as I known. In a time when Indian River boys were lying about their age to go and shoot Japs (or whatever they were) around the far side of the world, Aaron and I were the only ones looking at pictures of cars and women and drinking peanut RC at Marlin's store. That is until they shut the farm up; until they cut the cross high up on the barn's forehead.

Aaron and I had come back up the road one night to find the gate pushed closed and locked up right nice with chains and Schlages. At first, and for damn near twenty minutes after, the sheer look of it all put us in a heightened state of confusion and unrest. The gate hadn't ever been closed. It was a strange happening that heralded the coming or going of an age, and we were rendered mentally and physically incapable of reckoning the gate's foreign posture or what it meant. Neither one of us had ever seen an image so dark and forlorn. From the outside it appeared as if our tribe had closed up shop and took to the road like circus folk. In an odd way (and almost with a refusal to simply climb over), we waited for a sign from God on how to approach or address such a mercurial event. We were hopelessly lost for procedure.

It had gotten a good bit darker then when Aaron finally decided we had best climb over for fear of one thing: if our assumption was wrong about Momma and Daddy and the brothers and sisters up and leaving town to join Barnum and Bailey, Momma would be right pissed a closed gate kept our asses out of those dinner chairs, so we moved. First thing either of us noticed upon scaling the farm's new battlements was the tip of the sword on the ground near the inside of the gate. Truth be told, it wasn't a real sword, but a trick the light from the barn played on the yard. It was cast by a familiar shape that had been fresh cut out of the new barn's face way up near the roof that wasn't there yet. A cross, no doubt near the same size of the one used to hang the Christ all those moons ago, had been carefully sawed out of those gray and unpainted slats. And a single illuminated work light shone through. It wasn't an image either of us would rightly soon forget. A neat circle of blonde pine dust covered the ground lightly inside the barn door, like a colossal carpenter bee had come and made his home high in the eaves. In the midst of the dust, leaning against the unfinished seal, stood the remnant, its arms outstretched like a man awaiting embrace, but without indulgence.

We stood stone-still where we had landed, observing that plot that seemed so alien to us then. The residual light from the barn cast a diminutive cone of perception over our narrow corner of the world as if to subtly remind us or allude to the truth that there lay much more beyond its yellowed reaches. But at that moment, we did not believe. The glow was only enough to convince us that our world had shrunk to the size of our front yard and the red clay drive, alone. All else were the black walls of eternity. It seemed to us that if God were to have turned on all of heaven's lights at once to reveal our relationship to the whole of Earth and Indian River, there would have been nothing but this mere sliver of our farm, floating fragmented and alone, in a galaxy of nothingness where Aaron and I had suddenly become a lot bigger, or a lot smaller. Night was full then. I looked over at Aaron for solace; for warmth, but all I remember of his face was that last bit of guiltless inquisition before we learned all the things we wished we had never known.

2

As soon as we neared the house close enough to realize all was accounted for, Aaron's face lit up, and he insisted we go in guns out like we were pissed as fire. He reasoned it would catch Daddy and Momma off guard, thus inciting our immediate forgiveness. I protested mildly but then almost immediately gave in. Aaron oversold from the first word and let out several strings of accusatory statements, standing posed in the doorway after having forced his way in. To aid Aaron, I growled once in mock frustration (for want of a better expression) as Momma and Daddy turned about to pause, shocked with faces frozen in a wild stupor. Momma's immediate reaction was to aim and slap Aaron where his sharp cheek met his stony neck. Aaron damn near hit the floor. Then she threatened us both with the woods (which was a virgin proposal for me). Soon as Daddy saw Momma had command of the situation, he turned around in his chair and went back to eating quietly.

We made haste to our seats after that and were shoveling tomatoes and rice into our heads with fluid dexterity before Daddy finally spoke up.

"No more hittin' the road after tonight. We're stayin' put," he said after one bite and before the next, like he would never speak on it again. He had paused to say it, with his spoon suspended half-mass between his bowl and his mouth. His eyes were glued on Momma's twin glazed ceramic goose salt and pepper shakers. Each bird was unpainted, and each held a scroll across its breast; one said "blue" and the other, "ribbon." I didn't know what in hell it meant, and I guess Daddy didn't either, as he locked onto them each night with even more intensity than the last, helpless to pull away as he ate and ate, often until his plate were clean or Momma took it upon realizing he had raised three or four empty spoons to his dried mouth.

Aaron and I hadn't moved a finger since he spoke. Instead, we turned to Momma with blank stares as if to elicit confirmation that times were truly as different as we had gathered. Without seeing us, she sat down across from Daddy and responded to our apparent confusion, knowing Daddy wouldn't.

"Those outside our gate are afraid," she said plainly. "The plague has stripped this town of its vocations." She took a single bite then set down her spoon and wiped her hand—front and back—on her apron. "This land is closed to the wretched ..." Momma took a drink of water and went on eating tomatoes. And that was that. Daddy had geese in his wide eyes. Aaron and I settled slowly back into our bowls which appeared to be devoid of all former color, taste and warmth when held against the last thirty seconds of speech that had occurred across that narrow, wooden plane. Oh yes, times were different indeed.

Thankfully for Momma and Daddy, there was a knock or two on the door as the thickness at the table had become straightways unbreathable.

"That'll be Virgil," Momma offered without looking up from her bites. Virgil was Pastor Obis' Christian name, and I only ever heard Momma and Daddy call him by it privately. He usually returned the favor by calling them Joe and Maya, which always felt wrong to me. Momma wiped her mouth and made for the stockpot on the stove which was set aside each night for the brothers and sisters. Daddy pushed back his chair and walked to the door with a spoon still in one hand, half re-tucking his shirt with the other. He opened and braced the door, which swung outward. It was the one tweak Daddy had made to our home in my twelve years that was anything close to a precautionary improvement. Someone in Indian River had become exhausted by coastal storms with hundred mile an hour winds blowing their doors in and had the bright idea to reverse the hardware, which everyone in those parts seemed to adopt. It was cheaper than bricking the house, which appealed to Daddy, but it had still yet to be tested, given that we hadn't had a proper storm since its installation. He seemed to be pleased with it, though Momma went on and on about how wrong it felt to enter a house like you enter a wardrobe.

I watched Pastor Obis' broad figure spill into the door like a thick caramel bubbling through a pie lattice. It was only after he had entered fully, and gave his apologies for being just late enough to disrupt dinner, that I noticed he had with him a guest. Daddy's spoon went back in his mouth as he closed the door behind and studied the stranger, unabashed. Aaron and I noticeably snapped to attention like dogs.

"Joe, Maya, this is Peter Langford." Pastor Obis poured to the side and revealed a young, clean-shaven negro man, near pygmy in stature and wearing two pieces with the third about his shoulder. "Mr. Langford arrived earlier this evenin'." Pastor Obis smiled.

As the short man removed his houndstooth fedora, he spoke with such warmth and civil candor that the very walls of our house retched with nervous disagreement.

"Wonderful," he started, racking his hat and coat on his left arm and extending the other to Daddy for a shake. "So very pleased and delighted to finally meet all of you." Daddy took damn near thrice as long to oblige as the short man had taken to offer his small hand. Finally, after a dang age, and with much palpable hesitation, Daddy grasped the short man with his leather paw, and that quick-formed, clandestine ball of tightly-bound tension exploded simultaneously with almost audible declaration. Daddy withdrew the spoon again and clenched it low with his free hand.

"Have you waited long to?" Momma asked with thinly veneered derision as she relinquished the stockpot to Pastor Obis.

"Pardon?" The short man smiled greatly with his white teeth bearing a stark contrast to his midnight skin.

"Have you waited long to meet us?" Momma clarified. The short man delayed a brief second before his clean, Yank tone found words again.

"In my travels, I'm always happy to come into a home full of welcoming faces. And I heard more and more of your family the closer I neared Indian River."

"Oh?" Momma asked.

"People say your farm receives unerring direction from some unseen entity during these lost and despondent days." Obis shared strange looks with Daddy as the short man gripped low on the burly flank of Pastor Obis' bicep. "But now I see with my own eyes where your help comes from! How fortunate to have a man of such wisdom among you! The letters did not do your shrewdness a proper justice." he smiled and slapped Pastor Obis heartily on the small of his back.

"Well," Momma started, in what I hoped would be a saltless response, "with any proper stretch of time, Pastor Obis would make you privy to the fact that he's nothin' more than a vessel. Our help comes from the Lord."

The short man smiled politely as Pastor Obis spoke up.

"Mr. Langford is a recoverin' agnostic," Obis smiled and laughed apologetically, desperately hoping to appeal to Momma and Daddy's more patient sensibilities.

"Not recovering," the short man corrected Obis, laughing. "Card-Carrying, I think is the term." he smiled with all his proud teeth, as if expecting to be accepted warmly. Daddy turned his back on the stranger and walked the spoon over to the empty bowl. Geese swam in his eyes.

"If by some saintly miracle, an angel of the Lord saw fit to bid you safely by the flamin' sword that blocks the way to this place, then he must have his own business with you," Daddy said, turning his head to Pastor Obis. "In his own home."

The short man deferred gently to Pastor Obis who smiled a thin smile and shuffled awkwardly.

"Right," Obis hesitated, situating the stockpot snuggly inside the cleft of a single, massive arm. "Well, Mr. Langford, we'd best keep makin' our rounds."

"As I said, it was very nice to have met you all," the short man added as Pastor Obis gathered him up and made for the door. Momma didn't speak. She only stood there as she had been. Aaron and I exchanged non-verbals as we absorbed what we could of the subliminal conditions. Daddy kept his back to our guests and stared evermore into the glazed geese, silently. The door opened and closed a final time without further warmth of a departing word from anyone. As soon as their voices could be heard fading down the steps, Momma piped up.

"Did you know about this?" she said, instantly eyeing us and making a regretful note that she had asked him then.

Daddy stood without a word and retreated straightways to the den. Momma gave Aaron and I each a once-over. She had let us in on too much already with the question. Dinner was unceremoniously finished. She snatched our bowls as we went on sitting there, waiting to see which of us was gonna be dumb enough to comment.

"Does Obis mean to keep him here?" Aaron questioned bravely. "Is he gonna be our brother?"

"Pastor Obis," Momma corrected him. "And I don't know. You're Daddy and Virgil—"

"—Pastor," I said beneath my breath, not expecting her to hear. Momma stopped and looked at me wildly for a long moment and then turned to the sink.

"—They'll need to discuss it properly with..."

Momma trailed off vacantly as she stood there (or rather, her form did) completely void of any convincing signs of life. It was like her soul had unzipped her skin and flown away into glory while we were all left unawares. Now only her shell remained, balanced there curiously, caressing those soapy dishes in long strokes, circular and careful.

"With who?" Aaron asked. Momma remained silent and still as she stared out the window above the sink and into the deepening black of the southern night. In an instant, the house had turned tomb-quiet, and the kitchen was a catacomb, cold and wet, that stretched and twisted between her and us. Each and every nook and room of the house suddenly became a sacred place where secrets lay buried away in stone coffers, almost dead but still breathing. The dark from the yard seemed to pervade Momma's face as if on window glass, and the pane before her bore no reflection of her likeness; only a deep pitch that seemed to seep steadily in but failed to breach our house fully. She looked down briefly before she snapped to and awakened with reins again.

"...Each other," she returned in almost a whisper. We had almost forgotten why she had answered. "He might remain here a few nights...but he most certainly will not stay!" She paused, then snapped. "None of it's your business anyhow. Chores, baths, The Word, then bed!" She yelled, shooing us once without a look.

There were more questions floating around my skull than I could remember having in a right long spell. I had gone to our room and briefly attempted to share my thoughts with Aaron, but he wasn't the type to do his mental meddling corporately.

"I'm going to sleep so I can escape you people for a few blessed hours," he said as he climbed to the top bunk and rolled into his sheets, still wearing his clothes and shoes. He did that often; slept full-on dressed. I wasn't sure if it was an expression of pure exhaustion or some sort of malformed modesty, but I had figured out on my own (upon attempting it myself as one of my first studies of Aaron) that the feeling of sheets wrapped around boots was about as wrong as an out-swinging door.

Aaron always managed getting to sleep without a bath, chore or prayer. I reckoned it was because he knew as well as I did Momma never cared much herself to have a look in on us after nine or so. To her, she was off clock after supper, unless she caught wind of one of us being out of the house past then. I reckoned I did a fair share of Aaron's more noticeable after-hour duties; ones that would have gotten him red-assed in the morning for neglecting, but he had never noticed once (or cared enough to give me thanks if he did).

My reflection against the thick, clouded slab of still bath water was the bile shade of greenish-brown from the mixture of Ivory and sick that the bodies of my family had accrued collectively throughout the previous couple days. I sunk low into the fragrant broth, the surface of which cut a strict line of offensive cold and stagnant warmth across the pits of my eyes, which welled with tame tears from the rising fumes of oil and clover. The residual heat in the basin had a better chance of being a result of Momma or Daddy's warm blood proximity than leftover from that clear and steaming spring that flowed, on brief, rare occasions, from the mouth of the faucet there. I had quite seldom in twelve years seen it for myself, but when I was fortunate enough to witness the chaste clarity of Adam's ale spilling furiously in steady streams; in a million scalding storms. Those three holy minutes alone were enough to usher in a heavenly host, bearing gifts of pleasure and brail skin and proud hairs that collectively bore the ability to mend souls and burn sins with mock-baptism of the purest sort. But the ability to give that isolated gift lay only with Momma or

Daddy. In other words, I was straightways cursed if I dared touch the faucet or release one drop of precious hot water.

I bore my questions unto God there in that shallow reservoir. Night after night. I didn't mind the conditions of the water. The thought of what survived there—of what my family left behind that could undoubtedly attach itself to me—never held my attention for any period of time. My mind often drifted to less realistic scenarios; ones that found me pretending I had just awoke in a foreign place without the ability to recognize it. I saw that small washroom as an alien world, and I imagined that even commonplace utilities like doorknobs, hinges and hand-towels were among a family of appliances whose functions I could not comprehend. I pretended not to wonder what lie beyond the door, or that I even had the option to break its seal. Instead, it would become my plight to freshly educate my virgin mind on the mechanics of things and plot my escape.

Even after the dampness had long gone out of my short hair, the questions remained. Strange ones. Even for me. None, however, that might traditionally pervade the wits of a young boy in the midst of tangible changes or perfect strangers, but of one who stood on the precipice of a toppling paradigm. These were questions birthed from a desire to reckon the hierarchy of a people. The place of Daddy. The place of men. The place of me. How did the short man, Mr. Langford, fit into the piecemeal mosaic of our farm? Where had Daddy and Obis been repositioned on the chain? Who pulled it? My whole world was shaped in the presupposition of my father's rank in relation to those above or below him. I placed my faith in his position as a means to assert my own someday; to interpret my own worth. My unerring dependence on his hierarchical orientation, when weighed against my neglect of all else, had fostered in me the truest dichotomy of faith and distrust. Who was I without him?

Upon returning to my room, I noticed Aaron had already managed to escape into sleep. His tanned and spotted arm protruded lazily from the top side of our bunk bed, as it did most nights. I reckoned it was the prerogative of a brother; of an older brother; an older brother of the '60s, to demand the top bunk and stay there until death. It was only right; an established hierarchy of our own, and I was made comfortable by it. I only wondered if it hurt to leave himself bent that way for any length of time.

For the time being, I put aside questions of oddities and returned to the familiarly dark and perilous wood of my twelve-year-old existence, which positioned me geographically on that most awkward border of child and man. My clothes were too small. Aaron's old ones were too big. The joints of all my bones jutted this way and that. I had new muscles, like baby teeth, cutting through my limbs, and all of it together likened me visually to a rope ladder with large knots and braided strands. The smell of me was new, but wrong, like one of Miles Beckins' Mexicans. Worst of all, most nights I would awake from sleep having done more than piss myself after dreaming about Ms. Claudette Colbert (or someone like her) in a milk bath, like the scene from *The Sign of the Cross* (which was burned into my brain since the night Aaron sneaked me into my first picture). When I asked Aaron what in hell was wrong with me, all he managed to do was make fun of me, paying careful attention to point out my knobby frame, my infinitesimal muscles and my unmatched skill for "spilling my kids" all over my bed. He didn't think I knew what it meant.

I should have known better than to ask Aaron Cotton such things in the first place. That's why I didn't speak a word to him of my newest adopted pastime. It seemed I had developed a particular habit for wandering late at night, after all my family had fallen prey to deep sleep and gone beyond any prospect of rousing. I would do my chores slow after dinner and take my time washing, allowing myself to drift deep into reflection of the day's gone-by affairs. After toweling off, I would take it upon myself to feed and water the farm hound, Charles. I supposed he was my hound, given that he was only truly survived by me alone. Momma would throw him old food or table scraps on occasion, which might have just barely been enough to keep him alive without me, but I had readopted him a while back after he had gotten years of stink on him and wrecked himself into a dirty mop; a sad departure from his former resplendence as a shiny Christmas pup. Oh, the foul stink on the poor dog. One touch of him and the stench would become you, overwhelming the pores with lupine oils and other horrors.

Things seemed to go that way quite often on the farm. Nothing was truly cast away, only abandoned. Animals migrated away from the house and made their homes in older structures like squatters in our little city. Toys went missing and remained hidden after play on distant mounds, never revisited. Tractors sunk low into warm blankets of tall grass, left equally unchecked, and disappeared for ages at a time. It was a menagerie of neglect; a boneyard of the Aggie-American Dream. If it was possible, the night tended to reveal those hidden things even more.

Those late evenings, after tending to Charles, I would steal away down the side of the unfinished barn and wander alone into the night. I had known of that spring since I was old enough to tread water. Aaron would teach me to swim out there on hot days in the middle of our chores when Daddy would head into town for errands. He would teach me to cannonball. The Freedom Spring, we called it. It was during those times that I developed an honest dread of the unknown; when I would dive with conviction into those royal depths and never feel the bottom. There, in the quiet reaches of cold water, I would fear to open my eyes, lest I see nothing below me, or worse, everything.

It was on one of those most recent crusades into the dark that I had first seen her there. I had become skilled at arriving just before she did most nights, usually with enough time to conceal myself atop that foreign, white oak amidst that sea of middle-aged pines way out beyond the bunker. All the bark of that choice branch, from my waist to as far as I could reach was stripped bare for all the waiting I had done in that tree from night to night. But the waiting was well and damn worth it, even if I knew I was going to hell for what I had seen there. The night was usually quiet. I often could see the orange light emitting from a single, caged bulb above the door of the bunker, still quite a ways off.

I would sit there picking at my branches, dozing off and almost forgetting why I had shown up in the first place, and then she would come quietly along through the young trees. The mild low-light from her lantern would knock gently on the fallen lids of my eyes, beckoning me to come to life. My vision took flight, hastily at first, then slowing to rest gracefully upon her dark locks. Even with the light she carried, it was difficult to make out much more than her shapely silhouette on nights during the emptier cycles of the moon. Regardless, I trained my eyes on her every step as she moved wantonly through the pines, paying careful attention not to step on roots or fallen cones. Always, she walked with bare feet, clothed with a thin cotton robe, her hair already let down.

I had stumbled easily upon her the first time while making my rounds during a routine night wander. I had just reached the rear of the old barn where I could see the bunker light bouncing off the back of its technicolor coat. It was then when that orange bulb seemed to split in two and send its brother off floating toward the Freedom Spring out in the trees. At first, I was sure it was an apparition, so I followed it from a distance. Needless to say, part of me changed that evening, and I saw far more wondrous things than ghosts. That was during the prime of summer, when it was a good deal hotter. It was still hotter than the devil's hell then, only not as much. Weather around our region liked to change so sporadically, however, I figured it would be getting too cold to bathe outdoors before much longer, even in Indian River. That was a black day coming I didn't much care to dwell on the thought of.

She stuck her toe in, the same as ever. That frigid water took bravery at any time of year. One wicked touch would sap the body of all formerly collected comforts. But she challenged it brazenly, and the water itself seemed to draw away in tidal gestures, for fear of what was about to breach its shores. Then, she pulled gently on the cloth rope that held her robe closed against her navel. I glanced quickly to the light from the bunker. No one stood outside from what I could tell. From that distance it was damn hard to see anything, save for a faint luminescence from that bulb, which might have been a mirage by then. Maybe it was even God telling me not to look, but my eyes returned and adjusted before the robe had even left her shoulders. It was almost as if she had waited for me. Like she knew it was my favorite part. I wed my vision to her skin, and then down it went, without warning. The sacred vestment slid off her back like the skim of a wave on a sandy beach shore, slipping away into the dark for the millionth time.

My mind pieced the rest together from nothing more than bits and fragments I had collected over the previous few months. It was the most lamented of all fantasies; the kind that stands naked before you, but must be viewed behind the eyes, given the darkness of reality. In spite of that darkness, however, I knew well the cut of her legs, the breadth of her posterior, the braided muscles of her back. She was a working girl, Sarah Obis. There wasn't a doubt about it. I waited patiently for my recollections to be proven, when suddenly, for three brief and bless-ed seconds, I saw plainly the orange light of the lantern slide vertically against the entire length of her brawny and buxom figure as she left the vessel on the rim of the pool and disappeared into its frigid waters. Her form rose again shortly, and the lantern light told of her shimmering defi-nition. Her newly-filled breasts bobbed upon the water's surface (like Claudette's), and then rose, dripping beads as she waded toward the shore and twisted the lantern valve into utter darkness.

3

It wasn't so much the sound outside that woke me as much as it was the sight of Aaron's arm flinging to attention when it woke him. When I had laid down to sleep late the night before, after returning from my wanderings, his limbs were still painfully jutting this way and that, extended in all directions like planks on a pirate ship, and I knew he was none the wiser to me being gone. Well, the sun was up then, and Aaron climbed down, aided by one rung on the ladder, and taking two paces to the window. He stood there for a minute, bare-chested in his drawers, damn near breaking his neck to see where the clamor had come from. I pulled my blanket off and sat up, rubbing the sleep from my eyes as Aaron took another two paces into a pair of Lees and shoved his arms through the first dirty shirt he could find. I stood quick and tried to mimic his fluidity the best I could, but failed when I stepped on the inside of my britches and hopped across the room with one leg free. Aaron was gone before I could recover.

When I came into the kitchen, Momma had already set out a small spread on the table. I had forgotten all about the sounds when I finally saw Aaron come back in the front door.

"What's goin' on down by the road?" he asked.

"Sit down and eat," Momma said.

"Is it Daddy?" he persisted.

"Moses, say grace," she ignored. It took everything in me not to go over and look out the window. I sat down and curbed my curiosity enough to bow my head. I glanced at Aaron with one eye. I hated when she made me do it.

"Our Father, who aren't in heaven—"

"Art," Momma straightways corrected me.

"Our Father," I started again. "Who art in heaven, hallowed be thy name. Thy kingdom come. Thy will be done, on earth as it is in heaven ..." I paused and looked up at Momma to see her open one eye at me. I was clearly distracted.

"Give us ..." she led.

"Give us this day our daily bread," I continued. "And forgive us our trespasses, as we forgive those who trespass against us. Lead us forever into thine temptation, and deliver us for evil. For thine is the kingdom, and the power, and thine glory, forever. Amen."

Momma near about choked in my last couple lines. I might have said something blasphemous or heretical, but I could tell she was over it.

"Eat," she said. "Aaron, Daddy needs your help out there soon as you're finished."

"What's he doin'?" he asked insistently. Just then, there was a crash and clatter out by the road. Some men were hollering.

"It don't matter!" she snapped. I held a piece of toast with strawberry jam suspended before my mouth, switching vision between Momma and the window. "Just finish your breakfast and get out there! I had to fight him off just to get him to let you eat. Now hurry up!"

Aaron didn't much care to savor his food after all that. His curiosity had already ruined his appetite. By then he was just shoveling enough toast and grits into his head to last him the morning; to make a turd, I suppose. He took his last bite, wiped his mouth with his palm and threw his unused napkin on the plate. Now, I, too was in a hurry to finish and see what was going on. I ingested massive bites, far bigger than was characteristic for me, as I watched Aaron step into his untied boots and push past the door. "First through the legs ..." he would always say in times like that. I reckon I knew what he meant, but it was only a half sentence, and stupider than hell. Real fitting for a simple shit like Aaron. Didn't make it any less true, though. The first into life gets first dibs on all the excitement. Only reason it was so for Aaron was because he had him a bigger tail when we was stuck up in Daddy's balls. I had been a tadpole long as he had been one, he just got out faster. I had reasoned we were technically the same age because of that.

Honestly, though, it was on days like those that I was glad to be the younger. Days when Daddy had the brothers performing some innately obscure chore which required them to exert most or all of their entire day's worth of energy in a single, wretched hour of animal labor. Labor in which they hadn't the slightest bit of true investment in seeing the results of, given that Daddy didn't hardly ever tell anybody anything. Most of those times I could count on either my ability to deduce what was going on from simple observation, or I could get enough out of Momma to last me until I did.

She and I stood there on the front lawn, me beside her and her beside me, our toes resting slightly on the red clay drive. As we surveyed the situation down on the road, Momma seemed to know less than me. The gate was still locked up right nice, the same as the night before, and it didn't appear that Daddy or the brothers aimed to unlock it either. What a stupid set of stubborn circumstances. Either Daddy had lost his Schlage key, or he was making a prideful point about that gate. I saw Mattie and Bill and Silas, and of course Daddy and Aaron, down there atop a flat bed crane truck, trying to secure a large piece of abstruse machinery with lengths of Nylon straps like Ford had started putting in some of their cars. The truck's engine was running loud, and it was right hard to make out what anyone was sayin, save for when they hollered it.

"Alright, everybody move!" Daddy commanded with a boom that cut across the morning. I reckoned it was the loudest set of words ever spoken in that particular spot. The brothers leapt from the truck as its arm began to raise up. It was only then that I noticed someone else entirely was operating the crane. I couldn't see who, but I figured it was one of Beckins' Mexicans. It certainly wasn't Obis. The Harbinger, Miles Beckins had one particularly big Mexican named Don Miguel; a bull of a man who he usually sent out on jobs as such. I reckoned it was him in the seat of the crane truck. As is true with most of Beckins' employees, Don Miguel wasn't from around there. He was immigrated from Coahuila in 1942 as a Bracero during the Bracero Treaty and was a part of the labor force that helped end the war. After spending a year as a tamalero on his grandfather's tamale wagon in Los Angeles, Miguel left and worked his way east until he arrived in Indian River in 1947. I picked all that up one Saturday afternoon, tinkering with an Indian dreamcatcher and eavesdropping over a Moon Pie in Marlin's store.

The crane had by then lifted the mammoth machine well overhead, and it was approaching the gate. Daddy signaled to Aaron, who then ran and straightways got into the pickup which stood parked reverse at the gate with a flat trailer in tow. Daddy then extend one arm to the crane, gesturing for it to continue slowly, and one arm toward Aaron, directing him to ease backward until the right moment. I was right jealous of Aaron once again. All the while, Mattie, Bill and Silas kept inside the shadow of the great machine with their arms extended upward, as if to suggest there was any chance of catching the behemoth piece of gear should it decide to snap loose and do anything but crush the three of them entirely.

The crane's arm continued to extend slightly as it sailed the innumerable weight of the unnamed machine over the locked gate and nearer to Daddy's trailer. The brothers and Daddy were walking well on their toes, then, guiding the colossal metal block with the tips of their fingers. They looked like so many geese, aimlessly waddling in one direction, extending their necks for a taste of stale bread to be sprinkled into their cursed bills; a helpless scenario. Just then, there was the terrible sound of an amplified string quartet pulling downward octaves in unison. Momma grabbed my shoulders as our heads snapped to the road. There wasn't one of us who had noticed the crane truck tipped on two side wheels, balancing gracefully between gravity and its extended arm. The integrity of many mechanized beasts were immediately told in moments like that; the way man first realized the advantage of one creature over another. The way God intended. Whatever the machine was, the crane truck was no match for its fortitude, even with Don Miguel at the helm.

The load lowered a foot and a half without the help of the crane's pulley. The brothers and Daddy backed off slightly, then gripped the edges full-on with their palms and fingers in helpless denial and suicidal bravery. It wasn't a second later that one of those seat belts suspending the machine in midair around its backside snapped and whipped loudly, causing it to shift violently in its tether. Daddy and the brothers ran like hell as the machine held still another few seconds, continuing to lower steadily to the ground against the fulcrum of the crane truck way out on the road. Don Miguel was damn near horizontal in the cab by the time the monstrosity finally touched down of its own accord and Daddy and the brothers were able to cut the remaining straps free. When Daddy machete chopped the final strand, the crane's arm retreated straightways and violently toward the sky, seat belts and all, like a medieval trebuchet firing a volley at an enemy stronghold. Down on the road, the truck returned to four wheels with a thunderous collision; the sounds of those hurled missiles making their mark on that impenetrable stone wall somewhere in my boy's imagination.

Momma knew good and well that was the most damn excitement I had seen in months, maybe years. She looked down on me and exhaled, deciding it was quite enough. I caught one last glimpse at the situation before Momma wheeled me around and aimed me for the house. Daddy and the brothers were shielding the sun from their eyes and steadily trading glances between the tip of the crane and the truck down on the road. Aaron stood on his knees, turned backwards in Daddy's seat with eyes wider than Christmas. Last thing I saw was a quick shot of Don Miguel rolling upside down out of the passenger side of that crane cab and standing to his feet.

Many hours later, when Momma had finally seemed to turn loose of me mentally, clearly replete of any further superfluous school lessons or indoor chores that needed doing, and her attention had been driven elsewhere, I wandered outside, half expecting to discover the brothers and Daddy still playing at the machine in the front yard, but everyone had long disappeared, and so had the crane truck. Momma caught me gazing from the front deck but didn't say a word. Instead, she quietly withdrew back into the house for a spell and returned wielding a shiny green Granny Smith. She handed it to me. I scraped the skin once with my index fingernail and watched the gloss gather beneath, leaving a dull stripe on the face of the apple.

"Momma, what is this stuff?"

She took the fruit from my hand and held it up to her observant eyes.

"It's wax," she said. Then she spat upon the apple and made it clean. "It won't hurt you," she continued, as she took the fruit in her apron and rubbed gently. When she returned the apple to my hand, it was free of its reflective surface, and instead of myself, I saw nothing but knowledge upon its emerald clothes. Knowledge that me and her were different. I no longer craved the apple as I had when she first handed it to me, varnished with a strange substance. The taste; her taste, that was supposed to be familiar, had suddenly become unbearable to me. The thought of putting my mouth where hers had been— unthinkable. It was then that I also came to note that I had begun to detest the brown and brackish water of the tub; that communal broth of familial filth. And from that second on, I stilled myself with resolution to never again submerge myself in its depths.

When Momma went back into the house without another look, it was her subtle way of implying that I had some deal of time to consume the apple and settle my curiosities privately before afternoon chores. Or at least that's how I took it. With that peace of mind, I leapt from the deck and made for the first sounds to come within earshot. I held on to the apple (though I had no intention of ingesting it). I traced the sounds of hammers hitting nail heads and men growling unintelligible obscenities beneath the chug of a tractor engine until I came to a suitable observation point ten or fifteen yards from the source of all the day's toil on our tiny farm. The brothers and Daddy had pieced together a rather shifty looking framework for what I reasoned to be some sort of pulley system. It was constructed of several railroad ties and situated atop a large hole dug straight into the earth between the old barn and the ground floor of the hayloft where I watched, crouched in a wrinkle formed by three round bales pushed together with an open end. The hole in the ground was easy five feet across, and by the look of the pile next to it, I reckoned it was quite cavernous and must have been dug up that morning, given that I hadn't ever noticed it before. What in the hell were they trying to drop that machine down in that dirty pit for, I thought. I held the apple in my right hand and watched, quietly allowing my perched eyes to relay the story that unfolded before them.

Silas stood tall in his sportsman's frame, holding one nine inch iron spike after another in place as his brother, Bill balanced on the forks of Daddy's tractor and drove them in brutishly with a steel gavel. Silas would brave the first few frightful stabilizing strikes, shutting his eyes and turning his head quick with each blow, grimacing as he went. But when it came time for the killing stroke, Silas would release just before the hammer hit the head and sent the spikes singing through the aged planks. On occasion, Bill would give a truly terrible swing, barely tipping the corner of the nail head just as Silas had pulled away smartly. Bill would then fly into an outrage, blaming his brother for being a pussy and then swiping shortly at Silas' face with the mallet.

Mattie worked singularly at shaping crossbeams and support beams by cutting miter joints into shorter pieces with a large handsaw. Daddy and Aaron formed the third and final labor camp across the hole from Bill and Silas. Aaron, himself, it seemed, was holding the entire operation together with dear attention, clasping onto one of the two main structural beams and bracing it desperately with an arm stretched to the main crossbeam that spanned the two. From his command post on the ground, Daddy seemed to have an undue confidence in Aaron's ability to accomplish the task set before him. I figured I knew better. Aaron was strong, but completely without stamina. He would fold any minute then, like a smoker in a distance run.

I watched anxiously for a short spell, but was drawn away momentarily to bear witness to another diminutive struggle on God's great earth. Two chromatic creatures of reptilian impression, baring as many colors as the canvas covering of the old barn, scaled swiftly up one of the four

39

stilts that held the upper loft in unaccountable suspension above my tiny head, and were now weaving about the rafters violently; one in pursuit of the other. On occasion, the one giving chase would make contact and expertly savage the other in many blurred and murderous transactions that ended as speedily as they had began. I wondered what drove creatures of such indistinguishable character and appearance to do combat with one another.

No sooner had my attention been taken by the curious exchange than my gaze was recaptured by the sounds of a thunderous thud and clamor. Upon looking down and allowing my eyes to return to sunlight, I saw Aaron had indeed buckled in the fashion I had expected of him. He had grown weak in his requirement and had nearly fainted from nothing short of pride. Well, the whole mess of beams and supports had collapsed and the better part of it had been devoured by the gaping chasm below. Daddy didn't curse or kick Aaron the way any other self-respecting Indian River farmer would do his son. Instead, he tiresomely removed his baseball cap and wiped his balding head once with his sleeve.

"Have a seat," he said in more than mild frustration. It was subtle enough to humiliate Aaron in a manner that merited no form of retaliation whatsoever. He had made a fool of himself in front of the brothers, and there wasn't anything he could say or do for it. I ducked as Aaron turned and walked straightways from Daddy toward me, head sunk and staggering in exhaustion. It was then I realized he might have damn well dropped those beams on purpose. It seemed like something Aaron might be capable of; feigning weakness to escape responsibility. I crouched low and turned to sit down when he didn't change his course.

I half thought he might have seen me just before I sat, or at least picked up my scent. Sure enough, around the corner he came, right to me like a hound and stood over me in a posture meant for intimidation; a gesture made to recapture whatever pride he had lost down that hole. I regrettably bit the apple in embarrassment and looked up as he spoke.

"Jackin' off back here?" he said.

I was disarmed.

"Heh," I nervously pretended to laugh as a symbol of submission. Aaron looked over the hay bales and toward Daddy and the brothers.

"I gotta get off this damn farm," he said.

I extended my apple in reply. He grabbed it without looking and sat down to bite it.

"Are we gonna be rich?" I asked.

Aaron paused.

"Rich? Why in hell would you think that?" he took another bite. I looked halfway in the direction of the machine and at the ground in heavy thought. I felt Aaron look at me. "It ain't no oil drill ..." he paused his chewing like I was crazy for thinking so. He let out a single syllable chuckle and was back at the apple, shaking his head.

"... Well, what is it, then?" I asked.

Aaron swallowed and paused again.

"It's a water pump, you dumb duck."

I stood and peeked over the hay to view the machine with the new knowledge and was right shocked at what I saw. It seemed Aaron was the only thing that had held up the brothers and Daddy in their progress. In the mere moment he had sat down to rest, the pulley had been, for the most part, reconstructed and Daddy had slowly begun lowering the great machine into the hole with true horsepower. Inch by inch, Daddy's tractor delivered the payload; braking it's way forward against the uncountable tonnage that heaved mightily on its prehistoric steel bones. Black clouds of exhaust spewed from the tractor's growling, rusting innards with pissed tones and demonic snorts. The combination of chains and what-not and leftover nylon straps had been braided together to form a taut and powerful chord in that infernal tug-o-war.

I bent my knees and slowly lowered my body alongside the machine in subconscious unison, sinking low beneath the hay until the worst happened. With less warning than before, the weight of the machine once and for all proved itself victorious and broke free of its suspensions, disappearing into its own chosen resting place with ungodly sounds, and I saw it no more. My eyes widened to near splitting. Aaron rose to my side to bear witness to what had just happened. Daddy and the brothers were staring silently into the hole as an enormous brown cloud of dirt rose like a monstrous, volcanic belch. Daddy raised his hand to his brow in quiet frustration. Aaron and I lowered once more to our seats beneath the hay.

"Shit," Aaron said.

"... Where'd it come from?" I asked.

"I don't know. Somewhere out west," he spilled nonchalantly. "The Harbinger brung it on a plane as a favor to Daddy."

"Miles Beckins gots a plane big enough for that?" I asked.

"Beckins has got all kinds of airplanes," Aaron replied, pitching the clean apple core. "You need to find a better damn hidin' spot, by the way."

I frowned.

"You've had this one since all the way back when we watched Daddy mate them two paints." I turned my head quick at the joy of Aaron's mention of it. He laughed a little. "I'll never forget the look on your face when that big boy climbed up on that mare," Aaron slapped his knee. I faced forward again.

"It weren't that what give me the face …" I said. Aaron laughed even harder. I smiled. I always liked making him laugh. It was usually on rare occasions, when we were brothers and he wasn't thinking of me as a coworker in the place he hated most. We sat there and shot shit for a while. We were brothers then, and for a spell, he had convinced me my attention was as valuable to him as his was to me. I had given him an apple, and he had given me a moment, and it wasn't a moment I would right soon forget.

"Now get your ass out of here and go get your count," he barked. About right. Aaron was always spot-on with timing. And with that, we parted for the afternoon.

The rest of the day was about as normal as could be expected. After lunch I went right down and refilled the water in the four pens on the back fence closest to the bunker and caught no sight of Sarah Obis. I shook off one flake of hay for each of the four pens (since we were rationing) and then rattled the single gate until I saw the tenants come moseying up from the bottom of the pasture. After that I stripped two whole stalls, making sure to remove all the turds and wet shavings until I could see the clay floor of the barn. Then I shoveled in nearly a foot of new pine and left the doors open for whoever would be inside them that night.

By the time I got out to the front pasture for my final chore of the day, it was nearly twilight, and the sun had just gone down far enough behind the trees that I could look directly into it without going blind. I stood for a moment and observed the oddity of all those twine squares floating six or eight inches above the ground at various intervals throughout the field; like one of Dottie's crosswords or a piece of Miss Melba's mathematics paper. The front pasture was the expanse of our property that stood between our house and the northwestern reaches of County Road 1. It was triangular in shape and flanked on the longest leg with woods that belonged to our neighbors just north of us. The middle bore a few jumps and barrels for training, but it was mostly comprised of thick, dead tufts of hell grass and hay that shot up sharper than bamboo shafts, and shrubberies and small bushes left to their own evolutions that would crunch loudly at the mercy of boots or hooves. I often would pretend to be a titan or giant traversing a long-burned wood where all the trees were without tops, and each dead and true stick of grass was a free-standing trunk to be trampled. I would level uncountable forests as such.

Over the years, a deep and sugary rut had worn right down past the roots of that hell grass; past the mole crickets and beyond, forming a deep path, or ditch, of sand that marked the pasture's edges, where horse and horse rider wandered ways predetermined by restraints that had long-governed that space. In a dream I had, I saw hard rains return to Indian River and penetrate the baked earth. They flooded the foxholes of our enemy, and streams began to form and rush forth from all sides, causing the ever-deepening horse path to be filled with deluge and dead crickets. Then I saw the pasture rise from its seat, and its ties to the earth washed away. It floated upon the ocean that was our farm and carried with it only myself and my hound, Charles. We rose high above the earth and saw the end of the plague. The end of the whole world.

My final task of the day was a simple one. From the pocket of my jeans, I produced a length of twine and a fourth-folded scratch of paper with half a pencil. I crouched down and took the twine in my hands, stretching it neatly between two sticks of grass and wrapping it once around each end. I then repeated the method on an adjacent pair, and then another, and another until I had closed off a rough one foot square with twine turnbuckles at each corner.

With my hands, I began pulling away at tufts of grass and overturning handfuls of earth until the square was crawling with every bit of life below. All in all I counted fifteen or so; mole crickets, that is (give or take a couple I may have counted twice). It wasn't a bad count necessarily. It wasn't a good one either. Numbers weren't up since the day before, but they were consistent with the rest of the month. Whatever Beckins was dusting with every morning, it wasn't working.

It wasn't ten seconds after the thought that I felt an evening breeze come across my back and carry with it the swift and fortissimos sound of a low-flying prop. I ducked with instinct and watched as the belly of the cherry red craft passed overhead. I clearly read the words "ST. SIMON'S" at length in large, white block letters and then saw the tail pass by. The violent rise and decay of the plane's thunderous buzz as it tore through skin and bone across the sky within what seemed to be an inch of my ear, was gone as quick as it had come. The drums in my head rung with residual tones as all sound began to sweep back in after the whole of my observable world had been violently unzipped and ripped asunder by the screaming craft.

Speak of the devil and he doth appear. What in the hell was The Harbinger doing out that late, I thought. I had never once seen him out past morning. I had seldom seen him at all, save for once or twice when I had been up ungodly early performing some task in the wee morning hours that couldn't wait. As a matter of fact, I had never even even properly met the man. Well, he went on past me, over the tree line that struck our property, and then he banked east toward the Mennonite place. Maybe he dusted for them, too, I supposed. Chances were slim, though. Those hankies would have been expressly opposed to putting chemicals on anything of theirs. They were a queer type that kept solely to themselves, making cheese and carving shit from wood blocks.

Anyways, it was funny that I got onto thinking about them, because of what happened later on, just before dinner. After I took record of my count, I came back up to the barn and went on to help Daddy and Aaron water off the four back stalls once more before dinner. It was still right hot during the day, and the horses would come up several times between afternoon and evening to lick their buckets dry, so we did our best to keep them full for overnight. Because of such, we were out past sundown that night, which wasn't too terribly unusual.

I had just cut off the water when we noticed something give spook to the animals as they came up from the foot of the woods. By that time, it was too dark to see what it was from where we stood close to the bunker. Daddy, however, was suspicious of wild dogs, like coyotes, and he wanted to take a closer look. He let Aaron drive the truck while he shined the spotlight. I stayed out to let them through the gate. As soon as they had gone by, I closed up the galvanized steel panel, chained it and ran to catch up with the truck so I could hop in the back. Aaron idled us slowly down the hillocks that led to the far tree line, occasionally swerving to avoid big piles of cow shit that would have likely got us stuck.

When finally we arrived about midway through the pasture, Aaron slammed on the brakes hard, and I went sliding off the wheel well and wrenched my shoulder on the rear glass of the cab. Daddy threw his arm back and pounded once on the back window, absentmindedly, as if to tell me to knock it off. I was still recovering and busy picking myself back up off the truck bed long after Daddy and Aaron had opened their doors and stepped out in silence. They must have found the coyote, or at least seen it cross in front of the truck.

"Did we hit it?" I asked, standing to my feet and vaulting off the side. No answer. Daddy and Aaron stood at attention on either side of the high beams, staring away in silence. When I came around the front of the truck and stopped next to Aaron, my eyes had to make sense of what they saw. A monster longhorn, white as a sheet, stood resolute in our path, unmoved by our arrival. I swore on the devil if he wasn't big as the truck, he wasn't an inch. We watched as his muscles raged and his red eyes pulsed. I imagined fire from his nostrils. He seemed right anxious to gore the three of us on a single horn.

"Don't spook it," Daddy said with his left arm extended toward us. He had been holding the spotlight in his right hand, facing it at the ground since he had stepped out (as if it would add any more irritation than the high beams were already).

"Whose is it?" Aaron asked.

"Neighbor's," Daddy replied as he eased forward, tall as ever. The bull turned his head to the woods, stomped once in a dust cloud and gave out a long and boisterous call before looking back at us. Daddy took a step back.

"Turn them lights off," he commanded Aaron in a whisper. Aaron turned and made for the cab, but before he could reach the door, the steer turned and bumbled off thunderously to the north, taking shelter through a hollow in a thin line of trees that cut the back pasture in two. The ground shook as he went.

We followed the large and cantankerous beast as it went on out of sight. But then, without warning, our eyes were whipped back at the sight of something strange. Off toward the bottom of the pasture, in the direction of the woods, six or seven small firelights had suddenly appeared at the tree line. They were tiny, but still fairly obvious as they bobbed and swayed mildly in the darkness. Torches, each no more than a foot or two apart, several hundred yards off.

"Who is it, Daddy?" I asked.

"Mennonites," Aaron replied.

"Close your mouth," Daddy snapped. "Get them lights off." Aaron instantly took to the cab and pulled the light switch. The beams faded, and I watched the coils in the bulb closest to me fizzle into oblivion. When I turned back, the only thing my eyes could find were those lights off in the distance. Aaron came back around, and then Daddy crouched instinctively.

"Get down," he whispered. We did. "William's queer about things like this," he said.

"How do you mean?" Aaron asked.

"I mean, he ain't too keen on transactin' with folk who ain't his kind. He'll do his best to get that bull back with the least collateral exchange as possible."

"I don't know what that means," Aaron noted.

"Do we fear 'em?" I asked, questioning our postures. Daddy ignored me.

"I reckon I better go say somethin' in good manners."

"TO THEM MURDERERS?!" Aaron shouted.

Before I could even comprehend what had just been said, Daddy struck Aaron backhanded and laid him out real proper. The slap reverberated across the pasture like a stone clack in a canyon, bouncing around for embarrassingly too long. Then there was stark silence for a moment. I watched on with eyes wide. Daddy's were still on Aaron.

"Close your mouth. And stay put." he glanced briefly at me, as if I had been mistakenly made privy to something he would have to deal with later. Then he up and vanished toward the lights.

Aaron recovered without a word, rubbing his face with about the same expression he had after dropping those beams earlier. We watched as Daddy's silhouette against the torchlight got smaller and smaller. But then, before his form descended the last visible hillock, the flames drew together and extinguished, and Daddy was lost. I looked at Aaron, stricken. His eyes were glued where the lights went out.

"What in hell ..." he spoke. We lowered to our bellies and watched intently for several minutes to see any shape break the still dark. My curiosity got the best of me.

"Aaron ..."

"What?"

"Do you think William is Him?"

Aaron looked at me in my eyes and then glanced once at my whole form laying there, as if to remind himself of my size and age and ability to tender an occasional shrewd observation.

"Who?" he asked. "The Man? ...That shit ain't real."

I remained quiet and reckoned we both partly wondered if Daddy had been killed or kidnapped, but it were plain he was still a good ways off when the lights went out. We laid there for a witch's eon, it seemed, until we heard a voice that spooked us proper.

"Get up off the dirt," it said, annoyed. We jumped to see that Daddy had come and doubled back behind us. "Momma's got dinner waitin'. I smell it. Let's go."

It was evident Daddy had as little an idea about what had transgressed in the pasture as we had. We didn't speak any more about it. Upon sitting for dinner, I half expected another strange visitor to show, but it seemed our farm's cup had indeed run over with oddities, and life would surely return to normal.

4

Temperature had dropped right frozen over night, and I had unfortunately been there to witness the whole disagreeable transition. Up in that tree, near midnight, I had waited patiently for the object of my lechery to appear, knowing full-well the freshly born cold had every intent of keeping her from me. The spring by no means changed moods as violently or as often as Gulf weather. It was in every likelihood that she had decide not to come, given that it would have been a strange ordeal to enter into its icy depths then. But in a spell of pure astonishment, against all my preconceptions, she came. Like a message in a storm, she came. That was the night previous, following the business with the steer. And there was nothing special to note of the frigid Sarah Obis' sapped and adamantine manifestation. Not then, anyway. Not to a boy of twelve.

One occurrence that took place just after dinner did give me an honest spook worth mentioning. Just after feeding Charles, I made my way around the far side of the house, nearest the gate, for reasons I wasn't entirely sure of, other than the fact that perhaps I craved a bit of new scenery in the night, and I hadn't traversed that path in some time. Regardless of the fact, when I came to the red clay drive and looked southward, I damn near pissed myself proper at what I saw there beyond the gate. The sinister figure of a dark man loomed still between the horizontal slats of the closed gate. Behind him, County Road 1 lay desolate and unmoved like a river bed, dried in the summertime. Despite the fear in the pit of my stomach, I could not help but stay and look on as the strange being produced a bone white finger and bid me come to him. And against my greater judgement, I did not refuse.

"Come 'ere, boy," it said in eroded tones. "Come closer." As I neared the figure slowly in the quiet night, his body seemed to draw away at intangible measures, and yet remained close by. Regretfully, I was unable to make out the color of his hair or the weave of his coat, which I reckoned to be one of standard military issue for cold weather.

"Can I help you?" I asked in the way I imagined Daddy might have, with a slight twinge of inconvenience in my voice as to assert myself as less patient than I actually was.

"Much obliged for a biscuit and a cup of water."

"I can't give it," I replied nervously. The dark man's shoulders dropped visibly and he stood silent for a moment.

"How do you mean?" he asked. I took an imperceivable step backward when I observed the change in his voice.

"Th-That is to say...we're all rationed out."

"For the end of the world..." he added. I stared at the figure without a word for fear I would add myself to a dark gospel I didn't want to be part of. Mixing further words with the shrouded man became something I much intended to avoid. I thought on the disciples of Jesus and how they had known nothing of the longevity of their dialogues, and I suddenly became aware of my own speech. Should it have ever been recorded, I had no desire for any of my words to be idle ones taught to children as lessons of unfavorable virtues when the histories of Indian River's apocalypse were written in ink. "Why close up so tight and tidy at such a time as this?" he asked. "Does The Family Beyond the Gate bear no conviction?"

That was the first time I had heard us referred to as such. "The Family Beyond the Gate." What a terrible presumption the name implied. As if all of Indian River was once uniquely dependent on us, and its people had then been given to a bleak and starved existence at our hand. The words slipped off my tongue.

"...This land is closed to the wretched," I quoted with a coarse heat of bravery and regret in my veins. The look on the man's face as he trailed away and disappeared into the night was one I would never forget. It wasn't the last time I saw dark and shrouded figures gather at our gate and at different lengths of our property's edge to make ambiguous threats birthed in jealous anger neither. It became a regular occurrence to see the angered citizenry of Indian River gathered together like undead battalions, leaderless and broadcast, awaiting the chance to storm our keep and reclaim the last stronghold against the onslaught of plague. If only a leader or inspiration strong enough would rise up and make straight their path.

The next morning, we awoke on the first Sunday of our existence where worship wasn't on the agenda. When Daddy had closed up the farm, he meant for us to stay put, and the town to stay out. And I had grown thankful for the gate after what I had witnessed there in the night. Thankful for safety and provisions untainted. Momma had fixed us a breakfast of corn muffins, apple-butter and bacon, even though I knew it was inevitable she would run out eventually. She was grooming us for hard labor. We always knew we had an honest day's toil ahead of us when Momma fixed a proper breakfast. We indulged all the more because of it. I had an oversized glass of milk the same temperature as the tub water and resolved to swim my bacons through a pool of maple syrup. Aaron had black coffee. He bashed his muffins to crumbs and mixed in a God-awful marriage of cane syrup and butter until there was no longer a conceivable manner for knowing what it was. He then scooped the contents into his abysmal maw, one dripping fork-full at a time. I wretched and left the table before he chased it with steaming hot Folgers.

"Get your winter clothes on," Momma said as we stood, and she took up our plates. "It's cold out, and Daddy's got you boys up on that confounded barn roof all day."

Aaron and I straightways ran to the hall closet and pried open its hellish jaws, praying fervently that we not be crushed beneath a host of falling keepsakes and contrived heirlooms. But inside, nothing moved. It was a wall, bricked and mortared by blankets, shoeboxes, Christmas favors and Holy Bibles (since Momma thought it sacrilege to throw out any copy of the Word). Near the top, and just out of my reach, was a large box labeled "COLD"; a brazen intimation as to how often or how long winter weathers were likely to happen upon Indian River each year. We both tore into the box and did our damnedest to discern what belonged to whom. As per usual, Aaron left me in a heap as he stepped fluently into his long-johns, zipped up his coveralls and slid through a rubbery windbreaker just before stepping out the door. Momma came over and helped me locate my possibles. I stood there, shamed that my impotence had called upon her against my will, as she dressed me in an extra pair of jeans, a hooded coat, a scarf and a knitted hat.

Well, we weren't up on those sunny barn rafters ten minutes before we were out of every damn bit of those extraneous coverings. And it wasn't ten more before we had been in and out of our jackets three and four times over, given to pure confusion. The wind was colder than a witch's tit, but the sun was violently elemental and drawn. Not to mention, our chief cross to bare was two and a half burning tons of tin roof sheets to be hoisted one-by-one onto the unfinished rafters and handled into place manually for nailing.

Why Daddy had chosen to have me and Aaron up on the eaves and the brothers in the assembly line down below was beyond me. He had formed us into the best shape of efficiency he could assume, with Bill, Silas and Mattie all moving the metal (which was already partly rusted from sitting so damn long) up to the trusses where Aaron and I would hold the sides for Daddy to nail in steady. The conditions were probably the worst possible for the work we were having at. The wind whipped violently from one end of the structure to the other and made it right difficult to maneuver those titanic metal sheets without feeling as if the right gust would take you sailing away with it. On occasion, a good wind would rise up in the right circumstance and gather a foothold beneath that metal before Aaron or I could wrestle it down. I would see visions of myself toppling backwards off the eaves with a sheet of that razor-clad tin pinning me to the ground, chopping me asunder and protruding from my corpse like a battle standard. I would snap out of it with Aaron in my ears.

"Hold still!" he would say, and I would realize my eyes were fixed far below on the ground. I would recollect my senses and straighten up my end. It was obvious we had been handed a job that was pretty iconically Bill and Silas. It seemed only fitting that they be in our places, taking jabs at each other and near blowing to their deaths.

My attention would be drawn off someplace else in an instant. The top of the barn was probably the highest of heights I had ever been to. I could see all the way from County Road 1 to the house, to the bunker, and everything in between. I reckoned it was about a minute-and-a-half between each sheet, so my eyes had some liberties to wander. That particular time, there was a hold-up down on the ground. Silas had sliced his hand real good, and Bill and Mattie were tending to it quick as they could manage, so I was able to get a proper look of the grounds at a vantage point I had never boasted.

The view was unmatched to anything I had been en-lightened to before. I watched as the distant and perpetual gray stroke rose from the bunker and disintegrated into a wide and voluminous path, fading steadily into clean, win-tery blue. I saw the tops of Mennonite structures beyond the back pasture. Their whitewashed and chaste steeples, only ever seen from above, were then undressed by my waking eyes upon them. I drew my vision closer, and saw the alien browns and golds of my peeping tree as it stood transfigured in the midst of resolute and evergreen pine needles that refused to fall until the last exquisite ray of heat was long gone, and sometimes not even then. The house, of course, was the closest and most plainly seen of structures. Its roof, which leaned and sagged longingly toward the ground at the Southwest corner, was darker and more soot-covered than I had imagined. I reckoned it was the absence of any fair amount of shade that permitted the sun to visit wretchedly upon the rooftop and caused it to adopt characteristics of a freshly tarred thoroughfare. I imagined Beckins landing one of his planes there, from time to time. There certainly seemed room for it.

There was an impression in the ground none of us ever seemed to notice whilst regularly traversing the baked soil below. Just at the corner of the house, where the roof dipped low in humble submission to the earth, there was a basin of red earth, sun-sapped and bone dry where one could tell the stone clay had been utterly pounded and patiently negotiated into submission by years, decades, centuries even, of rainwater which had collected in haste at that southwest corner and plummeted ruefully to an infinitely useless and inevitably potent end. I thought then on the house as it might have stood a hundred years ago, with acorn oaks all around, shaded and hidden on all sides, but instead of that hole down there being bone dry or full of rain, I saw it overflowing with acorns, and I quietly wished I had been born in another time.

My attention was drawn off to the track in the front pasture; an endless and infinite rapid of white water, carrying horse and rider around and around until the current, like Jonah's great fish, would expel them upon dry land, where the green shore met the calming shallows. I saw County Road 1, an ever-imposed and equally obligatory birthmark that drew attention (like most birthmarks do) to some face; the town of Indian River. And finally, away in the south, my eyes met that darkened path into the woods; a tried and unwavering course that led either to the beast, or to the allegory. In due course, the inevitable collapse of my suspension would lead me there. It was something I had become certain of.

Daddy seized all attention there on the roof.

"Boys!" he said with a crooked smile at the tail end of a bitter wind. He held up his hand and brought his thumb to almost touch his pointer finger. "It's about that cold out here!" We smirked, for fear that audible laughter might be too much, and we didn't dare disturb the prescribed somber working conditions there in that cold, regardless of if Daddy wished us to or not. But inside, we laughed heartily. Then, as if cued by the uniform silence following Daddy's joke, a frightful and garish sound cracked and buzzed loudly at our rear. When our gaze met the tree line, a bright red duster rose high and protracted above the back pasture. It's engine seemed to cut dramatically at the peak of its climb where it floated and broke free of gravity for just a few seconds. I read clearly the words in white block letters along its chassis. Then, in a horrifying display, the engine seemed to stall out, and the craft then proceeded to fall slowly, plummeting with no foreseeable pattern. The tiny plane tossed and rolled every which way until neither its tail could rightly be told from its nose, nor wingtip from wingtip. It dropped and spun, like a whirlybird from a pine tree, till, at last, we saw those red wings straighten up tight as a drum, scooping the duster back into proper flight at what seemed just inches from the ground.

When Aaron and I caught our breaths and looked up, it took everything we had to refrain from applauding the show. We then noted that the duster had left a snow-white curlycue of smoke, like an irksome strand of hitchhikers, stuck to the blue jean sky. We marveled at the contrast drawn between it and the gray line that rose high from the bunker fire. Two signals; essentially the same, but chemically different in every way. One, fed of dry and organic materials, moved unhindered by wind or control, but dissipated at an untold altitude, changing from black to gray to translucent hues. The other, characterized by the presence of water vapors, stood static and transfixed, a statuesque braid of ivory, as dense at its apex as it was at its base.

Aaron was soon bored with the observation and went on assisting daddy with another big piece of tin. I, however, continued to follow the convoluted trail as it corkscrewed low, finally straightening out and crossing far above my head. When I at last caught up with the red duster at the end of the smoke trail, he was way above the front pasture; so far out, I could just faintly hear his single engine cry out over the track. My eyes stayed with him.

"Daddy, you reckon that's The Harb-b-Beckins?" I asked, stumbling across my words. Daddy didn't appear to look up; instead, he murmured affirmatively to let me know he had heard. I gathered more than once from Aaron that Beckins was a peculiar character, often given to loud, public outcries of conspiracy or impending doom. A score of townspeople had taken to nicknaming him "The Harbinger" for that. I conditioned myself to assume that anytime I had seen hide or hair of Miles Beckins, it was in some way prophetic. I had grown fond of him that way.

My eyes, still trained on the flat, red paint as it moved further out toward County Road 1, witnessed something I didn't rightly expect to occur. Just before Beckins banked back northeast and went on to the old Mennonite place, I saw the smallest payload drop inconspicuously from the plane's cockpit. At once, the brow of my face instinctively furrowed, and I felt ripples crack across the sunburnt surface of my forehead. The feeling surprised me at first, but then I went on watching—nursing my brow—as the duster made its way back along the far tree line in distant silence. I quickly glanced at Daddy and Aaron to take stock of whether they had seen what I had, but they were hard at work, hammering in another sheet. My eyes shot back toward the front pasture, while I still had a moment. I scanned the terrain near where I saw the parcel come to its resting place, but it was damn difficult to spot anything then in that thick, dead hell grass. I would have to wait until the evening count.

Around lunch time, Momma came and made us all get down off the roof and eat a quick meal of lentil soup and fried cornbread. Daddy had, at first, insisted we eat in shifts, on the roof, as to keep a steady progress, but Momma wouldn't have it. She made every last one of us come down backwards off the ladder with a rope tethered to our waist. Daddy and the brothers felt a fool for it, but I was honestly right relieved Momma had come when she did. I was getting weary doing my piece of a man's labor at only twelve years of age. It wasn't that Daddy had intended to exasperate me, it was simply that I wasn't aiming to forfeit my work and thus appear weaker than my much older and much stronger fraternity. I reckoned it was my responsibility to say when I had quenched my thirst of it. That being the case, Momma might have right well saved my life.

Daddy stayed on us throughout the better part of the following twenty minutes or so as we mechanically consumed bowls and bowls of lentils while sitting at a row of benches beneath the shade of the barn's eaves.

"Drink up," he said. "This ain't no birthday party." Daddy slurped the last of his soup without a spoon. Momma cringed. His formidable frame was cast in stone above us as he posed with one leg on the remaining sheets of tin. I looked around and wondered what in hell he was speaking of. Daddy wasn't innately gifted in metaphor.

After lunch, I briefly saw Sarah Obis walking and talking to the new Langford fellow as they tailed Pastor Obis on what seemed to be a guided tour of the property. Had I been able to boast a single hair on my young chest, it might have damn well stood straight up on its own when I saw that short man go and remove his jacket and place it on Sarah Obis' shoulders. I frowned and reckoned it was a gesture of some sordid motivation. After that, Pastor Obis turned them down a corner behind the rainbowed backside of the old barn, and they were gone from my sight. The thought of that versed and venerable tongue spinning words with Sarah Obis wasn't something I could very well contend with in my head whilst attempting to work simultaneously. I quarantined my observations to the roof, refusing to allow any further questions to pervade my mind which was already imbued with inquisition.

Nearly three hours later, I found myself traipsing wearily beyond the front paddock gate and into the shallows of that dying hell grass; to the front pasture where I would make my case for both the current state of our pestilence and for many newly-adopted quandaries. The feverish anticipation of finding that mysterious parcel promoted itself fervently inside me, and my once brief and incendiary crossness with the stranger, Mr. Langford, for his gilded and clever gallantry, had all but resolved. I likened it to a residual and faint ember's glow at a wick's tip; one that smokes on and on and leaks one putrid and poisonous fume at a time, administering no light, but is never extinguished.

I trudged with heaviness, devastating tiny forests beneath my feet, without possessing the least bit of sprightliness it took to enjoy it. I did, however, begin to feel the slightest touch of curious wonder resurrect itself inside me as I neared the grid of squares where I had seen whatever it was come floating down through the heavens from Beckins' red duster. I stepped lightly, surveying the ground carefully for something magnificent. My spirit of inquiry was fully awake then, and I sniffed and leapt and crouched, in my subconscious, as a puma or some other large and bush-bred feline predator might have done.

I could sense it was near. Something alien, or otherwise perverse lay in my vicinity, mocking my every step toward a colder bearing. I felt the ground move beneath me. It truly did, as the shapes of those crickets appeared and reappeared in the corners of my eyes, swimming dexterously above and below the sand, never stopping long enough to make their full forms readily seen by God or me. I halted and stood upright, turning my head and body in full rotation, where one was always behind the other. I drew my focus sharper and scanned the ground again. The more desperately my eyes searched, the more important it became for me to recover that lost and invaluable relic. Each passing second, it became, more and more, the most significant treasure in modern history. Suddenly, I had gone paranoid, assured that even then, curators from the Smithsonian Institute were hiding beyond my sight, peeking over our farm's fences, crouched in ditches and waiting for me to abandon my search or uncover the parcel in a moment of complete and utter vulnerability.

I decided to tone down the rummaging and do my best to appear calm. I breathed a steeled breath and shut my eyes for just a moment to regain self-possession. As soon as I had done so, I felt that cool recollection of sanity blow over me like the winds at the black bow of a mighty rain. At once, I reached deep into my pockets and withdrew the materials needed for my survey. I squared off an all new section, completely divorced from any preexisting side or corner (I fancied gathering an entirely unique sample every so often).

I turned three or four tufts of hell root and brushed my dirty hands off on my jeans. Seventeen. I made a mark with the half-pencil on my tool of paper and briefly visited the somber thought as Daddy might; or as someone might who had a particular investment in such information. I thought on what it truly meant, rather than what I had come to take it as. My concern was often more-so for the look in Daddy's vacant eyes. The burden of the news itself. It was a hell of a thing to be a boy and poor in 1965. Especially one whose chief responsibility was to bear creation's grievous tidings unto a family of faith. The weight of something like that was more than plenty to make a young man collapse beneath the rich pang of guilt.

The urgency to retrieve that fallen parcel had not gone from my consciousness when I decided to begin my long walk back. I knew that somewhere in those dead blades lay the key to my mystery. Some sacred moonstone or bit of coveted knowledge that just might reveal even a singular piece of enlightened instruction. An arcane transcript or instrument of innumerable wonders that might bid me resolution to that present enigma. I resolved that whatever it was, its ability to elude me would also prove its ability to elude others, and I would undoubtedly have to wait until a later day.

The sun was lowering its head once again on our tiny farm, and I saw the black shape of Momma against the red sky go and ring the dinner bell. The sound found my ears faintly, what seemed several seconds behind her swing of Daddy's old shoe hammer. And almost as if on cue, I heard even further tones ringing in the distance. The Indian River First United Methodist Church steeple spoke back where Momma had left off. I stopped and stood entranced, given that I had never heard them from our farm before. The gongs, which I always fancied as real bells when I heard them in town, were more than likely just a fancy set of phonographs set to a timer way up in that church tower. They played the Common Doxology. I turned and watched the echoes bounce wildly off the near and distant trees, up and down County Road 1. My head moved slightly to follow, and my lips subconsciously mouthed the words, wrongly, I'm sure:

Praise God from whom all blessings flow;
Praise Him, all creatures here below;
Praise him above, ye heavenly host;
Praise Father, Son and Holy Ghost.
Amen.

When I turned around, my eyes met the floor of the pasture, and at my feet was the tightly bundled and gift-wrapped answer to all of my God-forbidden quandaries thus far.

5

Dinner went on without hitch, and I would say mightily so because of my own willing it to. I sat there for nearly forty-five minutes without airing a bit of speech, and eating at a steady and quiet pace. Conversation was sparse, save for what words Momma tried to force, and the small exchange she'd had with Pastor Obis when he had come for the nightly stockpot. I wasn't being terribly observant, but I hadn't seen Daddy even gesture at Obis when he walked in to greet us. His eyes stayed glued on the geese as he fed himself slowly. Obis watched the back of his head with a kind of inquisitive smirk, the occurrence of which established he and Daddy as equal partners in a business dispute. That was fine by me. My world hadn't been shook up too rough by it.

I reckoned Daddy was still steamed at Obis for bringing that stranger, Mr. Langford, onto the farm, post-closure, without first consulting him about it. Leastways that's how it seemed based on their exchange of non-verbals and

Momma's slip of the tongue a couple nights before. At any rate, I didn't care enough right then. I sopped a leftover morning biscuit in a puddle of chuck gravy on my plate and stuffed it, while my other hand probed the shape of a surreptitious bundle in my pocket. I had indeed recovered that lost parcel after which I lusted the entirety of the day prior. It then laid tumbling quietly over and over in a secret place below the table. How I had spotted the object at such a distance (one I had managed to fit into my pocket) was beyond me. It was, after all, quite small. I hadn't yet inspected the interior for myself, nor had I pierced its protective wrappings. Though I commanded my own set of highly unlikely and hypothetical estimations for what contents lay inside; gold, a note, a thousand mole crickets, I had patiently resisted my own inconceivable urges to strike open the parcel and invite the inevitable revelation to wash over and anoint me with understanding.

I was the type of strange and private son who much preferred the gratification found in the modest and uninterrupted consumption of a reward, as opposed to the feelings of vanity and discontent that often resulted from brash or public overindulgences of mysteries found at the end of books or in the taste of sweet morsels. As a result, I elected after dinner to stay my curiosity until I had at least bathed. Given my obvious inability to secretly harbor the parcel within my mouth or a cleft of my naked form, I refrained from any attempt to bare it into the washroom along with me. Instead, I resolved to the lone debriefing of my thoughts.

I stood there, staring blankly at my clear and accurate reflection on the mint glass of that still and stagnant pond before me. The essence of the soapy brine had already begun to permeate the pores of my face and call water to the corners of my eyes. Yesterday (when Momma gave me the apple) I vowed never again to break, with my body, the malarious surface of the bath. I had been made conscious of the truth both there and inside the waters. Each and every night, as I had yielded to that brackish baptism and basted with the refuse of my family, I had consigned myself a little further unto the most cardinal of all human covenants; the one which bade me ingest each of them, until I at last would become them. My opposition to the water had less to do with my averseness to become like Daddy or Momma or Aaron, but rather a deep desire within my own soul to experience truthful and utter refrain for the sake of divergence. To simply decline that which wasn't inherently wrong, only easy.

What happened next was a metaphysical battle which occurred alongside a course of physical action. My arm plunged the depths of Daddy and Momma and Aaron and found the rubber stop which stood barring the way to the drain. I removed the stop, with the dumb bravery of a man-child, and watched as the opaque liquid left that tribal basin in a rushing stream and whirlpool like the one I had dreamed about picking up the front pasture with me astride it. As soon as the water had fully gone out, I saw a whittled bar of Ivory sitting at the bottom, which had been used previously to cleanse all of our forms of filth for days and days over. I reached forward and withdrew the bar with one hand, placing it carefully on the rim of the tub.

I thought deeply, then, (for the sake of being conclusive) about that which I had already and clearly made up my mind. Though my hands moved unapologetically, the consequences still raged across the synapses of my brain.

In a gesture that was half made of intention and half of hypothetical recollection, I began to twist knobs until that clear and icy spring came forth from the laughing mouth of the faucet. I felt the cold stream in my hands and twisted further; right this time, and then left with the other. The sound was overwhelming. I spoke shapeless words and mumbled unintelligibly to test whether I could hear myself over the endless fall and splash of the liquid column. I could not. I saw steam begin to rise from the glassy surface of purest water. It was only a matter of time. Any blessed minute, that washroom door would swing open and I would get hell beat for the atrocity unfolding around me. I stripped fast and sat crossed in the shallows. My skin went brail and I shivered as the small hairs upon my body stood to attention.

For a moment, I shut my eyes and allowed myself to be swathed in the rapture of the singular event. No thoughts perfused my mind at all. My head was empty and numb, devoid the mysteries and disquietness of the farm. I strayed into serenity for what rightly seemed a life age. Then, I was suddenly drawn back to consciousness by the lucid and perilous prospect that Momma or Daddy could indeed be hard at work, beating my physical body even then as I navigated that paranormal plane. When I opened my eyes, however, no one was there to chastise me. I waited and waited, assured that my just deserts were on the other side of that door, but still, no one passed through it. I heard the utterance of the water. I considered the sheer amount of time I had spent there and the closeness of proximity the washroom shared with Daddy and Momma's bedroom, and I gloried in the wonders of it all.

I was alive in the water's love. Something in me argued that even on the most toilsome of days, in the midst of so many mysteries or the undoing of my world itself, there was always that. There was always the water. A momentary escape; one that usurped sleep because of its ability to be done in consciousness. Its ability to be remembered without the aid of good or bad dreams. The steam, the hot bath was always good. I truly knew so, because on the few precious other occasions I had been permitted to sit still in that heavenly broth and cook like a fresh picked spud, it was when I had been sicker than hell, puking ponds and shivering my bones to shatter. And even then, the hot running bath was enough to cause me to trade the loathsomeness of those days for the blessed recollections of goosebumps and rapture (and don't think me too chaste to lie about my condition on various other occasions in order to stew there from time to time, neither).

The door to our room always remained open wide, and most often, the light was left on by Aaron, whose arm I had narrowly escaped decapitating myself upon when I swung around to my bedside to release my towel and then stand naked for a moment. In my normal, self-learned conventions, I would have stood with caution, watching Aaron's eyes and hastily trading the towel for my jeans in a breakneck transaction, thus only exposing my maleness to the elements for a short time. That evening, however, my modesty, which had always been a great deal more than Aaron's, had gone from me, and I no longer had any concern for who or what might bare witness to my most unadorned state.

There I stood, bare and cold, but open. My back was to the bed, and I peered past the open blinds of our window and into the shorn thumbnail of the moon. The stars were out but bore little light, even compared to the thinness of the far smaller lunar crescent. It was going to be damn hard to see Sarah Obis on a night like that. That is to say, if she even was to decide to show with such a pernicious wind chill in the air. One could see the still, black cold hanging in the air; even from the warm side of a window. Say it was my optimism, but I gave her one more night before she would call it a season.

I reapplied my jeans (which seemed counterproductive) and made sure to lay my fingers upon The Harbinger's parcel before leaving the room. After a momentary visit with Charles, I led myself away from the house by the barn light; first by the sword in the yard, then by the yellowed tones at its rear. It was enough to move me past the old buildings and haystacks, but beyond that it wasn't much good. It wasn't so dark, however, that I wasn't able to navigate with an amalgamation of that which I was able to see and that which was stuck in my head from repetition. My lustful and beating heart did guide me, as well, but none of it lasted for too great a distance before the light of the bunker fire picked me up and finally strung me along into the saplings of the Freedom Spring.

I navigated my way, by memory, to the foot of my peeping tree. I took note of the woods. The night was as still as a corpse, and damn near as cold. It sat there—the cold—in a dense, omnipresent vapor where the summer earth had drawn up the moisture from the ground and laid it to hang eternally on her clothesline. The sudden chill had crystalized each particle until the very air was frozen, but still passable. Every breath drew in a billion specks of icy fog which stuck fleetingly to my throat and made their home there for only a split second, until finally succumbing to the rich and overwhelming heat inside.

I scaled my tree and positioned myself comfortably within a low cleft upon the second tier of branches, just above the leaf line. There, I began my patient work of waiting. I reckoned I had arrived maybe half an hour early. I sat quietly, picking at what bark was left on the higher parts of the branches. In my nightly waiting, I had stripped that tree of whatever clothes it once had. I figured the things I had witnessed there, and the things I done to that tree, made me a good bit preoccupied with nakedness.

Had any right-minded woodsman come across it and stared down at its base to see that white sheet of bark all strewn about the floor, I supposed he would have immediately dismissed the notion that something like a hog had come along and scored the trunk, given that the bark didn't even start to disappear until halfway up. He might have also defused in his head the suspicion of a deer shedding his velvet against the tree for the same reason. A moose perhaps. That was all well and good, except I had never once seen or heard of a moose in Indian River or within three thousand miles of it. I reckoned it wouldn't have taken him long after his observations to conclude there was nothing less than a peeping boy living in that tree, given the close proximity to the spring, and the regular foot paths leading to both.

The nook in which I sat felt almost as if it had been made for me, or even by me, imposed upon over and over until wearily submitting to the mold of my form; a humble response to my many visits. It was right then, when I had settled down into that familiar place and attempted to clear my head of all lingering forethought, that I heard it.

"She's early," I said so far beneath my breath that I mistook it for a thought. Sounds had begun to claim seizure of my senses. Dried leaves split and disintegrated below foot. Sticks and twiggery snapped so loud their shrieks echoed across the pine-peppered landscape, bouncing freely between trees, but never beyond the straw-covered floor and canopy. The signals, however, were coming from a different direction than what was customary for Sarah Obis' approach. I sat indian still for several moments and heard nothing further for several more.

Suddenly, it seemed the shadows changed shapes behind me, and I heard a dull thud, like that of a horse's hoof to bare earth or a kept pasture. I turned straightways and saw it, sticking out like a bold gesture; like one of Charles' white spots. It stood there, chewing brazenly, about eight or nine feet off. A ewe; as certain as I had ever laid eyes upon one. The second I had seen her, I was sure she was the smallest, most lily white creature in all the world. She had come up from the direction of the front pasture, grazing lazily on sprigs of grass and whatnot between the tree roots. The damnedest thing was, we had never kept any sheep, and I hadn't known a soul else who did.

My first and rashest inclination was to scare it off in order to keep Sarah Obis from seeing her when she did finally show, but then, I began to watch her. She was unblemished and frail as pewter. Healthy, but delicate; no bigger than me, and damned if she had ever been sheered. My eyes were transfixed upon her for a spell. All else was reduced to a blackish-blue haze, and I caught myself, several times a moment, holding back breaths without thought, attempting desperately to keep from breaking that hallowed and silent moment. She moved with angelic grace, gliding between

72

trees and bowing low over and over again to humbly partake in the sparse blades of sustenance scattered about the terrain. My eyes were locked on her like Daddy's had been on those painted geese.

I had almost come to predict what step or posture she would take next, when all of a sudden, she spooked. The moment broke as I saw her look on past the spring and then turn to make haste in the opposite direction. I turned in the nook and saw the smooth silhouette of Sarah Obis standing there naked as the tree I sat in. She watched, stretching her neck longingly, this way and that, to see where the ewe had escaped to. She hadn't noticed me, though her gaze had to have struck my tree several times in a row. She dipped low to see in all directions, sometimes taking a step forward or backward to command a better vantage, but to no avail. Soon, it seemed she had given up trying to spot the creature, and instead turned to face the spring.

She bowed low and scooped up her lantern, which seemed to already emit the smallest starlight. She brought the lantern to eye level, hanging the device in front of her face with one hand on the simple wire handle, turning the valve with the other. Suddenly, her face shown clear as I had seen it in times around the bunker fire, in the cold of Christmas as we sang carols with the brothers and sisters. Sarah Obis' voice wasn't the creamiest tone one had ever heard; in fact, she seldom produced notes on key and never failed to project rogue harmonies at soloist volumes. All such thoughts, however, went away as soon as she released a little more fuel into that glass terrarium of fire.

The synthesis of where the light chose to break upon her breasts was more than enough to cause pain and stress in my heart of hearts. It was then and there, spellbound

Nick May

in a prophetic moment, that I did see my future and felt
the near encroaching of my manhood. Soon, my thoughts
would be solely fugitive, in all moments, to a temporal
force more alluring than adventure, than Aaron, than even
God. Woman. As if my mind, in idle moments, wasn't
already given to long-drawn meditations on the sleek and
robust form of Sarah Obis standing unclothed before a
version of me many years older.

She sipped at the water with her toes, as she always
did. The black and bitter cold glass of the spring took in
nothing of her. Instead, it merely stood aside, motionless as
the tip of her foot moved in and out, likely without a drop
shed. The surface of the spring was like chilled mercury,
unmoved save for a slight and imperceptible rise in volume.
Sarah Obis shivered visibly, and from all that ways off, I
observed the perfectly uniform brail patterns ripple across
every square inch of her skin. Her body seemed to raise and
shrink as her features tightened and changed hues in the
cold. Then—brave as ever—she went under.

The spring enveloped her fully, and she seemed to lose
her breath as the water graced her navel. She gasped loudly
and then produced a short and audible strain just before
she dipped her head. I rose slightly with eyes wide, pulling
up on a higher limb to see her emerge. When she returned,
she was facing me. She kept her arms close, holding them
against her breasts, which caused them to escape bulbously in all directions. She shook loudly and stood higher to
squeeze the black water from her hair. When her arms lifted, her breasts bounced back to attention and stood blued
and noble.

It wasn't going to be easy for her to get used to it; in
fact, she might have never recovered any sort of comfort

74

whilst captive to the frozen chambers of the spring. The cold would do nothing but eat away at her ever-renewed warmth. The body and blood would give, but the dark cold would take away, and so on and so forth. It was push and pull; never enough to help her adapt to the water, but always too much to oblige hypothermia. I watched her close, knowing full well this was my last evening with her until the warmer months. At least until April or May. I saw her still herself, sinking to her collarbones in the cold pitch. I trained my eyes closely and did not blink. Her eyes were closed. I watched her chest rise and fall mildly upon the black skim of the spring. Water pulled away and gathered in small drops, nearly frozen, as the beads stuck stubbornly to otherwise air-dried and volumous hillocks.

I revisited her shut eyes between long and drawn glances at her sapped features. Her wet locks were pulled around to one side and laid upon her left shoulder, drinking thirstily from the creek down around her arm. I turned briefly to see if I could manage a final glimpse at the ewe, but she had gone on through the trees to a place I couldn't tell. When I turned back, my eyes fell again to the warm glow against Sarah Obis' deepening bosom. I felt expressly wrong, but also blessed. Suddenly, I became chilled with my attention locked in that place. I couldn't bring myself to look into her face for fear of what I felt I might see. I was being watched, and I had known it for a good half minute since I had turned to search out the ewe. My sin had found me out. It wasn't immediate, but as soon as I found the grit, I raised my vision slowly, climbing along her chest, then her neck, then her jaw, to her temples, then finally to her eyes. Indeed, they were trained on me.

I stared deep into the black windows of Sarah Obis' soul. Neither of us moved a muscle or hair. Her stoic fortitude challenged mine as we sat in stalemate, without blinking even once between us. That moment went on in eternal stretches, reaching deep into my past and far into my future. Sarah Obis could have been dead in her stillness, frozen solid in the waters of the Freedom Spring's winter countenance. Something in the calm of her face told me it wasn't the first time she had noticed me. And not once in that boundless moment had she reached to cover herself in any fashion. With each added second, I grew more and more awkward, and she became less and less concerned.

Finally, in a gesture that wasn't quite submission, her eyes fell away from me. She then turned, and even smiled slightly. Her arms rose to the top of the water, outstretched in a wide span, with her hands gently treading along the surface. She was playing for me. I snapped and swept two half circular fields of vision to my left and right, barely assuring myself there weren't other souls present to witness the madness. I pinched myself violently and was soon back upon Sarah Obis with eyes wide and heart pounding beyond comprehension. I was then full at her rear, but she had risen fairly from the water. The muscles in her back worked artfully beneath her young skin as she raised her arms to gather her locks in her hands and wring them dry. Her face turned, and parts of her profile seemed to withdraw in a modest corner smile once again.

It was simply too much for me to handle the notion that Sarah Obis, object of dark fantasy and erotic reverie for every good man, was standing before me, willfully revealing herself in immodest shows of beauty and flesh. My mind would need weeks to digest and disseminate the images; a shock equal to witnessing a murder or being victim to rape, but nowhere near as mournful. No words were spoken. No sound was uttered. We remained there together in that moment that seemed to only make sense to half of us. I yearned for it to last longer and longer and pledged in my heart to remain there in that tree until the sun rose and fell a hundred times over if it meant I could continue to look on her grand image and admire her formidable presence from every aspect.

I had forgotten about the ewe or how long I had been gone from the house. I had forgotten about my family, the machine, and The Man in the Woods. Then suddenly, my hand latched to my leg, and I fingered the outside of my pockets until I felt the Harbinger's parcel there in that cold denim. Later, I thought. Then, my attention was drawn back to Sarah Obis, who had begun her ascension from the spring, almost having noticed my momentary wane in fealty to her show and ritual. I begged forgiveness silently for my betrayal as she rose from the water, hoping desperately that she would see reason and stay, but my heathen prayers did not avail. When Sarah Obis finally came fully out of the water, she did so in three or four agile strides which revealed the fullness of her statuesque tail and the seamless communion it shared with her braided lower back and the upper reaches of her crafted legs. My breath stopped and I shook with untold surges of near pain.

Sarah Obis stood there, trained away from me as she took graceful lifetimes to unravel her robe. The lantern shone full on the entirety of her form as she towered above the Freedom Spring. Her gate; unfettered. Her posterior; stalwart. Who needed the moon, I thought. The untold guilt had already begun to settle inside me even before she had turned to make her way back up the path to the bunker, but I could tell it wasn't a sensation that would see fit to last long within me. I watched her noble eyes as she tied her robe and found her footing against the path. Not once again did she acknowledge me, and I wasn't sure I would have wanted her to. She was well out of my sight when I finally released captive breaths and damn near choked. I drew in and out in long strides in an attempt to regain composure and slow my child's heart. The excitement left my body, and things seemed to subside the longer I waited. My thoughts, however, still fought to pervade my peace with what I had seen.

Sarah Obis had been revealed to me in all her bodily splendor, and only after having uncovered my deviant soul floating in that tree. In all my visits to that bit of woods, I had arrived each time with the hopes that my presence there would go unnoticed, and that with each sojourn to the waters of the spring, Sarah Obis would grow more and more agreeable with the conditions and become more and more likely to reveal herself the way she just had (as if there was something I hadn't yet seen). Each night, I went there in search of something new, knowing full well God had not seen fit to add to her any one feature the way he did with Eve. So I would sit pleased but unfulfilled until I had seen her in what I could justify as a different light. I had become slave to a useless practice which was a clever trick of my mind to tell me that any new image was indeed different and new and had never been encountered before. It was a cycle inescapable, and it consumed me.

I cast it away; the thought, at least. Reaching into my pocket, I withdrew the crumpled parcel, which was nothing more than a thrice folded scrap of cardboard wrapped tight in some sort of cellophane property as if to prevent weathering. Altogether, it was about the size as Momma's solitary lipstick tube. Momma was expressly opposed to the use of "such cheap parlor tricks" as a means of embellishing a woman's presence in a room, claiming it was "nothing but idolatry and conceited vainglory." She had stated before that her reason for owning such a heinous device was only as a tool to remind her daily to demonstrate "chasteness and modesty," but I could have sworn to have seen her on one or two isolated occasions with the slightest touch of red to her lips, pouting subtly in the window reflection when she thought no one was looking.

I thought long on continuing to put off reading what might have been the most significant message of my life, at least until I had retreated to warmer lodgings but ultimately decided in favor of finally releasing whatever spirit was hosted inside The Harbinger's parcel. It was too damn solitary out there to be challenging thoughts bigger than me, and too damn cold, but I had already begun to pry apart the wrappings with my ghastly fingers. Once I had removed the outer skin of plastic, the most peculiar thing showed through. As I unfolded the bit of cardboard that had been held in awkward contortions for hours, I understood it to be the innermost cone of a toilet roll, folded neatly on the ends (just like I imagined one of Don Miguel's tamales) and rolled horizontally into a smaller cylinder. I observed it for a moment, turning it this way and that, and then forcing my thumb and pointer into the opening on the end.

Inside was nothing more than I had honestly expected; a rolled message no bigger than a smoke. I retrieved it and held it there, spanned between my two cold hands. I was just as afraid as I was ecstatic about the prospect of what it told. I had not yet relinquished the reality that I was just a boy of twelve who could have full well breathed a very long life into a very short string of slightly peculiar events that, in every likelihood, I had imagined was anything more than a well-explained and logical scenario which I had willed into a mystery of the grandest variety. It was in that thought that I unravelled the message and gazed at the six words that heralded the great call of my life.

6

"So there I was, seventy-eight nautical miles out, stranded on a sandbar no bigger than your bunker, standing ankle-deep in the warm Pacific waters when I heard it." The brothers and sisters gasped as Mr. Langford continued with a story that had easily captivated me, Aaron and the rest of the morning onlookers. "Ooooogah!" he expelled with a grand gesture, raising his arm and pulling down on an imaginary horn tether. Mr. Langford would be dead before dinner. "Ooooogah!" he repeated with a contorted face and round mouth. The small crowd erupted jovially as they stood gathered outside the front of the barn in the freshly dried morning air. "The little tug had returned!" he shouted, almost evangelically. "I was saved!" he continued. "Yes, it turns out the French Quartermaster had been aboard the only ship that suffered any real loss from the skirmish and had not drifted far whilst sleeping aboard the wreckage. With a bit of luck, the captain was able to reacquaint Corporal Jean-Luke Baptiste with his lost and recently victorious flotilla and also manage my rescue on the return journey." The brothers and sisters began to applaud the short man for his heroism. "Indeed, the lesson here, ladies and gentlemen," he continued as he quieted them with his hands, "is never to draw the short stick when the wage is giving up your spot on a tug boat for a marooned member of the French Navy!" he said, nearly bursting to laughter with each syllable uttered until finally, he did.

The family was mad with celebration and hysterics. Even Aaron wrapped his lips tight around his teeth and bit to resist the urge to smile. The rest laughed for a while, and even I joined in mildly as I regathered what I had understood of the tale and gave myself permission to engage. Walter sat stoic just beside Pastor Obis, unable to hear, and therefore unable to process the wit in Mr. Langford's yarn. He also displayed the slightest twinge of jealousy for the short man (who Pastor Obis often favored with hearty slaps on the back and primal bouts of laughter), letting slip the occasional scowl through the thick brush of facial hair about his eyes and mouth. I watched the reactions of the brothers and sisters closely. For the most part, Mr. Langford had seemed to earn exclusive approval of all but one in the company, in only a matter of three days.

"There ain't no such thing," came a familiar and wooden tone from the rear of the rhetorician. Daddy stood poised against the seal of the feed room door. He shoved off with a flex of his arm and approached Mr. Langford casually.

"No such thing as what, dear friend?" the short man asked with a polite smile.

Daddy spat. "No such thing as luck." he came within inches of Mr. Langford's impeccable face and froze for a moment. "Luck...There ain't no such thing as it." The small assembly of brothers and sisters hushed, pretending not to pay attention to the confrontation and soon turning inward to conduct spurious discussions in scattered groups, leaving only Aaron and I to mill about awkwardly until Mr. Langford's reply.

"Pardon me, friend," said Mr. Langford finally, "but tell that to a man rescued whilst cupping his hands for a drink of salt water." he smiled.

We stood speechless; the idle murmurs yanked violently from beneath us. Our faces were made stone in the midst of the civil row. Daddy turned his head and then snapped his vision to a place straight through the lot of us. He began to walk, and we parted in humble submission.

"The good book does say," he proclaimed, "'if any man will not work, neither let him eat.'" Daddy's face was iron as he moved patiently to the remaining stack of sheet tin; nearly two tons of sun-brazed blades sitting neatly amidst a year of uncut weeds. He looked back at the short man through his wake in the onlookers. "You plan on eatin' tonight, friend? Or you hopin' you'll get lucky?"

Shit, we all thought. Some looked at their feet or stretched their necks in an attempt to conceal their desire to receive the short man's rebuttal. Others, like me, shamelessly returned their gaze openly to Mr. Langford as he began to slowly approach Daddy. On his way, he removed his houndstooth jacket and hung it and the matching hat on a nail protruding from the outside wall where Momma occasionally hung Christmas wreathes made from fake spruce found seasonally at the farmer's market in town. I heard the signature of the sawdust from the new cross crunch softly beneath his feet. The collective beating heart of the small ringside audience which featured all the brothers and sisters, including Mamie and Dottie, were audible and accorded to one another. The short man rolled up his sleeves in what seemed an open defiance of Daddy who flexed up and steadied himself on the firm red clay drive.

Mr. Langford would be dead before dinner. If it wasn't for his last minute change in perceived motive, it might have happened just then, but just as we thought the short man had left all words behind and had resorted to a more universal set of communications, he did the unexpected. Throwing on Daddy's own gloves, he took the end of a line of coiled rope on the ground without question, fed it through a rivet in the topmost sheet of tin and climbed the ladder to the eaves.

"I thought you'd never ask!" the short man said, smiling and swinging his arm free like Gene Kelly in a number. We watched in shock as he singlehandedly heaved the giant slat to the top of the barn. His smallish form burned a black silhouette into the center of the sun, and our eyes began to water and turn away. Daddy looked down and removed his hat, wiping his brow clean against his forearm. He had won and lost. His attention then turned to us.

"What's everyone doin' then," he muttered, replacing his lid back where it fit in the threads around his skull. Aaron, me and the brothers and sisters leapt to duty as if our legs were whipped with a crop until bleeding.

Aaron and I harnessed up and were first on the ladder to follow Mr. Langford. Once to the top, I could see the brothers and sisters had begun to separate and scatter like ants atop a stomped hill. Each went to their respective toil. I reckoned the day had it in the cards to be rendered right interesting as soon as that soft-handed Mr. Langford decided he was done proving his point to Daddy. I wasn't sure, however, that I was looking forward to more confrontation between the two of them. The short man and Daddy were both equal matched for different modes of conflict. While Daddy was given to his talent for threatening with postures and striking fear with passages of scripture, Mr. Langford had established himself an eloquent craftsman of words and diction, so much so that one could not help but want to stand in favor of all that the petite and scholarly negro had to offer.

It was obvious Aaron thought different of the scenario. I could tell part of him wanted to see Daddy strike the stranger and cast him from the barn's apex, but he wouldn't have minded seeing Daddy put in his own place with a few choice morsels from Mr. Langford's mouth, either. Aaron knew there was nothing more damaging to Daddy's inside man than to be outwitted in a way he couldn't rightly combat with holy rebukes or physical strokes of brawn. Mr. Langford's agnostic prowess was the one thing to disarm Daddy from all power there on that roof, and Daddy knew it. That's why he had been so disrupted by the short man's arrival. I reckon Daddy didn't count on Mr. Langford to oblige his offer to work. He at least didn't mean for him to do it with such enthusiastic buoyancy that he leapt up the ladder and hoisted his own materials into place.

Yep, we were dead wrong about Mr. Langford's ethic. Pure and dead wrong. Not only did the short man keep up; he set the pace for the majority of the morning. Before the first hour was out, Daddy had attempted to take control of a situation already claimed. Aaron and I watched as every command voiced from Daddy to Mr. Langford was accepted warmly, and then subtly rejected in favor of a different idea which the short man would then instate passively. In no time at all, the separate engine of Mattie and Kenzie had splintered off down the far backside of the barn, and with the help of the brute brother and sister, Mr. Langford had begun laying shingles at an ungodly rate, faster than me and Daddy and Aaron could hope to combined. Aaron and I took regular breaks to glimpse at Mr. Langford's methods in astonishment. Daddy didn't look up once, but almost seemed to understand subconsciously what was occurring in his periphery.

In a sort of telepathic fashion, Aaron and I began to try and instate certain tactics that Mr. Langford was employing down on his end of the trusses, but each and every time, as if out of instinct, Daddy would rein us in tightly, often yanking us violently along from the other side of a width of sheet or length of rope, still managing never to look up once at what the short man was playing at in his rebellious coup. I suppose it wasn't as embarrassing as some things your old man might find you doing, but it was more than the feeling of being found out that called me to shame for forsaking Daddy there on the roof. It was the sudden and apparent conversion that had taken place in my wicked heart when I had traded wisdom for reason.

We were slap beat harder than normal when we finally came down off the roof for lunch. I reckoned it was all the superfluous effort, trying to match the pace of Mr. Langford and his quick converts. Daddy didn't aim to appear weaker or slower, so Aaron and I got our asses handed to us up there. Daddy was destroyed likewise, only he didn't aim to show it. Aaron probably desired the opposite. He complained all through lunch, carrying on about how cold it was, and how we were "workin' harder, not smarter."

"We need to group up, fellas!" he yelled, breathin' heavy with his sandwich fisted in his hand.

Momma had brought each of us two peanut butter and jelly sandwiches and a huge vat of creamy tomato (which everyone thought was a right queer combination, and didn't dare dabble in the marriage of the two, with the exception of Walter). We sat in two groups, spread apart along the eastern barn face in the shade of the eaves, devouring the meal. "We're up there working in two camps," Aaron continued. "I just reckon it's settin' us up for failure." It was often typical of Daddy to allow such rants to occur on the clock, especially during the lunch hour. I reckoned he felt it was a man's right to speak his piece while at labor, and I figured he and everyone else were intrigued by Aaron's passionate discontent of the situation. Of course no one knew what he meant. The underlying spirit of competition on the barn roof was just what might have gotten those sheets laid before Christmas. That was the real problem Aaron was poking at, but he was too afraid to say it—like me—in front of Daddy. The newly adopted rivalry between him and Mr. Langford was causing us to work twice as hard at twice the pace than normal. We might all have been dead up there before the week was out. Mr. Langford would be dead before dinner.

"Now, Joe, please tell Mrs. Maya that this were a wonderful soup, here," Walter said through a brief rustle in his brush. Him and Pastor Obis had traveled down from the bunker to check on the progress, conveniently so at lunchtime. I watched Pastor Obis as he kept a constant sideways glance at Mr. Langford's crew down on the far end of the wall. Several times, he turned and began forward, but was conveniently interrupted by Daddy or Walter. "Pastor, you ought to try the soup with the sandwich," Walter said as he dipped a corner into the blood red broth.

"No, thank you, Walter," Pastor Obis replied as he again inched himself in the short man's direction. He itched to say hello.

"Pastor, a word?" Daddy asked without looking up from his soup (which he had elected in place of the sandwiches).

"I reckon I need a word as well, Joe," said Walter, merely trying to match Daddy's relationship proximity to Pastor Obis.

"Excuse me a minute," Pastor Obis replied, dodging the advance and making his way down the exterior of the barn, oblivious to all but his desire to speak with the soon-to-be-late Mr. Langford.

We looked on in disbelief. Even Daddy came up for air to witness himself shunned for a stranger. Pastor Obis reached Mattie, Kenzie, Mr. Langford and Ms. Mamie (who had also come down to visit). We watched silently as the short man stood to extend a warm hand and a bright smile, just out of earshot. In no time, they were laughing and carrying on larger than Daddy could stand, and he was back up the ladder with five or ten minutes to spare. It was possible Walter brooded even harder than Daddy. We left him sitting there in his favorite straight back barn chair that used to be Daddy's until Momma found newer ones for the kitchen at the Feed-n-Seed. I had aimed to make my own climb back up the ladder and work out the remainder of the afternoon, but Momma came and fetched me out around the same time she came to collect the dishes. She had me drawing cursive letters at the kitchen table by twelve-thirty.

The better part of the afternoon passed by without occurrence. Momma let me out to go get my count when I had become too stir crazed by fractions. She said I could take it early so long as I came back and finished what I started. I obliged happily as I slammed through the door and walked briskly across the red clay drive as if to appear to be on important business. I had glanced briefly to the top of the barn, only to see the arched backs of Daddy and Aaron, ridged and black with cold sweat. The moving forms of the others were disappointingly hidden from me at that particular vantage. I crunched through the hell grass and soon stood surrounded by hundreds of tiny, square fragments in a patchwork tapestry. I stuck my hand in my pocket and looked casually upon the barn roof from the view of County Road 1. It was only half as covered as the other side was, and there was no one setting any decent work to it, yet. I did, however, see two and three black dots bobbing up and down along the apex on Mr. Langford's side.

From my coveralls pocket, I withdrew The Harbinger's previously parceled note. I freed my thumb and pointer from my glove, but left my other members inside, unravelling the tiny scroll with experience. I looked down at it and read it, in secret, for the fiftieth time since the night before.

The plot is poisoned Moses Cotton.

When I had first read it, the shock was almost too much to perceive. I thought I had imagined it or even willed it to speak to me (and perhaps I had). Maybe my consciousness had overpowered The Harbinger's original hand and caused the very words to change shape from their intended script and appeal to only me, I thought. Maybe the letters themselves twisted and turned till, at last, they relented in order to escape the torturous bonds of my in-domitable telepathy.

What had it said originally, I wondered. Who was the note intended for before my will had subjugated its contents for my own gain? I reckoned the thought first crossed me upon my original reading of the text, wherein I noticed the line had been written and erased a dozen times before the author finally got it right and settled on verbiage that suited his tastes. It was then that I saw each of my thoughts from the moment I witnessed the parcel drop from the duster and had formed my own hypotheses about what privilege it might entrust me to. I read it again without even attempting to discern what it meant. If it had come from my own brain, I sure as hell didn't understand what it implied. A hunger raged inside me for another. I felt straightways entitled to a torrential downpour of scrolled instruction from the heavens, but none came that day, and I worried it might have been the only one I would see.

Twenty-two was the count. The plague was spreading, or at least multiplying on our cursed bit of soil. I shouldered my concerns and made my way back to fractions. I often wondered why Momma and Daddy had toyed with sending Aaron to Miss Melba's class in Indian River but had never once questioned whether it was proper or not to provide my schooling at home. Aaron had abused his opportunity to broaden his stroke on mankind and didn't right have the capacity for it, neither. Had Momma opened her eyes, she may have seen that I had shown true promise for growing into a creature of intellect and wit, but in any instance that I had presented a question to Momma about how many times one number went into another or who killed whom at Bunker Hill, she would act ignorant as all hell and flip aimlessly through my books with one hand, like she had just seen something in her free time the day prior that I should read in order to refresh my memory. She would turn pages until her thumbs bled or she got called away to something else.

Later in the afternoon, we were in the middle of one such aforementioned episodic equivocation when Ms. Mamie came running up the steps to our front porch and proceeded to pound on the screen door, screaming for Momma.

"Maya!"

Momma come rounding the corner from the den sooner than I could manage to push my chair back from the table and escape its grasp. I cursed in my heart that I was never fast enough. Momma pushed the screen door out to commune with our guest. "Maya! Someone's hurt!"

"What's happened?" Momma asked, alarmed. I could see on her face she assumed Daddy was to blame for whatever had transpired.

"I think you had better just come quick," Mamie said, considerably calmer then, since she had spoken to Momma. It was as if all her excitement had been wrapped in the prospect of being first to share with Momma whatever horrific events had occurred, and since she finally had, nothing was as immediately pertinent as it seemed.

"Moses," Momma said whilst dressing in her sweater from the closet nearest the door, "Don't you leave this house. Don't you go near that window." She never looked at me once and was out the door, leading Ms. Mamie away in seconds.

The screen door slammed behind the two of them with a clash that would have, on any other day, scared them both into muzzled curses, but had merited ignorance in light of recent events. I stood poised in my socks in that chilled block of crisp air existing in and through the fine wire mesh of the screen door, opened as a testament to the first true signs of fall; before the scent of leaf piles burning or the deafening silence of a Southern night with no native sounds to drown out the quiet. I shivered once and stepped forward in defiance of the cold, favoring my curiosity which had overtaken any need for warmth. What had happened out there, I wondered. Momma had warned me against going near the window, but she had failed to mention the door. From there, I could tell the roof of the barn had been utterly abandoned. The ladder stood still and quiet, reaching to the eaves from weeds taller than me in several places.

I listened for sounds, but heard nothing. It was then that I noticed I wasn't as drawn to attention as I should have been. The products of the last several days on the farm had done more to numb my young consciousness than anything in the short list of significant occasions I had witnessed in the twelve years since I was born. Then it started to well up in me that someone could be dead on our farm. I saw the only reason for the full evacuation of the roof being that someone had slipped or been tossed from the pinnacle and—like in my own visions—had plummeted to their death to be spiked upon a rogue sheet of tin. I entertained gruesome images of Bill or Silas suspended upside down with an overturned blade of metal embedded in their skulls and staked between them and the ground.

My heart began to race. The longer I stood there, the deeper the silence seemed to grow. It wouldn't be a stretch to wager the only sounds I heard then for the ten to twelve minutes that followed were those of easy wind whistling against the siding on the house, and perhaps the hum of a few distant autos passing unassumingly by, way out on County Road 1. I readied my socks and shoes in the event that I might be called away from the house to help with any and everything. My first plan of action, however, should I see Momma, was to leap from the doorway and get at least two steps through a numbers problem (regardless of how late it was getting to be) and look as believably uninterested as possible before she came back through the door.

The static on the mesh screen hissed softly, caressing the hairs of my cheek as I stood idly by the door, awaiting the promise of honest stimulation. Then, with a start, I saw a flash of movement at the barn door, and I reset my gaze on Aaron, who had just emerged from whatever debacle was unfolding at that very minute, and was then striding casually across the red clay drive in a diagonal b-line for the house. The static popped and stung my face violently as I opened the door to call out to him.

"Ya'll need me?"

Aaron looked up at me as he reached the steps, scrunching his brow as if staring into the sun.

"Get back in the damn house ..." he said, almost readying his backhand to put me wherever he assumed was my place. I backed up and let him catch the door on its backswing. Aaron passed right on by me and made for our room, looking as if to retrieve something and head right back. I decided against trailing him that time and stayed put, confident I had a better chance of getting something more substantial from him in a short burst. He passed me again and went into the kitchen carrying a pillow and reaching for one of Momma's big steel pitchers on the shelf above the window.

"How bad is he?" I asked, fishing for hints with nothing more than an assumption. I had hoped I was right enough that Aaron might believe Mamie had spilled already. Aaron shoved the pitcher under the faucet as straight as he could, turned the cold water on and glanced back at me.

"... Bad."

I felt my eyes widen as Aaron tightened the knob back and pulled the fresh water with only a few splashes wasted on the counter and floor. I would mop the spots later. Aaron made for the front yard and pushed the screen to open the door, classically disobeying Momma's omnipresent instruction never to do so. I followed close behind and caught the door as it swung back, my heart pounding evermore.

"Is he dead?" I yelled. Aaron turned his head and spilt another half ounce or so, casting a crimson blot on the red clay drive.

"For now," he called back.

7

Someone had fallen from the barn roof, and when I had asked my brother, Aaron if they were dead, he had answered me in the worst way possible. For him to have said "yes" would have honestly been an easier thing for me to consume. For him to have said "no" would have oppositely been difficult to reason—having fallen from such great heights. Instead, he had replied, "for now" which held in it the connotation that the party in question was indeed deceased at that present moment, but that the brothers and sisters had perhaps resolved to attempt a resurrection; a feat I had only ever heard accomplished in modern times by one man; a faith healer prophet called S.M. Stagwerth. He was a kind of figurehead to spirit-filled Southern families like our own. A prophet man and faith healer said to have literally walked on water and raised the dead before his own untimely passing over a decade prior. Momma had made us read about him and others like him in books and old writings, same as Jesus, claiming they were the great proph-

95

ets we would someday grow to be. Unlike Jesus, however, S.M. Stagwerth had been unable to cast his own stone aside when the time came, thus he remained a pile of bones to that day in a tomb somewheres in midwestern Alabama.

It was almost visible; that moment when I noticed the impulse overtake me and assume control of my faculties. I stepped into my boots, like Aaron, and pushed through the door, ducking low to avoid being spotted by any and everyone. I had enough faith in my own adeptness for not being seen; it was in my capacity to beat Momma back to the house that my faith wavered. I decided to brave the odds anyhow, but before I could damn near step from the front porch, I noticed movements near the barn's rear. I decided it too brash to traverse the east wall, which was subject to considerable foot and eye traffic, given the current circumstance of construction, so I resolved to pass on the barn's opposite face and hide amongst the manure piles as Aaron and I once had when watching Daddy mate those two paints.

From my approach, it would have been right hard for anyone to spot me before I was able to dig in against the rear wall of one of the larger heaps of horse and bull shit. I slammed into the flat side of the mound like I imagined the boys on Normandy had. The dugout was formed from Daddy cutting in and lifting scoop after scoop of shit from one end of the pile with his smaller front-end tractor attachment. My whole arm could near about fit in the tooth marks left from the forks. The smell wasn't too terribly god-awful. I was, for the most part, able to bear it; especially given that it was the cost of knowing full-well what had gone on. I knew that from where I sat, I would be able to look on just about the entire situation unfettered as it unfolded.

I steadied my footing and reassured myself that I hadn't merited anyone's attention. I then reached up and pushed into vantage. The first thing I noticed was the obvious huddle near the rear of the barn, surrounding some motionless form on the ground, which I then attempted to confirm was Mr. Langford, given his indisputable absence in the crowd. I then saw Momma at the head of the gathering (near where the short man's face was likely settled). She looked to be administering some sort of treatment, while the others—Mamie, Mattie, Kenzie, Bill, Silas, Aaron and Sarah Obis—drew close by, fully concealing the static body between them.

The next thing I saw was Daddy and Pastor Obis standing off to the side covertly. They looked to be having a tense discussion on the current matter at-hand. Daddy's motions and body language seemed to be speaking volumes more than that of Pastor Obis, who appeared intent on quelling Daddy's quiet tirade. One would have had to be observing them on purpose to realize they were in a heated discussion. It didn't appear they were so much crossed with one another as they were in passionate opposition.

When my eyes fell back on Momma and the others crowded around what I thought to be the corpse of Mr. Langford, I noticed something completely different. Perhaps I had returned at a slightly amended angle, or maybe they had all assumed different postures than before, but there appeared to be no administering of medicines or therapy. It then occurred to me that nothing had actually changed at all, only my interpretation of their actions. It was clear to me then that Momma was speaking prayers, and that the rest of the brothers and sisters were gathered in tight, with hands laid on the short man's lifeless frame. Just then, when I had sensed it strongest, Aaron's head rose from the huddle and stared directly at me. As if he had remembered our spot and coupled it with his brotherly instinct. He smirked an evil smirk and bowed his head once again. He wouldn't tell.

Suddenly, I saw the prayers begin to rise in earnestness, so much so that it drew the attention of Daddy and Pastor Obis. Momma and Mamie began to speak words I didn't know, fiercely and with loud expressions of their womanly figures. Pastor Obis left Daddy and came to join the hullabaloo down on the ground. He took the short man by his lifeless feet (which I could then see full well), and began handling Mr. Langford violently. Daddy and Aaron shared the same reserved behavior, only my brother had been forced by Momma to stay in place and hold Mr. Langford at his shoulders. Daddy paced back and forth near the second horse gate to the front pasture, looking on at the situation with visible worry and stroking his bristled face.

Aaron's eyes rose and fell upon me several times in those following few minutes, as if to make certain he wasn't being judged by me for partaking in such a strange ritual. The scene was then in full convulsion, and I couldn't rightly tell if the tremors were caused by the intemperate rattling of the brothers and sisters, or if they were a result of Mr. Langford's returning to life from the grave. Either way, there was power there from one end or the other. Then, like a bullet from a gun, Momma's right hand shot straight up, and I saw the tips of her fingers wriggle and shake as if she had teamed it with her other, steady at the short man's head, in order to create a steady conduit for channelling the electric spirit of God through her own body and into that of Mr. Langford's. Mamie immediately followed suit and raised her left arm to form what appeared to be an exit route for the power of God to leave Mr. Langford's body once it had traveled through safely. Now, I wasn't truly sure what the holy rabbit ears were poised to accomplish, or if one even noticed the other, but it seemed to be a choreographed effort wherein Mr. Langford would soon be effectively raised.

The terror that would later haunt me from such an unearthly practice being made before my very eyes was enough to make me wish I had never witnessed it or known the wills of my brothers and sisters to cause something of the sort to take place. There was nothing expressly dark or infernal about it—I imagined Jesus and the disciples doing similar things in their own time—but who were we to assume the Lord Almighty hadn't caused the short man to slip from those eaves and come crashing down on his own misplaced faith? Maybe he had intended for Mr. Langford to die, and we were like Saul, calling up the dead against the will of God, or perhaps Mr. Langford, himself.

Mattie and Kenzie and Bill and Silas were then in full-on seizures of spirit with their hands upon the body. Had I seen their faces up close, I might have observed their eyes rolled away to reveal milk-white orbs, like pearls of legend hung deep and large betwixt their ears. The cataclysm of tongues and tremors formed moving windows beyond the fray. With each shake and gyration, I was able to recollect this piece and that part of the man sprawled out on the ground. It was then that I was first able to see the corners of my pillow. Aaron had liberated it from our room, favoring it against taking his own. It was then covered in what appeared to be blood, from what I assumed to be the short man's ears. Through the fidgeting fence of buzzards, I could then distinctly make out the shape of a body, only, I had then become unsure about it belonging to the short man. My mind wandered beyond the scene and back to the front of the barn where I had made a distinct note of the absence of Walter from his chair. The elderly gentleman certainly wasn't a part of the gathering. I then opened my mind to the possibility of other victims (in keeping with the fact that Aaron had confirmed the subject of attention were indeed a man or boy).

Could my assumptions have so blatantly betrayed me, wondered. Could it indeed have been Walter laying there with his head to my pillow, bleeding blood older than the ground it was spilt upon? My perspective straightways changed, and I raised my head unabashed for a more proper look. If only the brothers and sisters would clear away for just a single fleeting moment, I could manage to rest my worries and go about my life of solitudinal wonderment. Any minute, I expected to see Walter come hobbling around from underneath the striped eaves of the old barn, or the short man, Mr. Langford to come rushing to speak one of his agnostic blessings of reason over the victim, pretending to have known the man for years, kneeling to wipe his brow and comfort his motionless form. I had decided I wasn't the biggest fan of Mr. Langford, on a count of his perfunctory charm and rehearsed courteousness which seemed to pervade his being at every corner.

I was not only unmoved by the prospect of Mr. Langford lying dead there on the ground beneath the wails and rattling of Momma and the others, I was concerned at the possibility of Walter. There was something about the old man's tales of simple work and arduous times that I much preferred to Mr. Langford's outlandish yarns about his many adventures in recent history. Walter had lived once, and I was without doubt that he had seen more in his inconsequential and patchwork Southern existence than the short man had seen or prayed to see in all his two-bit excursions along the curves of the world. Still, there was mystery still surrounding Mr. Langford that I had high hopes of getting to the bottom of, but the Lord's will is the Lord's way, and I wasn't at liberty to protest.

The sun had begun to lie low in the West. Daddy had already gone and returned from letting out the horses, and it was getting to be about the time when Momma would usually go and ring the dinner bell, calling us from the four corners of the earth to come and feast hungrily at her table. There was no dinner to be consumed, though. We had stayed and prayed there—myself detached from the rest of them—for nearly an hour when I finally rose again at the visible signs of resignation. I watched as Daddy came and crept up behind Momma, bending low to talk in her ear. The episode had quieted to nothing more than sporadic meditative murmurs and subtle readjustments to combat the needles of enervation. Momma accepted Daddy's negotiations and rose from the ground, holding his arm with one hand, and bracing her aching knee with the other. The brothers and sisters sat back on their haunches and opened their eyes to the darkening sky as Pastor Obis retreated slowly to the inside of the barn.

I had been so taken by the fresh stir that I nearly forgot to more closely observe the body on the ground, since the spot had begun to clear. Just then, however, in that singular and revelatory moment, Pastor Obis emerged from the barn with a large, striped and knitted riding blanket and draped it lazily across the stagnant remains of that once bold and golden temple. I sighed in quiet frustration. Then, as Aaron and the brothers and sisters pulled each other to their feet and dusted off what they had taken from the foot-path, I noticed there was oddly no ceremonial rite or last look. Instead, they simply followed Momma and Daddy away from the scene and left the creature lying there on the ground, alone. Pastor Obis took up the rear and did the same as he went.

I sat there for a moment, staring at the poignant lump, wondering how in the devil's hell the family could justify something as impetuous as abandoning such a misunderstood thing to be consumed by weather and curiosity. What if a coyote or some other ravenous mammal of the wild were to wonder onto the farm and come poaching for whatever lay there, casting that scent of death into the air for miles and miles. Even more dangerous was the liberty I had suddenly been granted to reveal unto myself who laid beneath the veil. I knew, however, that if I had even took one minute to satisfy my inquiries, Momma would have arrived back at the house before me, and I would be up shit creek. I decided, that if the Lord willed it, and if the body was still there, I would return later that night and have a look.

I was able to seat myself awkwardly at the dinner table just seconds before Momma came walking in the door. I tried to make a normal amount of expectant eye contact with her, all the while attempting to conceal my shortness of breath. She walked to the kitchen and left the door open for Daddy and Aaron who I saw coming across the dark-ening yard after closing down the barn and switching on the sword. I thought I heard Aaron pestering Daddy with a few quiet questions. He was carrying Momma's steel pitcher, but was without my pillow. Daddy put him off with a few one syllable answers in his patented deep tone. I faced forward as they came in the house, and I decided to play the role of the withdrawn son who was without privilege. My woe and despondency, however, was hardly enough to draw anyone's attention from that which plagued all of our minds.

Momma set out bread, butter, a few apples, some leftover lentils (over which Daddy staked immediate claim), some canned carrots and a carton of milk. She wasn't in the business to impress that night; not when she had just negotiated with spirits and wrestled with the dead all afternoon.

"Momma, do we have an extra pillow?" I asked plainly. It had come to me in a split second, and I didn't hesitate, given the projection of innocence the question put forth toward my family, and the answers it demanded of them. I realized it was perfectly posed, and I had no apology for it. Before she could answer, however, Daddy cleared his throat.

"Where's yours?" he asked.

"Aaron come and got it earlier, with the pitcher."

Daddy looked at Aaron and cursed him in his eyes for being so obvious.

"You can use his tonight," Daddy said.

I heard Aaron's spirit leave him, and I saw him lower his bread in my periphery. He spoke up.

"... How do you reckon I should—"

"Figure it out," Momma said, assuming control over the question, which had been made hers to deal with in the first place. So much for telling reactions. I tried a more straightforward approach.

"What happened this afternoon, Momma?" I asked. "Why was ya'll gone so long?" As I expected, there was a protracted silence at the table, followed by Daddy's ever deepening retreat into the ceramic geese, and Momma and Aaron's cold stares.

"...Walter had his self a bad spill." Momma said. Aaron looked at her. Daddy even gave her one free eye. "He's better now." And that was that. It wasn't entirely obvious to me why Momma had lied, unless I was to expect there was foul play involved in the death of Mr. Langford. Still, I found it right curious and vowed to question Walter the first chance I got.

A little later, as the family slipped off one by one to retire, I stole away for my evening bath. Since the night before, when I had summoned up the bravery to run fresh waters into the tub, I hadn't questioned the prospect that I would do it again and again. The truth was (as contrived as it might have been) I knew in my heart of hearts that Momma wasn't keen on answering all the questions she knew good and damn well were welling up inside of me, nor did she mean to even provoke such inquiries. Her and me, somewhere over the course of the previous week or so, had formulated an unspoken pact wherein strict boundaries were set between us to prevent her bearing down too hard and to bar me asking too many probing questions. It was how I could afford to run clean water from then on and never fear having my ass handed to me for it. Concerning other things, Momma reserved the strict right to chastise me for doing anything against her will for the purpose of answering such probing questions. It was all stated in some discrete clause or fine-printed set of bylaws somewhere unseen.

I laid there in my thoughts for a short while, aiming not to miss the opportunity to settle my query before the body was extracted by any number of unseen forces. Pastor Obis had yet to come and retrieve any sort of dinner for the brothers and sisters. I didn't expect he would, given the unusual circumstance of the afternoon. He and Daddy had argued briefly about something at the barn. I had noticed they were more at odds with one another then than they had ever been before. Momma had certainly acted well into her charismatic capacities in the afternoon. It was something I had observed regularly of her any time I would find her in weighty scenarios of the spirit which I was often too timid or too young to join in on. It was always a mild shock to witness her take up those tendencies in rare moments of desperation.

That was about as far as my meditations took me before I was nearly pruned and ready to wash out. I half feared Aaron wasn't quite all the way to sleep by then, but I aimed to make confirmation by laying eyes on his arm, stretched proudly like the wooden sign on Marlin's store. Momma had gone from the kitchen nearly seconds after we had left the table. There wasn't much to put away. Daddy was either in the den or already in bed. I elected to spend a little more time doing some of Aaron's chores before going out to retrieve the knowledge my well-baited mind so fervently desired. I put away the steel pitcher, tied up the trash, threw the soiled towels and rags into the wash basin to soak, stacked my schoolbooks, rehung Daddy and Aaron's work jackets in the front closet, swept under the table and then folded bed sheets until I was sufficiently assured Aaron and the rest were fast asleep.

My final task before heading out was to feed and water Charles, but before I could make my last quiet steps across the kitchen, I observed Daddy had left his Word sitting boldly atop the kitchen counter where Momma would have been right pissed to find it. I measured the consequences of moving the book myself and suffering Daddy, or asking Momma for permission to move the book and leaving Daddy to suffer Momma. I figured Daddy would prefer the book appear in its place unannounced. I gathered up the immense codex in my arms and trembled slightly at the thought that I had often seen, but never held in my own hands, that worn, and tough black leather champion. I felt the Spirit of God reverberate inside me, like a tuning fork in my bones. The binding was resolute, like a tortoise shell, and the pages had been turned so many times, they frayed at the edges like a old flag. I reckoned it merited confession that I had never known Daddy as well as I did then, whilst holding his Word in my own hands.

I decided it was best not to leave it in the open, but rather, to return it to the den and lay it beside his chair. I hardly ever ventured into the room. None of us did, save for Daddy. It was a dark and subterranean place, without windows and riddled with books and antiques; things like stained glass lanterns and brass-festooned ornaments that I despised. The room was tiled with the morbid faces of kindred strangers and ghosts; framed photographs of a hundred dead family members I had never known, all looking down on me, crammed so close together, one could scarce make out the wall. To be entirely truthful, I was right terrified by the space. We all were, and Daddy knew it. I reckoned that's why he retreated there so often; to keep away from us when he was in need of solitude.

I had set the Word down on the hearth next to Daddy's reading chair and was already on my way back out when something caught my eye. I turned my head and stopped briefly. It was a book I had never seen before on one of the shelves. Granted, it might have been there my entire life without my detecting it, but their was something that made me suspect I had never observed the particular binding upon any of my hurried visits to the room in times passed. I sidestepped back to the case and ran my finger along the spine of the alien tome. It was a black and gold leaf-stamped Bible, not unlike Daddy's, with the exception of its slightly more modest size, soft cover and newish condition. I touched where the pages met the binding and pulled firmly, having to brace the works on either side with my free hand in order to liberate it from the grasp of Daddy's overpacked library.

I damn near tumbled to the floor when the book finally turned loose. As I flipped it in my hands, I noticed the thing had scarce been read at all, if even touched. The stained edges were still dark red, and the publisher's name was clearly visible on the spine; SOLOMON. I searched for a "KJV" signature the way a seasoned drinker might spy out the maker's mark of a fine whiskey, but there was no other trace to indicate much else about the thing. I wondered if it might have been a gift to Momma or Daddy from a close friend, either from recently or long ago. I thumbed through the pages, undoubtedly taking with me the first unseen rubbings of that rich red edge. I heard the bones of the book crack and the pages peel loudly away from one another in crisp exchanges of static discharge. There was nothing to give away a single hint as to where it had come from at all. I thought perhaps it had found its way out of Momma's Bible closet.

I decided it best I get out to the barn and uncover the body before it was too late. Distractions weren't getting me any closer to doing so. However, just as I raised the curious book to place it back on the shelf, something struck a chord inside me and bid me keep it, if only for a brief while, to give myself a proper look, in a more favorable light. I enclosed the vacant space quick and shuffled the flanking books lightly to conceal the hole left by the Bible. It didn't take much to hide. The already claustrophobic conditions of the case were enough to gladly fill the void, and even press tightly against itself, as if there were never a tenant there in the first place. I admired my work casually and then left the room with the Word under my arm.

After stowing the treasure beneath my bed, I made straightways for the back door. I fed and watered Charles with careless intention, stroked his rank back once and was on my way. I contemplated my approach on the side of the house by idling briefly over which path to take to the body. I decided that perhaps the cover of the barn itself might be safest to conceal me from any watching eyes. Upon reaching the doorway, I pulled the plug to the work light in the eaves, which caused the sword in the yard to flash away instantly, and with it, I felt the protection and favor of God go from our little piece of earth. It was necessary, however, to keep cover of darkness.

I crept eerily slow through the barn; past stall and stable, keeping close to one side. There was nothing; not a sound at all but the soft crunch of clay crystals beneath my boots and the occasional swish of a horse's tail to shoo a fly from its ass. I felt like a murderer. Like I was planning something evil and wrong. I always did wonder how the lone lurker felt. Those killers and dark stalkers of the night. Robbers and rapists and such. If the only thing in the night to fear is your own company, is there much else to look after, I thought. I wondered how often criminals felt threatened in the night whilst attempting to enact threats of their own. Does the devil fear anything but God in the darkest reaches of hell and earth?

There was some light in the barn still, but only from the missing tiles in the roof and the square ingress and egress points in the north and south. Both doorways were made of blueish hues and speckled luminescence from the heavenly bodies. The angle at which the moonlight shined through the gaping construction holes in the roof caused it to play oddly upon the floor of the barn, forming a jagged and convoluted path from the back all the way to the front. Altogether, the light created a passage; a gateway from reason to truth, or the other way around. I was traveling through the middle, in a darkness that could have easily stretched from eternity to infinity on either side of me, and I would have never known. It was the first time I had felt such a way since the night Aaron and I had come back from messing with the oddities at Marlin's store. I thought fondly on that night, then. Though it was probably the last bit of honest ignorance I would ever entrust myself with, it was the night I had last lived unworried. The starkly unadorned and wholly unmitigated ending to a transient childhood. I reveled in the moment.

Then, voices. I broke free of thought and dove headlong into an empty stall. The reaction was animalistic. I wasn't sure where the open door came from, but I had landed on a coarse and dampened composite clod of horse piss and pine shavings which had separated upon my fall and released the most horrid and odorous stench of ammonia to ever permeate my lungs. I stood to my feet instinctively and stilled myself to try and hear again what I thought I had. There; the low hum of men's voices reverberating off the barn's wood panels, somewhere opposite me. I listened further. It was no doubt an exchange of voices happening near the rear of the barn, close to where the body lay, undoubtedly.

I slid serpentinely from the open stall, lightly brushing the pine shavings from my thermal shirt and blue jeans. The thin curls stuck to the frayed shoelaces of my boots, and my hands shone wet with horse piss in the light of the moon through the open spaces in the roof, but I ignored it all for the sake of the mission. As I came closer and closer, it was easy for me to distinguish the voices of Daddy and Pastor Obis. I stopped every few steps to see if I could discern anything at all. They seemed to be talking in the same manner in which they had in the afternoon. It was as if their spirits had never left that spot, and they had continued to remain there, arguing in quiet and insistent desperations, but had yet not gotten anywhere. They pleaded with one another, and in my head, I heard the words only as they were meant to exist; in man-sized hollers and shouts. They were real careful, however, not to draw attention, and so they conversed in less than a whisper.

I continued to step slowly forward until I at last reached the rear doorway and tucked myself into the lip of the seal, which was formed where a large, round telephone pole support beam met the residual wall panel from the last stall. From there, through a hole in the particle board, I could actually lay eyes on the two men sparring with hushed words and loud gestures in a cloud of foot-stirred smoke. In the midst of the dust, where the body of a Walter or a Mr. Langford had lain, there was—aggravatingly, but not shockingly—no corpse to be seen; only an empty space where an experienced gumshoe might confirm a body had once been. The striped horse blanket Pastor Obis had used to cover the corpse had gone, too. I crouched low against the stall door and watched intently.

"... She's gonna get us all in a whole mess of trouble, Virg!" Daddy said, gesturing to the bunker, or somewhere beyond.

"She's only doin' what she feels is best," Obis replied.

"Exactly! What she feels is best ain't what he feels is!"

"I just don't see your reasonin' there, friend."

"We're supposed to be able to handle this, right?"

"Yes, I do believe so."

"Well, isn't that exactly what we're provin' we can't do? handle it?"

"If our faith ain't great enough—"

"—If our faith ain't great enough, and he starts to believe it, who do you think's gonna catch hell, Virg?"

I had never heard Daddy speak so many words in such close and passionate succession in the whole of my life. He went on.

"And what do you think He's gonna do when he finds out you let a stranger and a heathen on the property, huh? That's why I told y'all you should've just let him be after he fell!"

"Maya thought it a good opportunity to exercise a—"

"—Don't tell me what Maya thought!" Daddy took a breath. "Virgil, there's two souls accountable for this place, and that's me and you," he said, shoving his iron finger into

Pastor Obis' chest. "If you really thought it a wise thing to bring that viper to this farm, have him fall off a roof and then act as a exercise in faith resurrection to try and prove somethin', then you and me; well, we've turned different corners in this whole thing!"

"Well ..." Pastor Obis started, letting loose a deep exhale. "There's a part you ain't full-on privy to, I suppose."

"What are you talkin' about?"

"Listen, don't blame me, friend. I didn't know how much he'd told you."

"Then don't," Daddy commanded. "If he told you somethin' and didn't tell me, it's obvious he meant for it to be that way. Don't meddle with it more now by oversteppin' your bounds."

"It's just—"

"—I'm serious, Virgil! Don't." Pastor Obis backed off, physically and conversationally.

I was sorely disappointed. Daddy had ruined an obvious great reveal with his pious, blind faith in something unseen. At least I had confirmed who had fallen (wherever the short man might have been at that point). My heart still sunk at the thought of a death on the farm.

"We'll just see what happens," Daddy said. "Either He'll welcome it into his own hands, or..." he shrugged. Pastor Obis looked up.

"He did it before."

"Aw, you know this ain't nothing like that!" Daddy scoffed.

"I don't see how it's different," Obis replied. "Maya would have died givin' with Moses inside her if we hadn't got a little humble."

My eyebrows touched and my chest began to pound.

"And after that, there were a lecture a mile long with emphasis and fire on gettin' our faith straight!"

"And we did!" Pastor Obis lit up. "The lame walked! The blind had sight again! But this is the grave, Joe. It's different."

"You see?!" Daddy demanded.

"... It's out of our hands," Pastor Obis clarified. "He knows that full well."

"I think you're gonna be wrong," Daddy concluded.

What in the hell was going on, I thought. Had Momma really almost died for my birth? Why keep it from me? If it truly was the case, it wouldn't have been characteristic of Momma's more manipulative tendencies to keep a fact like that from rearing its head in so many instances of convenience when guilt or respect were straightways demanded. If I was being completely honest, however,(withstanding the moral precedence of such things) the part to that whole midnight unveiling of mysteries that had me most spooked wasn't the fact that I had possibly almost killed Momma whilst coming into the world, or the fact that Mr. Langford's body had somehow freed itself of the ground with the help of some blessed third party (who I assumed, only through intuition to be Mamie). It wasn't the fact that the brothers and sisters had knelt patiently around the short man's limp and lifeless frame for more than three hours that afternoon in an attempt to raise him from the dead. It wasn't even the secrets of germane nature Pastor Obis so desperately desired to share with Daddy. It was the "He." There was a "He" and "Him" then, whom somehow, in a matter of whispered lines unfurled across thirty seconds of epochal revelation, had stepped into the fray of my upturned life, inorganically and unceremoniously unannounced, with the authority of the Godhead, three in one. After all, he had supposedly kept Momma from death.

Then, it struck me, but I was straightways forced to suspend my thoughts for a spell as Daddy moved on my position. I froze, without breath, in the dark of that cold cleft where I had chosen to conceal myself. Pastor Obis had parted, and Daddy had come walking briskly back through the barn, never acknowledging twice the prospect of a lurker, but instead, kept moving right on by me and away through the arch of reason (or truth). Soon as he was clear of my sight, I rose slowly and understood what I had forever known. There was always a "Him." For as far back as I could reckon (and obviously before, given my apparent eventful exodus from Momma's womb). He was always there; in my dreams, in Momma's yarns, in my deepest pit of fear. To me, he had shared faces with all the puzzled men of my life; those whom I thought to be enigmas or wild hairs. Men like Miles Beckins and William Justice. Men whose faces I had never seen, but whose reputations I had known and recited in my heart for as long as I had been able to cast suspicion. At times, I thought myself to have him pinned. Most recently, I had liked him for the Mennonite, or The Harbinger before. But I had been wrong. He was someone else entirely, and he had run our farm (perhaps our town) my entire life. I saw it then, plain as day. In every stalled word of my mother. In my father's every quiet thought. He was a shadow grown in whispered secrets, the shrouded origin of orders, and the all-too-true farm local folklore meant to distract boys like me from what was real by dangling in plain sight. The Ivory Colonel of Indian River. The King of the Mill Lands. The Man in the Woods.

8

I remained there in that cold cleft for more than twenty or so minutes, allowing my thoughts to drift from one end of the barn to the other, long after Daddy and Pastor Obis had dissolved into either side of the darkness. I sat still in a chilled fear of understanding. My hierarchical orientation had begun to spin once again. Who was I in this whole mess of men and power, I thought. Clearly, someone out there (Miles Beckins, maybe) thought I had a bigger part to play, yet. Standing to my feet, I reached into my pocket and felt The Harbinger's message, still scrolled and riddled in my cold and near dead fingers. It was starting to freeze outside, but I was in no mood to call it a night after what I had just witnessed. The restlessness had overcome me like a storm or a curse, and I had no hope of catching a wretched wink presently.

I settled on wandering with hopes of pouring slowly over the queer and revelatory nature of the night. If I wasn't able to sleep, I reckoned I could at least attempt to study on my thoughts and recollect some of the previous hour's more noteworthy perplexities. Maybe I would take another look at the words of Miles Beckins. Maybe I would see something there I hadn't reckoned before. The truth was, the night only held in it the proclivity for growing stranger and stranger as the hours rolled on. Neither my family nor that doleful patch of earth was beyond the norm for struggles and assertions of power when held against the rest of the dark, dark world. It was the same in there as it was beyond. A span of time laid between the present and the future of our farm and our town and the current and impending masters therein. Great lots of time passed in hours of sleep. In hours when lurkers and dangerous folk did their business, taking steps toward usurping one another by any patient and brutal means necessary.

The vantage I commanded from within the farm's embrace (especially of those gathering slowly at our borders) was enough to gain for myself a loose understanding of what was perhaps occurring elsewhere in Indian River. I knew not who or what had gained influence or leadership, but I discerned that many if not most of the townspeople were dissatisfied with the current state of affairs; whether it be because of tyranny or exclusion. I was reminded of it each and every moment when my eyes had set low on the gate or the endless lengths of fence at the edges of our property, where, in the recent days, it had become a regular occurrence for the darkened shapes of women and men to appear at sporadic increments and peer evilly into the world of the Family Beyond the Gate. It was of no wonder I did most of my probing in areas far from County Road 1.

I made my way, slowly, and by no concerted effort of my own, to the rear of the farm. Toward the glow of the bunker. I stepped lightly, paying careful attention not to pound the earth in any way that might have woken or startled a watcher and thus drawn them to look on me. I stopped cautiously at every sound of a night bird or flap of sheet tin turned loose in the wind at the corner of some distant structure. I felt illusory, but with no motive other than to wander. I would have been right lying if I said I had no hopes of stumbling upon a clue, but it wasn't in my implied objective for my walkabout, neither.

As I walked on, the glow residing at the top of the back pasture, which centered around the bunker, seemed to split and form two separate lights; one at the bulb above the door, and one on the ground in the fire. The artificial light was pale and corn-yellow, and emitted a sickening incandescence only suited for necessity and appearance. The fire danced shyly below, red and pregnant with life. Two silhouettes stood poised before it, and all I could see in contrast was the black contour of faces and arms and legs. One was clearly a man; smaller in stature. The other was Mamie. I was certain of it because of her overlarge breasts and prim ponytail. They were too far off to hear, and there was no hope of me closing in further without being discovered, so I let it be.

My attention turned to the trees of the Freedom Spring. And in an instant, my vision was wed to a peculiar thing amidst the deepening trunks and infinite blanket of fallen straw. Something ashen and ghastly moved with wanton mystery beyond where my young eyes could tell, but I knew it was there, nonetheless. It was like I had fallen headlong into a dream of sleep and had lost all communion with any realm or reality where most things I witnessed happened without cause or commonplace. I strangely had no desire to learn any waking reason—only to experience it.

I swallowed hard any lingering trepidations I might have had and allowed my body and soul to be lured headlong into the young pines. Behind me, there was the corn-yellow glow of the bunker light. My shape on the ground flicked and swatted haplessly before me as I aimed to keep low and enter the trees without being made. As I moved deeper in, I noticed the bars of orange begin to exchange themselves for more frequent pillars of black until there was nothing of the light to be seen except to turn and search for it desperately through the staggered ranks of pine. Though I had never traveled there, I imagined (and Aaron had once confirmed), that the planted trees of the mill lands were much different than those wild pines I stood amongst then. The planted ones had the inability to break light or conceal a man at any short distance. There, one could walk on for miles and miles down a machine-sewn row of aged giants and never once step beyond the moon's gaze or escape the watching eyes of a hunted creature standing at a diagonal vantage.

I reckoned that was why it was right difficult for me to lay sight to that paleness which had previously emitted from the place before me. In that deep thicket of Mirkwoodian witchery, far beyond my normal perch near the spring, I crept with a bravery that could only accompany a spirit of inexplicable curiosity and a hunger for the unknown; that, coupled with the truth that I had no hope of learning what was being discussed by Ms. Mamie and her veiled companion, led me to seek satiation where I could rightly find it, but I had lost the clue that led me away from the bunker to begin with. Whatever it was had gone on deeper into the trees or had circled back behind me and was then stalking my person with quiet steps.

I led with my eyes and focused them desperately with all hope of uncovering that spectral grace, and thus proving my own sanity on an evening completely devoid the need for it. Over vine and under limb, I progressed forward until I felt somewhat afraid and had at last come to a point where the wild seemed to close in on itself as a wall of darkness and bound foliage, and I realized then that I had wandered too far. I turned and found myself completely encompassed in not only the darkest of night, but also the truest void of air, space, time and heavenly bodies. The apparition had led me there, and I had followed it blindly, not anticipating the lesson might have very well been the end, rather than the seizure of a symbol or the discovery of a message. I was meant to stand there, in that place, and ponder.

I turned and stood calmer than water and stiller than truth. There I remained for the utmost of two and a half minutes, watching intently through the dense picket of trees for any tell tale sign of that ethereal entity. I ceased my own breathing. A couple more minutes passed, and I heard the clear crack of pine straw underfoot, followed by the faintest voice. My eyes widened, and had I had lids in my ears, why they might have widened, too, but my body did not forfeit an inch. A little more time passed, and it came. I saw her there and became petrified.

She wasn't at all what I had expected to come across in the cold, which had all but gone from me. Only my eyes moved to follow her pale, white form—stripped of all her clothes—making her way to the spring. She was careful in the darkness, tip-toeing between roots, rocks and other such harmful materials of earthen quality. She hadn't noticed me when I thought she might have. Instead, she passed in front of me in a peculiar way I hadn't seen her use before and moved gracefully to the water. Then, bending low, she took a drink, and I knew in my heart, right then, that I had never felt more uninvited to look upon anything in my entire life; to see nature borrow upon nature in so pure a way. I witnessed one being take what it needed from another in a fashion that had probably gone on a thousand times without my help. I saw God at work there, and I realized then, the world would go on right fine without me there to make sure of it. I turned my head in shame. My eyes shut and remained that way until I felt her go.

When I rose and opened my eyes, she had indeed gone. I felt her essence leave away as it trailed up the path toward the bunker. I wondered why she had come without clothes in such cold. Only then did I notice how entranced I had been by her. My spirit had awoken to take her in, and it stayed that way to call my senses back to life after she had gone. I was suddenly afraid of where I stood; of what I was capable of in desperation. I had become addicted to those regular occurrences of strange phenomenon. So much so that I expected them and readily embraced the recurrent opportunities to partake in bizarre realities and wild goose dreams.

I climbed my way out of the thicket and did my best to navigate through the darkness back to a place of familiarity where I would no longer have to depend on my eyes alone to lead me. Soon enough, I emerged from the trees and found myself a hundred or so feet behind the bunker. I was in a sort of ditch that led itself around the back pasture just in front of a thin line of trees which divided the space in half. A lanky barbed wire fence ran through its middle, held together every few yards by an ancient piece of railroad tie. The young trees had grown up alongside it as a result of the horses steering clear. Sometimes, I liked to look on the older structures of the farm and guess where they had come from or how long they had been standing in place. I would commit my own brand of reconnaissance every so often to gain insight on how various things had come about. The fence, I learned, was put in place before Momma and Daddy had come into the land, but Daddy had known the man who built it. He was a Mennonite named Eli. Eli had erected the makeshift barrier as a boundary marker before the property on the other side had been sold to our farm's previous owner during the depression for a fifty dollar bill.

The price tags on transactions like that never quite made sense to me, nor did the fact that people could own such intangible things as land or life; cattle, for instance. I pocketed my obsessive quandaries for the moment and held fast in wait for a decent time to break from the ditch. I scoured the landscape for tell of Mamie and her shadowy converser, but it seemed the bunker and surrounding areas had been cleared for the evening. Then, just as I poised to set foot across the pasture, I spied something right curious and ducked back down to conceal myself. From where I sat at the rear and south of the bunker, I saw a stream of light pour onto the ground near the dwindling fire as the door to the old structure swung open. Forth from it came a number of unidentified brothers and sisters, but just as I had seen what appeared to be the lank profile of Silas, the lights were shut off from inside. The pale corn-yellow glow disappeared from the front of the building, and all movement turned to that black tar crawl that occurs whenever staring too long into darkness.

I sunk low into the earth—what seemed a foot in depth—as to rest assured in my camouflage. I watched as what was left of the fire on the ground split into many smaller tongues of flame and rose to land head-level near those gathered around it. I felt, straightways, as if I had lain there and witnessed a new Pentecost, and I wholly expected to encounter, with my ears, a series of loud wails in a host of other languages, but the night remained silent, and the tongues of flame bobbed reservedly as they awaited something unknown and illusory.

Several moments later, in an instance many less observant folk may not have espied, a triad of additional tongues was suddenly alight amidst the court of flames. I knew so, as I had double checked with a count and noticed there were presently twelve where there had only previously been nine. I became concerned that what was taking place had the potential to be something more directly related to myself than I wished to give it credit for. I shuddered. With each passing second, I sold myself more and more to the notion that a search party had been formed to locate me. I locked into position as the tongues began to move once again. They drew together and formed a steady queue, one behind the other (which I remember thinking was queer), and marched off into the east. The flames, however, were too far away and held too high for me to make any sense of who stood where, or who indeed could be confirmed present for the strange ordeal. I watched partially in expectant bewilderment. The nature of the evening had not warranted anything personally startling. Not until right then.

On and on down the hillocks they marched until they were nothing more than the size and shapes of fireflies or those flames we watched that night we saw William and the steer. I waited until I knew they were fully gone before I crept up off my hands and knees and out of that ditch. At that point, I had no reservations about marching right on across the pasture and climbing through any barrier I fancied in order to make my passing to the house faster and easier. I was right scared shitless and didn't mind showing it to whatever lurker might have been spying me. It was one thing to imagine the brothers and sisters disappearing late at night (as they had been known to for days at a time), but it was another thing entirely to think that those three added lights belonged to Daddy, Momma and Aaron, and that an entire gathering as such had been called in regards to my going missing. I needed to confirm my suspicions as false.

Though I hoped in earnest I was wrong, I knew deep in the pit of my soul I was alone on that farm, then. The lands had emptied into the trees of the back pasture. The validity of the theory of the search party grew in my mind the closer and closer I neared the house. I was going to get my ass whipped seven ways to Sunday. I marched through the barn without apology, knowing full-well there was no one around. How had they known, I asked myself over again. Then I remembered Aaron. Though I could have sworn to have witnessed his arm planked out from the top bunk in honest sleep before I left, I might have never actually returned to the room to be sure. He might have very well heard me leave and then laid in wait just long enough to leap from bed at the realization of my departure, with zealous anticipation to tell on me to Daddy and Momma.

I ran around the back of the house, finally giving way for more caution, and raced up the back steps in two soundless bounds. I entered through the back of the kitchen and straightways noticed a lamp turned on that wasn't previously. The coat closet was left open, too. I was in deep shit. I reckoned the best thing for me to do was to get in bed and feign sleep until I fell asleep in truth. At least that way I might have had a chance of escaping a berating until morning. Furthermore, if Daddy and Momma did come back with intentions of dragging me from bed and beating me silly, I would have escaped to dreaming for just a little while, and therefore will have eased my own worry in what small way I was able, for what short while I was able to.

That last bit of patient reserve left me when I rounded the corner of our room and realized Aaron was indeed gone. I quickly undressed and climbed into bed beneath my quilt. Its cavernous deeps were enough to soothe my worries for a minute or so, as I felt the warmth of the bed against my legs and the soft folds against the pads of my feet. The comfort, however, soon escaped me, and my mind began to wander again. I would have laid there and turned for hours had I not fortunately been so damn tired. Though I was racked with the thought of Momma coming in at any moment and snatching me up like a fiery chariot, I was fast asleep in no time, without an ounce of recollection.

Some time later in the wee hours, I awoke with a start. The room seemed darkened, save for a spout of moonlight coming through the doorway from a window in the hall. I realized my position in the bed was fetal, and I had wrapped my quilt around the top of my head like I had been camping in the cold. It was a posture of defense I had formed in the subconscious of sleep, in preparation to be disciplined. With my one free eye, I watched the door intently and saw shadows and shapes moving in the hall, but no voices could be heard. It was coming; the most biblically-sized ass reaming anyone in Indian River had ever played witness too. And I could be assured, Aaron was going to be right there through the whole of it. Perhaps Sarah Obis had even made Daddy and Momma privy to me peeping her at the creek. That would have added insult to injury. I would be marched to the woods for sure.

The steps became familiar and close, so I shut my eye to squinting and trained it on the door. Sure enough, Aaron's black shape came gliding through, but he didn't check for me first, like I thought he might. Instead, he quite casually walked from his clothes, kicked them aside and then started for his ladder. Then, and only then, did I seen him turn and stop dead. My heart dropped with pain. His eyes were on me. My own face was veiled by darkness, so I watched cautiously through my flickering lashes, just enough to see his shape and movements. He was observing me for signs of waking. There was a doubt in my mind about it. I could see his silhouetted form slink down on me quietly like a demon, and I was instantly afraid. I closed my one free eye and prayed, full-on expecting him to rouse me himself with a swift kick to my chest or holler for Momma and Daddy at any moment, but he elected, instead, to remain there, staring down on my body and haunting my spirit.

Then, to my continued surprise, another twenty or thirty seconds went by with him just watching me in that stillness, but neglecting to raise any kind of alarm whatsoever. He never did, in fact. Instead, the most unbelievable thing of all occurred. My brother turned on his heel and scaled the ladder to his bed. Simple as that. I froze to an even deeper stillness—if possible—till the bed stopped creaking and I saw Aaron's arm come lowering down like a slow drawbridge. Perhaps he was simply too tired to call me out right then and there, and he had decided to wait until the sun come up to rat me. Perhaps Daddy and Momma had told him to let me be so they could have their own way with me. "'Judgement is mine' sayeth the Lord," Momma often misquoted. Maybe Aaron just wanted to let me think I got off for his own pure joy. Whatever the case was, morning would tell, and we were damn nearly there.

9

The next morning I awoke and found I had pissed myself in the night. I changed my drawers and made it all the way to the washroom before I remembered the catastrophic shit storm awaiting me in the kitchen. I had been distracted by my situation and hadn't even noticed passing Aaron in the hall. I stood froze in the washroom mirror with my toothbrush paused in my frothy maw. A drip of foamy dental cream plopped in the porcelain reservoir below. I heard it sizzle against the silence of my contemplation. As much as I longed to turn the bath water on and abandon myself unto its depths, I decided to face my demons head on and be done with it once and for all. Anything was better than suffering under the torment of uncertainty one more minute.

I opened the sink faucet and filled my hands. My frost-bitten tongue became enveloped in the cool water. I shook my head violently with tradition and spat the refuse into the drain. My face remained there in the mirror for only seconds as it spoke strong words into my soul, then it left for the door. When I rounded the corner from the hall, I saw Aaron headed out for work. He turned and saw me but didn't miss a beat. He was out the door before I could sit. Strange, I thought. The kitchen was empty where I had expected to see Momma, but there was a meager spread of cheese toast, apple slices, Quaker oats, coffee and milk. I sat and picked at the food modestly as to avoid an overabundance of embarrassment or defenselessness should Momma come rounding the corner, aiming to snatch me up and castrate me.

Aaron's actions and non-actions had me right surprised. It was completely out of his character to leave a caught fly living that long. He'd had, in the least, three separate opportunities to either rat me or play audience to my getting beat, and he had passed them all up in silence. Either he was being promised a reward for his reservedness, or he was avoiding the conversation just like I was, possibly for fear of being asked the same questions he had wondered of me. For him to challenge me on my whereabouts the night previous, he knew it meant I would earn the right to challenge him on his and Daddy and Momma's in return. The thing I didn't understand, however, was that Aaron had himself a right strong alibi. At any point in the confrontation, he could have merely pointed out their objective to find me. I would be out of luck at that point.

I had already consumed an entire apple with half a glass of milk and had just crunched into my first bite of sticky cheese toast when Momma came marching through the kitchen.

"Moses!" she stopped on a dime upon seeing me.

I dropped my toast and licked my teeth. The baked film of that American yellow was stuck to the roof of my mouth, and there was nothing more important—not even Momma's reckoning—than scraping it free. I was unavailable to focus. "Moses!" she repeated, reaching over and grabbing my arm. The distraction left me. "You've got some explainin' to do, boy!" Momma yanked me out of my seat and damn near dragged me across the kitchen to the back door. I could barely think straight. "Don't you dare ignore me again," she barked as she opened the screen and pointed my head down at the back steps. "What is that right there?!" she demanded. I stared at the empty dog bowl before me and wondered what it had to do with any of my current plights.

"... Charles's bowl?" I guessed.

"Charles' empty bowl," she growled, forcing my face closer. "Charles don't ever empty his own bowl before mornin'!" I gazed with oblivious wonder. "... Did you feed and water him last night? Poor dog ain't got nothin' to drink neither!" She squeezed my neck hard.

"I did!" I replied, wrenched with pain. "He must've gone and got hungrier than normal, Momma! Ouch!"

She bore down one last time, even harder (if it was possible). "Ouch!" I repeated. It was a right awkward situation. I had every expectation that the confrontation was about my absence the night before, but it was nothing more than typical. Momma eased up. I felt my muscles loosen and my body relax for just a moment. I remembered I might have paid Charles less attention than he deserved on my last visit, but I wasn't planning on making Momma wise to it.

"I sense the devil's lies in you, son," she warned. She turned loose of my neck. "If I find out you're fibbin' to me, or if I catch you neglectin' your chores, we're gonna have a come-to-Jesus."

Momma was playing at my sensibilities. She knew I was frightened of many supernatural and spiritual elements; especially those having to do with judgement and the apocalypse. I came out with it not too long ago when she had started trying to push Aaron and I down to the altar at church to receive prayer by the laying on of hands. I would shake uncontrollably, either from the Spirit or from being scared out of my damn mind, and we would be corralled down front in a flood of forward moving souls all seeking the same thing; some vainglorious and desperate satiation in obtaining for themselves a piece of tangible power that was, for some reason, more "real" than any knowledge of or comfort in a savior.

Those relics of faith were often found in the form of addictive manifestations which, while clearly nothing less than otherworldly, seemed to have an eerily brief shelf life in the hearts of those who often continued to seek stranger signs and bigger wonders. Though he often facilitated these events (which became more and more frequent before the farm closed up), Pastor Obis never seemed a threat to my comforts. Many times, traveling evangelists from distant places were the ones to come, claiming to have access to some privileged avenue for the Lord. They would push on your head and say, "FIRE!" and teach you how to roll your R's and blow air over your tongue to speak spirit languages. There was nothing the least bit natural or right about it.

There was something else present in Momma's rant, however. A subtext. Like she was warning me against more than just leaving Charles's bowl in less than fair shape. The idea, when it came upon me, seemed to pose plausibility, that she might have indeed emptied the contents of the bowl herself in an attempt to pin me with something small enough to scare me off larger carrion. I replayed her words in my head, as if she had spoken plainly to me about going missing. It was evident that the bit of discipline which had just then transpired was about more than dog food. She had just threatened to take me to the woods should she ever catch me sneaking off again. I turned and watched her as she carried herself back through the door. She turned and caught the screen just before it slammed.

"And Moses, you're done on the roof. I don't want you goin' up there no more." I choked on a syllable of protest. "—I already spoke with your Daddy," she interjected. "Mind me, boy. You're on thin ice." I lowered my head and reached for the spigot as she left the doorway.

"Momma," I caught her once more before she went out of sight. She come back and gave me daggers through the screen. "Sometime, will you tell me about the day I were born?" She hesitated momentarily, as I expected, and I saw her swallow her heart back down.

"... Most painful day of my life," she said simply. And with that she was gone from the door as quick as she had come back. There wasn't much else that felt worse than my own mother telling me all the feelings I brought with me into the world were of pain. I coupled it with the quiet knowledge that I had almost killed her upon arrival, and the despair of it all doubled me over until I could scarce draw a breath, and I wept bitterly.

The rest of the morning was spent in action to keep my mind focused. I finished six lessons in social studies and three in mathematics. I was desperately trying to appear inanimate, asking nothing of Momma, as to minimize the opportunity to draw her on me again. My presence at the work table in the front room went unnoticed for the better half of the morning until Momma asked me to help her make lunch for Daddy and Aaron and the brothers. We fixed up a right handsome batch of biscuits and peppered white sausage gravy. I stood on a chair, cutting circles into the softened dough she had prepared earlier. I added small handfuls of flour where needed on the stickier bits, and rerolled the remaining scraps into smaller and smaller cakes and cut circles until there were no more circles to be made. Momma was always slightly annoyed with my ability to render far too many biscuits from the amount of dough I was given.

She was keeping me close, but I managed to aid her without being as present as I might have been under different circumstances. I ached badly to be on the roof with the brothers, gathering any slipped and surreptitious morsels about Mr. Langford. If I could have convinced Momma to allow me to help serve lunch, even, but I could tell there was no hope in that. She was keeping me from the exactness of what I aimed for. She knew I was the most curious of types, and Momma was convinced it was her duty to safeguard as many answers to oddities as she could well manage. Childhood renders the young man unworthy of knowledge (or at least the grown man believes).

I had just handed Momma the picnic plates—a mint green set of plastic discs that more closely resembled bucket lids than items for actual eating from–when she handed me the heavy basket of vittles and told me to meet her outside.

"I'll be out with forks and whatnot in a minute," she said casually. "Go on." I stood still for a second, perplexed by her choice as she turned and disappeared around the corner. If there was one thing I was sure about, it was that Momma positively meant to trap me inside her dungeon all day, but the Lord laughs at what we claim to understand of one another. I kept my mouth shut and was out the door in two shakes.

The first thing I made eyes for was obviously the barn roof, but I couldn't manage to see much, not even heads bobbing. I reckoned they were working on the back end, on the far side. I cursed and searched the yard and surrounding areas, but there was no one to be found on the ground or on the roof. I knew in my heart of hearts, however, the day would reveal something, and part of one mystery would be solved.

I made for the picnic table and did my best to set out lunch in the manner in which I had seen Momma do it before. I dropped one or two biscuits and had to fend Charles off the sausage gravy with a stick as to avoid touching him, but Momma had soon come walking down the front steps to takeover in a way that awfully reminded me of Aaron.

"At this rate, there ain't gonna be no food left edible," she said. "Back away. Go hit the bell."

I didn't hesitate once at the command. Ringing the dinner bell was an institution both Aaron and I were right enthralled by, and fought each other over any time the prospect arose. The rusty dinner bell was an ancient and mammoth thing taken from the steeple of Indian River First Church (which was presently Indian River First United Methodist) nearly fifty years ago, following an areawide fire that spread from a nearby crematorium and burnt up damn near the whole county overnight. Rumor grew that the flames had begun when a madman escaped from a prison work camp near the mill and went and abducted his own family. The unconfirmed story goes that he then proceeded to burn them alive—his wife and three children—in the crematorium's kiln.

Being as that it was before Indian River had its own volunteer fire squadron, many of the town's men and women were awoken in the middle of the night and called to pass buckets of water in an assembly line all the way from the creek north of the town, down to the church and surrounding buildings. Nearly half a mile. By the time the fire was either extinguished or had burned up most of the buildings, it was estimated that nearly the entire township had been present in the bucket line. But the excitement wasn't over. A boat carrying a team of log drivers sent word to Indian River's leaders that the woodlands south of the creek and east of the town (much of the same pinewoods which existed above our own farm) were ablaze and unable to be contained. Whilst the townspeople fought hard to save their homes, the forest burned with ever-growing speed and ferocity. It was decreed that the town of Indian River should be abandoned, and its citizens were instructed to flee to nearby Pinehelm.

Several days passed before it was deemed safe for the townspeople to travel home and begin salvage. What they discovered upon returning was far worse than they had originally hoped for. Indian River was awash with soot and carbon piles ten and twenty foot high (or so they said), and the forest was burnt so far, many boasted to be able to see from the church all the way to the smoldering Gulf water where hundred foot burning pines had fallen headlong into the surf and still smoked in clouds that rose a thousand feet high. Ash rained for nearly a week, and the cleanup took more than a full year.

The great bell from the church steeple, which was three foot tall and nearly ten foot round at its lip, was amongst the only few artifacts to be recovered from the devastation; a half ton relic in memoriam to a time gone by. It was the last great piece of one of the Gulf's first establishments, swallowed by the flames started in four souls wailing in the night. As for the madman, nary a tooth nor bone was found of his body. His alleged family, however, was completely accounted for amidst the ashes of the crematorium. How we had come into owning the bell was still a mystery neither Daddy nor Momma claimed to know.

I stuck my foot up into its mouth and gave the clapper a stiff kick with my boot. The resulting toll was one that started sharply and then called out across the acres of the farm, singing back several times before its deep and operatic vibrato gave way to wind, which whisked it far out to County Road 1. I waited eagerly to see if the speaker bells in the steeple of First Church would answer back as they had before, but the sun's place showed it was probably closer to eleven than noon. A swift wind picked up nearby and carried off west. I turned and started again for the picnic table when I heard it, far out in the trees. At first, it seemed to almost come from behind me, in the mill lands opposite the road and rear of us. Then it switched positions almost instantaneously. I swore to have heard the high notes of the Doxology cutting against the wind. Though I was then certain of it coming from the church (if it indeed they were bells), the wind was most resolvedly fighting the sounds off my ears with terrible force. By the time I moved on, I had almost convinced myself it was all in my head.

As I met Momma at the picnic table, I saw the backside of Daddy coming down the ladder with a host of silhouetted figures behind him. I held my gaze into the sun as long as I could, but withdrew when my eyes welled. Around the time I rubbed them clean, my vision caught something that interested me a good bit more than usual. Shuffling slowly from the barn, looking typically unhealthy and right on cue as ever, was the old man, Walter. I immediately abandoned the table with intentions of speaking with him. He didn't see me take note of him until I was almost right upon him, and then he looked up with a start.

"Moses, my boy. Good grief."

"Sorry," I said.

"What can I do you for," he stated ceremoniously as he carried his course forward to the picnic table in my periphery. The rest of the brothers and Daddy and Aaron had already come down the ladder and gathered there. I turned and walked alongside him.

"How are you?" I asked. The old man looked upon me weirdly.

"Right as rain, boy. Right as rain. Where's the pastor?" he replied quickly, looking elsewhere.

"On his way, I reckon. No broke bones or bruises?" I drilled further. Walter stopped and looked at me directly, laughing once under his breath.

"Young Joe, you're full of it today ain't you?" he proposed in his High South toothless Mississippian. Young Joe was his nickname for me, on a count of him thinking I looked like Daddy. He flicked his mustache twice as I searched for a response.

"It's just...well," I started. "I know I weren't there to see, but I heard you had a spill." I saw the lights come on in Walter's eyes. He looked around to make sure no one noticed him take me aside and put his arthritic hand on my shoulder. Momma had seen. She didn't want me talking up Walter, and for good reason. He looked me square in the face, without detecting Momma, and addressed me with an air as stern as stone.

"Now here," he said. "Might be best you back away, Young Joe. There ain't one bit of that's true, but somebody told you as much to keep your young head out of deep water. If I's you, I'd heed wisdom."

I had never once seen Walter so on edge about anything. It seemed to me he was aiming to scare me off a bit of bad mojo. My best judgement told me to leave him be and go on under the long-confirmed assumption that Mr. Langford had fallen off that roof and that he had been long buried or cremated and scattered on unsanctified earth far from there. The lesser part of me said I ought to keep hounding the poor fellow until he bled.

Just then, the old man glanced casually over and turned a double take in what seemed to be the grasp of horror. Walter was pale as purity and appeared to have seen a specter of terrible magnificence. I joined his vision and at once was encircled in the same horror which had arrested him. There, amongst the brothers and sisters who had joined together at the picnic table for lunch, were the keen black edges of Peter Langford, risen from the grave and standing quite alive there, spooning sausage gravy into his gullet on beds of buttermilk biscuits. Had Walter not seen him first and confirmed my hallucination true, I would have thought him a ghost.

I continued to look on as Sarah Obis got up from her seat and engaged Peter in conversation where he stood. I was straightways puzzled by the lack of blatant disbelief amidst the meal-takers, so I begun to look below the surface, where there was subtext inscribed upon every living thing. Momma's attention caught me first. It was on me. She was taking note of my expression to see what I had surmised thus far. She flicked her eyes back and forth from Peter to me, knowing full well my mind was wrought with suspicions. The next thing I saw was Mamie, and only cause she was the furthest away from Peter Langford, and damn near departed from the group entirely, which I thought odd. Lastly, I observed Aaron, who appeared to be quietly angered in a manner I had before seen. My heart skipped a beat at the realization he was watching Sarah Obis, whose attention was half paid on Peter, and half back on him. As for Peter Langford, he didn't seem to be doing much in the way of talking (which I also found right strange), so Sarah Obis managed to do quite a bit more than bat her lashes and breathe heavy breaths whilst making every possible effort she could to keep Aaron's eyes trained jealously upon her.

Then, as if we had been gone for days, attempting to unravel the burdensome charade that was unfolding before us, I looked down and noticed Walter no longer beside me, but instead, laying flat on his back with a dusty spittle cake at the side of his mouth. I fell immediately to my knees, but seemed to be too late to the occasion. Momma and Mamie were already upon him. Within seconds, the whole scene was alert and moving with great haste. Daddy took charge against Momma's clear will.

"Bill, Silas, get his legs!" Daddy ordered, taking the brittle old man underneath his arms.

"Ya'll shouldn't move him, Joe," Momma said calmly, to which Daddy replied with a look that put her in a quiet place.

"Ain't ya'll gonna pray for him none?!" I demanded without a thought. I froze in fear of what had just come out of my mouth. The scene were suddenly even more silent than my regret. Bill shuffled his feet in dumb obliviousness to what had just transpired.

"Silas! On, now! Move it!" he commanded. But Silas's eyes, like all others, were on me. Even Mr. Langford had seen and heard. I looked to Momma for direction or recovery, honestly hoping she would provide a handful of words to ease the tension and refocus the party, but instead, she chose to hide me.

Seconds later, the situation was back fully mobilized, and Momma had me talon-gripped by the shoulder, heading me for the pasture gate.

"Go get your count," she demanded. It was early, but I didn't protest. The instant she released me, I felt I had narrowly dodged a bullet. I opened the gate, saw the gargoyle sitting there, and closed the gate behind me as a result. Momma had already turned back around and started a swift trot back to the house where it looked like the others had taken Walter for sheer proximity's sake. I was expected to be gone forty-five minutes in the least.

I stomped my way through the hell grass and thought of those boys way out across the waters, trekking through those jungles where there were laid traps for them in all manner of ill-intended scheme. I once read an article in a magazine at Marlin's store that said savage warriors in primitive times would dig holes and fill them with sharp sticks coated in poisonous frog blood or some shit, and then cover them up and wait for some unsuspecting fella to come step his leg in it and get himself all nice and mangled up. The savages believed it was better for to waste the time and resources of the enemy than it was to kill them off. I reckoned Vietnamese didn't have a conscience, either and were probably doing something similar. A sharp stick hole was something I imagined Aaron might have dug up for me out there in the pasture, should I ever piss him off enough to warrant a punishment at his hand, so I watched my footing.

It seemed the pandemic of the mole cricket plague was only getting exponentially worse as time drew on. Seldom had there been a day when I counted a square that wasn't twice as large a number as it was the day before. It was growing into a damn chore; one that lasted near a half hour. I had started pinching the heads off the ones I had already counted, just so I could keep track in my brain. At that point, I wasn't quite sure what exactly Daddy had me doing it for. The pasture was all but desert by then, and rife with dead hell grass. Our farm was lost, and so were the lands of everyone else in Indian River. The plague had won, and a white hot sun orb was melting persistently through a dirty grey canopy of dust. It had at least seemed that way since Aaron and I came home to that locked gate.

All that was left then was the weeping, I thought to myself as I made my return journey to the house after near an hour being gone. I wondered if Indian River would have to start again like in the olden days. Would our family have to leave for a time and then return when the mole crickets had all but burned in the blazing desolation of our farm? There was no sense in fleeing to old Pinehelm. The place was nothing but a square of unused brick buildings somewhere deep out in the mill lands, in some bit of wild pines where it sat forgotten and awaiting development ever since

Ortega Paper bought it half a century before. Thoughts passed as I walked and planned our survival.

The crunch of the hell grass beneath my feet had become a familiar sensation, that was why I was immediately taken when my foot tread upon an alien bit of earth whilst halfway home. I looked down to find my foot perched upon a lump of soft plastic goods that looked to be well-weathered, either beaten by the sun or chewed by the plague. I moved my foot to reveal a likely sight. It was a message from The Harbinger. One I had missed. Perhaps several days old since Beckins had dropped it. I picked it up excitedly and observed the parcel inside its taped container. As per usual, The Harbinger had brought a gift well-suited to withstand nuclear blasts. I used my half pencil to rip through a layer of brownish Scotch tape, releasing a plastic bag, which I tore through instead of wasting time trying to get to its opening. Inside was the trademark tamale of a toilet cone. I couldn't manage to understand Beckins' final barrier of protection as his chosen method to keep moisture out, but it was bone dry, nonetheless.

I unravelled the expected scroll immediately and read the mangled lettering inside, but not before scanning the perimeter of the field to be sure no lurkers were spying me.

Stagwerth

That was all. At first, I was right agitated by the lack of guidance and sheer stinginess of information the cryptic message boasted. I was additionally concerned that the message might have been several weeks older than the first, perhaps from when I had first started the count. If that were to model The Harbinger's pattern of communication, I shouldn't have expected to receive another for at least a month. A tiresome disappointment washed over me; so much so that I dropped my hands to my side and searched the skies once or twice over for Miles Beckins himself so I could curse him with futility from the ground. Then, however, in a moment of purest eucatastrophes, the tide of my mind reversed, and I was brought straightways to revelation. The message wasn't as cryptic as I had initially thought; in fact, I had known precisely right what it meant, and I was at once bewitched with such a jovial spirit that I twirled in place and held the note skyward in praise.

Had any soul ever warned me I would someday be caught in the midst of an intrigue so perplexing that it caused me to question my place in time, in a hierarchy, or in the spiritual realm, and that at such a juncture, my knowledge of certain personalities of my faith would be called upon to aid me in answering some of the questions asked of my own life in order to situate me concretely in any of the aforementioned places, I would have thought they were mad. Then, I would have said they must have been even further crazed to assume my piddly circumstance of a life could possibly lead me into a communion with so widely-revered a figure as S.M. Stagwerth.

My brain immediately and independently began making recollections of all the details of the man that it could muster. Beckins was attempting to get me to recognize a commonality between me and The Prophet. Perhaps there was something about his life that I was supposed to discover in order to guide me some bit in my own. At least, that would be the case if my assumptions were true that The Harbinger's intentions indeed were to aid me in some way. Hell, for all I knew, he could have as well been leading me into my own self-imposed apocalypse, and I was just following along willingly.

I remained there in the field, studying longingly the lone scribed word. S.M. Stagwerth was about as well-known in Southern religious spheres as Harry S. Truman was to damn near everyone else. It seemed like everywhere we went, someone was saying his name in the background; like the underlying score to a motion picture. It had been ingrained in the oral tradition of Indian River for years and years.

"The man had faith like Stagwerth!" someone would say.

"By The Prophet, she's getting big!" another might state, using only his nickname. None, however, was a bigger proprietor of Stagwerthian heirlooms and mythos than Joe Cotton. Daddy, on two distinct occasions, had allowed Aaron and Momma and me to sit silently in his den whilst listening to old syndicated radio programs of the prophet and faith healer. Daddy would catch tell of Stagwerth reruns and sternly corral us into the dimly lit room as if to suggest it were high time to secure ourselves against the crossbeams of the house and brace for Holy Ghost twisters.

One could attest to the felt powers that seemed to go forth from that speaker box in those times. Stagwerth, in the pair of instances I had encountered him with my ears, seemed to be a bold and venerable man of terrible imposition, capable of containing within himself a portion, if not all of the Spirit of God, as well as the pitted fear that accompanied it. He spoke with a rust in his voice that was almost certainly caused by his aptitude for casting prophetic messages at upmost volumes from behind pulpits (which he had done for thirty-some-odd years). The hoarseness of his voice only added to his foreboding nature, implying that he indeed spent much of his time in loud contest with sin and the devil.

His final and most well-known of recorded sermons, which was one that I had heard partially on the radio (and one which Daddy had made Aaron and I memorize by heart) was entitled, "Devil in the Sidecar" and the frontis-piece went something like this:

> Be not deceived; God is not mocked: for whatsoever a man soweth, that shall he also reap. For he that soweth to his flesh shall of the flesh reap corruption; but he that soweth to the Spirit shall of the Spirit reap life everlasting.' To each of you, a field has been given. One full of rocks and hell grass and hard pan as far as the eye can see. And unto each of you was given the task of making for yourselves a crop, capable of sustain-ing life. This task cannot be accomplished alone. Simply put, it is the single greatest impossibil-ity and plight of all human existence. And yet, you attempt each day to shoulder the burden on your own, lifting rock by rock out of the hard clay. Pulling weed after weed and casting them into the fire, when little do you know, the flame to which you feed the waste of your field was first stoked to consume you! The simple truth, is that you are already a corpse, and your field is doomed. You could move those rocks for years and years, and until that hard pan with great and powerful machines until the day is done, but you will never be! Unless I go with you, you will toil aimlessly until your bloodied hands cease their

fruitless toiling and you fall, beaten and utterly spent, into the dust of the ground. For it is from dust that you came, and to dust that you shall return!' Most of you sow iniquity into your field as you go along, removing rocks! What foolishness is this? Uprooting one stone and planting another! It's like the man who, with the purpose of fleeing the devil, bought the fastest two-wheeled car he could find and made haste into the setting sun, but not before attaching a sidecar to carry with him his own fleshly corruption. You see, the man was too comfortable with his earthly things; his stones and weeds and hard pan. So even as he fled, he carried with him the very devices of his own damnation! You are that man! Repent! Leave the sidecar and flee on foot or be dragged screaming into the abyss, where for all eternity, flesh will burn away and regrow again and again in agonizing and eternal punishment for your deplorable transgressions!

Many folks claimed that an unfortunate circumstance induced the prophet to undergo an inexplicable change immediately thereafter. They said in strange appearances following, that Stagwerth's countenance had turned to that of a bitter and violent charismatic. The very same October night he delivered "Devil in the Sidecar," S.M. Stagwerth was attacked whilst traveling back to his hotel room in Pensacola. Stagwerth's biography (which Daddy had read to us from on various occasions) stated that the prophet was on a Southern town circuit and, only hours before delivering the famous message at Seville Square, had booked a stay at the new Hopkins House in Pensacola's North Hill district and eaten his weight in fifty-nine cent fried chicken. Late that night, as Stagwerth stumbled—holy spirit drunk—to the Palafox Street trolly stop, a group of inebriates from a bar in the quarter robbed and shot the prophet in his head.

The story held that Stagwerth was discovered only moments later by a lone Samaritan, and was taken to a nearby hospital where he laid comatose for three days. On the third day, attendants claimed Stagwerth sat straight up in his bed, removed the bandage from the entry wound on the back of his skull and marched away from the hospital in nothing more than a dressing gown. The orderlies did their best to restrain and detour Stagwerth, but in a way almost evasively Christlike, he managed to slip by them unstoned and untouched. When he exited the building, Stagwerth was met by the man who had saved him in the street only days earlier. The Samaritan, who remained nameless in the biography by Victor Luccano, reportedly awaited the emergence of S.M. Stagwerth the full three days, sleeping in his truck in the hospital parking lot as not to miss the release of the prophet, despite reports that he wasn't expected to survive the ordeal. The hospital staff, confused only by his attire, saw Stagwerth partake in a short conversation with The Samaritan, and then leave with him in his truck, making west. They later noted the oddities surrounding the man known as The Samaritan, saying he had a great deal of questions about Stagwerth and had stated he would not leave until he had seen the prophet.

The Samaritan allegedly drove Stagwerth directly to the boarding house where maids witnessed a male, who wasn't Stagwerth, go into the prophet's room and retrieve his belongings. Several hours later, two strange men walked onto a stage at The Royal American Fair and proceeded to accost the crowd with spits of scripture-induced rage until they had gained the ears of all in attendance. Witnesses said the tirade went on for the better part of an hour until the sheriff came and had them both booted from the grounds. It was later reported by one of the railroad carnies that a hot air balloon had been commandeered and was last saw floating off east in the direction of Blackwater. A photo from the scene later positively confirmed the two to be S.M. Stagwerth and the man known afterwords as The Samaritan, but the hot air balloon was never seen again. It was widely believed the craft went down in Blackwater River soon after lift off. The unfortunate event was officially pronounced the death of the two after the river was dragged for weeks to no avail. Some time later, the skeletal remains of a male in his forties, which many assumed to be The Prophet, was discovered, but a second body never surfaced.

I awoke from my daydream. The recollection of the Stagwerth story had taken me for God only knew how long. By that hour, the sky had darkened to an amber window unto the sun, and I watched it dip low as I walked with my head up until I reached the sugary dip of the horse track. I had never seen the fabled green flash at the end of a sunset (which apparently only sailors and Aaron ever claimed to), but I watched for it at any opportune moment I could. I thought long and hard about what Daddy was going to think of the count before I lifted the gate and passed by the gargoyle. He sure as hell wasn't going to like the report, which is why I decided on letting him have his peace for the last few hours of the work day. I rolled The Harbinger's note in my hands and stuffed it deep into my jeans pocket "Stagwerth," I thought. What an unusual and surprising circumstance it was to receive such a defined granular stroke on this broad and wondrous canvas of obscurity.

10

As I passed by the barn, I noticed the brothers had taken the afternoon off the roof and were now on to other chores elsewhere unseen. As soon as I entered the house, Momma came rounding the corner like a dog and put me on books at the desk in the living room to keep me occupied whilst she and Mamie tended to Walter somewhere else in the house—more than likely, my bed. It was the only place of rest that made any logical sense to bed down an old man. I had resolved to that much before I even left for the field. It wasn't until I had opened up my phonics book that I noticed Ms. Dottie sitting behind me at the kitchen table. I turned violently in my chair when I heard her old voice rev into speech like a slow swinging stall door.

"Prophet's name, that man's gonna be mad as a March hare when he hears about all this here." She remained facing forward, nearly losing all her breath with the delivery of every "H" and never once acknowledging my presence. I waited for my heart to recapture its former pace and replied suspiciously.

"What man?"

Dottie looked at me square and paused briefly. She swallowed once and spoke. Her voice cracked. She tried again.

"Pastor."

We looked at each other for a long moment, knowing full well the house was a crypt of secrets, and that she had nearly breached before me the grandest sarcophagus of all. I turned slowly in my seat and removed the tallest pencil from a sterile Campbell's can with no label. I felt her cold eyes on my back as I turned the page in my phonics book and attempted fruitlessly to read. The room was properly spooked and made silent for several minutes; each one of which, I felt Dottie come closer and closer to inquiring of me something she shouldn't. And Rightly so, for there was no topic I wanted to avoid more than the man she had actually referred to. If I couldn't ignore his existence altogether, I at least wasn't ready for it yet. Some things I just as soon would have rather figured out cumulatively on my own; the way I did with phonics. I wasn't too big a fan of the promised awkwardness birthed in a powwow like that, but it came, nonetheless.

"You know, don't you boy ..."

The words—spoken in soft wooden tones—sent tingles down my spine. At first I ignored her, pretending to go on about my work as if I hadn't heard a thing, but Dottie kept on as I figured she might. "Don't ignore me, boy. There ain't no one who can hear me besides you."

I set the pencil down on the table gently and turned about, looking at Dottie with fear from the corners of my eyes. There we remained for several uncomfortable seconds, staring at each other from opposite sides of the room until she finally screeched again. "How long?"

"...I don't know nothin' about Him," I relented.

"What do you know?" she replied immediately. There was something about her persistence and line of questioning that drove me to believe Dottie wasn't truly the Dottie I was used to. Like, somehow, deep under the feathers and lace and pomp of those Sunday hats, she was more than just a simple aged bell.

"...I know it ain't Pastor Obis you're worried about."

"...Hellantarnation," Dottie said to herself. My ears perked as her head snapped to attention at what she had just uttered. Her piercing eyes sealed in me the audible transgression, never to be relinquished. I couldn't rightly believe the conversation that was taking place. "...Go on, son."

"...I know Daddy and Pastor Obis hear instruction from somewheres else."

"And where'd you pick that up?"

"...Watchin' the two of 'em," I shrugged.

"Spyin' the two of 'em, more like," she attacked. "I ought to tell your mother. She'd ring you up so good, it'd—"

"—What's all the whisperin' for?" Momma appeared without warning. She stood shorter than normal in her bare feet, waiting on an answer. Me and Dottie froze.

"...Your boy's pants are soiled up," Dottie improvised. Momma looked at my legs and face and then back to Dottie.

"Dottie, I told you we ain't got the time for your unhelpful High South prejudices. This here's a farm." Momma walked over and grabbed me up by the arm.

"What are we farmin', dirt?" Dottie added.

Momma stopped and looked at the elderly inquisitor who had just turned her head nonchalantly from the conversation at hand. It was true. There hadn't been a head of cattle or horse on our property that wasn't our own since the start of October. It was nearly Thanksgiving then, and I hadn't pulled up a green blade of grass in weeks. My original estimation had undershot on the timeline but overshot on severity. The cows were the only steady dying animals we'd had. We watched them close until every last one was gone. We'd had each of them butchered for meat and froze at Marlin's so he could sell the meats on consignment to rare and well off folk. As for the horses, well, those whose owners wouldn't come and claim them, we had all but turned loose of or sold off at silent auctions on Saturday mornings before the gate was locked up. What indeed were we farming, I thought.

Momma stared in silence at Ms. Dottie for another five or ten seconds and then yanked me off in the direction of my room.

"What is it, Momma?" I asked. We stopped just outside the bedroom door, which was closed up. Momma bent down to eye level and brushed off my jeans.

"Mr. Walter's callin' on you. He wants a talk. In private." I looked at Momma with curiosity.

"Is he ok?" I asked.

"The old man just had himself a little spell." It seemed like more than that to me, and I partly thought Momma might suspect I knew the truth. "I ain't sure what he wants, but you can expect to give me a full report when he's said his peace."

I remained limp and confused as Momma continued to brush me off violently with her leathery paw. A moment later, Mamie came sliding through the door, closing it gently behind her. Momma rose to meet her and they began exchanging words in the darkened corridor, barely loud enough to be heard. I reckoned Walter wished to finish the conversation we had started prior to his collapse. Strangely, it wasn't something I was right looking forward to; a further moment alone with the man who very well may have intended to relinquish the answers to every question I had postulated in the past several weeks. My hunger for that fruit of knowledge, however, had greatly subsided the second I realized the potential magnitude of what I was digging into. I needed a bath, and quick.

Momma situated me forward, to where the only thing my eyes could see was the cloudy brass doorknob. There I waited until the door suddenly opened, revealing what seemed an alien world to me. The curtains were all drawn and the lights were all off in the early afternoon. That was enough to immediately cause me to feel out of place in my own habitat (as if nothing else had thus far). I looked back at Momma briefly as she nudged me forward and gestured over to my bed. She closed the door behind me. For a second, I couldn't see to walk a step, so I paused and listened for his breathing. Every so often, I would hear a deep exhale, but then the silence would pervade for what seemed eternities as Walter took slow anonymous draws. Then, I could have sworn to hear his voice come low in my direction.

"Young Joe..." I thought I heard. I approached the voice with caution, listening carefully for what could have very well been my imagination's witchery at work.

When I reached the bedside, my eyes had furthermore adjusted to the dimness of the room, and I was then able to make out Walter's frail form as he laid atop my quilt. I got down on my knees and poised myself to rouse him. I'd had half a mind not to even wake him and tell Momma he had asked for a glass of water, but I didn't have the grit. I reached up and straightways shook his arm once proper. After all, I didn't want to have to do it again. The old man nearly choked himself into waking and turned his head to me. I couldn't map his face.

"...That you, Young Joe?"

I cleared my throat in confirmation.

"Yessir." I searched for Walter's shadowy features in the darkened room and listened closely for his next words, but they didn't come. Instead, all I heard were more of those long exhales and ages of silence in between. I shook his arm again, fiercely. He jumped and moaned, and I worried I had almost broke something in his bones. "Walter. You awake?" I asked.

"Young Joe?"

"Yes. It's me, Moses," I stated firmly, beginning to feel frustrated. "Are you awake?" I asked again.

"Y-yes, but I don't know for how long," he said. "The sleep, it comes and goes, you know."

"What did you want to tell me?" I asked. Walter paused again, and I almost thought he had slipped back into sleep, but then I saw his eyes open wide and white as he turned to me again.

"It's b-about that strange one. The boy."

"The boy?" I asked. "Mr. Langford?"

Walter's head nodded softly. His voice was weak as a newborn's.

"What about him?" I probed further. "What about Mr. Langford?" I waited. Another several seconds passed before I heard Walter prepare to speak further.

"That day. The day h-he fell..."

"Yesterday. So Mr. Langford did fall?" I asked intently. How much proof did I need, I thought.

Walter lost his breath and turned his head in defeat.

"I'm sorry," I apologized. "Go on. Please."

Walter returned slow and spoke again mildly.

"I seen it from afar. He weren't fell down, he were p-a-pull..."

My heart seized at what I thought I had heard. Even Walter's broken Mississippian was right difficult for me to understand sometimes, but it sounded as if he had implied Mr. Langford was pulled from the roof by another party. I adjusted on my knees.

"Pulled down?" I whispered. "By who? Why ain't he told no one yet?"

Walter shook his head in wide side to side motions.

"He don't re-m-member none. The p-passage of death erases..." he drifted away.

"...Who pulled him down, Walter?" I asked. I could tell it had become a great chore for the man to make words, so I tried my best to aid him along. "Daddy?" Walter shook his head. "Aaron?" No. "Bill? Silas?" Still no. "Miles Beckins?" I asked with curious bravery. Walter looked at me with the most puzzled and queer-eyed gaze I had ever seen, lifting his body to do so, then dropping back down in exhaustion and shaking his head.

155

"She tied the l-load," he started slowly. "The Mennna..."

"The Mennonite?" I questioned? "One of William's people?"

Walter shook his head. I sat back on my haunches, frustrated and impatient as all hell. I could feel him slipping away again, but then, I feared he might never come back. I sat up once more and planted my hand on his chest. "Walter! Who?!"

Just then, a pillar of light poured across my hand and Walter's profile. I turned swiftly and straightways saw Mamie enter the room. She came around next to me and bent low beside the bed, forcefully shoving me behind her. She hovered over Walter's face, her ear to his mouth.

"He ain't breathin'," she stated.

"He were, just now," I said. Shadows moved in the hallway. Momma came bursting in, wielding ten thousand questions. I was pushed even further back in the ensued chaos. No other brothers or sisters were in the house, but it was still mad. I expected Momma to lean hard into the spirit and begin praying wildly again like I had seen her do with the short man, but instead, she seemed to become progressively more docile and entranced until I could no longer recognize her countenance.

I listened, through the rustling garments and forced whispers and creaking of the bunk bed, for the sound of Walter's tidal exhale as Mamie began a primitive form of resuscitation. Joining both her hands together with fingers intertwined, she started at the old man's chest with unyielding blows which seemed to fall harder and harder with each murderous gesticulation. With every impact, Walter's body involuntarily gave up a dull and hollow moan. I cringed at the sound and twice moved to stop Mamie, once with my hand, and once in vocal protest.

"Quit it! You're gonna break him apart!" But Momma's dead eyes found me slowly, and there was a red evil in them I had neither seen before nor aimed to contest. I retreated to that former ball of awkward and crippled impotence and watched helplessly as Mamie continued to pummel the old man's fragile frame. Tears began to drop from my face. I wiped the stream quick for fear of Momma's eyes finding me again. A cold suspicion seized me, heart and soul.

Suddenly, Mamie paused with her conjoined fists suspended high above Walter's chest. The room turned un-earthly quiet, and I watched and prayed as those fused tools of fleshly design slowly disconnected and fell to the bedside like dandelion florets in those quiet summer moments be-tween gusts of warm wind. Momma's eyes were closed then, and I witnessed the hope of life go out from her body. The two women wept in silence. Mamie fell upon Walter's body and his bones became enveloped in her strong arms and broad endowment. Momma stood and turned away but remained there with us amongst the presumed dead. I cried and snorted loudly as I watched Mamie (who I was, by then, gravely suspicious of) bury her face in the old man's neck, her head and pony still tightly covered in a Menno-nite's likeness with a white kerchief. A shrill of fear sent a metallic, dull pain through the marrow of my bones like a tuning fork. My suspicion had grown both horn and tail.

A short spell of time passed by in silence as I watched the scene and imagined ways to stop Mamie from doing whatever I had pieced together of her motive. Had she just killed Walter before my very eyes, I wondered. Had she done so in order to hide the fact that she had too tried to end Mr. Langford? It was then, amidst the questions and flood of inquiry, that I saw the faintest bit of movement upon the crippled fingers of the old man as he lay eclipsed beneath Mamie's Germanic frame. I looked to Momma, then to Mamie. Neither had seen the tell tale sign I had witnessed. My tears paused momentarily as I watched Walter's hand for another sign of life.

Then, without warning, those old organ pipes came to life in what I was certain was one of the familiar and deep inhalations I had come to know during the outset of our conversation only moments prior. However, in as quick a moment as she heard it, Mamie seemed to collapse even further upon the old man and overcome his gasps and moans with grunts and groans of her own. It was a clever and garish ploy to conceal Walter's honest condition. It was only truly then that I perceived Mamie's gilded character, as I watched her behemoth arms grow tight around the old man's fragility. In a weakened and futile projection of my own valor, I saw myself move from my situation and leap at Mamie, pulling hard at her ponytail and kicking her, horselike, until Walter was free of her titan's grasp. But in every ounce of truth, I had remained stunned and incapable of heroism. Instead, I heard with my own ears, the very cracks and shattering of the old man's ribs and vertebrae. I saw the light leave his eyes through the back of Mamie's head and float away into Heaven in the same place my vision disappeared each and every night before sleep. In shame, I had done nothing to stop it. In shame, I was unable to.

That bitter quiet came and settled on that room once more, only then, it was devoid the sounds of weeping. I had learned not to make much of my own sadness. Age and affliction had taught me to mourn in solitude, never in boisterous shows of lamentation like Momma had done only moments before. Ironically, it had been Momma who taught me never to do such a thing, especially in front of Daddy. I had never once seen a Cotton man cry. Though I never met either of my granddaddies, Momma said her Daddy was about as soft as a sandbag, and I believed her.

Momma was the first in the room to stand, then me. Mamie stayed put as we left slower than comfortable. As I crawled away, I remembered a flash of the black Bible beneath my bed. I had seen it there through my tears, but had dismissed it subconsciously; much like I had done right then. I had forgotten about it entirely. The thing warranted another investigation, but I had been so busy in my own affairs that I ignored the primal urges that first pulled me in its direction.

"Moses, come on now," Momma interrupted my thoughts. I couldn't bare to look at her in the eyes as she guided me out the door by my shoulder. Then, just as she said she would, Momma turned me around and bent down to interrogate me.

"Well?" she said. I did my best not to confront her ocularly, and weighed the options of whether or not to tell her the truth. "Don't lie to me, boy," She preempted. I was right sick of hearing that. Right sick of being lied to like it was everyone's job, and then being expected, in return, to be the zenith of forthrightness for all. I lied on principle.

"He told me to listen to you and Daddy and Pastor Obis and learn as much as I could."

I could feel Momma's eyes on me with a wild suspicion. "Look at me when you say it," she demanded, shaking me with force. I recovered, and my eyes found hers against my will. To my surprise, the deadness had regressed into her normal glare of intimidation.

"...He said, listen to my Momma and my Daddy and listen to Pastor Obis," I repeated masterfully. "And learn as much as I could." I took a small breath in order to seem less nervous than I actually was. Momma's grip loosened. Something broke then, and it seemed she believed me. She didn't probe further beyond that.

The rest of the afternoon was about as ill-favored as one could imagine. Momma and Mamie had left the house about sunset and gathered everyone at the bunker to tell them about Walter. I only knew as much cause I overheard them say it as they went. I imagined the typical brothers and sisters welling up with tears; Mamie, Momma, Kenzie, Silas, maybe Bill, Sarah Obis, for sure. Before anyone else returned, Mattie and Kenzie came and took Walter's body away, which was right strange to witness. I couldn't figure where they took him to, though. Dinner was awkward as all hell. The single moment I had reserved for the worst—the count—ended up being the one normal strand of short words in a long tradition of silence. Daddy even told me I didn't have to continue the confounded chore. I reckoned he had unofficially conceded to the plague then. Aaron didn't make eye contact with anyone, almost like he was on a different planet, anticipating something else entirely. The strange thing was, once I had noticed Aaron's demeanor, I observed it upon Daddy and Momma, as well.

The mood was downcast when we were finally excused from the somber collation. I took the opportunity to become enraptured in normal duties and force myself back into a routine that felt most ignorant of the fact that very strange and dangerous dealings were taking place never more than twenty feet from me. There was nothing more useful for growing a man than knowledge unfettered. Not manual labor. Not the touch of a woman. Not proximity to the sun. A man's marrow is learned in the consumption of awareness which was previously, but no longer, desired. In my heart of hearts, my only known use in gaining a further awareness of the happenings surrounding me on the farm, was in hopes that I would be able to use such a knowledge in order to put an end to our plight and steer us back to neutrality. I don't think one of us claimed to need harmony. We had never had that.

Momma remained in the kitchen for a short while, wiping down surfaces and prepping the over-warmed stock pot for Pastor Obis who was late on a count of the evenings events. There wasn't going to be much in terms of leftovers for Charles. Things were getting scarcer and scarcer as days went on, but in a conundrum of economic grief, Momma had resorted to feeding us our own cows, which was damn unheard of, even in well-off times. A small freezer truck from town had come in the afternoon and brought ten or twenty pounds of frozen meat encased in wooden shipping crates burn branded with Marlin's "M" inside a circle. Momma's continued patronage of Marlin's store puzzled me, given that she had recently voiced her expressed opposition to the man and his selling of "new aged" artifacts. I reckoned it was because he had the only deep freeze in town. She started into the shipment with the cheapest of cuts and fried up a few peppered chuck rounds, as to not put ourselves out should our situation drastically revert itself over night.

Once Pastor Obis had come and gone and Momma was clear of the kitchen, I swept the floor, put away the dried dishes, straightened the countertops and tied up the trash. I then threw some of my soiled clothes into the wash basin outside to soak, took the trash out, fed Charles from a slug-infested box of kibble, gave him a swift stroke across the back, then made for the bathtub. It was something I had been looking forward to since the moment I had last dried off. There was a prophetic element in the release of old and clouded thoughts in order to refill the mind with clear and coherent ones. I would stick my hand deep into the misty, lukewarm brine and release the rubber stop, and all the obscurity of my mind would go with it. When those burning crystals would flood back in, there was order made inside me.

The water trickled ticklishly into the deeps of my ears as my head bobbed with curiosity in the fullness of the tub. I turned this way and that to make sure the canals had become completely infused. Silence swept over me, and my mind was, at last, free to wander. I reckoned the first and most honest order of business was to address the disturbing fact that Mr. Langford had indeed fallen from the heights of the barn roof, (to his death, undoubtedly), and was then, at that present moment, alive. The sheer awe and terror which would normally be wrought by such news, against my greatest expectations, was something I had not felt at all upon seeing the short man before at lunch (at least to the extent I had expected). For some reason, it actually wasn't that peculiar for me to see a man raised to life from the dead, especially one whose death I hadn't witnessed. Perhaps, in my mind, he wasn't really dead. Or perhaps he had never died at all (though I found it right hard to believe a fall as such was without the guarantee of death). In my most forthright of explanations, I assumed it was both my present childlike faith and exposure to such things as a stark normality that allowed me to view resurrection as commonplace.

I full-on intended to question the short man, ever still, and thus, in a most desperate fashion, attempt to adopt some slight understanding of the weight of that situation, given that I was fully admitted to the fact that it wasn't normal for me to view such things in so calloused a way. A man, who was dead not twelve hours prior, was alive and walking at that very moment. Which begged the question as to why the body had been moved and where it had gone to the night before. It was evident the brothers and sisters had been without the faith, patience or fortitude required to raise the short man themselves, so an outside party was called in to take control of the affair. Before witnessing the brothers and sisters descend the back pasture hillocks to the woods, and before I had my strange encounter in the trees surrounding the Freedom Spring, I had overheard Daddy and Pastor Obis speaking curiously on the situation, wherein a host of new questions had arisen in my mind. In truth, I believed I had made a connection between the myth of The Man in the Woods and the anonymous vacuum of attention and obedience that seemed to permeate our farm since the days before I could remember.

The sounds and repetitions of my own voice in my head, which played at a thousand different volumes suddenly silenced themselves in the wake of revelation. I laid cold in those clear waters which still held transfixed upon their surface the steady presence of hot smoke against the chilled air of the house. The residual ringing in my ears came from the water which had laid itself so deep inside my head, coupled with the phantom sounds of all my voices

of thought that had spoken and screamed so loud for so
long and then suddenly vanished into ear-piercing nothingness at the thought. I renamed the events in my head;
in their simplest recollection. A plague. A gate. A traveller.
A message. A death. A quorum. A resurrection. A Man. A
Prophet.

The thought that had so laid siege to my desperate
mind, which then writhed in silence in every which way,
was that perhaps an honest figure of Southern spiritlore;
one that had personally aided S.M. Stagwerth himself, was
in fact never dead, but alive and well and living in our own
woods. The Samaritan's corpse, after all, was never found in
the high tides of Blackwater River. Even if he had died then,
I acknowledged the truth that death had ceremoniously
lost its bid on the inclusion of our farm with the return of
the short man. I pondered for a short lifetime of moments.
Ludicrous, I thought. Why in the devil's hell would The
Samaritan of the S.M. Stagwerth story be found in a wood,
on a farm, in Indian River, so many years and miles from
his fame and notoriety?

I closed my eyes and fell far beneath the water. I saw
the night sky above me as it had been on many nights prior,
when the fullness of the moon was veiled in shadow, and
the stars were out in clouds of celestial cream and strokes
so vast one could scarce tell they were stars at all. I then
watched on as every star parted from its partners, and there
was room enough in the whole of the universe to fit every
light. They continued to shift and realign until I, at once,
reckoned that which I had never been able to reckon before
in the shapes those heavenly bodies made together. I had
never been able to conceive the bravery of Orion; the Gran-
deur of Leo. The shapes, however, weren't the shapes I had

always heard tell of. They were the visual manifestation of my every thought; all cumulative and gathered information laid and planted in precise order upon the garden rows of my mind. I surely believed I would be proved wrong, but in that moment, there, I knew I had missed something terrible and huge. I had made myself ignorant (or been made ignorant by those I loved) to the fact that there was presently a titan of faith bending words with the stewards of Indian River, and every unnamed command or strange twist of fate was inexplicably linked to his power beyond my sight.

11

The matter which had survived the bathwater, and had, as a result, followed me all the way to bed (even to sleep, as I laid in Walter's final peace) was that of Mamie. It was naturally the last thing to be given the full-on investment of my conscious real estate. The fact was plain that Mamie's actions were the ones to be handled most careful, given her own newly discovered wherewithal to settle up her affairs by snuffing out threats with the prowess of a Methodist acolyte boy. Not to mention Momma's further proven custodial obligation to look after Mamie's interests, even to the extent of blinding herself from the truth that Mamie was indeed a murderous creature. I was afraid of them both; Mamie for the fact that she would kill me too if she found out how far my meddling went. I feared Momma (perhaps even more so) for the belief that she knew more about Mamie's plans than she was letting on. I hated my guardians for their secrecy and darknesses.

The weight of it all had finally started to sink in. Up to that moment, I honestly believed I was of the capacity to eat whatever pang of guilt or test of conscience should come my way, but the day's end was drawing too close, too quick, figuratively, and the twilight was near upon us. I could feel it. I had no choice to shoulder the burden of knowledge on my own any longer. What I was attempting to do was noble, just not practical. I had to tell somebody. I thought about Sarah Obis, but she was too close to Pastor for my comfort. That, and I was scared shitless over her since she had seen me peeping her at the spring. Mamie was straight out of the question, for obvious reasons. Momma was no good. Walter was gone. Dottie had daggers for me. Bill or Silas were too dumb to count, and Mattie or Kenzie were honestly too distant.

I had thought of Aaron first, but dismissed him as a last resort, given his propensity for treating my usual inclinations with disdain or neglect. He was the last person I thought would take me serious and give enough of a damn to help me sort it out past what the bathwater could. I supposed there had always been the possibility for him to betray me and rat me to any and every person he could catch hold of. I weighed the options, and the idea of suffering under so much undiscerned knowledge a second longer was enough to entreat me to mention it. That, and the feeling in my heart that Aaron would be too much a chicken shit to say anything once I had mentioned Mamie's homicidal tendencies. He was already spooked by her, and he wouldn't test it further.

I found him after breakfast, leaning against the paddock fence nearest the barn and the house, chewing on a bit of bobtail weed between chores. Momma had shaved his head not ten minutes prior, and he looked like G.I. Joe then. I approached him cautiously as he gave me his typical once over.

"What is it?" he asked, annoyed but cordial. I shrugged out of nervous hesitation, not wanting to appear to have an agenda. "Come on," he pulled. "Spill."

"... We need to talk," I said simply.

"You sure about that?" he asked with a frankness. I stopped and gave heed to what exactly he meant by the question. I looked from side to side and then nodded warily. "Alright," he said, taking his foot off the fence. "But first, I need you to balance this bobtail in your mouth."

"Why?" I asked, puzzled.

"Just do it!" Aaron's voice escalated uncomfortably. I opened my mouth as he laid the long and slender blade of forked grass across my lips with the twin black pollen buds bobbing just beyond my right ear. "Now, close your lips down and see how long you can hold it in place." I was bewildered by both the obscurity of Aaron's request and the simplicity of the test. "That's it," he said, reaching for the picked edge of the blade and pulling it quickly through my pursed lips. I spewed and spat the bitter black pollen collected at the corner of my mouth as Aaron bent over double in laughter. He braced my shoulder with one arm as I stood there in my stupidity, wiping my mouth with my sleeve. Aaron was in tears and speechless. I stood straight tall and blew the last of the foreign granules from my lips, looking around to make sure no one else had seen. It might have been funnier at a different time.

"So what is it you wanted to talk to me about," Aaron recovered. Together, we walked further down the fence line, almost into the back yard. Aaron was still smiling mildly.

"I know about Mr. Langford," I spoke bluntly.

"What do you know about him?" Aaron smiled.

"I know he were dead. Now he ain't."

"Well ring the dinner bell! Hallelujah!" Aaron scoffed. "Tell me something that don't already scare the shit out of me."

"I know who pulled him off the roof," I said.

"He slipped."

"Nope," I replied. "Walter told me before he...died. He seen someone pull him down." Aaron's face turned stoic. He'd known it was plausible because he'd seen Walter on the ground before it happened.

"Who?" he asked impatiently. I breathed. No turning back.

"Mamie." Aaron looked at me with a dead stare. I waited for the unknown. I weren't sure if he would scream, cry, dance, run, or just punch me square in the stomach. He took a step back, turned away and ran his hand over his fuzzy head.

"Sonuvabitch," he said under his breath.

"...What?" I asked, scared. Aaron turned back around and looked at me wild-eyed.

"That's how she managed to tell Momma so fast," Aaron looked off again. My heart was straightways soothed at the thought of him owning up to similar suspicions.

"Wait, what do you mean?" I spoke quickly. His eyes were back on me as he drew close in stern excitement.

"I seen her fat ass waddlin' toward the house before Kenzie even called it out," Aaron whispered harshly. "Langford weren't off the roof twenty seconds before then!"

"So you believe me?" I asked. Aaron laughed once.

"No, I believe me," he said. It was good enough for me.

"Then you're really gonna like this next part," I hesitated. Aaron's eyes widened. There was something I loved about being the barer of such terrible and privileged news. "...She done Walter, too."

"...No shit..." Aaron said with fire in his eyes.

"I seen it, myself," I kept my voice low as I watched the brothers and Kenzie climb the ladder to the roof. It was time for Aaron to go. "Heard his bones snap with my own ears."

"His bones?!" Aaron said with disbelief.

"She smothered him."

"Smothered..." Aaron repeated. "Now look, I can understand that know-it-all shit talker, but why on earth would anyone kill Walter?!"

"Cause he seen her do it to Mr. Langford!" I said in hushed tones. Aaron's stupidity floored me sometimes. "And Walter were busy rattin' her to me when she come in and started at pounding on his chest and bearhuggin' the fire out of him! He were dead in minutes!"

"So what makes you think she ain't gonna try and—" Aaron were interrupted by the clear call of Daddy's voice from the heights of the barn rooftop. Aaron looked back at me. I knew what he meant to suggest. I knew it cause I feared it too. "You keep this to yourself until after lunch."

"You too!" I said. Aaron ignored me and walked off.

As I made my way back to the front steps of the house, I saw the morning dew had particularly favored the red clay drive, transforming it into a caustic opportunity. If the dense gray shroud that had settled itself over Indian River indeed was rain waiting to spill (rather than the plague's further omen of dust and gloom that I knew it to be), then it had absolutely refused to relinquish its stores in the fullness of deluge yet, and instead had only greeted each morning with enough moisture to keep the mole crickets quenched, which was a cruel enough irony for any man. The clay, however, was a moment for me to boast in my genius. So without a further thought, I straightways stepped into the soft crystals and heard them squish and crunch beneath my boots. Once I had made sufficient hourglass prints in the drive, I tiptoed hastily to the front door and entered the house, disregarding the slightest hint of caution. I made for my bedroom with conviction in each step, being sure to shake off a pound and a half of red grime with each leaden foot. Upon reaching my room, I dismantled half of everything in my path and sat patiently awaiting my reckoning. The house was silent for exactly thirteen decisive seconds.

"Moses!" She screamed. I would act oblivious but earn a beating worthy of intention. Momma raged as she entered the room. You would think a boy had committed the most carnal of sins. She was unable to find words to suit her anger. I winced as she turned me around and yanked my britches down. My button popped off and my zipper straightways broke and separated as a result of the brute force. I saw the plated Levi's seal spinning on the wood floor and made it my focal point as Momma's bare hand met my pale ass with truth, plain and simple. Spare the rod and spoil the child, she reasoned with herself. The sound was about as offensive as an auto collision. "Moses Cotton, what are you thinking?!" the cadence of her words matched nearly every slap. My eyes watered. "Dragging all of Indian River into this house on your shoes! You must be possessed, boy!"

Once my ass was sufficiently red, she turned me around with my hands covering my boyhood and put her finger between my eyes.

"If you ever test me like that again, I will—" Then she noticed the room. The red rage that grew in her eyes was starting to make me regret. "...What in The Prophet's name has happened to this room?" She paused momentarily and scanned the dwelling with her mouth fell open. Momma reeled back to plant one across my cheek and then balled her fist to her mouth with deep breaths and closed eyes. "I am gonna lock you in this room and you're gonna clean it proper until your hands bleed!" It was right hard to stand up straight under the pressure of Momma. She was like every bit of the Holy Spirit that wasn't warm and tingly. I watched her face go from livid to reticent in a manner of seconds. "...Before the day is gone, you'll beg yourself bitter for the barn roof's perilous embrace..."

Shit, I thought. I hadn't reckoned on Momma becoming quite that poetically cross with me for what I had done, but there I stood, still shuddering with my balls cupped in my hands after she had gone out of the room and slammed the door shut behind her, knocking a wooden Jesus off the wall. My bones were straightways jarred from the encounter, but it had achieved the exact desired effect. Momma surely aimed to leave me to my thoughts and guilt as I painstakingly scrubbed and polished me and Aaron's communal quarters. My guess was that she would check in about the middle of lunch. The first thing I did was get the room back in order. I knew Momma had made note of my ability to do so in times previous, but I reckoned she had forgotten it in all her screaming. I boasted often in what I fancied a photographic kind of memory (which I didn't have), so I fixed the room back up with an added spit shine in twenty minutes flat. I had just bought for myself—with a brief spell of anguish—several straight hours of solitude in a row.

I peered sideways from the window to make certain Aaron wasn't coming down off the roof any time soon. I confirmed as I saw him and Daddy looking suspiciously on at recently resurrected Mr. Langford who had rejoined the alpha labor force with a grand, white smile waxed across his shiny, black face. I drew the curtains quickly and then double checked to make sure the bedroom door was closed up tight. After I had found myself to be adequately alone, I reached beneath the bottom bunk and grasped the crisp, crimson edges of that unmolested Word of God in bonded black leather. I held the book in my hands for a moment as I pondered where to start. I decided on combing straight through it, page by page, still unsure as to why I believed there to be some importance surrounding the book, other than the simple fact that I had never seen it. Some hidden aura upon the binding had gripped me from the instance the Lord set my eyes to it.

The inside cover was blank as slate, and the subsequent three or four pages were nothing more than filler, which I always supposed was for added favorable repute; the way ancient citizens and statesmen often took to wearing powdered wigs in public. I sometimes imagined God wearing one. I imagined he might don one as the judge of my life when the time came (which scared the fire out of me). That's how I saw those few superfluous pages; as the powdered wig of the Word of God.

Beyond that were several dedication pages and some lines for recording notes on whom all betrothed whom all and so forth. There were even some pages for denoting who passed when and who was born where and how to whom. I reckoned it wasn't unusual at all, but then I came to the publisher's info just prior to the table of contents, where I noticed two distinct items that caught my eye. The first was that the translation wasn't known to me. It certainly wasn't the King's.

"Revised Text of the Second Coming," I quoted under my breath. I stared at the strange title and suddenly felt I held within my trembling hands a tome of blasphemy; a book of practiced witches and gypsies. I straightways laid it on the floor, holding the cover flap ajar with one finger, and sat back with my legs crossed before me. I desired greatly then to separate myself physically from the work, for fear that it had already transferred some unwelcome spiritual property through my hands and leaked into my soul.

The second queer and vexing discovery was something I was actually right surprised by my ability to perceive as quick as I had. The publisher was a company called "Dozier-Powell" (whose names I recalled seeing on many of the Bibles stacked spine-side-out in Momma's hall closet). The part of it that straightways seized my attention, however, was the simple and disturbing fact that the name on the spine was completely left out of all distinguishing materials. Nowhere on the page was there listed a city, printer, subsidiary or contributor called "SOLOMON" as the outside adornment so ornately implied. I let go of the cover flap and allowed the book to close as I turned my neck awkwardly to observe the spine. My finger moved slowly across the shallow indentions of the gold leafed "SOLOMON" stamp, and I was rightly puzzled by it.

A further page by page scope of the entire Word (which took more than an hour) resulted in no added perplexities, save for one very fine underline marked in pencil by some anonymous hand in the Deuteronomist's second book of Kings. The scripture, which was the telling of the prophet Elijah's rapture into Heaven aboard a fiery chariot, felt an odd choice for a solitary inclusion. I held on to the thought, however, citing it as a possible reference for later, should someone suddenly disappear and last be seen at the end of a long trail of dirt and flames in the middle of the pasture. I shoved the book back beneath my bed and exhaled. I wasn't exactly stumped, but I had assumed the understanding that any further clarity would only be found in conversation and in dropping eave. Such methods had proven themselves worthy of my investment, given my recent run-ins with Walter and Dottie, the snooping I did on Daddy and Pastor Obis, and the brief but honest encounter I'd had earlier with Aaron. The time for clues and paper trails was long gone, and should I have continued on that course, I feared I would be lost or dead by Thanksgiving in three or four day's time.

My estimations of Momma's return were confirmed correct when she came charging in an hour later, after she had plated up lunch for the roof dwellers. I saw the prepared rage dissipate in color upon her face when she observed my work.

"Come eat," she commanded plainly.

Lunch was a smattering of Momma's own pickled garden vegetables and a plate of meat pies she had undoubtedly made from more of our own ground cows and po'dough (which was what Aaron and I called it whenever Momma had to skimp on certain finer ingredients to make biscuits out of necessity). I thought it right strange she didn't save a meal as such for dinner, being that it seemed more fitting for the end of the day. Most everyone passed on the pickled goods, save for Daddy and Aaron. I bit committed into a pie and was straightways pleased by the filling Momma had made, but the chalky white po'dough rock pockets were enough to kill the taste soon thereafter.

I finished my first and only meat pie whilst simultaneously noticing Mr. Langford crossing my field of vision near the corner of the barn. He was headed for seconds. It seemed he had quite fancied the things. I saw my chance then to have private words with the short man and probe gently at his recollections.

"Mr. Langford..." I said sheepishly, barely even certain he heard my voice. The short man turned with a smile and scanned my general area without making the connection. I waved and spoke once more. "Mr. Langford." he looked down and smiled wider, if it was possible.

"My friend!" he approached. "And how are you this fine day?" The short man bent slightly to match my height.

"Good," I said. "How are you?"

"Oh, I'm doing much better, thank you."

"Do you remember anything?" I asked.

"Well, I'll tell you what, I don't recall much before the great gust that took me and my sail away," he laughed, "but I do thank the Lord for the faith and prayerfulness of those on this farm."

I choked back a lump in my throat at the words.

"You mean, you ain't an acrostic no more?"

The short man laughed. Aaron was watching then from the table.

"An agnostic?" he corrected. "Oh, no. How could I be when such proof of God exists in the form of so tangible a man?"

"What man?" I asked hastily, seeing Momma approaching in my periphery. Mr. Langford stood up straight and faced her as she came and put her hands on my shoulders opposite the short man. "You mean to tell me our little fellow here has not yet met your local healer?" Mr. Langford asked jovially with his hands on his hips. I saw the short man's smile almost fully skulk away upon viewing Momma's reactive expressions (which I was unable to observe or read). I looked back at Momma, but the sun was orchestrated masterfully above her head as to keep me from telling facial knowledge. When I turned back, Mr. Langford was well on his way through the barn door. He nodded and smiled at me as he went. Momma gripped me as she usually did.

"I don't want you talking to that man," she commanded, taking my dirtied mint green plate and leaving for the picnic table, "even if he is claiming now to believe."

I figured it was Mr. Langford's color that Momma and Daddy were opposed to, or maybe it was something else entirely; his polished speech, perhaps. Whatever it was, it must not have been bad enough to keep the short man from sticking around or being deserved of fervent prayers when he was loosed from the top of the barn. It was both queer and convenient that the short man was told by some soul that he had been blown from the roof, but it made sense for Mamie's veiled innocence or the deniability of any other party involved. Either way, he had no idea what really had occurred. All he possessed then was an unwavering devotion to the brothers and sisters and a newly adopted reverence for The Man in the Woods, to whom he had unsurprisingly referred to as a "healer." It was becoming excruciatingly plain to me that there was a figure of great importance in the woods of our farm, and that his name was being screamed loudly from lungs and from rooftops. And I was fairly certain I had discerned him to be The Samaritan from the Stagwerth tales.

Concerning a somewhat separate matter, I had grown more and more inclined, over the previous day-and-a-half, to the idea of writing Miles Beckins. I truly wasn't sure whether or not I would see another of his planes or find more parceled notes in the pasture, but the odds didn't look good considering I hadn't caught fresh tell of him in over seventy-two hours, and the fact that I had been called off the count, thus nullifying any further daylight visits to the drop zone. To be completely honest, I had become somewhat concerned for the man. Something felt threatened about The Harbinger's marked absence from the skies, and I believed for some time that a third message might aid me in unravelling the first two, which was the reason I debated contacting him myself in order to keep the game afoot. I reasoned if I could appeal to Miles Beckins, that maybe I was a friend, capable of possessing clandestine information, then perhaps he would speak to me more clearly concerning his knowledge of the developing intrigues. I decided on letting the matter sit for the remainder of the day, until I could decide on a prudent approach. At the very latest, I would pen him in the evening and place the letter in the mailbox before bed or my nightly wanderings (though I was without knowledge of The Harbinger's proper home address).

I stayed opposite Mamie by any subtle means necessary for the remainder of the lunch period, and avoided the puzzled looks of Aaron and the inquisitive glare of Momma the best I could. It wasn't healthy to have so many enemies in one's home. I had become quite a dynamic figure on our little farm, with quite a large footprint, and I wasn't sure it was the wisest thing I had ever done. It wasn't an hour past noon and I had already gained the eyes of half the family.

The rest of the afternoon passed by without the least hint of interest; the fates and I made sure of it. Not to mention, without the count to keep my time bought in the afternoon, Momma resorted to encumbering me with more school lessons than were rightly deserved of any overly curious youngster. I writhed in frustrated boredom as my body revolted against the wooden desk chair in the living room. It was a ridiculous sight to behold; a boy working vainly at schooling himself in his own home.

When Momma finally came and retrieved me for Walter's memorial, my heart leapt in jubilation at the idea of trading pain for sorrow. It was near about sunset then, and there hadn't been a single Indian River boy in school for hours. Sometimes I debated just staying out of shit for the sole sake of keeping Momma from ladening me down with business, but then I would be rendered a creature of fettered curiosities, bound to spend my days in private meditations of the world around me, eventually resulting in a violent lashing out against humanity. That wasn't written in the histories, however, and I had already begun to understand my role in the small tale of the Cotton Farm that would fit like a fuse into the grander portrait of an Indian River under siege of plague and conciliatory dangers.

Walter's funeral was a place I hoped to perhaps get a look at a few telling expressions upon the faces of Mamie or Daddy or Pastor Obis; maybe even Momma. Even more, I hoped to win Aaron fully over and possibly gain an ally in the whole God-forsaken ordeal. Where we gathered beneath the dead oak on the far end of the front pasture, there were more long bouts of silence from County Road 1 than there were sounds of actual automobiles. Two parties had formed there at Walter's favorite spot where he was to be buried, but only one was there to mourn. We did not acknowledge the host of folk who stood picketed along seventy-five or a hundred yards of our property line.

For many of them, it was the first time they had seen the Family Beyond the Gate up close in a long while. For most of the brothers and sisters, it was the first time they had realized what we had on our hands was the potential for an outright dangerous situation. I sneaked as many glances as I could, but the rest of the family kept eyes glued to the ground or Pastor Obis with plastered expressions of embarrassment more than terror, as if they had greater things to fear within the farm than without.

"Brothers and sisters," Pastor Obis said, quiet enough to exclude the onlookers, but loud enough the Lord would hear and receive Walter into his hands. "Jesus said, I am the resurrection and I am life. Those who believe in me, even though they die, yet shall they live, and whoever lives and believes in me shall never die. I am Alpha and Omega, the beginning and the end, the first and the last. I died, and behold I am alive for evermore, and I hold the keys of hell and death. Because I live, you shall live also..." Pastor Obis kept on with his traditional funeral fare as I trailed off in attention. Had the townsfolk so desired, I reckoned they could have crawled beneath or through our fence, which was no more than a man high and consisting of two rows of horizontally placed timber, the same as any other ranch style barrier. I had no idea what kept them from sneaking across at night and throttling us in our sleeps. And though I greatly feared a breach by those angered souls, it was no more so than I feared what kept them out.

"Let us pray," Pastor Obis reentered my conscious. "We ask you now, dear Lord to accept this, your servant into your kingdom, that he may remain there with you for-evermore. In Jesus' name we pray, amen." he seemed to say it with increased speed and lessened sincerity as he went, closing his word with his eyes shut and anxious to leave. The gathering broke apart shamelessly, like a wrecked sea craft, without as much as an invitation to give kind words or speak final goodbyes to the man. There were no last looks or moment of silence. It was then I realized Walter was dead a long time before then. It was no secret he was a nuisance to most on the farm, which was a shame, given his kindness to and adoration for each and every one of us.

Ms. Dottie was awash in handsomely mitigated emo-tion, and though her flamboyant hat covered much of her powdered countenance, her truest fondness for Walter was told in that moment, then, along with her most disconso-late regret. Mamie fraudulently cradled her in the cleft of a single arm and walked her away from the scene. I hated them both for their charade. They had no rights to loose a drop of saltwater upon the earth I had tilled. The crickets would surely drink their tears and grow stronger in their evil trade. I watched as they went on, weaving through the squares, treading upon the plague wrought by me and my brother. I might have induced the plight, but people like Mamie and Dottie and Momma and Daddy and The Man in the Woods perpetuated it with their schemes and bigotry.

Had I paid the ceremony any mind, myself, I might have cried, but my attention had been forcefully and relentlessly held hostage at the fence and elsewhere. I looked down in mock mournfulness as we traveled back through upturned earth and hell grass, desperate to make out a partially buried note or even a trace of some alien material corroded by plague and time; anything to imply The Harbinger's continued good faith in my ability to aid him in his cryptic quest, but there was nothing at all. Miles Beckins had seen fit to tease my sensibilities with a pair of enigmatic missives which revealed to me exactly nothing. He could go to hell with Mamie and Dottie.

One hour later, I sat at the dinner table with only Aaron and Momma and a plate of roast before me. Momma had mentioned Daddy and Pastor Obis had something urgent to tend to, so when naturally I asked how the brothers and sisters would eat, she said Mamie would be coming to retrieve the stock pot. I realized then, from Aaron's reaction, that he had perhaps come to my side.

"That don't seem like a good idea to me..." he stated.

Momma laid her fork down and put her hands together in sarcastic patience.

"And why not?"

"Same reason we don't favor woman ministers," he answered, diving headlong for Momma's bait. "I don't reckon it's Mamie's job to feed the Pastor's flock."

"Hmm, well you've got something there, son," Momma said. Aaron gave a sideways nod and set his attention back on his plate, not expecting Momma to continue. "I heartily agree," she said. Aaron slurped and nodded again, but Momma wasn't near finished, and I knew it. She went on. "But if you think just cause your Daddy's away from the table it gives you grace to speak like the man of the house, you're dead wrong! You watch your mouth! Mamie's still your elder!"

Aaron looked at Momma, puzzled, with his mouth half full of stringy roast. Then I saw the expression on his face change from concern to redolent with reciprocal anger, like that of a soul suddenly overcome by the likes of a rogue storm (and damn near as futile in its ability to combat it).

"Takes more than age," my brother said. I gasped involuntarily beneath my breath and fluttered my lashes in precaution as Momma stepped once from her seat with hurricane force, screeching her chair and taking up Aaron by his shirt collar into the next room without a syllable uttered. I heard the singular flat pack of flesh against flesh, accompanied by the stiff sounds of a wordless struggle from the other side of the living room wall. Aaron emerged, still leashed at Momma's mercy and donning Daddy's work jacket and boots, untied and filthy.

"You wanna be Daddy, you're gonna need to wear his clothes, too," she said with the quiet ferocity of a spilt flame, and I at once understood. The last time Aaron had dared to do something as bold on his own, he was straightways steamrolled by Daddy and made to stand on the red clay drive full-on clothed in ten or twelve layers of cold weather attire in the treacherous inferno of Indian River's hottest summer afternoon. He damn near expired from heat stroke before the day was out, but he never dreamt of such disobedience again. Momma was aimin' to make Aaron appear drunk with belligerence before Daddy.

She opened the front door into the cold night and faced her troubled son into its eternal blackness.

"He's at the hole," Momma said. "Go and find him."

"...Ain't I just gonna tell him you dressed me up and sent me?" Aaron challenged.

"If you do, I'll deny it up and down," Momma replied. "Then who do you think he'll believe?"

"You wouldn't lie," he said.

"Test me," Momma concluded. And with that, she shoved Aaron out into the abyssal night with a push of her forearm as she simultaneously reached to pull the door shut. Aaron then disappeared behind the proverbial pulled curtain of our home and reappeared where God-only-known.

The evening dripped on past dinner, and as always, I waited in my bedroom for Momma to finally give up and vacate the kitchen. Instead of pouring over my own Word, however, I read from the Solomon Bible, perhaps hoping to find clues within the text. I was straightways confused by many of the verses, as they all seemed to speak loosely to the same sensibilities as were accustomed to me, only with different phrasings and peculiar rearrangements that made me feel as if I had uncovered some weathered yellow folder bearing the papers outlining my adoption. I considered opening my Word alongside the Solomon one and holding them in parallel next to one another in order to perform a thorough examination, but that was as far as I got before I heard plainly the sounds of Momma leaving off in the direction of her room for the evening.

Aaron had me the slightest bit worried by the time I finished the dishes and bleached a load of drawers and socks. Daddy, too. I was in a steady rush at that point to finish and steal away from the house with godspeed. The fiery broth of bathwater would indeed have to wait, as things of life—of subtle danger—had taken precedence. Charles wanted for nothing that night, as I skipped to the grass below the steps with a singular, dull stomp, leaving behind a pair of basins overflowing with scraps and kibble and fresh water. The pup was a king then. Momma would have no grounds to prosecute me for neglect (in disguise of something else). She would surely have to procure some other means by which to passively prune me should Aaron and Daddy evade me and reach home before I was able to tuck myself expertly into bed.

In the least, I knew the exact (alleged) location of the pair, which was more than could be said of my luck in most times precursory to a manhunt. I imagined Aaron had already been savaged once over by Daddy. There wasn't a chance in hell Daddy would believe Momma made him do such a thing, and given the history of the stunt, I reckoned Daddy would assume drunkenness or delirium of Aaron, one. Neither of which were good for my troublesome fraternal cohort. I half expected to find Aaron at the bottom of the hole, alone in the dark without clothes. And though I wasn't exactly right, I wasn't far from the truth when I finally came across him in a bizarre circumstance.

I ducked low in my stubborn vantage behind the hay bales; still unconvinced it was the terriblest of hiding spots, as Aaron had claimed. I knew, however, he would check there first, should he detect the slightest audible indicator, or feel the first chill of paranoia traverse his spine. Daddy was expressly absent, along with Pastor Obis, and the night was quiet, save alone for Aaron's frustrated interactions with the world around him. I made a hole between the bales with my arm and didn't dare watch along the tops, as was my custom. My vision was limited, but my brother didn't seem to leave the prickly-edged border of the bubble I had entrapped him in. I watched, bound in curiosity as Aaron loaded one incomprehensible wooden crate after another into Daddy's red wheelbarrow. A partially reconstructed haiku swam in my head, but I was alas unable to oblige the tip of my own tongue. He was retrieving the sealed boxes from someplace beyond the shadows near the maw of dirt before us. They were made of materials foreign to our farm, yet familiar to me. I studied the blonde pine enclosures and instantly recognized the burn brands on the sides. The capital "M" inside a circle was Marlin's crest (for lack of a better word), and the crates were the same crates inside which Momma had received her shipped meats previously.

I smirked mildly at the prospect of my expertly deduced and drawn conclusion, making note to myself that I hadn't had many since the start of that long and strange ordeal. The barrow was nearly packed full when I saw Aaron go and climb down inside the hole. He disappeared within seconds of mounting an almost fully concealed set of wooden rungs that I hadn't spied until that point. Soon after, the sounds of clanking metals and tools, either mistakingly dropped or angrily cast aside, accompanied him far away in the bottom of the pit, where the echoes and delayed dullnesses could have easily deceived one into believing the chasm was forty or fifty feet deep. What in the devil's name, I thought. Had Aaron been instructed by Daddy to perform a chore of such suspect? Or was Aaron acting on his own accord, perhaps committing a sin of sabotage in defiance of Daddy and Momma? My thoughts caused me to assume it was typical of disciplinary behavior for Daddy, thus indicating Aaron was there against his will. Either way, it was positively apparent that Aaron was pissed as fire.

Then, as if queued by a final and jarred metallic clamor, I heard the clear combustion of what could be nothing if not the ignition and steady, cantankerous gurgle of the titanic machine beneath the ground. It hummed and choked back infernal heaves as it went on and on and on without stopping. I turned and looked at the house, half wondering if the terrible sounds might reach out too far and draw the attention of additional spectators, but then I convinced myself it wasn't quite loud enough to break anything more than a low hum anywhere further than where I crouched behind the bales. A moment or two later, Aaron came back out of the hole, bracing the rungs of the ladder with his left arm and cradling another of Marlin's crates in his right. I watched as he handsomely sandwiched the final crate within the wheelbarrow's last conceivable vacancy. Aaron always took a knack for being able to make something out of nothing.

He disappeared into the black shroud of the old tack closet, which doubled as a feed room. It was nothing more than a caged stall near the end of the dilapidated structure of the old barn. I made a conscious effort then to observe a moment in the night sky as a single, silver-lined cloud rolled away like a tombstone and revealed the white moon underneath, which shone upon the old barn's roof and breathed many new and dazzled breaths into the colored stripes of the tightly stretched canvas canopy, and for a brief second, the marriage of it all seemed to carry with it such a wildly vibrant technicolor display, that I could scarce but wonder what gifted and charitable creature had bestowed such a masterwork of beauty upon so tainted a world, and whom had boasted gall enough to bring it to Indian River and have it hogtied torturously to so homely a framework. Aaron finally emerged with an ordinary brown saddle blanket and (in one of his trademark gestures of fell swoop fluidity) threw it expertly over the top of the load without rearrangements and wheeled the entire thing into the doorway of the large enclosure on the west side of the overlarge stall that housed our pine shavings. Then he left away.

I stood there, perplexed for a moment, wondering why in the devil's hell he would leave such a package so susceptible to random discovery. Every impulse in my body told me I should be deranged not to march toward those cases, pry past Marlin's crest and see what lay inside; every impulse but one. It was the one such impulse leading me to hightail it back to the house and beat Aaron to bed, lest I suffer a repeat of my former chastisement in twofold severity. When I rounded the front of the hay bales, however, and retraced Aaron's exit for confirmation of his whereabouts, I found myself staring at his back as he plodded along quietly through the dark and into the orange glow of the back pasture. I made a spur of the moment decision to continue with my crusade and allow Aaron to lead me on aimlessly to his undisclosed destination. I kept enough careful distance not to warrant the suspicion of my wayward sibling, but as much as I didn't care to admit, chances were he was already suspect to my following him. I didn't pay it any mind. He was too far ahead to double back and prove it.

Soon as he crouched down and slid sideways through the gate panel, I saw Aaron dip off into a darkened alcove of conjoined fences and wild shrubbery, much as he had before in the tack room. When he stood again, he brandished a long, broad and blunt object, shouldered it, and made his way onward to the bunker fire. I followed at a safe interval still, careful to turn corners only after Aaron had made several long paces onward in other directions. As I warily approached the area where Aaron had retrieved his curious instrument, I collapsed my profile and sunk into the same shadow he had. I had risked a good deal storming that particular position, given that the only bit of obscurity between Aaron and I was the contrast of dark and moonlight, but I had seen the integrity of the spot proven seconds earlier, so I decided to invest. My eyes followed Aaron's silhouette closely as it neared the docile flames of the bunker fire. As I backed slowly into the overgrown nook; a place where the wooden fence along the western side of the back pasture met the additional galvanized gate panels along its south corner, I stumbled clumsily into what felt and sounded uncannily like a whole mess of loose bowling pins or something just as clumsy.

I snapped to attention and froze inside myself. Aaron had stopped in that moment, undoubtedly upon hearing the racket I had caused. He turned ever so slowly as I balanced backwards with hands and limbs braced in all directions, attempting desperately to quiet the confounded wooden objects as they aimed to roll and settle beneath me. Aaron faced me fully in the dark then. From all that ways off, I could not make out his features, but the slow and antagonistic lay of his posture was enough to say, "I know you're there, fool. Just keep quiet, for Prophet's sake." Disarmed, as usual, I was once again straightways embarrassed at my own inability to do my work without being granted life strokes for apparent retardation. Even Aaron had to help me spy on Aaron. Well, he turned and unburdened his bowling pin, dipping it into the fire. The end of it lit away and instantly revealed to me its identity and application; a simple torch, no wonder. I was dumbfounded at my vapidity. At once, my hands clasped the nearest one and held it low.

I stroked cautiously along the object and learned its grain, but before I could allow my eyes to adjust and attain a proper look, I was alerted to the immediate presence of whispers and shadows which had descended upon me in rapid succession. They had come for the tools at my rear. My mind instantly flashed to the night I saw the brothers and sisters with the suspect torches traveling across the back pasture allegedly in search of me. I recalled how they had done so in such an odd manner; walking single file, and how Daddy and Momma and Aaron had all neglected to confront me afterward.

I stood quickly in an improvised survival reflex and began handing torch handles to the darkened figures. My heart pounded as the first silhouette gladly accepted the gift and moved on, followed by another and another and another. It was simply too dark to make out my height or contour, and the brothers and sisters went on unaccounted, as if it was part of the ritual. There was no question among them that one had assumed the responsibility for allocating articles of illumination. I swore to have identified both Momma and Sarah Obis in the fray of hands and feet as they shuffled by in an unassuming hurry. Some figure had lingered long enough to give me a slight feeling of discomfort, but was soon gone off toward the fire like the rest. I let loose a quiet sigh of relief as the brothers and sisters filed off once again and made for the bottom of the pasture.

I at once abandoned the theory of a continued search party. The party wasn't for me. They weren't searching then, and they weren't searching before. They were headed for the woods; for the far tree line, and I reckoned I had built up enough courage then to go on and confirm why. I felt my own body lift itself up off the ground and make way on the same bearing as the torchlight processional. I managed an unsafe distance, given that no amount of space out on those Indian River moors were enough to conceal a cast silhouette at any range. One foot after another, I ran as light and low as I could, whilst managing to keep my own shadow behind me. The glow of all those torches did much to drown out the celestial bodies and cause my movement to appear as nothing more than the far off dance of a flame held too high against a rear member of the march.

The ground beneath my feet became newer to me with every step. As strange as it was, I realized then that I had never blazed that far east on our property before; I reckoned for fear of being abducted into those woods and introduced to a terror of my childhood imagination. I wasn't certain of what dumbfounded bravery went with me then, but I was sure as hell headed straightways for the molten heart of fear at an unrelenting pace. The land underfoot felt alien as it rose and dipped in uniform successions of tiny hillocks the further and further it went, sinking low into the toes of the giant wild pines before me. My approach took a slight southern course as I attempted not to overcome the parade, electing furthermore to situate myself sideways and rear to their visual plane.

In no time at all, I was forced to stop and fall level to the ground (likened to how Daddy had taught us) as the torches went on through the teeth of that front row of trees and were swallowed whole by the darkness from the shadows beyond. One by one, I watched and counted as each and every living soul on our farm disappeared as nothing more than faded lights down a hidden path into the pines (even Mr. Langford must have been among them). When at last there was nothing but dark, I climbed up off my belly and sprinted full-on toward the place where I had seen the last light disappear. The persistent glow remained there, etched onto the softer parts of my eyes like an overlay from where I had stared directly into the final flame with the intent of recording its last known trajectory. When I reached the foremost tree amongst the edge of the endless ranks, I stopped to catch a breath and relinquish any fear I had shouldered in the last ten to twelve minutes (or ten to twelve years). The closest I had ever stood to such a venture was two summers prior, when I had fancied it a decent hiding spot during a game of sardines with some of my Indian River friends. I had stood at the top of the pasture, near the construction of the bunker, and watched the tips of those trees sway ominously in the cool wind of a summer afternoon. They were cut in stark contrast by the blackness of storm clouds rolling in behind their evergreen coats so high above me. I decided then those woods were evil.

The night made the trees look a good deal worse than an impending gale storm had, but I was also two years older than when last I challenged the idea of breaking the seal of my physical childhood boundary. I looked back, far up the pasture, over all the hillocks and beneath the glow of heaven, which was notably more visible then, and I saw the stars start bright and then fade away over the orange luminescence of the bunker fire, and I remember thinking I was as far from safety as I had ever been. When I turned my attention back to the woods, I recognized I was then sandwiched in a split second resolution between danger and ignorance, with the latter seeming far worse. It might have been one of the keystone moments of my life, wherein I was changed from boy to man, if in nothing but my priorities.

The first thing I noticed upon entering that black place was the sharp absence of sound. The decrepit foliage below, opposed by the dense canopy above and braced between by age-old heirloom pines seemed to form an auditory vacuum. I could scarce hear even the crunch beneath my boots or the sounds of my own breathing. I scanned for signs of light and at once responded with movement in a westerly direction, following a faint flicker which had just crested a bisected ridge on the trail ahead. There indeed was a trail; one I had neither seen nor heard of before, but it was more difficult to navigate with eyes than I anticipated. It wasn't cut away, but rather, walked in, from what appeared to be scores of night journeys down its winding way. What little moon and starlight did manage to pierce the veil of trees was far too faint to make sense of the path without traversing it oneself.

Several times, I noticed I had drifted away and found myself stepping into bald patches within the brush and having to turn back whilst keeping my eyes wed to the glow before me. Upon each new reintroduction to the trail, I felt the aura of the torches fade further and further away, until I eventually elected to abandon the path altogether and make a straight run for the lights. It seemed they had stopped somewhere ahead, beyond the hill in the trees.

I crept low and moved apelike, swatting away twigs and vines, and swallowing silk webs as my feet sunk regularly into moist micro ponds of muddied leaf sludge and compost. It seemed I had gained on the brothers and sisters, and, in a curious way, it was as if their light had grown immensely beyond the swiftly approaching hill. My pace quickened against what I thought possible for my state of fatigue.

As I advanced on what I had marked visually as the apex of the small rise, I felt the mounted fear, which had filled my soul with fast drips of cold pain, begin to dissipate in slow releases the nearer I came to the increasing glow. I once again moved to my stomach and crawled the remaining five or ten yards to the peak, in desperate anticipation of what I should see there. What I witnessed, in order of how things were revealed to me, was at first the far edge of a large convex in the terrain, like a natural bowl which started with me. I then turned my gaze to the fires in the trees and was straightways transported to what felt like a frightful dream. There were more torches, all gathered along the circumference of the indention and lit high upon the tree trunks, shining into the bowl's interior like a great high beam. Inside were the brothers and sisters—as well as my own blood—clearly seen then in more light than was necessary, all seated in handsome rows atop logs of pine, wearing the queerest of garbs; what looked to me like white sleeping clothes with hay ropes tied at their waists. They were still clenching their individual torches, in what had clearly become more ritual than necessity amidst all the other lights present. They were chanting something low and loathsome, and I was immediately filled with a sub-terrestrial terror, desiring nothing more in that moment than for everything to return to what was normal and good.

My final observation was of what laid before them; a great, crafted platform made of all manor of earthly articles—stumps and stones, logs and mud and debris—and finished with a proper pulpit that seemed to have no business amongst the other adornments, and could have easily belonged in some southern preacher's perish somewhere long ago, save for its ten point elken frontispiece. I cast my full weight upon the edge of the rise, attempting to fuse my very core to the earth, as to not be detected during that most crucial of moments wherein I had successfully procured a distinguished vantage from which point I should be able to fully witness the escapades that would indeed unfold themselves before me in due time. My eyes found Sarah Obis, and though she looked strange to me—dressed and modest—there was a beauty surrounding her I had not yet experienced, encompassed by the likeness she bore to the others, whilst still managing to stand alone, as well as her ability to, all at once, cause me to experience a stilled peace, when all I wanted was to spill vomit in great volumes for the twisted fear and disconcerted confusion begat by everything around me. I was in a bad way.

The undimmed, orange glow that began in the bowl and amongst the trees, seemed to fade noticeably as it rose into the tall trunks and finally disappeared in the midst of an ovular, black and starless ceiling high above the pine boughs. I watched the brothers and sisters and Daddy, Momma and Aaron, and Mr. Langford, even (with his black face in stark contrast to his white pajamas) as they sat still as toads upon those unshaped pine pews, awaiting something omnipresent, but yet to be shown. There was a moment then when I detected in myself the slightest hint of nervous embarrassment, as I looked to the creatures of the ritual to continue and spook me, rather than acknowledge what approached and stole their gaze. I saw their attention draw forward, but I refused to join, aiming desperately to pretend I had yet to witness the queerest of it all. Then, in a manner in which I could not have hoped to ignore, the place where we were gathered filled with what seemed to be the sound of a mighty rushing wind, and the fires danced wildly in the trees until the force become so great they were snuffed out all together, shrinking the light in the bowl to nothing more than a modest glow surrounding only those seated along the makeshift pews as they drew together slowly.

I felt the light detract from me, and I was straightways frightened anew. My heart pounded as a drum, violently, and a low and thunderous clamor reverberated beneath the gust as it drove away into the black and endless corridors of the planted pines. The phenomenon was then capped with a subsonic tremor, as the whole of Indian River seemed to shake, but only enough to make note of; as if somewhere far beneath me, there was a great stone churner, polishing primordial boulders in mammoth volumes. I reckoned the sounds of such a chaotic chore must have been deafening so far below the earth's crust, where noise and pandemonium were all too familiar parts of a cruel and tortured underworld. We all seemed to wait for the last of the manifestations to crescendo and fade away, but they continued, only rising.

In the distance; what seemed miles away, were the sounds of what could easily have been ranks of savage hordes, great in numbers, cooing ominously, thirsty for blood. The choral tides rose and fell with haunting tones which echoed through the trees and traveled in almost visible waves encircling the bowl. Then, the scene at once turned quiet; silent as indifference or unreciprocated love, and I felt the wordless transition of attention settle upon the darkened platform. My eyes searched the place, from where all light had left, following the initial manifestation of wind, and it was then, in that still and silent moment, that I knew he had come.

My vision was glued to the black, and I couldn't be certain whether the tears that welled in my eyes and fell to the earth below were because of my unwillingness to blink or because of the marked fear that had found its home in my chest. I wiped the wet from my cheeks and rose just a little, hoping to read the reactions on the faces of the brothers and sisters; namely Aaron and Sarah Obis. I wouldn't have minded catching the short man's either, to be true, but before I could manage to hone in on one of their glazed faces, a newborn light appeared on the platform, planted in the antlers of the pulpit, and I watched as the face of the man I had feared since before I could scarce utter his name materialized into being.

It was almost as if he had formed from nothing, wrought together from estranged molecules that only managed to conjoin when being summoned to craft the man on such occasions as then. He was etched in traces of shadow and light, drawn slowly, as rain tends to permeate clothing over time exposed. Before long, he was completely composed, and I reckoned then it was perhaps because of the ability of my eyes to adjust to new light that made him seem that way. He was right different than I had always imagined The Samaritan looked in the stories I heard from Daddy and various townsfolk. I supposed it was due to the fact that Daddy had first told us the stories, and I assumed the man would share a likeness to him. I realized then, however, what a simpleminded idea it was as I stared into the burning image of a man grand in stature, but not overlarged like Pastor Obis. In fact, his physique tended to be somewhat slack and accidental, giving the impression that he spent far more time tending to his mind and soul than to his mortallity.

The man was not the image of wild abandon or John the Baptist as one might so appropriately attach to his name. His boots were made of aged leathers (or leastways appeared to be from where I could tell). I fancied them to be the sort that zipped up and rose ankle high. They were black, and each boasted a distinguished silver buckle resembling something of pilgrim or Puritanical origination. The well-cut but unlined cuffs of his trousers hung high and hovered about his ankles, undoubtedly trespassing along his legs somewhere above his socks with a relentless, prickled itch. The rest of his pants were covered from above by a flowing, black vestment, the weight of which looked to be tremendous. It poured over his shoulders and down about his wrists where from beneath protruded a set of womanly hands that seemed unbefitting to the rest of his figure. On his right, index finger, he wore a thick, gold band that bore the likeness of a class ring or seal.

Near around his chest and neck, where the stitch in his robe changed to run horizontal, a great, white sash split and fell to his waist, which was adorned on the ends with twin red crosses before finally coming to separate points. I followed what I reckoned was a zipper, from below his navel to up around his neck where there appeared to be a strap and clasp keeping the vestment closed tight around his cleanly nape. His face was aged childishly, razor cut with that learned disdain for uncleanliness. Like Pastor Obis, he also boasted a side-parted, wet-combed tuft of hair atop his head (which could have been false), but wore no glasses. His broad, red forehead glistened with sweat or grease, or anointing oil, and I felt certain of what would have remained on my hands should I have touched his brow. Perhaps the man's most frightful feature—the one that set the nerves of my teeth to torturous reverberations—were the spaces above his eyes (where normal creatures of human persuasion possessed hair). Despite his unmistakable humanity, his face was utterly devoid of the feature, and I wasn't sure if it was because he had been born without, or because he had clean cut them away with straight razors, the way he did the hair about his neck, chin and lip.

His wide eyes seemed to protrude bulbously from his skull, but remained protected by cavernous indentions formed under the great mantle of his glistening forehead. His nose was inconsequential, but the skin below gathered around the lipless void of his mouth, from which would soon pour the textbook inspiration of fear. I was filled with dread for each passing second as the time slipped away, counting down to the moment when he would finally speak and perhaps have me the way He'd had Daddy and Momma and Aaron and Sarah Obis. He remained there, however, in silence before them, intent on building cumulatively upon that marked fear struck within every heart present.

Despite his memorable appearance, none of the man's truest ferocity were found in his physicality. All else was tied up in his aura and disposition of rare and authentic intensity that felt the most like God's fear as I had ever experienced in my young years. The greatest realization of which would have come in the form of physical contact. I feared I would be filled with great revelations or manifestations of the Holy Spirit that I were simply too entangled by to manage; things that might cause me to scream and shake and fall down weeping uncontrolled, if I were to be completely honest. The other part was the unadulterated terror he bore inside me. The man looked alert enough to gnaw the face from an angered bear and win at such a sport. Not to mention, I had incontrovertibly located the black hole of our farm; the one that seemed to at first sip, and then slurp thirstily at the attentions and allegiances of our home and the rest of Indian River.

He was at last there, before me, in real flesh and bone. If someone were to have come along and told me it wasn't real, why I would have right believed them, if only for the simple hope they were there to deliver me from the whole shocking debacle. At that moment, I was mostly unable to even return to acknowledging the condition of my family below. I had a great deal of questioning them to do yet, what with their robes and flames and strange behaviors. It was no family I had grown alongside and shared a home with. They were a people I hadn't quite yet had the displeasure of making acquaintances with, and I didn't aim to, either. I fancied the idea of pretending it was a dream or alternate dimension I had stumbled into, and that all things would be normal upon my returning home or waking in the morning.

Then, I felt the breath draw away from me, as if the bowl and the sky and all the world had been sapped clear of God's good air. I felt as if I had been thrust atop the highest mountain or tossed into the deepest sea, where neither air nor life had its place. The Man in the Woods was gathering breath to utter his invocation, and I was suddenly and voluntarily returned to the memory of a day long gone by, when I had come to be engaged in my first physical struggle. It was a proper earned scrap of boyhood; a passage. Aaron was there, and he would have sooner died than allow me to see it by. There was no turning back as a son of earth and toil; only one door stood before me in a concourse of growth and bitter graduation from child to god. My contender's first blow was the most memorable. He was a good deal larger than I, and commanded a force in his punch that woke the dead parts of me. It landed below my ribs on the left bisector of my gut and evacuated me of all hope to draw breath for the indefinite future. Several minutes later, I came to with only Aaron standing over me. To that present day, he had never wiped that disappointment from his face.

When I had at last reached the point—laying there on my stomach in those woods—that I knew I could scarce draw another breath, I rose just a little; enough to forfeit some of my concealment and grant myself the best conditions of survival. Perhaps God would bring another mighty wind and flush cool air through my lungs, lest I lose my life there in the pine straws above my lost and ill-fated family. I tried desperately to find them in the dark as the flames in their hands seemed to wither and shrink, and I was sure then that I would die at any moment. Their bodies were buckled and bent, choking and wheezing, but staying put, as if they had expected to suffer under such prerequisites long before arriving there. It was almost as if they had adopted procedure for it, and did clearly better than me at fending off the basest of human struggles that we should have all bore equally. I gasped and clenched the straws with my hands, but just then, when I felt my time had come, and my body began to settle into the grave, the Lord sent a host of gales through the trees, reigniting flames and life and color. Our lungs were filled, as if with a wellspring, and our ears became brittle with humility as they encountered his first words.

"AND I HAVE FORMED MAN FROM THE DUST OF THE GROUND, AND BREATHED THE BREATH OF LIFE INTO HIS NOSTRILS; AND HIS SOUL HAS LIVED!"

Time stopped. The earth stood still on its axis and every star in the sky was rendered motionless, even to the most infinitesimal scale. All was silent, save for the crackle of flames in those trees and on the ground and at the platform, whose lights seemed to grow and swell incoherently beneath the operatic commands wrought from our host in that terrible but true phantasm. The inside of me shook with tremors of the macabre, as if I might die yet upon hearing another bout of words from the man. His voice was too intense; too unearthly for me to focus even on what the words meant when added together in purposeful succession of one another. I had not truly processed a single word he uttered, only the sounds of his voice and all physical and paranormal manifestations that accompanied it.

I unhinged my eyes from The Man in the Woods (if the name still suited Him) and attempted desperately to look upon my family. Oppositely of what I had expected to behold, it seemed the twelve had settled into the intensity and stood seated inside themselves. A watchful peace was upon them as, even before my eyes, they began to separate visibly as islands unto themselves along the wood-hewn pews. They were still standing, but not for long. Before I could prepare myself and brace rock or root, the force of his voice eviscerated my thoughts and tossed me raggedly about as Daddy had expected Stagwerth's might have done in those recorded radio addresses.

"CHILDREN!" he started. The boom of his voice set the wind in motion again. The trees cracked and the flames damn near fell out of their places. "THE TIME HAS COME FOR CLEANSING! CHOOSE YE THIS DAY WHOM YOU WILL SERVE!" his voice was a chorus among the trees; a high tenor of hell's own opera, and I remember even likening it to The Prophet's. He held his hands out, and the earth came alive. The gusts bent the trees back, and the torches dropped tongues of fire on our heads. I patted away a rogue ember that bounced off my arm. When I looked back, I saw tears falling from every eye and noticed not even my own was spared. Momma and Daddy fell prostrate to the ground, and the brothers and sisters followed, weeping violently with loud wails and moaning. Sarah Obis was shaking with violence, and I watched as Aaron's forehead touched cold dirt in a way I had never seen him do before. My hand went over my own mouth without command, and I choked on tears as an unknown power surged inside me, unwelcomed. His voice continued to echo in those trees long after he spoke, and all I could do was weep to hear the words of The Man in the Woods.

12

I couldn't quite say how I drifted from that breathless place among the pines back to my bedroom and further on to sleep. It was a thoughtless set of motor gestures that bade me return to the realms of physicality; the only one of which I remembered was the moment I had stopped off in Daddy's field office (a red-dusted and shabby space across from the barn's tack room) and liberated a postcard of the 1947 Blue Angels in diamond formation, props and all. It was part of a set of U.S. Navy collectible mailers I had eyeballed since the summer prior, when I stumbled upon them during a routine snoop. I lifted it with the intention of writing The Harbinger, Miles Beckins; an idea I had settled on whilst laying there in that fearsome scenario, wherein it seemed I had witnessed the end of any kind of kindred agreeability with my family. That is to say, I doubted intensely, then, that I would be able to voice concern to them about what I had witnessed.

Aaron and Miles Beckins were the only souls in Indian River who had given any kind of rise to my attention concerning danger on our farm, and seeing as how I had outed Aaron as an initiate of a secretive ritual which had gone on for God-only-knows how long, it was my understanding that The Harbinger was the only individual I could hope to gain any kind of undisclosed education from concerning the whole God-forsaken affair. Not to mention, the man must have known something about the late Stagwerth, thus pointing to his assumed ability to confirm The Man in the Woods as The Samaritan. I scrawled a few words in my best cursive hand, but tried to keep it cryptic, should the message be intercepted by enemies.

"Which plot? Stag's man? Talk soon?"

The night was so damn queer and incoherent, my mind only recalled short, blurry images of hopping the gate to the road and tossing the postcard in the mailbox. I tried to remember whether I had raised the flag, but then hoped desperately I had not for fear I might be found out. It was then, as I rose to the sounds of Momma rousing us with racket from a pot and spoon, that I feared the worst. What ignorance was I to claim should The Harbinger write me back through traditional post? Daddy would sure as hell think it was trouble to see an envelope or postcard addressed to me. All I could pray was for Miles Beckins to continue delivery by his usual means; in dropping unhelpful clues from the sky.

I kept strictly to myself with a harsh sense of territory throughout the early morning. I tuned out the chatter at breakfast and ate as quick and dutiful as I could manage without once looking up. I half expected Momma to challenge my behavior, but she didn't. Aaron didn't dare question me either, given he probably knew I had snooped him in the night, which meant I had made visual confirmation of his activities. He was either sworn to assume ignorance or too embarrassed to converse about it all. Plus, he didn't have real proof anyhow, considering he knew he wasn't in the house and able to confirm my whereabouts. It was a political deadlock neither of us cared to pick apart.

Daddy had me gathering scraps of construction from beneath the barn's eaves which had either fallen from the roof or been left behind in the wake of industry; sheet metal screws, strips of cut tin as sharp as kitchen knives and old rotted truss wood that had seen too much sun and rain before Daddy had decided to cover them proper. I kept a watchful eye on the pasture as I bent for handfuls of metal and grass, knowing good and damn well the mail wasn't even picked up most days until ten or eleven. I figured I had a small chance of seeing a reply from The Harbinger around sunset, if the systems worked well enough, and if Beckins found himself feeling particularly responsive, but it was nowhere near then. I only ached vainly for it to be.

Around noon, I had nearly filled a half gallon bucket full of screws, rusted nails, sheet scraps, forgotten tools and other hazardous hardwares, as well as Daddy's old wheelbarrow with all the larger pieces. It seemed to be taking me twice or three times as long as it rightly should have, but only because the barrow was rusted out and flatter than hell. I thought once about using the handsomer red one I had seen Aaron with the night prior, but I elected against it, seeing as how it was in play, and I didn't dare disturb events that were unfolding in my favor. I had complete intentions of spying Aaron again that night, and I didn't want to do anything to hinder his work.

It was right as I had hoisted the bucket of miscellany into the rusted barrow that I saw her making straight for me. Mamie was approaching with purpose, and it was undeniably me she had such urgent business with. I stood froze with thoughts of fleeing, but I stayed my ground, covertly taking hold of a small claw hammer I had liberated from the tall grass below the eaves. I observed her volumous gait hidden beneath her full skirt as she progressed toward me on the red clay drive, her mighty bosom moving unhinged like a brace of water buckets strewn about the neck of a great mare. My hand clenched the hammer tight as I readied myself for the encounter.

About the time she neared me within ten or so feet, she produced a postcard of some sort and held it in my direction, her face remaining stalwart. Before I even knew what it was, I extended my arm in trusted response as a blind gesture of submission or pseudo-friendliness and collected the familiar article. I was straightways startled to see the name "Miles Beckins" scribbled across it in my own fledgling cursive hand, followed by the cryptic message I had penned only hours prior. I looked dead into her eyes, ready to be killed, or in the least, beat.

"You're gonna need to include the address if you're aimin' for it to go anywheres..." She eyed me suspiciously. I grinned worriedly with instinct. Mamie knew my handwriting from tutoring me in my schooling from time to time. She made no mention of the message, but I immediately gathered (without understanding fully why) that Mamie had contemplated my intentions and had settled on the fact that my attempted communications with The

Harbinger must have been at the bidding of someone close to her. She wasn't in the least bit privy to the fact that she had made me out. Her response was simply too trusting. Things weren't exactly sensical in her eyes, but she had been trained not to interfere with errands of mysterious coincidence.

I remained there, holding the letter with both hands as she walked on past me down the side of the barn toward the bunker. I turned in place to watch her leave, wondering what in the hell had just happened. Furthermore, I became straightways embarrassed at how utterly dense I had been as to imagine an article might find its way to a desired place with only a name, even in a town as small as Indian River. To be right truthful, I remembered nothing about what I had written on the card in terms of delivery, but I was then subject to an honest predicament. I didn't have the slightest clue how to acquire Miles Beckins' home address. I recalled on several occasions spying a mailbox—one of the last before coming into town—that read "Beck" in crooked adhesive lettering across its chassis, but I couldn't be sure it was any indicator The Harbinger resided there at the far end of a dirt drive that ran over hillock after hillock of old planted pine.

I folded the card horizontal and packed it carefully into my back jeans pocket, then transplanted it to my front for fear I would lose track of it again. As I made my way around the back end of the barn to offload the scraps into their designated piles at the salvage shed, I saw Mr. Langford on a morning stroll, fully dressed, holding his coat over his left shoulder and smiling that big dumb smile. I spied him momentarily as he picked a weed and chewed it with noted disdain, but my attention was soon stole by the learned laugh of Sarah Obis.

My head snapped away, and I instantly saw what I had no desire to; Sarah Obis sitting right pretty atop a fence near the back paddocks with none other than Aaron Cotton. He had her giggling about God-knows-what. My blood instantly boiled as I dropped the old wheelbarrow slow and pretended to take a rest, wiping my forehead clean of imagined sweat.

"Why ain't you usin' the good barrow?" Aaron called out to me about as pompous as ever. He knew good and damn well why not.

"...Daddy said you was usin' it for night work," I tested. A questioned look came over Sarah Obis' face; one that made Aaron right nervous, I could tell. I figured since we were deadlocked, I might as well have had some fun with it.

"Daddy tells me you got night work of your own," he bit back. I froze. "Pissin' your sheets," he laughed. I would have liked to grab my brother on his throat right then, but I would have lost the endgame. Sarah Obis bowed her head in embarrassment for me. Aaron had bested me for the day. There was no more I could do or say, so I lifted the old barrow and started away. To my surprise, I heard Aaron come down off the fence soon as I had turned. Next thing I knew, he was at my side. I had always been impressed at his ability to leave Sarah Obis there, likened to so many dirty rags hanging on a fence, with never as much as a second thought.

"So, you wanna walk to Marlin's after work for a drink?" I stopped and turned to him curiously; half because he wasn't being himself, and half because he was testing the fates.

"You know we ain't supposed to leave..."

"So..." Aaron said, producing an apple from nowheres and taking an obnoxious bite. "I can't stand bein' penned up here no more. I gotta get out and catch my breath." I turned and looked briefly at Sarah Obis. Aaron's eyes followed mine. "Fine, be a square little daisy," he concluded, setting off past me, leaving Sarah Obis there alone, as was his specialty.

I knew why Aaron wanted to get out for a bit. It was the same reason I craved it. Things had gotten right heavy in few days' time, but I wasn't one for doing something that was deliberately going to put me out or put me around a tree. He could go on and do what pleased him.

I gave Sarah Obis one last glance before hoisting my load again and making way for the scrap shed. She was perched there looking at me, clothed in a kind of modern dress, altered to be low cut against the neckline as a kind of mating plumage for Aaron who had managed to escape the girl's wide-cloven breast tops bathed in the morning sun a right sinful way. I would have given a leg or a few toes to watch her again at the spring where I could look on her for long stretches without fear of being seen. I couldn't do so there by the fence, in the daylight, with work in tow. She smiled at me and raised her hand to bend her middle and ring fingers twice in a kind of petit wave. I swooned in my heart of hearts and fought the urge to pretend I was an older, more confident man and approach her. I kept on towards the shed, against my greater judgement, and lost track of Aaron soon after. He was off to complete more adult chores with Daddy and the brothers.

Later on, after several toilsome hours of bone-chilling labor, the sun had gone high, but the cold created an impenetrable barrier between it and us. The scrap shed, which was no more than a meager box made of scrap (mostly tin in composition), had become a formidable deepfreeze amid the frozen winds and dense, chilled humidity, and I reckoned it wasn't smart to reside there much longer, lest I harden into neat blocks and proper scrap stacks of my own flesh and bone, never to be used again. When I made my way back up to the house, I looked out toward the front pasture and saw Aaron creeping off down the diagonally drawn fence that cut across the face of our property and ran along County Road 1. He was ducking along, all those acres out, trying to stay hid by the taller crops of hell grass. I stood there for a minute watching him, and watching to see if anyone else were watching him. There was no one who had seen him or paid mind to wonder where he was just then, save for Sarah Obis. She was spying him, same as me, but from the other side of the picnic tables betwixt the house and the barn where the brothers and sisters were slowly congregating for a midday meal.

I knelt in response to Charles who had come to sit right on my foot and spread his rank nature across the whole of my body.

"Hey, boy..." I said piteously. There was no doubt the hound had learned the slow and somber tone of indifference that it seemed all humanity had adopted for his touch.

"Moses, where's your brother?" Momma suddenly called out to me from amidst the crowded tables. She had already rung the bell once herself and wasn't going to hail him again. I stole a quick glance at the pasture, but was unable to locate the boy. He had more than likely already gone on through the fence and skipped the ditch. I looked briefly at Sarah Obis who was also scanning the perimeter in a modest fret. I had just started to prep my best lies when Daddy spoke up from his approach near the barn.

"I got Aaron doing something for me out back," he said. "He'll eat later."

"I'd like him to eat when we all do," Momma argued instinctively. "Can't it wait?" Daddy casually spoke something in her ear as he came upon her and kept the attention to a minimum. Sarah Obis and me caught quick glimpses at each other out of mutual suspicion. Daddy was certainly lying about Aaron, given he was easy a mile from any of us by then, and Daddy knew it. I reckoned he was giving Momma what for in her ear for adopting habits of questioning him in front of his subjects, but when the two parted again, it wasn't a face of scorn that came across Momma's face. It was a nod of agreement followed by neutrality as she went back to feeding her people.

Daddy had just let Momma in on a detail I surely wasn't privy to. Aaron wasn't sneaking off anywhere (at least not from Daddy and Momma). I wondered what would have transpired if only I had agreed to go along with him. Would I have been dismissed from thought as well as Aaron had, charged with some secret task in Indian River? I surely thought not. My ass would have been beat hard for leaving without permission, and Aaron's a little less, merely for allowing me to accompany him. My mind raced with wonder until Momma called me over to collect my scoop of dumplings. It was easy my favorite of Momma's recipes, and by my estimation, the last bit of poultry we had on hand at the house or in some offsite rented freezer space, but I couldn't bring myself to pay it any mind. I swallowed spoon after spoon of the thick and savory broth without tasting as much as a bite. My mind was elsewhere, studying the possibilities of Aaron's clandestine chore.

Charles and me were sitting there beneath the shallow shade of the house eaves, away from the tables, minding our own thoughts over those tasteless and unmemorable bites when a long shadow came and joined itself to mine. I looked up and saw the memorized figure of Sarah Obis. I snapped to attention; not because she was suddenly within my field of vision (I had thankfully gotten used to that), but because she had come for me. There was no mistaking the reason for her choice to situate herself within my circle of immediate awareness. She was in my space, and she was there to have words with me, only me, for the first time. I smiled with instinct (a mechanical function that pervaded many, if not most, of my initial nerve-racking exchanges).

"Hey there," she spoke gently. I cherished the words and witnessed their longevity in a futuristic vision as they sat weighted in my heart for all time.

"Hi," I squeaked out in the first manifestation of dual-toned pubescent embarrassment. I cursed myself internally, but the girl was already kneeling to face me with Charles between us. The sun and shade shared a line across the middle of her exquisite face and rationed its beauty into opposing images of watercolored innocence and sable desire.

"Charles, right?" she asked.

"Moses," I said dumbly. She pointed to my hound. "Oh, yes. Charles." I pursed my lips in frustrated shame. Sarah Obis smiled and bounced once with a laugh.

"I know your name," she said, stroking Charles without reservation. I smiled back and figured it was better if I didn't try and respond just then. Another several seconds passed in torturous silence. "Thought that brother of yours was a goner there for a minute," she proposed. I looked beyond her into the pasture and absentmindedly touched Charles' beard. He didn't have the slightest clue why his luck had suddenly changed, resulting in so many hands upon him, but he didn't care any.

"I reckon Daddy's got him doing something he don't want none of us knowin' about," I replied.

"That's the thing about this place," Sarah Obis started.

"What..." I asked, hoping desperately to form another ally.

"Well, we're a secretive bunch for a group of people who call ourselves a family."

"True," I said, waiting.

"And incestuous," she added, making eye contact.

"What does that mean?" I asked.

"It means there ain't a lot of places to turn our eyes, so we often turn 'em to one another." We broke vision again. I knew exactly what she was referring to, I just didn't have any means to parry it.

"I seen you in the woods," she said. There we were. I sprang into guilt-ridden apologetics.

"Now, listen, it were an accident the first—"

"—At the rite," she stopped me with a short smile.

"The rite?" Sarah Obis didn't care that I had seen her naked time after time. It were clear to me just then.

"In the woods behind the back field," she added. My heart dropped three stories.

"When?" I prodded.

"Last night!" She seemed shocked. I kept silent. "Oh, come now," she said. "That ain't the first time we've locked eyes in a dark wood." I was blushed beyond recovery, most-

ly at her subtle returned references to our encounters at
the spring. It was true I had witnessed the rite the evening
prior, but I was stumped on which moment we had made
contact during the ceremony. "Well, I'm not telling anyone," she concluded. "But you should find a better spot." I
stayed quiet for the sheer sake of my own safety. She went
on. "I don't know why you'd watch it. When you're old
enough to go, I doubt you'll want to."

"Do you?" I asked plainly. She hesitated.

"...This ain't good talk for right now," she said.

Charles was on his back then, and Sarah Obis and me
had both begun stroking his soiled belly.

"Tell me a story," she said with a smile.

"...Like what?" I smiled back, aching with so much
nervousness it near about made me numb.

"Tell me something about Aaron," she said. I shrank.
"Something old that no one knows." I turned my head in
thought, searching desperately through the caverns of my
mind to locate something that might make my brother
out to be more of a villain than Sarah Obis liked him for.

"I know one," I finally said. "He made us kill every
caterpillar on our farm once."

"Why on Earth would you do something like that?"
she questioned. I suddenly regretted the story, as it impli-
cated me in the apparent crime as well.

"...We were just being stupid I suppose." My head
sunk and then snapped back to attention suddenly. "One
time Aaron cussed Momma!" I continued. "Actually, he's
cussed her a lot."

"Moses Cotton, are you trying to paint your brother
in a unfavorable light?" She smiled.

Sarah Obis had just used my whole name for the first time, like she knew me in my deepest parts. I fell in love with her even more for it, if that was possible. It meant she fancied me a person all my own, more than just by what was polite to call me. Moses Cotton was my name; only mine, and in that moment, she had addressed me in the most personal manner anyone could. Call it what you may, but the utterance of such a thing from the lay of her lips was enough to cause any young man to shudder.

"Well, you better try harder than that," she added. "Do your worst. What's the big secret? What's the unpardonable sin?" She dug deep and smiled a sinister smile as if she enjoyed collecting Aaron's transgressions in her heart because it made her hotter for him.

I sat quiet for a moment, looking down with serious doubt that I should go on in that transaction which had straightways changed from whimsical to melancholy in a matter of seconds. I cleared the reluctance from my throat and rejoined her at her semi-sadistic table as the world seemed to fade away in volume and vision.

"…The summer before Aaron started at Miss. Melba's, back before he got his new friends and fell in love with spirits and mischief, it were just the two of us. I don't reckon Aaron needed or craved friends besides me then. We'd always been close enough friends." I looked up at Sarah Obis to make sure she was still following me. It seemed she was highly engaged, so I went on. "That summer, we got into burnin' through Roy Rogers comics at Marlin's store, and we both wanted to be cowboys and carry sidearms. That were the first time we started to pay any mind to the horses here; when we realized cowboy heroes always had trusty steeds. When Daddy'd go off on trips for several days, we'd spend our mornin's doin' our chores, then we'd steal us a horse and make for the freedom spring—" I stopped dead in my words, realizing the place I had just described and the awkwardness of it all, which seemed to keep finding a way to crop itself up.

"I remember that!" she exclaimed with beautiful, wide eyes. "I remember seeing the two cowboys on Mr. Bellview's paint and thinkin' it were the most ridiculous thing I'd ever witnessed! Didn't you have a rifle?" she asked.

"Yeah!" I said, surprised. "That's the next part actually."

"Oh, I'm sorry," she apologized. I smiled faintly.

"Aaron's first order of business were to get us a couple proper sidearms. He'd found the perfect set of dead twin pine elbows to make his self a couple handsome Colt pistols with, and I'd given him my materials for a stout twelve-inch live oak Winchester. Well, he started whittlin' away at them twigs day and night for a week and a half 'til they was ready. When he give me mine, it were better than I'd even thought. The details was mostly all there, the size were spot on from what I could tell, and he'd gone and sanded them both real nice 'til they was smooth. I'd never loved somethin' so much in my whole life."

"Can I see it?" Sarah Obis asked, excitedly, "Up close."

"Well, that's where the whole thing goes sour," I said. "We played with them things for the whole rest of the summer, battlin' and carryin' on. The gun never left my side. That is until the first day of school, when Aaron came back up the road on his walk home with a couple new boys. I met him at the gate to start our day's battle, but Aaron had a devilish look in his eye, and he took my rifle. The two boys he had with him laughed a bit and watched my brother, admirin' him wildly.

"I was afraid, and then I saw him grip the gun in front of me with both hands and snap it crossed his knee. He smiled and tossed the pieces to his friends and pushed on past me."

Sarah Obis sat there looking across at me with her mouth gaped in utter silence. I had stunned her good with the tale, and I was straightways afraid in that moment that I had sold it too harsh and painted Aaron in a light she would never forgive.

"Has he ever said sorry?" she asked me.

"...In ways," I said. "But it ain't never been the same between the two of us. I figured after that, we were through being friends in a sense." The silence continued for more than a couple minutes as we both sat stroking gently at Charles, who, in a move quite telling, up and stood to make his way toward the dark underworld of the front porch, where even creatures of rank disposition could retreat when suspect to doleful moods that seemed to befall scenes of comfort.

The call came from Momma at just the right time.

"Moses, come here please." She had a knack for waking me from dreams I didn't wanna be woke from. "Come help me clean up," she said from near the picnic tables. I turned my attention back to Sarah Obis for a moment as Momma went on stacking plates and silverwares.

"Well..."

"Good talk, Moses Cotton," she said. I smiled so genuine it caught my own attention.

Later that day, I found myself several times bouncing between thoughts of the conversation with Sarah Obis, and the predicament of the mailbox. I would then straightways become downcast upon remembering the folded mailer in my pocket that had been returned to me by the killer, Mamie Dixon. How in hell's name was I to procure The Harbinger's address, I wondered blindly. At that point I would have considered spelling out my request across the pasture with twigs and twine for him to see in his red duster if I thought he would actually show again. I imagined to him, our pasture must have looked like it was entrapped in the biggest mullet net Indian River had ever seen; one that I had woven together singlehandedly and painstakingly over the previous several months of my life.

I thought regularly over the following hours about my conversation with Sarah Obis and played it back again and again in my head, cursing myself for the weaker points, and swooning over the finer ones: the otherwise invisible lines in the closeness of her face, the lay of her hair, the start and finish of her contagious laughter. I was all the more impassioned by her then, and I began to devise a plan for how she and I might leave Indian River and pass the rest of my adolescence together until we were ready to make a family. I did the math the best I could, and reckoned her and me were the same distance apart in years as Daddy and Momma, and that felt promising to me. Surely she had felt the same way. There was a spark in our exchange more real and intoxicating than any time I had observed her at the spring, in secret, beneath the silverest of moons, and I loved her then.

Night was closing in on our little hamlet of arcane ob-scurities, and I reckoned there was no amount of mystery a simple basin of warm water couldn't help sort out, if I could just make it through dinner first. I had things to think on. I had forgotten more puzzling tales and events than I could recollect. I needed to gather upon my current state of affairs and devise new strategies for reckoning with them. I didn't have the slightest idea how to approach something so sinister as murder or a "poisoned plot" or The Man in the Woods, or if I even should try, for that matter. All I knew was that my family was in the midst of something I didn't quite understand, but was indeed certain I would find myself folded into any day. And I had no desire to be subject to any of it. I feared if I didn't find a way out while I could still claim ignorance, I would soon be absorbed in it as a result of either my coming of age, or my meddled self-inclusion. Seeing as how I couldn't help but meddle things that occurred before my eyes, I reasoned there was only one choice left for Moses Cotton of Indian River.

I was straightways relieved when Aaron finally showed back at the house only moments before dinner. I could tell Momma was on edge (and right cross with Daddy) about Aaron being out loose in such a tumultuous time. Rumor had given rise to people getting sick something horrid, even dying in worse cases, and that it was a result of some homemade fumigation remedy tests going on across the other side of the river in the North where the plague was most fearsome. Right spooky shit, if you asked me. I supposed Momma wasn't as scared that Aaron would return having contracted an illness as she was afraid he would be killed for being recognized as one of The Family Beyond the Gate, but she still looked relieved to see him home when he came in the door about the same time she was setting a modest portion of fried potatoes, biscuits and several thick, pan-seared steaks on the table. The choice cuts of beef were feeling more and more ridiculously unmatched to the times, the further and further the days went on. No one seemed to complain, but I was growing tired of red meats.

"Want me to ask the blessing, Momma?" I offered first for fear of being commanded to.

"No," she answered in a snap. "I'll ask it."

Suddenly, all our attention was on Momma as she bowed her head strangely and took the reins of something she wasn't typical to volunteer for after laboring to conjure such a warm meal from scratch. We bowed our heads low, in expectation of what she needed to say to God. "Great Judge Above, we now consume this meal as your body and blood. Spare us in this perilous time, but keep us not from your righteous punishments for the wickedness of our own souls. Place a hedge of fire around this holy encampment and set ablaze them who might seek to harm your servants. Let this plague be your cleansing, and let the coming judgement separate the wheat from the chaff in your storehouse. We thank thee, Oh Lord, for your great works and signs and wonders. Amen."

The three of us—Daddy, Aaron and I—sat silent as Momma raised silver and began cutting away at her meat. None of us had ever heard such a practiced and disturbed prayer in all our waking lives. It was like a spirit had entered Momma's body and spoke it from the dark recesses of her subconscious. It didn't sound much like Momma's voice when it came out, but she sure was keen to speak it. One by one, we slowly relinquished our attention to the meal at hand and were through in minutes, having spent no time conversing for lack of lofty or normal subjects to speak on. I got the hell out of the way as fast as I could and made for the bath to take inventory of the eerie.

As the warmth settled in, and the steam began to rise forth from the scalding hot and eternal spring, I crossed my legs and entered a trance of metaphysical thought. I lost all control of my mental recollections, and instead, found myself lost in a dreamscape of prophetic and non-prophetic symbolisms. I saw a dark man negotiated forcefully from a rooftop, then resurrected and displayed for all to see. I saw a bright white ewe, fully clothed, walk across a crust of ice upon a frozen spring and then disappear into its black depths. I witnessed a young boy with tears in his eyes, searching desperately for signs and wonders. A duster without a pilot. A girl beneath a tree. A mole cricket. A bile green mist. A creek. A cross. A bell. The joy of a man's face hearing a familiar voice in a radio. And finally, a colossal engine below the earth, stamped with secrets.

My physical eyes opened wide and I saw that space again which looked so unfamiliar to me, until my memory served to remind me what it all was. I had awoken in the washroom, my lower half pickled, like something in a jar of white wine vinegar. I had been preserved there for God-only-knows how long. My fingers were well past shriveled and the water was right frigid. In all truth, the mystery of how long my body had sat unattended in the tub was un-important. All that mattered was that I believed something had been revealed to me in those visions; something imper-ative to my understanding of what me and my family were into, and perhaps what waited for us in our near futures.

When I emerged from the washroom, Aaron was al-ready gone from his bed. It must have been later than I had originally thought, and well past my usual wandering time. Something in me was so tired, though. I half considered leaving it all be until morning. I also feared ending up back where I had found myself the night before; at the mercies of The Man in the Woods and his words and the many unconscious meanderings that would undoubtedly follow, leading me back to my bed with several curious regrets. But yet again, in lieu of my better self-advisements, I gave to the yearning for answers inside me, knowing that if I heeded my intuitions that night, I just might have found those answers, as well as Aaron. It was a good bet they would be together, as well.

I stood half but overly clothed, poised between Daddy's dozer and the big shavings stores perpendicular to my normal hiding spot just across from the hole. Aaron was undoubtedly already inside. I knew so because I heard the typical racket coming from down under as the machine pumped and choked loudly while Aaron worked to gather whatever he was gathering from below. There was also a hainted glow of orange light emitting from inside the hole, more than likely from one of Daddy's many kerosene lanterns he was so prone to leaving forgetfully in curious collections all over the farm. Only in a chore sanctioned by Daddy could Aaron do such a thing without drawing queries from the house or the bunker. There was no one to come along and ask questions or poke around the hullabaloo but me. I reckoned Aaron knew I was there by then, but he wouldn't concern himself with me.

The regularity and frequency of sounds escaping the pit was enough to indicate he was moving at a right quicker pace than the night prior. I heard strange sounds, like glass shaking against glass and the knocking of wood against wood. I watched intently as the first signs of life showed from the hole. One of Marlin's crates seemed to rise all on its own, as if levitated by magics, but the illusion was soon broke as Aaron's iron arms rose to follow. I was right amazed at his ability to ascend the ladder without a free hand to aid him. He did that six or seven times over until

Daddy's red wheelbarrow was full to the brim, and then to capacity, and then some. The glow went out of the hole. He didn't even look once in my direction before covering the load with a canvas tarp and leaving off toward the barn with it. I did, however, see him several times steal glances at my regular spot, from where he assumed I was watching him.

As soon as he was out of sight, I leapt from my post and made straightways for the ladder in the ground. I feared that to follow Aaron again meant he would lead me once more into the darkness of the woods where I would be forced to endure the further dismantlement of my family and the more unsettling notions of God's loving kindnesses which were subject to The Man in the Woods and his seemingly protracted grip upon the people I knew. I didn't dare give The Samaritan another chance to cast his handspun words within earshot, given my assuredness that I too would become prey to his wills and be made to fall prostrate in tears like the others. There was a power in his words I had only ever experienced at one other time; whilst in range of his master's voice.

I clung to the ladder as I descended, without fear, into the breach. Ten steps later I was standing upon a gritted dirt surface. My face found a structural beam of some sort before my hands were able to locate one of Daddy's forgotten lanterns. My arms were suspended before me, the tips of my fingers probing for signs of anything but dirt and hell grass root and haphazardly-placed wood supports until they detected the presence of residual heat surrounding a nearby source. I straightways withdrew for fear of hearing the sizzled sounds of my calloused fingertips against fire-softened glass. I smelled the kerosene burn mixed with the overwhelming scent of freshly turned soils. The combination was damn near enough to knock a man over, but I grew quickly to like the earthiness of it all.

The valve was just below the heat emanating from the lantern's glass hood. As I twisted it open, I thought about the revelation of Sarah Obis' body to me, and for the first time, noticed the blue and silent light of the lantern's soul as it rose from almost nothing and came to life from whence it lay dormant upon Aaron's departure. In seconds, the small cavern came alight with new dimensions I hadn't realized. I saw light and shadow break and run upon a convolution of earth and wood and metal. It was more primitive and unrefined than I had expected, and from all directions, the roots of ancient hell grasses reached out at me like a thousand tiny hands grasping for resurrection. I half expected to observe fossilized mole crickets from plagues gone by. All of it bent in humble submission to the centerpiece.

The machine was a grand composition in shattered fragments of shadow and light. Its many pieces and contrived parts seemed to join and leave each other in ways that eluded my perfunctory efforts to reckon with it. I couldn't command the slightest idea for how the prodigious automaton carried out its work or if it did so properly at all, but luckily enough for me, an understanding of its operation wasn't what I had gone down to gather from the machine's metallic husk. I searched high and low for the stamp; the one I had seen in my hot water visions only a short time earlier. It were true, the hull of the great metal-bellied beast was branded with all manner of markings and etched industrial prose, but most, if not all of it, was indiscernible to me. I wasn't exactly sure what I was looking for, other than the fact that I figured I would know it when I saw it.

For a time, I traipsed around the perimeter, kicking up more dirt than was needed to cloud my vision. I scoured the blunter pieces of the machine for distinguishing signs or symbols, and all the while found myself distracted by its elements whose sole purposed looked to be the removal or mangling of limbs rather than the collection of water. It was just as I had contemplated climbing atop the great subterranean engine that I saw the thing which seemed to free me, heart and mind. Two letters peaked from below the dirt floor where the sleds or kick plates of the pump were buried half into it. I nearly collapsed upon the sight and began scratching and digging frantic as a hound against the side of the kick plate. I freed one hand to open the lantern valve fully. A flood of light poured upon the characters as they adopted their meaning. I let go and pulled back to observe the entire composition.

C.O. Miles M. Beckins
6119 Open Pond Rd.
Indian River, FL 32465
U.S.A.

Why in the hell a manufacturer of such an object would etch the name and address of the person providing airfreight for one of their products upon its outers was beyond me. Perhaps it was Beckins himself who did the etching for safety reasons or to avoid questions of ownership or stewardship or what-have-you. I didn't much care. All I knew was that my premonitions had come true and I was further along in the mystery that had become my life than I had been in a good while. I recalled the house numbers along the stretch of County Road 1 best I could, and it only made logical and geographical sense that the number on the "Beck" mailbox (before it had been worn away by time or weather or force) was previously a match.

I scanned the room quick for final clues before making my way back up the ladder with nothing more to gather than a leftover piece of counting paper I had used to perform a primitive carbon transfer of the crude etching against the side of the machine. I saw nothing but a few carpenter's nails and some shards of glass. I made a passing note of my inability to locate the pump's ignition, and set plans to visit The Harbinger the following morning.

13

That night, I dreamt a frightful dream that caused me to wake myself moaning Aaron's name incoherently. Embarrassed, I stood to see if he had heard me, but it was obvious, even at that late hour, he was still away, pushing a barrow or laying prostrate wherever the Lord willed. My dream was of The Man in the Woods, but it began with the ewe. I was at the spring, feeling the water and parleying with its cold shores on whether to enter, when suddenly, she appeared. My eyes settled upon her; that snow white lamb, clothed again. Her beauty caught my eye, as it had the times I had seen her before. She was a vision of grace, like Sarah Obis, and her mystery was legend in my heart. I would have watched her for eternities to know her in the deepest way. I couldn't tell why the little ewe commanded so much of my adoration and enthrallment. Perhaps it was because of her grace, or her coincidence, or her proxy for some part of my childhood that should have remained frivolous. In any regard, her appearance, whether in dream state or reality, was always enough to beckon me toward her, forsaking all else.

I was drawn straightways from the water and into her wake as she lead me on past the spring and toward the bunker. I seemed to care little about my proximity to her, and she the same. It was almost as if she'd had intentions to show me something and possessed no fear of me at all. If anything, it was I who feared her, or her motives for baring me unto whom she might have planned. In my dream, I followed her headlong through the back pasture, down the hillocks and toward the darkened fringe of the woods.

It wasn't until just before we had arrived at the entry of that famed and familiar path into the trees that I adopted a sense of our true chore. I discerned that the ewe held an allegiance to me and gathered there was a plot afoot to bring about resolution. The creature sought to kill the King of the Mill Lands and do so by means of influencing my hand. When I looked down, I found gripped there a dagger covered in poisons, and I felt from within come a vain sense of protection and blind power that seized me and gave me a purpose I had not commanded before, like a man who joins a protest, not because of the rights for which it stands, but because of the brute mechanical power inherent in a mass of human bodies moving in unison.

The woods were like a Frost poem; dark and deep. The ewe traveled on and on, intrepidly, without stopping. I tightened my hand around the hilt of the blade as the blanket of pine straw seemed to grow deeper beneath me, and I became fearful of the crunch of my bare feet against the dead straws, wondering if it might draw out our target prematurely. The alarm and panic seemed to grow in me as we passed tree after tree, and I straightways realized the futility of the weapon I carried and the assurance it boasted. I felt my fingers release the instrument, and I heard it fall at my feet as I moved onward. The ewe then turned and spoke to me:

"You'll regret that," she said. A pang of sharp contrition tuned through my bones and heart, and I knew she was right, but I continued to follow her still.

It was in that moment that the path into the wood noticeably darkened, even more so than before. It wasn't a visible kind of darkness, however, but a spiritual one; one that penetrated my soul with a sickness, so I refused to go on. But in my refusal, the ewe continued, either in ignorance of or in protest of my decision to stop. She did not look back like I thought she might, but instead, went on far ahead of me until she disappeared into the black of the path, and left me truly alone. I fought a desire to flee in the other direction, but it was already too late, for he had come.

As I turned to my left, he revealed himself to me, stepping backward from behind a broad pine trunk and wheezing heinously with a smile. I screamed and tried to run, but my words fell short and my steps sank low. Within seconds, he was upon me, making ready to gore my face with his sharp mouth. I felt his warm breath upon my cheek, and I woke with urine in my bed and muddled words on my tongue. The voice in my head replayed the the call for Aaron, which inspired me to check for his presence in the room. I said a prayer for him then, in that haze of sleep and awake where things seemed to matter so much more than they would in full-on consciousness.

I stayed in that place of heightened fear and emotion for some time that night, lying flat on my back, watching the shapes of shadows twist and bend into imagined demonic hosts. I replayed the dream again and again, combing over each and every detail with analytical dread, and I reminded myself that time and daylight often did wonders for neutralizing thoughts and images which seemed so threatening in dream space. In the morning, however, when I expected my anxiety to be significantly dampened, I was actually somewhat increased in my trepidations. In my heart of hearts, I knew my family and our farm were in for a world of darkness, as was indicated by the many bad omens which had seemed to bring themselves to my attention over the recent span of time since the plague began. The only practical hope for easing the deep qualms in my spirit was the impending powwow with The Harbinger, Miles Beckins. It wasn't something I was expressly looking forward to, but I viewed it as a necessary discomfort that would afford me with some much needed help.

Following a quick spattering of fried eggs and breakfast steak, I made for my books with the advertised intention of spending the "fine morning" studying beneath Walter's dead tree in the front pasture. The look on Momma's face was puzzled at my broadcast. The day was actually more of a cold and overcast gray (one not typically suitable for such activities), but Momma wasn't the type to protest me happily performing my studies. I nested the modest bundle beneath my arm and forgot any manor of writing utensil. My feet crunched across the hell grass a full hour before I was used to seeing a soul other than Daddy at work.

I didn't reckon any of my family had thought twice about the possibility that I was making swift plans to leave the farm for the better half of the morning, which gave me a decent head start. After stomping through hell grass high as my head in some places and observing the innumerable hosts of mole crickets turning beneath each step, I came to Walter's tree at the edge of our property and County Road 1. There, I laid my books aside, made one final glance at the house and climbed through the dilapidated fence's wide berth, making note of how easy it was to do so, and wondering why the angry townsfolk hadn't tried. The truth was, I would never know if they had, but to progress further on that line of thinking would have lost me a good deal more sleep per night than I had already become accustomed to losing.

I crept low and listened carefully for the hum of approaching cars or trucks on the road. Every step seemed to find my feet and legs tethered and slashed by berry vine thorns. At one point, when I had gone on past the end of our property and come into view of a few mailboxes out on the road, I was forced to duck low and lay myself against the deepening ditch wall as an unfamiliar auto came whirring by at top speeds. When I had made sure the driver hadn't noticed me, I kept on, occasionally stepping out onto the road to try and spot the "Beck" box at the edge of the long, hilly driveway. The better indication was when I came upon the planted pines on the south side of the road. I could see the toes of the town in the distance and knew I was close.

There was a cold bite in the air, and the winds behind it kept me clung to myself and to the inside wall of the ditch when I wasn't peeking out on the road. Within enough time, I spied the chalk-white mailbox with the crooked vinyl lettering and stopped myself just opposite to it, amidst a thick blackberry bramble. Just when I had prepared to break across the full width of County Road 1, I heard the undeniable racket of a short, informal procession;

three cars approaching in quick succession of one another in the direction of town. I collapsed into a ball inside of the thicket and felt a vine of teeth saw across my face just below my left eye. I felt for blood but only detected a notable scratch that would undoubtedly draw questions from Momma.

When the vehicles had passed me and gone and made their way as far as I could see (which I reckoned was our gate and the edge of the red clay drive), I climbed up out of the ditch and felt the pricks and thorns pop and pull away at the cotton fibers of my outers until I was free of their grasp. I exhaled a few white puffs of warm vapor as I crossed County Road 1. A short several leaps and bounds later, I found myself poised at the edge of Miles Beckins' long and sand-packed drive. I stayed off the tracks for fear of leaving a print and thus sending tell of my presence to some future soul I didn't want knowing I had come. I did my best to stay balanced along the grass strip in the middle of the lane that wasn't beat down dead from years of heavy tire traffic.

Beckins' drive was flanked on one side by planted pine, and on the other by a field that lay open beside the home of a widower named Justice. There were remnants of a boundary or a fence there from a time gone by; made evident by the uniformly sunken posts at measured intervals along the drive, which carried shattered lengths of half buried planks and cross sections every so often along their battered remains. The planted pines were between ten and fifteen years old, though I couldn't recall the day they were sewn in such hansom rows along County Road 1, or a day before when it was all bare. One row I looked down seemed to half conceal something puzzled amidst a dip between trees. It was a porcelain toilet bowl, from where I could tell, and I couldn't help but wonder if it had once belonged to Miles Beckins, or perhaps one of his forebears.

As I made my way further on, with careful glimpses at my rear every couple minutes to catch the blur of a passing car out on the road, I began to notice more and more curiosities among the pine rows. They were close enough for me to tell their shape and likely origin, but too far off for me to observe in detail. There was what appeared to be a doghouse, parts from an engine, an upturned icebox, the bones of what might have been an airplane chassis, and a clawfoot tub; all becoming more and more frequent the nearer I came to the clearing ahead of me, which I assumed surrounded the dwelling of The Harbinger. The meaning of that title came and rested in my thoughts then. It was a curious thing, that all his life, Miles Beckins had been referred to as such with right negative connotations. Only then, in a boy's hour of desperation was he being sought with the expectation that he fulfill his namesake.

I had come alongside a thickening backdrop of aged pines at the rear of the Justice property; one that I reckoned shielded Miles Beckins' full endowment from the view of the road. When that wall of hundred foot pines to my left broke and scattered about sparsely on the opposite side, I found myself standing amongst the largest piece of open range I had ever seen. It was thrice as big as our front and back pastures combined if it was a square foot. It went on and on so long, it seemed to bend over the very edge of the Earth before it found edges against a distant tree line joining the planted pines, which stretched from my right, what seemed miles out. The land was dotted throughout with fifty or a hundred of the eldest and largest legacy pines in Indian River.

In the middle, towards the end of the white sand drive, stood a structure more derelict than the worst on our farm. It was a trapezoid of a house, whose roof seemed to have suffered a stroke some time ago, with one side upright and the other dipping so low it nearly touched the ground. In fact, I was quite certain I could have mounted it with no trouble at all. Beyond it was a great, square-formed enclosure made of crimped tin or aluminum sheets like the ones on our barn roof. I reckoned the building was where Beckins kept his many planes, which I imagined was a collection as great or greater than the one that lay freely strewn across his lands. There, about the grounds, were all manner of appliances, utilities and machinery. It was a ghastly boneyard of any and every rejected creation of man; a space which boasted a treasury far superior to any we had passively gathered over the years. I marveled at the wonder of it all. It was as if the red sea had parted once more and revealed to me all the fortune and antiquity left behind by the pharaoh whilst in pursuit of the Lord's people all those many moons ago. How could one man curate such a hoard, I thought.

In spite of the vast trove of unique and varied objects about the place, it lacked one thing. There was no sign of The Harbinger inside or out. I knew so for the single mocking bird alight the eave above the door in perfect calm, and though it was a disappointment in realization, I felt it pertinent that I stay and survey the grounds a while longer. I knew I had bought myself a decent share of time to wait, and I had plenty to keep me busy whilst doing so. The immediate problem was that I scarce knew where to begin browsing. There was so much to see, I felt I could wander forever—twisting and turning past one artifact after another until the sun's dull glow had gone down behind the trees—and I could still never manage to see it all.

I stood there, my feet still planted on the green grass in the middle of the drive, and surveyed the littered wilderness, where the man-crafted objects seemed to rise up with the grass and become a part of the very landscape, likened to some futuristic alien terrain or the remnants of some ancient civilization. Then, the air grew quiet and cold with a phantom swiftness, and I felt the familiar sensation of being watched from on high where the clearing was fully visible, and where my dot was a stain of intrusion upon that hallowed ground. Straightways I turned upon the object of my suspicion, which I confirmed with my ears first and then with my eyes.

It could have at first been a red bird, if not for the betrayal of that violent and thunderous buzz which tore at every part of me. My hands clove to my ears in instinctual precaution as the duster lowered steadily and approached at a speed which should have frightened me a great deal more had I known its true velocity. My legs began to stretch without my telling them to. As the plane came nearer and nearer, my body seemed to move faster beneath me than I could remember it ever having moved before. My head turned back and forth frequently, attempting to keep a record of what lay before me and how swiftly I was pursued from behind. The wheels had nearly touched down upon the white sand tracks that skirted my thin, green concourse.

I was then running at my full capacity as I felt the gears of the duster make contact with the Earth behind me. It was as if I had entered into a cowboy comic and was fleeing a stampede on foot in a dusty ravine. Something kept me locked to the middle lane of that drive, unable to alter my trajectory and perhaps duck behind some appliance I knew the duster would not dare to challenge. Instead, I continued, ever fearful that my premature stride would soon give way to the plane's tires and underbelly, and I would be chewed asunder, leaving me as nothing more than a mess of gore upon The Harbinger's runway. I began to feel as if I had no fight left within me, and in that moment, I collapsed in a heap of dust and grass and knotted vision. Each breath bore a withered and deteriorated signature as the cold air stabbed sharp at my lungs. I laid on my back and awaited my doom as the craft drew nearer, its single prop still spinning violently even as I heard its engine cut away. The worst part was that I knew I would be alive when the blades started to eat me apart at my feet. The pain of such a thing before me was more than I could bare, and I began to pray loudly.

"Are father who aren't in Heaven, Hollywood be your name!"

I felt the wind from the propeller come near me and wed the cold air to the sweat on my face.

"...And for giving us dress pants, as we give dress pants to them amongst us!"

The cool turned to warm as the heat of the engine neared my feet and slowed. The detail of the craft had become so great, I could hardly take note of it all.

"...For thine is the kingdom and power and glory forever and ever and ever amen amen amen!"

I embraced the warmth and comfort of the engine and accepted my fate with placid passivity, the same as one might have upon drowning. I closed my eyes and awaited the great pain. Then I waited, and waited, and waited, but it never came. When I gathered enough bravery to open my eyes, it was in time to see the duster's metal prop slow to barely moving and tap gently against my shoe, then recoil. Standing over me, silhouetted in black and casting a great shadow, was The Harbinger, Miles Beckins, in his honest flesh.

I stared up at him, squinting through the dust. Then I saw his black figure descend upon me. I flinched and tried to move, but before I could start myself, he was upon me with my t-shirt gathered up in his small, rough hands. He settled in a straddled position, as if we were wrestlers in a match, and he had pinned me good. That grade of physical contact was about as intimately and offensively obtrusive as I had ever experienced. The man was angry with me, but not for trespassing. The sun shown upon half his profile then. He had a handsome and chiseled face when finally viewed up close. A dark and red-leathered man, he boasted a thick, even brush of gray stubble about his neck, chin, jowls and mouth. The top of his head was covered with a red baseball cap which matched the underbelly of his plane.

"Who's else knows you're here?" he demanded. I hesitated apparently, and he shook me once with violence. "Who's else?! Answer me!"

"No one!" I replied with haste.

"Why are ya here?!" he shook me again. He was by that time holding me clear off the ground.

"I were gonna write back but—"

"Never write back!" he shouted. His face came closer, and his rank breath was enough to knock a puking buzzard off a gut wagon. It was reminiscent of Charles', save for the minty traces of whiskey and other spirits that accompanied it.

"I need to talk!" I shouted back. The pressure and intensity of it all was setting me on edge. Beckins braced to shake me again and opened his mouth wide enough to utter a single broken syllable, then stopped. We stared at each other for a good moment then, me looking uneasy and worried as ever, and him biting his lower lip and gazing at me with wide and crazed eyes, his head cocked slightly.

"What part of 'git out now' didn't ya understand, boy?" he waited patiently, my shirt still gripped in his hands, as I came to my senses. He was speaking of a separate message; one I must have never received but perhaps should have. "What part?!" he shook me. "Answer me! What part!" he shook me so hard and long then that I swore I would slip into seizure and awake with permanent damage. "What part?! What part?! What part?!" his voice vibrated with each convulsion, and I tried desperately to form words but couldn't hope to for the tremors. It was then that I realized Miles Beckins was more than mere strange; he was a mad and demented wild man with a profound and ernest conviction. "ANSWER ME!"

"...S-stag-wer..." I spilt in broken, near involuntary English. But he didn't hear.

"ANSWER ME!"

"...Stag-werth! Poi-sn plot!" I yelled. "The plot is poisoned Moses Cotton! The plot is poisoned Moses Cotton! The plot is poisoned Moses Cotton!" I repeated over and over in a sort of desperation chant until my tongue was twisted, and I choked on my own tears.

Suddenly, the shaking stopped as I felt The Harbinger's hands release me and my head hit the ground. I drew breath greedily and closed my eyes as the world spun and pulsed with dizziness and pain.

I felt spit and tears run down my face, mixing with the sand below. I grabbed my own head tight with both hands and wept on my back with The Harbinger still astride my small frame. We remained that way for some time, him in silence, breathing heavy, and me in shattered frustration and fear, unable to process a thing that had happened. The confusion and pain and fear of it all had compounded into so much unresolved burden that I felt the weight of the world collapse upon me, with the encounter with Miles Beckins appropriately as the capstone of it all.

He saw in me a madness unlike his own; unlike any he had ever seen, for that matter, and it was enough to cause him to stop dead in humble observance of it. I felt his fear of me; of the crisis that had consumed me on the ground. It was far more than what he had presumed to discover from on high or from outside the gate. I felt him shove off and shuffle into a fatigued posture beside me. My tears and wailing had subsided when he finally spoke again.

"...Ya don't know, do ya?" he stated calmly, in a tone I hadn't heard yet. It was simple and reasoned. I shook my head in response, my hand still clinching the corners of my eyes.

"...Only some," I said. "What I seen, I guess..." I opened my eyes and sat up to look across at him, against my desire never to behold him again. "Help me. Please help me make sense of it..."

We sat there for a long while after that, with a lengthy bout of extended silence and blank thought. Beckins then spoke simply.

"I can't," he admitted.

"What do you mean?" I asked, attempting to quell my growing impatience.

"I mean...I can't," he stood. "There's too much at stake for me, Lina." I thought he had called me by a woman's name. "If ya can't make sense of it, forget tryin' and git out. Leave, now hear? Leave Indian." he turned to walk away off toward the shack of a house.

"What about my family?" I asked, angered and standing to my feet with a brush against my jeans. "What's at stake for them?! For me?!" Miles Beckins turned and charged me with intent. I recoiled, but he stopped and lowered himself to my eye level.

"Stay then. Stay and die like the rest of 'em," he spoke calmly and spat. "But they ain't goin' where he claim."

He said it with such matter-of-factness that I scarce noticed him turn about a final time and make straightways for the house. My thoughts dwelt there still where he had drug me in his valediction. Such ponderous and consequential words had escaped his lips that I felt a grave difficulty in taking them to heart, for fear that they were in every way true. I wanted to agree with the whole of Indian River that Miles Beckins was indeed as bent and foolhardy as they claimed him to be, and yet for some reason, it seemed as if The Harbinger's ludicrous tidings were as sensical as anything I had heard since it all began. He had implied that I should leave, which was exactly what I felt confirmed in doing for as long as I had suspected anything amiss. He also made it clear that he had retained some feared obligation to whatever was transpiring in Indian River, but felt that it was a great and false yarn spun by The Man in the Woods, which was a belief I had no trouble subscribing to. My only bit of trepidation was in his complete and utter disregard for the wellbeing of those who were tied to me by certain familial obligations. It was indeed true I had intended to leave off with Sarah Obis and never see my family again, but it certainly wasn't without my own share of reservations, or the design to return some day when I was much older and able to explain myself without fear of consequence. No matter how cross or bitter I had become with my family and their lack of discretion, it didn't change the fact that I wanted them to live full and happy lives; especially Momma.

I returned to my mental faculties with enough time to witness Beckins draw closed his single pale curtain. I took the opportunity to vacate the premises without plundering his little menagerie any further, given that I wasn't keen to relive the tumultuous event of being tackled and questioned over again. My return journey was marked with failure and the express absence of an exit strategy. I was torn in the grandest way. On the one hand, I knew without a doubt it was in my best interest to leave Indian River and narrowly escape the coming deluge, but on the other, I felt a deep and pitted sickness at the thought of what my family had been dragged into (and were presumably willing to give their lives for). The truth was, I didn't fully understand (or understand at all) how honestly brain-dead and unapologetically fanatical they were until later that night. Before I could get there, however, I was greeted by the numbingly normal day before me.

After returning to retrieve my books, I walked home, completed a lengthy list of chores and was scarcely noticed at lunch, save for when Momma brought up the scratch on my eye, and I lied, saying it was from dozing off at the tree. I then worked at a mathematics lesson and re-cleaned our room until I was called away for evening feedings. As the day drew darker, I made a noble but fruitless attempt at bathing Charles, which I was convinced afterward only worsened his stench, given that the wetness seemed to accentuate his odors and draw him to roll swinishly in the deepening dirt beds of the back yard. Following dinner, which Daddy and Aaron were absent for, me and Momma parted ways silently for the night as she retired to her room and I cleaned up the kitchen, all the while bearing thoughts of what I supposed was next in the tribulations of Moses Cotton.

I skipped my bath and forewent my nightly devotion upon seeing the Solomon Bible protruding itself from beneath my place of rest. There was nothing that could have suited to draw me further from God than the thought of him in all the recent lights he had been shown to me in. Somewhere down there was a God I knew and loved, but I wasn't strong enough in faith to rebuild him quite yet from those shattered infernal fragments he had been brought to way out there in the woods. I laid in my bed for what seemed like an hour, waiting for Aaron to show back up so I could gauge how the rest of the night was going to play out, but when he kept for another forty-five minutes or so, I decided to try something I hadn't before. I didn't like it when Aaron knew I was spying him, so I stuffed my bed with a likeness of myself made from what was available—spare blankets, pillows and the like—until I was adequately satisfied that the figure beneath the quilt was accurately representative of my smallish wireframe. In truth, the effigy was far too long and boasted much too big a head for me, but it wouldn't matter in the dark. The hell of it was that my artful construction had a better chance of being prematurely dismantled by me than discovered by Aaron, given that he was gone and probably wouldn't return before I did.

I was right tired that night when I stole down the side of the barn in my usual way; a right bit more tired than normal. It seemed my routine of late nights and inundated mental status had grown into unhealth, and I had begun to feel it earlier and earlier. It was almost enough to still me and cause me to return home in favor of sleep rather than another night of malformed questions and anxiety-ridden concerns. I just wasn't quite ready to quit my family just then, however. If there was any foresight I could have gained from observation; any tactic I could employ upon a turn of luck, I had to stay awake. I had to remain watchful as I had been. I had to believe that something was going to reveal itself to me like a beautiful flower of knowledge.

As I approached the hole, I heard the regular sounds of Aaron in his enigmatic waltz with the machine. My unofficial objective for the evening was to at least get a look at what he was peddling inside the barrow itself. I had my suspicions; given that there wasn't much else that could come out of that hole besides the elements, but I still meant to lay eyes on it and at least try to discern what he was doing it all for. As I sat crouched there in my place between the tractor forks and shavings, I witnessed my brother emerge from the ground several times carrying crates, as he had the night before. After three or four rounds up and down the ladder, I saw Aaron cover the barrow in a dark colored, cloth tarp and tuck in the sides handsomely. Then, just as he had hoisted the load and started the wheel-a-rolling, he stopped and looked back at the hole. To my surprise as much as his own, he had left a light on, and there was a terrible orange glow emitting from that hellish pit that might have drawn even the most raven of creatures to stare into its hollow gaze. It was a sight so unnatural—the light which spilled out onto the earth without order—that I wondered how I had missed it as my brother had.

Aaron straightways left the barrow and made several swift strides back to the top of the ladder, where once more, he disappeared into the hole. I knew without a shadow of a doubt that it was my appointed time to swoop down upon the load as a bird of prey and make haste in learning its composition. The moment my legs lunged me into action, I knew I was a committed and moving part of the story that had only previously unfolded before my eyes. I was most certainly suspended within the realm of real risk. Should Aaron discover me, I wagered he would punch me in the stomach and leave me in the hole without a ladder, only to be discovered by Daddy the following morning. The thrill of it was both exhilarating and sickening to me all at once.

I was a right bit more quiet than I thought I might have been, running along the wet, trailed shavings. When I reached the load in the barrow, I traced my finger along the rim and found a compromise in Aaron's tuck job; one I knew I could recreate in the tarp without him noticing. One thing the boy could never do was a proper house chore, tucking his sheets was one of them. As I lifted the tarp with both my hands, I saw the light in the hole go out from the corner of my eye. I caught a glimpse of seven or eight wooden crates with lids tight before my panic caught me and took control of my motors with a surge of animal adrenaline. In no time, I offloaded a crate damn near as big as me, stashing it nearby and replacing it with myself, curled and pained near the front of the barrow. Just before I re-tucked the edges, I saw with my dilated vision the ladder rocking a bit as Aaron neared the top. I left a loose wrinkle in the dark fabric, the same as he had, and watched the hole through it with hopes I would somehow earn a share of luck and not be discovered until I had gathered something of use.

I didn't reckon I had much faith from the start in my ill-devised and spontaneous scheme which landed me in the covered barrow, praying to the Lord God Almighty that my weight was matched to the crate I had offloaded. When Aaron lifted the handles once more and turned the laden bucket with ease, I felt the slightest inclination that I could maybe do anything. I smiled to myself beneath the tarp and tried not to expel sounds with eyes wide when passing over deep dips in the path as we made way from the old barn. Things would undoubtedly go easier out on the road, I thought. It was only when we had turned right instead of left out of the back stables that a sharp pang of fear pierced my heart deep and I was filled with a grave regret for what I had done. My internal compass was at odds with the direction in which I believed we would go. All turns and trajectories aimed us at the place I had come to fear most.

One rise and drop after another, we descended the hillocks of the back pasture. Aaron didn't seem to struggle at all at the mercy of the great burden. My heart, however, felt heavy at the thought of being uncovered before Daddy and Momma and the brothers and sisters. And him. Of course, the idea of being found out whilst far from home (whilst wherever I assumed Aaron had gone all those nights with Daddy's wheelbarrow) carried with it little to no risk at all, given that mutually assured destruction was imminent in such a case. In other words, should Aaron tattle me, my family would have to explain his chore. The same would indeed happen in the scenario before me, but only after having my ass beat, and only after being forced to participate in or witness the great spirit havoc that unfolded in those woods.

To my utter relief (and in a further confirmation of my turn in favor), I felt the barrow come to a halt before crunching along the straw coat beneath the trees. I peeked from under the tarp as Aaron lay the sleds down and disappeared free-handed into the woods not ten feet off. I sat there in quiet disbelief for a moment, and then when the moment had passed, I remained there still; quiet and breathless, attuned to the night and the air. Out there, it was as the world had been before man; no light but the stars, no sound but the soulless.

Several times, I moved to step myself out of the wheelbarrow and make for the house at the expense of potentially learning more. I had a stronger desire to avoid being discovered than I did to discover something myself, but each and every time I leveraged against the brim of the barrow, I imagined Aaron calling me a pussy in front of Sarah Obis. Though it was Aaron I was spying, it was still his voice all the same, jeering me for not being man enough to find him out. What a shame-as-shit way to go, I thought. I would be damned if I was going to be caught taking scorn and derision from Aaron for lacking the sack to spy him proper. So I stayed (and for longer than I cared to count). I caught neither sight nor sound from amongst the trees. The night—already wrought with a bite—was growing colder and colder as I sat curled there in that crowded metal cradle. My legs were long asleep then; so far gone I scarce dared to move them at all for fear I would feel a thousand tiny injections upon the soles of my feet; or worse yet, that my foot would fall off altogether and my body be drained of blood where I lay.

Of course, those were all hallucinatory notions brought on by what I felt was a prolonged imprisonment. In all reality, it had probably been something more like twelve or fifteen minutes when I finally heard the scream. It rung out clear as Momma's bell, but then tread jaggedly across the still night, like a perforation sundered into ruin. It was a woman's shrill tone that echoed far out across the planted pines and diminished in an arched fashion which fell somewhere far east of me in a strained gargle followed again by utter silence. I sat still and alert, wondering if I had imagined it up. Perhaps it was one of those instances wherein I had drifted unknowingly into the beginning stages of sleep and been awoken by the sound in a dream, but when I heard it a second time, in almost exact uniform to the one previous, I leapt mad and drunkenly from the barrow and fell upon myself in many loud clamors, struggling to my feet. It was Sarah's voice I had heard. I was sure of it. Panic-stricken, I waited there a half second more for a third cry but became instantly overrun with impatience and rushed off headlong into the tree line.

I forgot all about the contents of the wheelbarrow and any fear I had once carried for what might befall me upon witnessing the ritual again. All I cared about was the condition and safety of Sarah Obis. No plan seemed to form in my head for how I might manage such a rescue as I was indeed committed to, I only knew what was convict to my spirit. Love was nothing if unwilling to lay down its life for another. My face, legs and arms were whipped red by brush and twiggery, until alas, my feet found the path and moved nimbly down its winding profile. It seemed I had missed the ritual of wind and flames, and was instead left with the deafening silence following the pitched screams of Sarah Obis. I would have almost preferred the bone chilling manifestations to the uncertainty brought on by silence and cold, dead air. I felt assured I should have seen some sign or heard some sound by then, but nothing stood up or rung out amidst the great, darkened bowl before of me.

When I reached the brim of the basin, I sunk low to my stomach and pulled myself forward. A marked distinction in temperatures existed there. Where the air about me was cool, the space about the edge and below was unmistakably colder; so much so that it reminded me of the Freedom Spring and the stark contrast between the water and the air of summer. The void was utterly dark and without definition, but I came to detect subtle movements on the surface. The longer I remained there, the more I seemed to see. Before long, the shy little candlelights in the trees found their place about my periphery, and the movements on the ground felt more and more like those sluggish shapes I was so accustomed to seeing about my bed and walls when all was comfortably dark and quietly evil in my room. I willed myself desperately to make out the lines of Sarah Obis, but there was nothing for it. Soon, my search was drowned out by the low rising and haunted tones of many whispered litanies. It was a ghastly, spoken chorus that gathered volume until it had well-passed the window to be discerned in words and became so loud and tormented that I caught myself moaning involuntarily as a means of covering the collective, sinister plea.

Then, as soon as it had come, it was over. At the apex of the swells, the chorus had ceased, and I felt my heart thump back to regularity against the dull earth. In the resumed silence, I saw her, and it was only because I had already learned her shape out of necessity. There was no other curvature like it on our farm, Indian River or in Heaven above. She was prostrate in front of the platform, and only then did I notice the rest of them in definition, laying behind her in many scattered arrangements, all flat on their faces, the same as her. In the quiet night, I heard muddled murmurs and stifled whimpering from about those cold forms down on the ground. They seemed to all be in a deep trance of worship, and I weighed the option of going down and standing among them to try and ascertain the condition of Sarah Obis. But just as I had come to the mental crossroads of whether I would or wouldn't, I was interrupted by the resonant vocal tones of the master of ceremonies. Like the uneven rumble of thunder and storms on a distant plain, his voice never clapped like it did the night I first heard him. Instead, it stayed low and lucid, but just as poisonous.

"Eternity awaits those who would earnestly seek to breathe the mighty rushing wind, but all who desire a means to escape it can only hope to expect eternal torment and death." I searched for the genesis of his voice and seemed to locate it centralized around an upright and mottled black form there on the riser before Sarah Obis who remained sprawled upon the frozen floor. The words poured forth from his unseen lips as seamlessly as if they were lost scriptures that only he had the privilege of hiding in his heart. I thought of Miles Beckins' and the warnings of such promises. The logic behind The Samaritan's statement was unsound in the mildest of interpretations. I gathered from his words and the aforementioned words of The Harbinger that some manner of doom—aside from me and Aaron's plague—was perhaps set to be visited upon Indian River, and that furthermore, The Samaritan was urging my family (and perhaps many others) not to seek refuge from it, but instead to refuse escape and swallow death whole, with little-to-no amount of query, in expectation of Heaven's wide-swung gates. My young brain seemed to drop to my heart and hemorrhage within me at the thought of it. Then, it came to its worst. The darkness of The Man in the Woods spoke again, but then, it was familiar. Then, the revelation took root in my memory.

"Unless I go with you, you will toil aimlessly until your bloodied hands cease their fruitless toiling and you fall, beaten and utterly spent, into the dust of the ground. For it is from dust that you came, and to dust that you shall return." My hand gripped its fill of pine straws and tightened. My heart thumped once more against the cool earth, and my breaths drew deeper. His voice, in such a tone, was undeniably familiar to me. I knew in that instant I had heard it before, but was unsure of where. Only the fact that I had recognized both his voice and his words in perfect sequence was what set me on edge and made me fearful of what had occurred. There was no reason I should have rightly possessed memory of it. The only other time I had ever heard him speak, he wasn't speaking at all, but hollering at the top of his lungs. I started to question whether I had been brought to the Ritual Ground before I was properly cognizant, but I felt that if I remembered something as specific as a voice from all those moons ago, I would likewise remember the place or something about it, which I couldn't claim to. My heart and soul became straightways filled with secret fears as attributed to the new territories into which my mind had most recently wandered.

Soon my curiosity concerning Sarah Obis' condition was satisfied as much as was possible, and my strong desire to leave had overcome any valiant character I had almost channeled. There would be no rescue that night; not while The Man in the Woods held so fierce a dominion over such a quorum. I retreated with much guilt and made quick work of the worn footpath back toward the tree line at the edge of the pasture, but just before I came within line of sight of the barrow, I was straightways overtaken by a force both reckless and familiar. At first, I didn't have the slightest idea what had hit me when Aaron came barreling along up the path from behind and waylaid me with ruthless abandon. I reckoned he didn't know either, until his teeth found the back of my skull and we both collapsed into a god-awful pile of limbs and cursing.

"Prophet's fuggin' sake!" he said with panic followed by swift realization. I hollered with the same amount of revelation and pain and did my best in the dark to untangle myself and climb back to composure. "What in hell's name are you doing?!" Aaron exclaimed. "Peepin' on me at the pump ain't enough?"

"I heard a scream—"

"—Nevermind," he interrupted. "Daddy's right behind me." I looked at Aaron's dark face with unadulterated panic. "Go!" he said, shoving me forward and near about rolling me over again. Our two bodies moved almost in unison—his feet stepping into my prints as we ran full-on into the pasture. "Here, hide in this!" he said forcefully, lifting the tarp covering the barrow, but before I could climb in he noticed my handy work where I had hidden previously. "You little—"

"AARON COTTON!" came the call from the trees. Daddy was close to surfacing, and he sounded pissed as fire.

"Get in," Aaron said. With that I climbed back into the barrow and slid into place. Aaron covered me over and did a right shit tuck job, as was expected. I tried to catch my breath quietly and waited for the encounter.

"Don't you run from me boy!" Daddy had come out of the woods, it was evident in the clarity of his voice.

"I'm right here!" Aaron called back. "You damn fool..." he said under his breath. For several seconds I heard nothing save for the sounds of Daddy's approach.

"What do you think you're doin'?" Daddy asked in a voice a right deal calmer than I expected.

"I'm headin' to Marlin's," Aaron answered matter-of-factly.

"You can't show up in the middle of a rite and leave ten minutes later," Daddy said. "You were supposed to have this done already!"

"I thought I were bein' watched," Aaron admitted. I bit my lip.

"...By who?"

"Langford maybe," Aaron lied without skippin' a beat.

"Damnation!" Daddy cursed under his breath. I had only ever heard him do it in extreme cases of exasperation. It never ceased to stop me cold though. "How could you let this happen?"

"It's a big hole in the ground, Daddy. You don't think somebody would eventually get curious?"

"It's a well, son!" Daddy snapped. "What's there to be curious about?"

"It ain't no normal well," Aaron replied.

"And the only reason it got such a high profile was you not bein' careful!" Daddy said. "Look at you, trekkin' the load all the way down here! It's like you're askin' to be followed!"

In the ensued silence I pondered the clues and postulated several new theories in my head. What in the hell was it then, if not a well pump, I thought.

"I tried!" Aaron fought back weakly.

"And so you bring it all here where everybody can see it?" I assumed he was referring to the wheelbarrow. "And tonight of all nights, when you think you been made?! Langford's down there, son! You know they're close!"

"What do you mean 'close'?" Aaron asked.

"Come on!" Daddy started. "Wake up! Ever since Solomon brought him back He's been usin' him to make sure we're in line! If we're sloppy, we're done; you, me, your Momma, Moses. Everyone!" I was stricken suddenly with a flash of the Bible beneath my bed. My mind was at once seized and beaten senseless with questions. The pump. The crates. The short man. The name; Solomon.

"Marlin knows," Aaron said. Who was Solomon?

"You're right," Daddy started. "And he's havin' a hard enough time tryin' to keep the town from knockin' down our gate!" Were Solomon and The Samaritan synonymous?

"So let 'em!" Aaron spoke free. "We'll point 'em right to Him! We'll point 'em right to the man with the plan! Here he is ladies and gents! Your righteous judge and eternal jury! Solomon Marrower Stagwerth! In the flesh!"

The voice. The name. The message. The stories. The Man in the Woods wasn't The Samaritan from the Stagwerth tales at all; he was S.M. Stagwerth himself. My thoughts took my breath and commandeered control of my nervous system. I gasped loudly and then swallowed the sound with quick-resumed control.

"...What was that?" Daddy asked.

"What were what?" Aaron replied, trying to cover for me. Three seconds later the tarp was flown clean of me and Daddy's wide eyes were on my fetal form.

"Get out," he commanded. I moved swift and speechless to the edge of the barrow where Daddy took hold of my shoulder and lifted me clean out with one arm. I stood next to Aaron and awaited Daddy's next words. "You still sure it were Langford that watched you?" he asked Aaron. Aaron thought long and looked up.

"...No," he said. We both looked down submissively.

"Did you know he were in there?" Daddy asked. Aaron paused. "Don't lie to me. Because you know he won't," he added, gesturing to me with a nod.

"...I found him just before you come out." Daddy took a breath.

"Here's what's gonna happen," he said with resumed power in his voice. "You're gonna take your brother back, then you're gonna deliver the load." I turned and made ready to leave, showing Daddy there was no questioning his orders. "I ain't done," he added, looking directly at me. "You can forget what you heard," he said. If Daddy had known half of what I had heard in recent days, however, he might have well killed me and made it easy on himself. "I know it ain't realistic to think the both of you ain't tunin' in from time to time," he spat. "I know I can't stop that. But you will mind me." I gulped. The finality in Daddy's voice was enough for me to know it was safe to turn away, but Aaron then said the words that set the whole damn thing into the beginning stages of grand culmination.

"To hell with it…" Aaron said back, and it was the single most foolhardy thing I had ever heard. Not in my twelve years had I witnessed something so radically insolent. I couldn't right believe my ears. Daddy didn't even try words. Instead, he lunged at Aaron with the force of that great albino bull, but Aaron was too quick on his feet, and he parried Daddy's advance until he had outrun him. I turned to watch the short pursuit up the next hillock, but Daddy had already stopped with his hands at his side. He wasn't going to be made a fool of. Aaron yelled at him from a ways off.

"A man who has to sneak around to do what's right ain't no man at all," he said. "Ain't my father."

"And no boy who abandons his family is a son of mine!" Daddy's retort was severe, but equally matched. I swore I was in a dream.

Soon as Aaron had spoke, he turned and started off toward the top of the pasture in the direction of the barn. He mumbled something and kept right on walking. I couldn't accept that he was actually leaving. Much less could I believe the previous thirty seconds had even occurred. What took place next wasn't just out of some dormant wickedness in Daddy's heart. I knew right where it came from. So when he wandered over and backhanded me, I understood it was out of a frustrated embarrassment for what had just happened with Aaron. It was justified by my actions, but far too late to be respectable. I didn't hold it against him past the pain though (he had slapped me right on the spot where I had been thorn-slashed earlier, which was both convenient and agonizing). He needed to reassert his power, and not just from Aaron, but from the situation in general. Part of him knew Aaron was right, and that was the part that slapped me. The part made of steel bone and dried leather flesh. I needed him to reassert as well. There was never a man in my vision who ever held more control than my father did. It was all I ever understood, and all I could ever place honest faith in, aside from God, but Daddy's sovereignty always made more sense to me than God's ever did.

Daddy motioned over for me to get up off the ground. The impact had lifted me from my feet and set me down several paces away. My skull throbbed, and I thought of a time when Momma refused to let me sleep a night after bumping my head something fierce on the bottom of Aaron's bed.

"Get the wheelbarrow," he said. I straightways approached the vehicle with requisite certainty and grappled the handles stoutly. The wheel began to move, but despite my fullest efforts, it wasn't enough to steady the great vessel, and the whole load began to topple. But then, something happened. Just as I had postured myself vainly to absorb the inevitable spill, the front of the barrow rose up off the ground and became near weightless in my arms. The sleds below made tracks in the grass, and it was then that I looked onward and saw the massive working form of my father, striding stalwartly with his back to me; one hand free and one hand gripped at the lip of that burdensome wheelbarrow. The cool fog of his calm breath came and went like that of the bull, and in that moment—despite what Aaron had said—I knew he was working things out. I knew he was man.

14

Aaron didn't come back overnight. He didn't come back the next night neither, or the next, or that whole week, even. In fact, Aaron stayed gone a day short of a month's time. It was two days then until Christmas, and there were no signs of him showing back up any time in the near future. I honestly expected he would; not because of his character, but because of the way the universe worked. I waited as long as I was physically able that night in November, but I soon fell prey to sleep. After Daddy and me had dropped off the loaded barrow at the shavings barn and hid it proper, we returned home instead of to the ritual. Daddy made straightways for his den where I assumed he stayed the rest of the night, waiting. Momma went to bed unawares of what had transpired in the pasture. It wasn't until the next morning when she spat out of her room looking madder than hell, muttering curses for Aaron and Daddy, that I knew she knew too.

I started keeping count a few days before Thanksgiving, only after Aaron had been gone three nights in a row. I liked to imagine him out with those dead boys, smoking and drinking and throwing dice. I tried not to think of him starving or sleeping in a tree somewheres. I tried not to think about how his days were probably spent in preparation for his nights. The nights had changed for me too, while some other things stayed the same but only grew in complexity. Daddy avoided dinner conversation with geese in his eyes, as usual. He would then retire off into his den where he would listen to loud radio broadcasts at night (many of which were of S.M. Stagwerth; the man I had confirmed to be alive and well and living in our back pasture). I stopped my wanderings and found myself bypassing fresh baths in favor of luker waters. Nothing could have deadened the revelation of The Man in the Woods so anticlimactically as Aaron being gone (not to mention resurrection was becoming a regular occurrence around the Cotton Farm), and so my taste for personal luxuries went out the window in favor of more answers—real ones; unlike the ones I was picking up from my family and others as Aaron's proxy.

I was let in on some necessaries, but not many. There were some things I simply couldn't break Daddy or Momma for (some I refused to even try). One of which was why the brothers and sisters (including Pastor Obis) believed the woods were their true church, and Stagwerth, their appointed spiritual leader by God. I assumed it was because of his reputation, and when someone like that comes within arms reach, there demands a following be made. I supposed it could have been because he had a knack for raising the dead (Himself included, apparently). That was another thing; the second half of the Stagwerth lore remained undisclosed to me, and I foresaw no hope of hearing it any time soon. I wasn't even sure someone actually knew it in full, save for maybe Daddy or Pastor Obis. One thing I was made privy to was the fact that, before Aaron had left, he had been loading large crates full of something from the hole and bringing them to Marlin in Indian River for distributions. Maybe it was a peace offering to ease relations with the locals who perhaps felt threatened by The Prophet or some power, wielded only by those on our farm. Maybe it was some kind of manufactured pesticide to rid the town of its plight. I wasn't sure, but the more I asked Daddy about it, the more he clammed up and became angered. I told him I felt scared, and he told me there was nothing to be scared for.

It was around the same time I had started marking Aaron's absence on the slats of our bed that Daddy approached me about fulfilling my "duty to the family." I was to continue Aaron's unfinished chore of delivery, only I wasn't allowed to know the contents of the crates or why they warranted distribution.

"Pry one lid and Marlin will tell me," Daddy warned. I had asked him about the packing of crates, and he informed me he would be readying the parcels himself, stating that there was "no need" for me to become accessory to what was going on, further than what was necessary. When I further inquired why he didn't just deliver the crates himself too, he said it was important that he be amongst the others at the rites (which I assumed was his alibi). Then he beat me conventionally on the ass and told me never to question him again.

Unfortunately for me, the deliveries were never as eventful or informative as I hoped they would be. In theory, they were to be completed rather early (most often immediately following dinner and sunset), and given my size, I was forced to use Daddy's older and much smaller barrow, which meant lesser loads, more trips per night, and furthermore, that I had to deliver four nights a week instead of just two as Aaron had previously. Marlin was never once physically present at the drop off point, which was nothing more than a hollow on the roadside just beyond our property. Daddy apparently wasn't too trusting of my ability to make it all the way to town, and thus had negotiated with Marlin for a closer rendezvous. I was also required to do as Aaron apparently had been instructed and abandon the load should I be seen by any townsfolk or lurkers.

Even more unfortunate for me was the fact that on the fifth and sixth nights of every week, when I was without deliveries, I was most always drawn inexplicably to spy amongst the ritual Ground in search of answers and satiation for my curiosity. Oh, the nights among the trees. It was there that I witnessed a host of things that grew me much too quick; things I would have rather not seen or heard in twenty lifetimes. A man wishes for the faith of a child that he might see things he thought not possible. A child wishes for the doubt of a man that he might avoid such things. That was me; weeping and shaking nightly, promising myself I would not return, only to find myself there again, night after night. I sometimes went even after deliveries. It was only the consecutive nights without clues that made me consider staying away, but the times I would feel he was talking directly to me were what beckoned me there again and again. The Prophet's voice was tidal and hypnotic—His words, tactile.

"A plague has stripped this land bare of its inheritance. What end, then, for that which rises against us? I SHALL CAST A GREAT AND MIGHTY JUDGEMENT UPON THE WICKED! And every tongue will confess, I AM LORD!" he quieted once more. "One amongst you has possessed thoughts against me. One amongst you has had dreams. You remain hidden, for now, nursing an urge to come forward, but you are fearful." his tongue collected a salivary discharge that often seemed to gather in the corners of his mouth during prolonged diatribes. "Do not be afraid, for I have come to deliver you from fear." It was during such moments when I was both entranced by the certainty in his voice and perplexed by the economy of his words. Was he merely regurgitating the red letters, or was he plagiarizing in the name of God? It was hard to discern.

It was the day before Christmas Eve, and The Harbinger was on my mind. The sky and air and earth seemed to be growing evermore ominous—black and clotted and dead—and it was in times like that when I thought of him. Times when even the hell grass looked grim. Times when The Prophet's words seemed to feel more and more cryptic, and awfully more dangerous. It was likened to the waters on a shore retracting in silent preparation for what came next. I could almost hear the calm hiss of a billion strangled bubbles on the sand, and I feared what it meant.

It was already well after lunch when I crouched in the front pasture and inspected the ground curiously on my way to the outer reaches of our property. Daddy had me on a mission to the hollow to check one of the drops. Apparently, Marlin had phoned him in the night and claimed he was a container short (I seldom ever heard the telephone ring and often forgot we owned one). I reckoned Daddy didn't think it too dangerous for me to venture out during the daylight hours and check on the situation. Maybe he thought it was unreasonable for maddened townsfolk to attack The Boy Beyond the Gate during broad daylight. They sure as hell didn't mind in the middle of the night though. We had undergone six intrusions since Aaron left. Six. One nearly resulted in a breech of the house, and another got as far as the old barn. I reckoned they were headed for the bunker. Each time, Charles had alerted us with long and guttural grunts that didn't stop until he had seen Daddy. It was a sound he only ever produced when he felt he was protecting us from something.

As a result, Daddy had led the brothers and Kenzie in constructing a sort of watch tower he dubbed The Sentinel. I wasn't sure of its precise Biblical orientation, but was sure it had one. It was nothing special; a four post structure supported by x-framed cross beams and equidistant geometry, situated just in front and to the left of the barn. It rose high enough over the barn's roof that a watchmen could see both the town and the glow of the Ritual Ground at night with full visibility. The crow's nest on top was nothing more than a wood-made box with a slanted sheet tin roof that could accommodate one person comfortably. The brothers began taking shifts at night around Pearl Harbor Day and had foiled three advances since then; a couple with multiple enemies. By foiled, I mean either Bill or Silas shot at their feet with a scoped and dialed 22 caliber until they were sent reeling. Daddy did allow me to climb it once on Thanksgiving day under his supervision. Mattie, Mr. Langford and the sisters (including Sarah Obis) all watched and cheered me on from the picnic tables as I climbed the fifty-one-rung ladder of scrap planks which meandered itself to the top with less than half the nails I would have been comfortable with (it was the most joyous I had seen any of them in a long while). Against my prior judgements, the crow's nest boasted a much more sizable view than the barn roof did. Not a soul but The Harbinger had seen more favorably.

So there I was presently, dressed warmly and stopped in that cold and windy pasture in the heart of a southern winter, where for the first time in over a month, I bent low on a whim to free a tuft of hell grass from the withered soil and was shocked to learn it was devoid of mole crickets. I pulled another, and another and confirmed the unthinkable! The plague, in the least, was lifted from our plot! I of course had a fool's hope that it was gone from Indian River altogether. I turned excitedly in the direction of The Sentinel, but Silas wasn't paying me mind. I felt the same as I did when I had first found one of Beckins' messages; a moment I had nearly forgotten. Apparently there was another one out there somewheres, but I didn't reckon I would ever discover it. It had allegedly warned me to leave in haste. and I had kept every intention to until Aaron beat me to the chase. There was no way I could leave the family then; even if things did seem to be getting progressively more dire.

My thoughts were almost always on The Prophet in those days; on The Man in the Woods. I had a grave fear I would encounter him on my own in time, like I had in my dreams. Though I had never met S.M. Stagwerth, it still felt as if I had stood there with him atop all those train cars; beneath all those pitched tents, where curious congregants would gather momentarily and at once be swept away by his saline verbal prowess. He could, all at once, make you despise his teachings and heed his word. There was a measure of fear associated with it; a measure of reverence. And all any of us wanted was to dodge his gaze and know him more. Truth be told, I had readied myself for the day when his attention would be paid to me like it so often was to Sarah Obis, but for that moment, she was his example for all things requiring corporate demonstration, and she seemed, oddly, to revel in it. The Prophet would use her to teach tongues, apologetic scenarios, the casting out of demons, prayer and worship postures and as a test conduit for his unmatched powers. She considered it an honor, I supposed, though I often questioned whether her tears meant she was battling something underneath all the laudation. There wasn't a day that went by where I didn't imagine what it would be like to save Sarah Obis or my family by means of subjecting The Man in the Woods to his desserts by the mercy of my own hands.

I approached the fence on County Road 1 with caution. I was doubtful Silas's weapon could sharpshoot that far, even if his attention had been drawn on me. The silent barrier (which might as well have been a metaphor) seemed to be unadorned with onlookers; a lucky stroke for me, so I slipped sideways through its aged arms and went down into the ditch, where I asserted that my idea of secrecy had changed quite drastically in one month's time. Before, it had meant pulling the wool over Daddy and Momma with the intent of not being caught and punished. It had since come to adopt a good bit more danger of bodily harm and possible risk of death, but still retained the same amount of excitement. I hadn't even considered expressing a concern for my own safety to anyone. Aaron was gone, and I prayed desperately for his safe return, but I had finally earned a certain set of provisional rights that I wasn't ready to forfeit.

I could see the hollow from my usual checkpoint in the ditch, and noted I did not have to duck much. The day was unusually bereft of inconveniently paced automobile traffic and eerily quiet. The cold air sat contented beneath a white-gold core at the center of a gradient overcast, and all around, the sky was pregnant with weather and darkness, as it had been for so long, without rain. I saw my breath then in that bitter cold and cursed the remnant humidity which had seemed to freeze and suspend itself for my consumption. I hated the cold through and through, but the extra layers helped, and they also kept me from sustaining unwelcome cuts and scratches from the host of native foliage in the ditch along County Road 1. When enough time had passed for me to accuse myself of being overly cautious (which was what Daddy had instructed me to do), I climbed out of the ditch handsfree and crossed the worn and aggregate roadway.

It was as Marlin had said. There was no sign of a crate forgotten from the night before, which left only three explanations: Marlin, me or someone else. Marlin was long a friend of the family and had never once done a thing to cause Daddy or Momma to question him as far as I knew, so I ruled out him stiffing our family a single measly box of whatever objects of inscrutable import I had delivered. On a side note, I had reasoned that inside said crates was perhaps a gaggle of glass jars containing some manner of liquid, judging by the sounds they gave off. There initially was the thought that it could have been just water, but I ruled it out based both on what Aaron had said in the pasture the night he left, about it being more than just a well pump, and on the clear notion that a crate full of glass water jars was a right queer thing to keep hidden with such surreptitiousness.

I also knew I had counted the crates in the barrow three times over before finally reaching the hollow the night before; once at the hole, once in the front pasture, and once as I carried each individual container through the ditch and across the road for stacking. So it wasn't me. That left the final supposition that the missing crate had been taken from the hollow, by someone who not only knew me or Marlin had business at the hollow, but who also possessed a tight rein on both our agendas, some time between my departure and Marlin's arrival, and whoever it was had most likely watched me the entire time. The thought of it sent chills down my spine. I scanned the area but didn't see or hear anything save for the faint sounds of what I soon recognized to be a prop slowing in the distance. Beckins was landing his duster home, and I wondered.

Sure, it could have been anybody who liberated the crate, and I was no detective, but it made as much sense as anyone. Not to mention, I hadn't paid The Harbinger a second visit as I intended, and I was curious to know anyway how his suspicion-laced fidelity had progressed to match my mounting vexations. The last and only time I was there, Miles Beckins had reduced me to tears and panic in a matter of seconds, only to retire without offering up any real petition to leave other than what I was already subscribed to. It didn't make a great deal of sense that I should want to subject myself to such a treatment again, but I felt the terms had somewhat changed, given that I commanded a much larger allowance of knowledge than I had the last time, and a slightly larger fiber of confidence as the new Aaron. I settled on it in my mind. The Harbinger's white sand drive was only another half a mile up the road, and I was empty-handed, despite believing I might find a neglected crate on the side of the road and have to haul it back as proof of Marlin's oversight. As it were, however, the crate was still at large, and I considered it my righteous charge to locate it and champion it home by any means necessary.

When I arrived at the mailbox marking the hilly, white sand drive through the rows of planted pine, the cold air had chapped me good, and I only questioned my decision in a physical sense. The rest of me had been confirmed stronger and stronger the closer I neared The Harbinger's place. I advanced down the rows, along that green strip of grass between the tracks, without as much uncertainty or questions as I had before. I knew what lie at the end and most likely the encounter I would have there, but I was readied a bit more than I had been the last time, and that made me feel safe for some reason or another. I observed each and every piece of abandoned treasure I had the time before and even noticed a few relics I had not seen previously. As I came to the clearing, the first thing I noticed was the plane; one I had not seen before. It was a well older model, white with bits of wood and scrap metal used to patch and repair places about its war-era physique. I noted it wasn't a duster; just something old used for recreation, I reckoned. I reached up and touched the underside of the wing as I came around it on my way to the house. My eyes were out for Beckins. I had alerted myself and took every step with stilled caution. I had resolved myself to not have a repeat of what happened before. I had returned with authority and cause (and a good bit of added muscle from lifting and hauling all those crates).

My eyes fell off the old plane and onto the house. Something had disturbed the single curtain in the window, and a bird had simultaneously flown away faster than I could tell its species. Beckins knew I was there. I was almost certain he would have a gun on me if I advanced any closer to the house, but it was a risk I was willing to take, in the least, to be a hero, and in the most, to earn the answers I had always suspected were there, hidden amongst his thoughts. I scanned my immediate area and then the perimeter. Me and The Harbinger were utterly alone with each other, and while that partly scared me, it also meant freedom to speak openly about topics of disrepute without the risk of being ostracized or worse. I took one step toward the house, and heard a deadbolt dislodge. I prepared to be shot through the head. The door on the house whined as it opened outward (same as ours) and Miles Beckins stood poised there in his Fruit of the Looms and nothing else. He was holding a fifth of Jim Beam in his left hand and smiling uncharacteristically.

"Moses Cotton!" he said. "I be damned!" he stumbled out the door, drunker than hell, it seemed. "I be damned to hell and back, get over here, son!" I remained paused, unsure of his monologue, but certain of his tone. It wasn't anger. It was genuine pleasantry. He was happy to see me and was convinced it was the first time. "Come on!" he said as he continued to advance on me slowly, opening his arms wide and smiling lazily. I only imagined how his body would smell once it had fully enveloped me; odors of labor and sleep brought on by days, if not weeks, of sweat without bathing, mixed with that minty smell of spirits. I had never regretted so much being so right. He pulled me in close and pressed my head to his bare breast. The one thing that stuck out past even the smell was the moisture on his body which stuck to my face, as told by the cool wind that followed. "What brings you my way, boy?!" he said joyously. My mind sought adjustment, the way one might adjust when speaking to a young child or infant. I had to tailor my speech to his debauched state.

"I came to speak with you, sir," I said quietly. "About the notes..."

"The notes...?" Beckins questioned cluelessly. "The notes, the notes, the notes..." A light come on his head like the lights of a house. "From the plane!" he shouted. I smiled with satisfaction at how advantageous the moment had proven. "The ones I dropped you from the Grumman!" he laughed.

"The what?" I asked.

"The red one!" he replied, pointing to the hanger beyond the house, where I noticed the single prop peeking sheepishly from behind a massive metal door.

"Right!" I confirmed.

"Well, whaddya wanna speak at me about 'em?" he asked in a broken tongue. I lowered my voice to a whisper and dramatized a sense of secrecy. Miles Beckins matched it and came down to my level as I spoke.

"...Would you mind if we spoke somewheres more private?" he looked around in agreement, as if there were spies all about the tree line. Then he motioned with a finger over his lips to be quiet as he nodded his head with earnest and led me toward the house. The truth was, the house was probably no more private than right there in The Harbinger's front yard, but I knew I needed him to be bought in so he would have no qualms about spilling secrets, and believing he was doing so under complete and utter discretion on his part.

As he ushered me inside the modest dwelling, the smell straightways overtook me. It was the stench of his body multiplied a thousand times over; a sour ammoniac quality that nearly gagged me dry. The air inside was stale as a cellar or the hole in the ground by the old barn. Beckins shut the door behind us and peered out the window with one eye. I partially feared the scenario I had just conspired myself into. The darkened space was only as large as the width of the house; maybe twice the size of me and Aaron's room. On one end was a modest living area with a couch, radio, and a couple homemade tables. On the other side was a kitchenette with a sink and single-burner stove. Off down the middle was a short hallway which led to a veiled view of a disheveled bedroom and another door which was what I assumed to be a commode. All about us, the place was adorned in trash, food waste and mechanical sundries.

"Have a seat, have a seat," Miles Beckins said welcomingly as he turned from the window. I turned and saw he was gesturing at a small wooden crate sitting upright on the floor. I didn't make the connection until I sat and the box rattled with familiar sounds. I froze momentarily while Beckins hobbled to the couch. He gripped his bottle around its neck and fell backwards into his seat whilst taking a shallow swig. I was certain the crate beneath me was the missing one in question. Why Beckins had taken it was beyond me, but if I could have marshaled it back to Daddy I knew I might well be perceived a hero. Surprisingly, Beckins offered me the bottle with his extended arm. I was at first stunned and then refused politely as a reflex. I soon after seemed to warm to the idea, certain that in my place Aaron would have taken the drink. I reached for an over-turned glass on the table and slid it toward The Harbinger.

"Attaboy!" he said, instantly taking the vessel with tremors in his hand and pouring much of the caramel col-ored liquid on the table.

"Cheers," I replied customarily as I accepted the wet glass back into my hands and raised it to my mouth bravely. It was only during that split second wherein Beckins took another swig that I chose to purse my lips and only pretend to take in the spirit. As our vessels tapped back down simul-taneously, my tongue reached out and touched the residual moisture about my mouth in order to sell the charade, and I wretched beneath my breath.

We sat silent for a moment until I mustered the gump-tion to speak first.

"Mr. Beckins..."

"Call me Miles," The Harbinger slurred with eyes half closed, but still on me. I dismissed the order.

"...About the messages."

"Oh, yeah," he recollected. "I realize they weren't much to go on. Weren't much to go on at all," he laughed mildly.

"I know about S.M. Stagwerth," I said, attempting to keep the conversation on track.

"Solomon," he said.

"Right, Solomon. Is he dangerous?" I asked. Beckins took a long pause, as if he was either readying himself to speak profoundly or preparing to disclose a sworn confi-dence. When his mouth finally opened again, it was the latter.

"Solomon Marrower Stagwerth is the prophet by which we swear." Beckins words ran together but were still easily discerned. "His knowledge of the scriptures and command of the Spirit is unmatched. He's a great and mighty man. He's revered by his followers. And yes, he is dangerous."

Beckins took a deep breath of recovery, lifted the empty bottle to his mouth and poured vainly. Upon taking in the last few exquisite drops, he hurled the glass container at the far wall, but it didn't shatter as we both expected it would. Instead, the bottle skimmed across the top of a table and spun into the corner of the room with several loud and prolonged clanks until it finally landed pointing upright against the wall in a peculiar fashion. I looked back at Beckins with my mouth opened wide. He had not even noticed the miracle that had taken place in his own home. Instead, I caught his open eye peering at my glass which was surely the last taste of alcohol in short proximity. I considered offering it up, but then elected to keep it as means for bargaining.

"Your first message—"

"—The plot is poisoned Moses Cotton!" Beckins interrupted loudly with a smile, his arms flailing high above his head in mock urgency. He laughed until he choked.

"Right," I confirmed. "Did it have to do with Stag-Solomon?"

"Well that's the whole thing ain't it?" he replied. I was still a good bit puzzled. "I seen that brother of yours last night." My eyes widened and my interest straightways peaked at The Harbinger's abrupt change in topic.

"Where?!" I near demanded.

"Here!" Beckins replied in direct mimic of my own tone. He gestured to the floor below me. "Brought me that crate you're sittin' on." I looked down between my legs, then back immediately, trying my damnedest not to seem too excited.

"What's in it?" I asked immodestly.

"Hell if I know. Heck if I know," he repeated with a drunk's discretion, as if to erase the prior reaction. "He just dropped it by and said it were for the end."

"The end of what?" I asked with unveiled interest.

"The world!" Miles Beckins shouted, attempting to rise, but falling quickly back to his seat on the couch.

I sat quietly for a minute, allowing Beckins to near about drift into sleep as I looked around the room and held my hand to the side of the crate.

"Let's open it," I said loudly in order to wake him.

"Be my guest!" he replied with eyes still closed. "You'll need to pry it," he added as I stood to lay the box flat. "Should be a crowbar by the door." I turned to the front of the room and located the iron apparatus on the floor. "Near about used it on your brother last night'." In seconds I was upon the crate with many fruitless negotiations until the vessel finally wedged itself against the wall and I was able to make a steady grapple. I noticed The Harbinger offer up a hand to help, which gave me just the right amount of hubris to finish the job. The lid came free with a rattle and swish, and Miles Beckins leaned over as I pulled it away. I was, in the least, dumbfounded to witness what contents lined the crate after all that time. Inside were three levels of four rows with four slots per row, each containing a solitary, corked, wide-bottom glass phial full of clear liquid which I knew (but couldn't believe) to be plain water.

"What is it?" Beckins questioned. I uncorked a middle row specimen and sniffed it heartily.

"It's water," I confirmed. "Plain old water." I didn't understand and was exceedingly frustrated. "Why would he bring you a crate full of water?" I asked. "what did he say again?" Beckins leaned back into the couch once more and furled his brow.

"He said it were for the end. He said drink it at the end..." I could tell I was losing him.

"Miles, you want my Jim Beam?" I asked, reaching for the glass. It was like waking the dead. Beckins sat straight up and extended his arm toward the liquor, but my hand was already waiting to pull it away. "Tell me more." The Harbinger sat back, defeated and slightly annoyed.

"No more 'til I'm quenched..." he slurred. I paused briefly, then improvised.

The Harbinger's eyes were closed when I introduced the uncorked phial into his idle hand. I watched as he took the water and imbibed it with one gulp. To my delight and his, the moment passed without the slightest bit of suspicion; the opposite, in fact. The Harbinger's taste was so impaired that he asked for another almost immediately. Given the supply, I indulged him with a second phial, then another, and another, until he seemed to experience such satisfaction I was confident he would never drink again.

"Now, what's the poison?" I asked with expectancy. Then, Miles Beckins took a deep breath, followed by a long pause and spoke with more coherence and presence of mind than I had heard him command ever.

"The hopper on the plane's full of DH-720, and I've got three others ready as contingencies incase something happens or a hundred gallons ain't enough—"

"—What's DH-700" I interrupted.

"Seven-twenty," Beckins corrected me. "The poison," he clarified without hesitation. "Strong enough to stamp out this plague. Would've been done sooner, but it took longer than we thought."

"We?"

"Me and Solomon," he stated. "What brings you here anyway, boy?" Beckins asked suspiciously. It was the first of that tone I had heard during the visit. I ignored the question and kept on, for fear he was sobering up.

"Is the DH-720 bad for people?" I asked. "Is that why you tried to warn me?" Beckins stood full and tall and walked toward me.

"Well," he started, "You can be sure it's strong enough to kill a man, but I ain't sure what warning you're speakin' of." I stood to my feet as my heart begun to race. Something was amiss. Beckins was lying to me and I didn't know what for. "Come on, son. You're making me say things I don't wanna say."

I had never imagined any inebriate soul could straighten out as quick as Miles Beckins had just then. Not only was he almost fully recovered, but he had reestablished boundary lines between me and him and was lying to save his ass.

"But you've been saying all along I should leave Indian River!" I contested. "I just want to know why!"

"I ain't never said that," he bit. Miles Beckins was going mad before my eyes.

"The plague is gone! I checked today! Gone!" I implored, attempting to reason with him, but he wouldn't have it.

"What are you doing with this?" he asked sternly, lifting the glass of Jim Beam from the table. "You start down this path, and you never come back." I watched with caution as The Harbinger drank the glass dry and set it back down on the table. Then, as if experiencing a momentary relapse, his head lowered a final time and he spoke several inane sentences to me all at once. "Mighty kind of you, but he wants us all dead. I tried to save Moses but he's dead too. The crematorium is safe, but it alone." Without warning he took two steps back and collapsed unconscious into the shallow embrace of the couch.

"Miles," I checked. "Miles!" I reached over and shook him hard on the shoulder, but he was out good.

I stood there for several minutes in the quiet dwelling as I contemplated what to do next. It was clear Miles Beckins was a great deal full of additional information I had been unsuccessful at liberating from his saturated cortex, but I had learned a good bit in a short while about the man's constitution for spreading tidings willingly. The Harbinger had to stay drunk to go on doomsaying; otherwise, he was only prone to encourage evacuation without detail. It seemed that in seconds of ingesting the distinguished liquid, he had almost fully recovered to sobriety and was aware of my intentions to coax away some truth from inside him. I loosely suspected his final words were some he had spoken to my brother the night before, and that he was reliving some moment wherein he assumed I was Aaron. Needless to say, his message had frightened me, and so had his explanation of DH-720 which seemed to bare in its design a capacity for the harm of more than just one species.

I gathered the empty phials that lay scattered across the table and loaded them back into the crate before closing the lid and hoisting the whole thing out the door. The weight and balance of the box made more sense to me having then known its contents. At first, I advanced toward the driveway and the road, but then turned and noticed the hanger in the rear of the property, closed and chained like our gate. Somewhere inside was a WWII era red duster loaded with a hundred gallons of homemade cricket poisons, which was suspect to me, but not quite enough then to give me cause to attempt a break in. I took one last look at the house and resolved that Beckins would more than likely be under for the remainder of the afternoon. It was nearing dusk then, and I knew it was in my best interest to get home before my family noticed I had been gone far too long.

I made it to the drop point opposite the corner of our property about the time the sun went down behind the trees and took my shadows with it. All I could think of then was Aaron. I was glad, in the least, that he was alive, and I wished desperately he was on my side. I wished anyone could have given me a straight answer without the looming fear that some terrible judgement would befall them, but the power from beyond the trees was too great and too strong for them who had long been bewitched by The Prophet's sable graces. It seemed there wasn't a soul in Indian River who wasn't bought by The Man in the Woods. Each of them seemed to have their own intermittent qualms of spirit, but none would fully denounce him who had done wonders amongst so many, spoke word into the depths of their souls and convinced the world of its utter depravity and death apart from Him.

I had seen it upon their faces, dimly lit by the glow of a thousand tiny fires dancing high upon the trees; a dependent terror. His words settled deeply into their hearts, and gestured chillingly at mine.

"Some of you look upon me with the doubt of the Israelites! WITH THE DOUBT OF THOMAS UNTO THE CHRIST!" he preached one night with sulfur. "As if you challenge the authority given to me by the Godhead! I am your covering! Did I not say that a THOUSAND may fall at your left side and TEN THOUSAND at your right, but it will not come near you?" I questioned the proclamation. I questioned whether I had heard it under the same context as all the others present. They had been subject to hundreds, if not thousands more sermons than me, and it showed in their submission. It showed in their thirsty expressions. It showed in their need to prove him wrong. "I tell you the truth," he spoke, stepping down from the platform with bare feet, soiled fringes and a face I had forgotten each and every time I deserted that place of visual advantage high on the rim. "You have known the dead to rise, but before this time has passed, you will see me tread upon the surface of the waters and rain justice upon this withered valley!"

It was a phenomenon I couldn't right explain as a twelve-year-old or a lifelong observer. I had only just been introduced, after all, to the notion that my family was sub-scribed heavily to the tutelage of a figure I had only ever known in one dimension. The eeriest part was the fact that I had started to recall various instances throughout the earlier parts of my life wherein I could trace the footsteps of such a figure with endless lines and dots. There was no way I could have truly known how long his influence had reigned in my life or the lives of those around me, but it was safe to say that most of my existence had been followed by the man. Every time Daddy had second guessed himself, every time Momma flinched at a knock on the door, the loss of sleep in Aaron's eyes as he slowly grew more and more exasperated throughout life, he was there.

I made a precautionary stop in the ditch beside County Road 1 to refill the three empty phials with cloudy skeeter water before doing my best to embed the nails back proper and inspect the crate. I thought about taking a phial for myself, but opted against it for the purpose of avoiding further suspicion. That, coupled with the fact that I knew always where I could find an endless supply, should I ever so desire. When I arrived at the barn and told Daddy I had found the crate sitting right where I left it, he straightways bought the story like he wanted, saying, "Marlin. Blind as a bat." he then commended me half-heartedly with a touch on the head as he shouldered the wooden box and carried it off toward the rear of the farm. He had no choice but to believe me, as I had presented him with the very object in question. I did feel somewhat poorly for making Marlin out to be the foolish one, but I didn't reckon it would do much to alter Daddy or Momma's view of the man as a reliable but dim character.

It wouldn't have been a stretch to say I felt a little mixed at dinner. I had learned Aaron was well, and I trusted his movements on the outside, but I missed him truly. Even still, I thought it was better he was opposite the gate, figuring things out, because Lord knew I wouldn't have been able. I neither felt I understood what he and Daddy hoped to accomplish with the water, nor was I allowed to speak to Marlin on such things (as per Daddy's request). The concept of Daddy's approval was a new one to me too, but I wasn't sure if I loved it or felt tethered to it. The truth was, aside from the part of me that just desired to be my own man with Sarah Obis, my longing to leave the farm and Indian River had comparatively grayed itself against where I stood a month prior. I still considered there was danger, and even continued to wrestle with the idea of leaving, but that amount of passion and fervor to leave was equal in proportion to the amount of ambivalence and duty that bid me stay. A single saline drop freed itself upon my cheek in the presence of Daddy and Momma at dinner, but they didn't notice. Their minds were so drawn away to faraway places and concerns in those days that I seldom felt we were alive in the same time.

That thickness of collective contemplation seemed to collapse on all sides when a visitor came pounding on the front door that night around six o' clock. I wiped my cheek, quick and discreet.

"Virgil? He's early," Momma said, standing to her feet with a confused expression. She laid her napkin down and made for the door, but upon a second bout of bangs, accompanied by what sounded like a call of distress, Daddy shoved his chair away and crossed Momma. When he unlocked the door and pushed out, it was Pastor Obis after all, but not in his usual fashion. He was mighty unkempt and breathing heavy, as if he had come running to the house, and he was redder than hell.

"It's the woods," he caught his breath. "They're on fire. You can see the flames from here." My face opened up wide. He pointed to the northeast. Daddy and Momma rushed through the door and stood on the steps, gazing into the distance with tongues of fire in their eyes.

"Stay here!" Daddy shouted as if I had already disobeyed him. The three of them then disappeared as the door came shut. I tried briefly to convince myself I was upheld then to a new standard of accountability; one under which I couldn't right afford to disregard a direct order. It was another chance to prove my quality, but it was all just utter bullshit. There was no way I could spare to bare witness to a wildfire. The second I heard the alerted tones and chatter fade away through the window and into the quiet night, I gathered the plates and silverwares from the table, dumped our bowls into the bunker crock and nursed several spots where molten broth had plopped across my face and arms upon doing so. I then filled the sink with hot water and suds and sunk the dishes and cookware inside. After I had wiped down the surfaces of the kitchen, it was six o' five and I was stepping into shoes and tripping over Charles on my way down the back steps in the direction of a great red glow.

I knew it were improbable as all hell, but I swore on the maiden I could feel the heat growing greater the nearer I came to back pasture. It wasn't until I passed by the trees of the Freedom Spring that I fully understood the threat at hand. The ritual ground was ablaze, and there was no obvious sign of The Prophet. From my place about the rear of the bunker, I scanned the scene for signs of a missing saboteur. There was no way I was buying that the fire started of its own accord or by the will of nature. Perhaps God was to blame, but I reckoned he was to blame, in some way, for all natural disasters. I counted eleven silhouetted figures, wreathed in dancing red contours, among the middle of the pasture. I ruled out Mamie and the rest, leaving only two explanations in my mind: either The Prophet was laying ground for some steeped lesson in the spiritual realm by striking his own dwelling place ablaze, or the townsfolk had gotten brave again and found a way into the woods from the Mennonite place. I tended to believe the latter, given its practicality, but that night wasn't much for practical.

Some time passed before the group at the middle of the pasture seemed to break up in search of fruitless methods for extinguishing the flames. Some shapes went past me and made haste toward the spring with vessels of various shapes and sizes. Others went further down toward the fire in search of weaknesses, I supposed. All of it was vanity, however. The blaze would find fuel the further north it went. It might have even taken our northernmost border by then, but one could only hope the Mennonites were keeping their end up (that is, if they weren't in cahoots with whomever started it). The southwest was nothing but pasture, and the northeast seemed reasonably contained by the scar in the trees. Something deep inside me swelled with relief at the idea that perhaps the fire had taken The Prophet's life once and for all. Maybe he had burned out there, caught resting in his home, which I always imagined was a stoic place, made from mud and grass and hewn from the roots of the ground. Part of me, however, felt conviction for having reveled in the idea of any man's death, even one whose intentions I wasn't sure of.

I laid there on my belly, as I had so many times in that pasture, waiting for the unknown to rear its head, but I saw only uniform commotion, and heard only the sound of the winds which seemed to come down from above me, above the spring, above County Road 1 and brush rhythmically across my back with measured breaks in their currents. The cool air seemed to ride in and fill up the space between the tree lines, as if to combat the heat and bend the grasses into submission, thus claiming influence over the land. It was only then that I noticed the gentle breeze had given way to a steady and constant gale which seemed to ever increase without respite. In due time, I had become straightways fearful of the unnatural winds as they tore across me, loosing my shirt from beneath me and bringing it to fly about my head and shoulders. The bunker took prolonged onslaughts from the wind, and everywhere around it, loose sheet tin banged and scraped, and I soon heard the voices of women inside, seeking refuge from the spontaneous upheaval.

No one was visible in the field or upon the hillocks when the very worst of it showed. I looked on as the flames rose and become straightways enraged against the wind. The range of heat and cool upon the skin of my face was a wild contention, and every second it grew, I feared our farm would be swallowed whole in the lick of a single cosmic flame. Then, as if it was a sign or wonder left unwritten from the good book, the wind rose a final time with such great force that the trees buckled, and I felt mist upon my face. The bunker was then lifted from its anchored place there at the top of the pasture and pitched listlessly against the buckled tree line below. I was straightways undone at the thought of Momma and Sarah Obis rattled around inside the flying tin can like a couple rag dolls. I almost called out, but then snapped to realize Momma, Mamie, Dotty and Sarah Obis had merely been left uncovered upon beds where the curvature of the bunker's roof had once stood.

Just as I had opened my mouth, I felt my voice escape me and take with it every last inch of air left in my lungs. The sound in the pasture was like wind in a bottle, and the pitch rose higher and higher until the woods at the bottom were filled with what seemed like every last breath in Indian River. The fire was stoked to its maximum, and I knew I needed to brace for something. With the last bit of strength left in me, I rolled sideways and allowed the wind to carry me into the cleft of the ditch beside that middle strand of trees along the old boundary fence where I had first laid and watched the torchlit processional all those moons ago.

Then, unlike anything I had seen before, and against all my possible predictions, something happened there that none of us were ready for. The wind stopped suddenly and completely. Silence fell over the field, the trees seemed to unbuckle and stand straight, and all manner of earthen matter rained from the skies. The fire, however, continued for several more seconds until, in a show of grand finality, the flames—some a hundred feet tall—fell from their places amongst the trees and disappeared into the black night without as much as a single ember left aglow. We watched in total bewilderment as smoke rose from the remnant and the sounds of a thousand hissing demons filled our ears. The sharp smell was overwhelming; like a campfire burned to ashes and dampened by morning dew. All was black and charred and ashen. I knew what we had witnessed there was more than mere coincidence. No wind was strong enough to surpass its own proclivity for feeding flames as such, and instead extinguish them. It was like the breath of a man upon a candle, only, the breath was finished before the candle had gone out, which was its true tell.

As the brothers and sisters emerged slowly from cover and rose to stand amongst each other, I entertained the possibility that the fire was started at Aaron's hand. Had he learned something in all those nights away, I thought. Was he sending a final warning to our family? Could it have been an attempt at assassination gone awfully wrong, foiled by The Man in the Woods' terrible power? Aaron and I were hardly ever on the best of terms, but I trusted my brother. And if he had found cause strong enough to attempt something so recklessly endangered, I had to believe he was on to something real. The only trouble was confirming it truly had been Aaron that started the conflagration.

Then, as if I had asked for it plainly, what seemed like confirmation shone out, but not in the way I would have preferred. It was a voice upon the air; one that seemed to come from the woods, but boasted such great volume and capacity that it could have just as well been many voices in one.

"DEATH FOLLOWS SWIFTLY THIS DISSENTER!" it said. "TO HIM WHO DENIES MY NAME AND SEEKS TO SUPPLANT ME FROM THE THRONE OF DAVID!" I felt in my spirit that same trembling fear I had known the first time I heard him speak, only, it was different then. A cold hatred had finally surfaced in him fully, and it seemed his very tongue had been transfigured into that of a diabolical beast. "THOUGH MY FLESH IS BURNED, MY VENGEANCE ABIDES, RESOLUTE AND TERRIBLE! AND NONE BUT THOSE UPON BENDED KNEE WILL ESCAPE IT!" The brothers and sisters instantly fell to their knees, as if hearing the voice of God. His words were unlike any I had heard him say before. The Prophet wasn't bending scripture any longer, he was writing his own, and something inside always told me it was only a matter of time. His last decree was one that sent chills of expectation down my spine. "THIS NIGHT, YOU ALL WILL GIVE AN ACCOUNT, AND BLOOD WILL BE SPILLED AS RECOMPENSE FOR MY OWN! BLOOD FOR BLOOD! COME TO THE

TREES." With that, the voice was done, and the brothers and sisters stood slowly.

There was no way I was gonna be caught dead counted amongst those in the trees or anywhere close by that night. I reckoned I should stay put for the time being until I could tell all was clear for me to make my break. I searched with intent for a moment to steal away with Sarah Obis. It would have been the perfect opportunity to make our leave from Indian River, if only I had known I could convince her to take me up on my illformed plan which involved great measures of patience and blind trust from all angles. I watched as the women gathered themselves up and dusted off their clothes. Mamie was suffering from a minor head wound. Blood dripped through her fingers but she wouldn't accept help from anyone, not even Momma. Sarah Obis was doing tolerable despite the fact that she, along with all those who called the bunker their home had just lost everything. I saw a moment approaching when she would be alone, so I stilled myself in preparation and rehearsed a few lines in my head.

Momma was attempting, unsuccessfully, to aid Mamie down the hillocks toward the burnt tree line whilst holding a kerchief to her head. Sarah Obis delayed momentarily to withdraw a darkened object from the waist of her skirt and observe it briefly. From what I could tell, the brothers and Daddy had also begun to descend the hillocks, and I felt providence urging me for such a time. I looked down once more to gather the reality of the situation I was in and then lifted myself out of the shallow dip. When I called out to Sarah Obis from behind, she was startled bad and straightways stuffed whatever held her attention back down into the folds of her garment. She turned quick and squinted her eyes into the darkness for several seconds before making out my form.

"Moses?" she said. "What are you doing?" I implored her with many hand gestures to lower her voice and come closer.

"...I'm leavin'," I whispered.

"Leaving where?" she asked as she approached.

"Home first, to gather up some things, then...on." I saw Sarah Obis' face noticeably change, as if the thought had crossed her mind more than once as well.

"...You can't just..." she hesitated. My heart dropped and I felt a hot sweat break across my body. Perhaps it was all a terrible misconstruction. But still, there was a reserved tone in her voice which begged that I still ask the question.

"Do you—"

"—Sarah!" came a worried voice from beyond the ruins of the bunker. I ducked, but there were no place to go. Pastor Obis were upon us. Sarah Obis turned and met her father's gaze which seemed to question heavily my presence in such close proximity to his daughter and the night's events. "Are you ok?" he asked her.

"I'm fine," she answered.

"How 'bout you, Moses?" he added. "Everythin' alright?"

"Y-yessir," I stumbled, afraid to say more.

"...It's about that time," Pastor said, with his large hand extended to Sarah Obis. He had one eye on me in a suspicious way. "Does your daddy know you're here?" he asked me. I froze.

"...Yessir," I lied. I reckoned I had never lied to a man of the cloth before. His eyes narrowed again as his daighter took his hand. He had heard Daddy tell me not to leave the house.

"Better come along with us," he suggested.

"No, I best be getting back to the—"

"—MOSES!" Daddy's voice was unmistaken. I closed my eyes in defeat. I felt Pastor and Sarah Obis turn away as Daddy exchanged places with them. "I told you to stay in the house..." he said, angered and regretful. I opened my eyes as he seized me by the shirt collar and dragged me away down the hillocks.

"Where we goin'?!" I asked, knowing full well what the answer was. Daddy stopped us. He turned swiftly and bent down to my level with a formidably grim disposition.

"When we arrive, I don't want you to be nobody special," he started vaguely. "I want you to keep quiet and make yourself small. Don't draw no attention. Be Moses." It was almost as if he was less mad at me than concerned. He was looking me dead in the eyes with his hand on my shoulder like he never had; like he cared more intently about me following those instructions than he did any others in my whole life. I didn't know why he was telling me all that he had, or what any of it meant, but I never felt more compelled to do as he said than at that moment. "Make yourself small," he repeated, as if to seal it in my heart. Then he stood and allowed me to walk freely with him and the rest of the brothers and sisters who had all seemed to accept my presence there without special attention paid. I reckoned it was what it had been like the first time Aaron was obliged to actually attend a rite and not just spy one. Something in me felt privileged and terrified all at once.

Soon enough, I looked up and noticed Sarah Obis had come alongside me there as we collectively descended the final few hillocks before the smoldering tree line. My heart habitually skipped a beat as my eyes performed a double take.

"I suppose Daddy foiled your plan..." she said. I didn't say anything back, just gave a side smile and kept on walking. "Just as well. I can't imagine your brother is doing much better out there on his own; 'specially after tonight." My head snapped.

"How do you mean?" I stopped. The look on Sarah Obis face was one of surprised regret. She had spoken too much.

"Sounds like you've already got a hunch," she observed. We continued walking.

"You mean the fire. You think Aaron started it, too."

"I think it's a pretty fair guess," she said.

"...I don't reckon it went the way he planned then."

"...No, I don't reckon it did..." we walked quietly to the edge of the trees and observed the blackened landscape for a minute, then Sarah Obis again reached into her waist and withdrew what appeared at last to be a stick of some sort. "I made something for you," she said. I swallowed my guts as she offered me the object with both hands, and it became clear what it was. She had crafted for me something of unspeakable sentiment. It was a masterfully made and meticulously faithful replica of the whittled rifle; the one I told her Aaron had made for me and destroyed. She smiled a perfect smile as she witnessed the utter shock and joy of my countenance. I would have taken a knee then and there, with daggers in my heart, and made her mine.

"...Did you make this?"

"Not such a bad whittler myself, eh?" she smiled again.

"How did you know?" I asked. "It's exactly the same."

"I told you I seen it before," she said. I ran my fingers along the grooves and ridges and sanded surfaces that made it uniquely superior to its predecessor.

"Thank you," I offered simply.

"You're welcome," Sarah Obis replied. A final moment passed quietly as we stood there together.

We turned slowly then to the woods and exchanged our levity for somber preparations. We were the last ones to remain on the fringe of the trees, and I once more thought about asking her to leave with me, but I slunk inside myself and shied away. There might have been a moment there or before, when she might have said yes, but I convinced myself that moment had passed, and that after we entered the woods, we would come out different than before. I held my tongue, and felt the fear and reservedness wash over me like a warm wave. It was something I bitterly regretted then and in every moment that followed.

The trees and undergrowth were burnt up black all the way into the center of the ritual ground; that bowl shaped, earthen amphitheater which I had only ever seen from its elevated rim. Though all the greenery above and below, was gone. What remained of the trees in the dark night still managed to make one feel secluded or concealed out there in the wild. There was no light but the stars and moon above, which seemed to shine on, despite the invisible plume of smoke above our heads. As we filled that intimate space with reluctant obedience, I felt Sarah Obis' presence part from me as she was drawn to the opposite side of the aisle with her father, and I was seated upon a pine pew next to Momma who looked both surprised and horrified to find me present. No one spoke a word. I watched as Mattie and Kenzie helped Dottie into a seat.

What, among the rest of us, did she have to answer for? I honestly wondered. Bill and Silas had taken on their more reserved demeanors as they often did at the rites and were having a seat in front of me and Momma. Mr. Langford was alone on a pew across the aisle from us, and Daddy was on the front row, which I straightways marked as odd.

It was then that I noticed, in my periphery, the black shape of the man Himself. I had almost forgotten our host until I saw a flash of his marred and pinkish face there on the platform, not ten feet in front of me as I scanned the night. I purposefully withheld my vision from falling back upon him. "Make yourself small." The words played again in my head. I looked down but detected his darkened presence only an eye's twitch away. I fought hard the urge to look in his direction again. Make myself small, I thought. From what I could tell of the image so freshly stamped into memory, Stagwerth had suffered some unfortunate circumstance with the fire. His skin shone like blown glass, waxed against the dome of his skull and his sharp, angular face, which was newly remade. It was an honest horror to behold, but I couldn't manage to arrest my desire a minute longer.

In an instant of brazen disobedience both against my father's wishes and my own best judgement, I turned my eyes upon The Prophet, but kept my head still. His form was more grisly than I had even comprehended at first. I straightways wondered how the man had survived such an encounter. I watched him closely. His vision was where I feared I might find it; upon Sarah Obis, and his face was one of momentarily distracted disapproval. I reveled, however, in a few stolen seconds of choice surveillance as I permitted Sarah Obis to dangle there as a distraction. Then suddenly, as if he had baited a trap hinged upon my inevitable foolishness, his eyes telegraphed mine with psychic precision, and for a moment I stared directly into the face of a man who seemed to have been waiting desperately to drink in my soul since the dawn of all time.

It was a perverse and unwelcome encounter that sent shrills of panic and anxiety through the deepest parts of me and lasted long after I had turned away in denial of the event. My heart pounded, and I grit my teeth together, breathing heavy as I realized what had just happened. I had made a terrible mistake. The Prophet had ceremoniously traded his attention from Sarah Obis to me, and I feared he would keep it there for the foreseeable future. Though I only looked into his eyes for a brief moment, I could tell he found pleasure and interest in me. I offered something Sarah Obis did not; a pure intention. I reckoned Stagwerth wanted to make me his pupil; not in the same sense that everyone else was, but in a different way I wasn't quite sure of then. His previous fixation seemed to have more to do with impure thoughts for a sexual creature. His fixation on me was academic, from what I could read.

I looked at Momma to see if she had caught the exchange. She was oblivious, but when I looked in Sarah Obis' direction, she was looking right back at me, and the expression on her face was one of concern and fear; not for herself, but for me. In addition, I reckoned I caught an undertone of relief upon her face, but not without a pang of worry and guilt, as if she had just broken a piece of my property and had been caught in the act. I didn't look at The Prophet again, even after his voice broke the settled silence.

"It was not an accident," he said. "An attempt has been made on my life this night. I will allow the penitent heart to come forward and seek forgiveness, but if one does not, I WILL CALL AFFLICTION DOWN UPON YOUR HEADS!" The woods echoed ten and twelve times over until all that remained was the hiss of the smoldering wild. Then, one rose from amongst us; one who I happened to know was not to be blamed. Daddy stood with words on his lips.

"Solomon, how can we be sure it was one of us here?" he questioned. It was the question on all our hearts. "How can we be certain it weren't one of the townsfolk who've been known to blaspheme you to their own kind? Ain't they got more cause for killin' than any of us have?" Daddy's logic was sound, and part of me reckoned he knew his son was to blame, same as I.

Solomon looked at Daddy a long while and then smiled confidently through his affliction.

"This land is closed to the wretched, is it not?" I had heard the statement before, of course; from the mouth of Momma, as well as my own, as I spoke it to the dark man at the gate that evening past. Little had I known then where it had originated from. Daddy answered.

"It is, but—"

"—Then how can my assassin be any but you amongst me?" he asked calmly. We watched on as Daddy did his best to contemplate the question in reality without offering another in doubt. Even I had to wonder what it really meant for our farm to be "closed to the wretched." It was as if he was suggesting a magical enchantment was in place around the farm's borders and hedges, but we all knew that wasn't true, as had made evident by the recent breeches. Even

The Prophet knew what he was saying might as well have been based in fiction. There was nothing about a closed gate or cross shape cut in light upon the lawn that could keep enough brooding hatred at bay. Daddy sat, defeated, nonetheless, and a silence fell upon us once again. It was only then broken by what we all recognized as a tone of finality. "Atonement must be made," The Prophet said patiently. "And punishment will be given." Not one among us knew what indeed it meant, but we were all pretty damn anxious to find out.

Moments later, we heard the quiet sounds of approaching feet and the faint cry of a newborn or something like it. In seconds, Mamie appeared from the shadows behind the platform carrying something in her arms and accompanied by a man I had not seen before, but by the look of his puritan attire, I reckoned it to be William the Mennonite. It all started to come together then. Mamie held Mennonite roots as well. I had always thought her kerchief head covering was peculiar, even by our farm's modest standards, but in such close context to the Mennonite, it was evident she was of his kind. Upon a closer look at her appearance, my eyes widened, and I recognized the thing she held against her breast. It was the ewe from my visits to the spring! She was milk white as ever, in a new coat of short fleece, and she wept like a babe, but quietly, as such a graceful thing might do. The Mennonite removed his round hat and held it where his suspenders clipped to his handmade trousers. Mamie handed the ewe over to The Prophet and I somehow knew what was coming. The creature began to buck and bay, and before long, I noticed many of the brothers and sisters either plugging their own ears or wiping tears away at the sight of it all.

"TURN YOUR EYES TO ME!" Solomon yelled. "YOU WILL LOOK UPON THE PURE AND INNO-CENT LIFE WHOSE BLOOD IS SHED FOR YOU!" Then, as if with inexplicable power, our visions were set upon the front as The Prophet drew a short blade. Its silvery edge shone in the moonlight and was all but identical to the one with which I had given hunt to The Man in the Woods in my dream. My chest pounded with blood and breath. I gripped the edge of the pine pew. The Prophet's hold on the ewe become so great, the creature quieted to nothing more than a murmur, and its head and legs ceased to move almost entirely.

As the blade moved into position, I stood from amidst the group and cried out, heedless of the consequences.

"NO!" I screamed, but the blade had already made its silent run across the ewe's throat. I heard only the echo of my own voice and the gentle splash of blood upon the wooden platform as The Prophet dropped the creature's stained and limp body to the floor. When I realized what I had done, I noticed all eyes were upon me, including The Prophet's. Daddy had turned in his seat with his face sternly lit, and Momma was grasping my arm with all her strength, trying to pull me down into my seat and away from my self-inflicted spectacle, but it was too late for salvation.

"I'm afraid so..." said The Prophet as he gazed into my eyes and walked ever so slowly towards me. His blood-soaked hands were out-turned and dripping as he made his approach. "The price must be payed. Blood must be spilled." I looked from side to side as he got closer to my face. The brothers and sisters and Daddy and Momma attempted only to make sideways visual contact. My legs burned as my courage emptied, and I stood there, wet in my clothes.

He was upon me then, his face maimed and flesh broken. He stopped. "We've been waiting for you, Moses Cotton," he said. "Long have you watched from the shadows, but never have you stood in my courts. We are honored," he mocked. I shuddered at the thought that he had known of my spying. I couldn't speak or move voluntarily. "The first lesson you'll learn is that there is no protest here. And the next is that there are no secrets." he paused for a moment and reached out to touch my chin. "Do you bring secrets with your protest, Moses Cotton?" I smelled blood on his hands and felt it stick, warm and wet, to my chin as he held my face straight. My eyes closed instinctively. "Do you?" he asked again. His face wreaked of death, and his breath was stale and unpleasant. Tears fell down my cheek, and I felt his thumb wipe me clean, leaving red smears upon my face. "DO YOU?!" he demanded. I shook my head franticly and felt his hand release with a shove.

The Prophet turned and walked back up the aisle.

"I CONFESS, FRIENDS, THAT I HAVE COME BURDENED WITH SECRETS!" he said. "Secrets that I no longer wish to keep from you; secrets that will startle you and urge you to withdraw from my presence, but will also confirm in your spirits that there is no way to eternal life but through me!

"There indeed is a cleansing on its way; one that will separate the wheat from the chaff. Most of you have suspected it goes beyond the plague. You would be correct in your suspicions. You will not know the day or the hour, but when the time does finally come, the wretched of this land will wither away. And it is your choice whether or not you wish to wither away with them.

"I will confess also that I ordained the assault upon one of your own." A light gasp traveled through the pews as Mr. Langford swallowed and looked at Mamie in sudden recollection. "I did so as a test of your faith. And you failed. Every last one of you! And when you could not raise him yourself, my servant brought him to me WHERE I SPOKE INTO HIS LIFELESS BONES, AND HE ROSE AND BREATHED AGAIN!" My eyes were set on Mr. Langford who seemed as moved by the revelation as we were. But even murder and resurrection seemed like nothing compared to what followed.

"How many of you knew that Mr. Langford was also sent here to investigate me?" Heads turned, and the tension became straightways palpable. The short man's black face was beet red, as if he had been both outed and reminded at the same time. There was no telling what kind of trauma he had experienced from the fall and being brought back to life. Who the hell could even know if he was the same person. "It seems the town law is too corrupted by and engrossed in its own sin to question me personally!" his vision narrowed upon Mr. Langford. "So they sent spies, unfamiliar to us, into our camp. Tell me, Mr. Langford, what report will you deliver unto your colleagues now?" The short man hesitated for a moment.

"…That S-Solomon Stagwerth is The Way. Th-the only Way—"

"—That's right," Solomon laughed a little. "That's right. OH, THE WONDERS OF DEATH AND RES-URRECTION!" he shouted. A few forced claps arose from the group, accompanied by one or two estranged vocal endorsements. I wondered if Pastor Obis would be The Prophet's next target, considering he had been the one to brought Mr. Langford onto the farm in the first place, but he was not. The blood had begun to dry on The Prophet's hands when he beckoned Daddy to stand again in his place. Only then did I notice Mamie had taken a seat on the front row of our side, and William the Mennonite had gone. I noted that he must have had strong privileges to be able to leave a rite where even Daddy reckoned he could not.

"I have just one more confession, in closing," The Prophet said as he stepped down off the platform and stared Daddy in the face. "I am EVER so aware of the counterplot to foil my plan for this wretched people." I felt Daddy's face sink from the back of his head, and I watched as a posture of shame overtook his body, almost as if he had stopped breathing. He lifted his head slowly to meet The Prophet's gaze. "But, my oldest friend," he continued, "for every ounce of grace and mercy you wish to impart upon this sinful people, I have in my heart A BURNING, RIGHTEOUS ANGER, TENFOLD, FOR THEIR TRANSGRESSIONS!" he screamed into the heavens, then looked back down at Daddy with a blood-crusted finger pointing. "And neither you, nor any drop of blessed water will safeguard them from my wrath!"

It occurred to me then that Solomon Stagwerth had a power of omniscience, and that at any moment, he was privy to any and every thought that swam in the minds of those in accordance with or in opposition to his will. It made me afraid to think certain thoughts, take certain postures, breathe in certain patterns and look in certain directions. My soul worked desperately and covertly to process and recover from the intense revelations that were being thrown at us from every which way. Nothing, however, could have fully prepared me for the true and final disclosure of the evening; the one that made all the sense in the world, but stood veiled amongst me for twelve years.

"HEAR ME!" The Prophet started again, addressing us all loudly. "THE SPIRIT OF JUDAS THE BETRAYER HAS POSSESSED YOU!" Then he looked at Daddy. "Even you, Samaritan. The one who gave me care. The one who brought me here." I ceased to breathe. The Prophet shook his head at Daddy. "You will see, though, that I am good. I will forgive you and cleanse you of all unrighteousness. COME FORWARD IF YOU WISH TO BE RID OF THESE DEMONS!" The whole of us shoved in the direction of the front. Even I was pushed, dragged and led forcefully by Momma and several others. The brothers and sisters weren't leaving anything to chance. We knelt around The Prophet's legs, and he raised his bloody red hands over us. I shuddered with fear and clenched Momma's dress with my eyes closed. "COME OUT, LEGION!" he quaked. "BE LOOSED INTO THE ABYSS!"

15

I awoke on my back to find myself staring at the slats under my brother's bed. It was full-on night still, and I was naked as a jaybird. There was no telling what time it was, but I wagered it could have been near morning. The last thing I remembered was the bare feet of The Man in the Woods and the warmth of many gathered bodies against the cold night air. Daddy must have carried me home, and Momma must have undressed me, which was becoming right embarrassing at my age. I tried to roll over until a more suitable light was at the window, but there was nothing for it. I was awake as ever, which was rare for me.

Tears had immediately begun to refill my eyes as my mind raced with images from the night; the slaughtered ewe, The Prophet's blood-red hands, Mr. Langford outed in his ulterior motives, and the revelation of both Daddy's betrayal of The Prophet and his true identity as The Samaritan from the Stagwerth tales. I figured it was as good a time as any to mull it over in the bathwater, so I got up and made my way down the hall. The light in the kitchen was on, which I marked as strange for so late at night, but I let the bath run fresh regardless. There was simply too much to process to let the water sit stagnant another time. My most primary consideration whilst sitting there cross-legged amongst the pouring hot crystals and steam was the idea that perhaps the authorities ought to finally be notified. Aaron was amongst those on the outside whom The Prophet had said would "wither away" in a coming time, and if his implication that only the twelve of us would survive was true, then a preventative action might have been in order. I feared after that evening, however, that further efforts of Daddy or Momma or any of the brothers and sisters were out of question in light of how things had ended at the rite.

The water did things to me. It attuned my body and made it aware of certain afflictions that had come against it in times as such. For once, I was conscious of the stress in my veins and that constant, rhythmic bombardment of my heart against my chest cavity. It was always there, only I had grown used to it. I placed my head in my hands and tried to breathe more air than I would involuntarily. My heart ached for Aaron, and my mind grew in fear of what was to come. When I opened my eyes, I felt the streams on my face empty into the ocean around me. I never even saw the tears. One minute, they were upon my cheek as the manifestation of worry, confusion and helplessness. The next, they were pouring over me in waves of comfort, warmth and grace, and it was all too soon interrupted with fists upon the door.

"MOSES COTTON!" Momma shouted, finally. She must have awoken from a dead sleep. "WHAT ARE YOU

THINKIN' RUNNIN' THAT WATER?!" I reached up and turned the faucet tight to listen. "GET OUT HERE RIGHT NOW!" I thought it quite odd she was making a to-do of it after all that time. It was the last thing I had expected.

Once I toweled off and did my best to wrap myself around the waist the way Aaron did, I braced the doorknob and opened it slow. Momma's arm then came straightways through the opening and pulled me out into the hallway by the scruff of my neck. She slapped me plain a simple and meant it. We floated there together for a moment, in silent anticipation of some further cause of reaction. Then, like a castle in the sand, I collapsed in tears and let my mind well up with residual emotions. It was the first time she had seen me like that in a long while, and it broke her.

"I'm sorry, son," she said, bending down to put her arms around me. It was altogether alien, but familiar; like a queer and comfortable memory, and I welcomed it. I stood there for several minutes with my arms tucked into her loose embrace, hoping she would hold me tighter, but she never did. I cried and cried until I was red and dry, and then I looked up at her. Her face was cold and honest.

"Is Aaron gonna die out there?" I asked. Momma hesitated, looking down first, and back up at me. She then spoke the single longest strand of words she had ever said directly to me in my twelve years of life.

"Aaron made a choice. Now, we've raised you boys in the best way we know how, but in the end, all you can really do is make the best decision based on the circumstances God gives you. We're your coverin', and Solomon is ours. In the same way that you don't often understand what your Daddy and me want you to do, we don't always understand what Solomon wants us to do, but we do it because without direction, life is vanity. All we can hope and pray is that He's right." Momma wiped my face and pulled my hands down to my side. "And while you're here, that's your job, too."

I remained there and wiped my own tears away as Momma loosed herself and stood.

"You know better than to run that water," she said gently. "Don't let me catch you doin' it again." I nodded as she turned and made her way back toward the kitchen. The tone of her voice was that of someone who had spoken in vain and knew so. It wasn't until I had gotten fully dressed and looked at the clock on Aaron's dresser that I realized it was ten and the sun had yet to come up. When I turned around in shock, Momma was at the open door. "You slept all day," she said casually. "Daddy tried to rouse you, but you wouldn't move. Mamie thought you was dead for a spell." I gasped at the thought of Mamie kneeling over me in my sleep, enforcing another of her inept diagnoses.

"It's Christmas Eve?!" I said, stunned.

"We saved the last advent candle for you," Momma confirmed as she looked around the room once and turned off down the hall quietly.

What in hell had happened, I thought. Could it really be night? Could it have honestly been possible for me to have slept all through the day? As much as I had desired the entirety of the day to contemplate the events of the night, it seemed my body had finally taken emergency control and foregone my own ability to fight against exhaustions and fatigues both physical and emotional. My night's sleep following the rite of confessions had felt just like any normal slumber, but it was clear I had indeed skipped a full day of my life. It was Christmas Eve then, and Momma had invited me to do what only Aaron had in years past, but seemed only fitting for me to do in his absence; to light the center candle of the advent wreathe. It was a prestigious honor in our tiny quartet culture, and I wouldn't have dreamed of passing it up, even in a time so bleak.

It was typical of Daddy to let us into the den on such occasions. I reckoned he figured the advent tradition was important enough to take place within his sacred vestibule. It was seldom I had ever ventured inside the room when Daddy was actually present as well. He didn't seem his usual somber self in that moment, though; in fact, he almost seemed to smile in the glow of the lit candles, all nestled around the skirt of the advent wreathe. He held it low enough for me to reach. There was a reluctance in his spirit as a result of my disobedience to him the night previous, but Momma had convinced him to let me light the final candle anyhow. In the ancient tradition, the four candles surrounding the middle were lit during the four weeks leading up to Christmas, with the middle "Christ" candle lit on Christmas Eve. Momma had crafted the wreathe homemade from dried leaves and twiggery she had hot-glued together. It always smelled the same every year when she pulled it down from the hall closet; like the stale cinnamon scrolls she had woven inside, mixed with burned glue and oak leaves.

I was allowed to strike the match against the box, which I supposed was the grandest part. The swift and sulfurous fume stung my senses and turned my head. Daddy watched the tip of the wick and waited patiently for the flame. It was a special moment that caused me to forget that which was potentially in store, should a ritual be called in the night. We stared collectively at the five tiny fires as

Daddy raised them to the mantle and allowed them to burn free. Tears had escaped my eyes once more.

"...What's gonna happen tonight?" I asked generally and quiet, as a dark intuition seemed to seep back into my mind. It took a bravery in me that only could have been solidified in the fear that we were all in the company of a danger greater than the sum of both Daddy and Momma's wrath in response to my curiosities. Momma looked at Daddy. Daddy kept his eye on the flames and spoke.

"Nothin' at all," he said. "We're gonna stay put right here and observe the holiest night."

I supposed he meant to impart a kind of comfort in some strange way, but all else pointed to the fact that a climactic evening had finally come, and all that Daddy's deceptive comforts managed to do were induce me into panic.

"Is it something bad?" I asked, beginning to shake. "Are people gonna die? Us?" Daddy had heard enough. His attention upon the candles had broke on me and my worries, and Momma looked on both of us with unspoken concerns.

"Work's work, and dead's dead," he said authoritatively. "No matter how you use one to get to the other. God's gonna take us all one day. Either by famine or by sword, but in the meantime, we're gonna worship." Daddy had intended for it to stop there with his patented string of philosophical jargon, but certain circumstances had endowed me with a set of inviolable freedoms to continue in my line of questioning.

"I'm just afraid cause—"

"—Get your chores done and get ready for bed," he interrupted. "Not another word." There wasn't an ounce of concern left in him. All compassions had gone. All discernment had been abandoned. I turned my back to him and straightways left the room without another syllable uttered.

Never before had I been so sure I would leave. Being a Cotton meant you weren't always guaranteed the reassurance of a father, or the loving kindness of a mother. I supposed I had come to terms with those facts, but they never got any easier to swallow. I often imagined other boys my age and how they managed in their fears (especially in my part of the world). It was probably a safe bet to assume that many of them experienced the same kind of emotional disregard as I had, but also like me, none of them probably knew a difference. None of them had ever felt the full embrace or words of comfort from a vested guardian. I had stumbled headlong upon a juncture in life where I coveted the words of my father; that everything was going to be alright. And he had denied me that. He always had. If someone had asked me if I knew whether or not my Daddy and Momma loved me, why I would have said probably so. Then I would have made sure the two weren't listening for fear of being beat.

I reckoned it made it easier for me to go through with whatever I had planned, having Daddy and Momma act in such neglect. I could easily justify gathering what was most important to me and leaving all else behind, but I didn't want the fear of what approached to be my driving force. I would have much rather left on my own terms, with a decision in my heart and a course on my mind. Aaron hadn't left in a favorable manner, but it felt as if Daddy and Momma had oddly respected him for it. I wasn't sure if Daddy and Momma's respect was important to me, but I sure as hell wasn't going to be labeled by them as a deserter for the rest of time. I reckoned even a family as cold as mine could understand pure fear, so I assumed that was what I would be forced to go on.

I went outside to find Charles more rank than ever. I figured he would die of reeking despondency one day shortly after I was gone. It was evident I was the only thing that had kept him alive all those years. I briefly considered inviting him along, though I was certain he would survive longer on the farm than he would in my care on the road. I began to weigh the cost of leaving; what I would miss against what I would never think twice about. The truth was, most of the things that came to my mind were already long gone; my brother, Walter, my youth in innocence. I supposed there were aspects of Daddy and Momma that I would miss; certain soft corners of their hearts that I saw poke through in the lesser moments of life, but as sad as it was, it wasn't enough to keep me subscribed to their expectation of silent compliance, or to the tutelage of The Man in the Woods.

Something felt strange about that night, ripened, as if Christmas Eve had been it all along. It was god-awful cold too, and damp. My coverall sleeves were wet to the touch, but not from rain. There was a bitter fog on the air, which all but froze in place due to the cold. I pondered the idea of traveling alone down County Road 1 on such a night, and it made me wish the time for leaving had come sooner than later. I knew there was no hope of me making such an escape with Daddy and Momma still in the house, but it felt advantageous to go ahead with it once they had gone to bed. I would be found out in the morning, but I would rather have risked a beating than have been stuck another night on the farm where certain danger loomed.

I stayed with Charles for a while and then went inside to mill around the kitchen until I heard Daddy and Momma make off toward the bedroom in two distinct retreats (as to avoid the false appearance of intimacy). Once they were out of sight, I sneaked back into my room and packed a small, blue canvas duffel as conservatively as I could manage. In it went the Solomon Bible, a flashlight, a pair of blue jeans, two cotton work shirts, the rifle Sarah Obis had crafted me (which had somehow made it back to my room), The Harbinger's notes, three pairs of drawers, four pairs of socks, two smashed Moon Pie's I had smuggled home from Marlin's store and the survival issue of Boy's Life Magazine. When I finished, I went back out and stashed the duffel in the bed of an old horse trailer near the front gate. The next priority was to have words with Sarah Obis, but even I had come to terms with the idea that I was probably faced with leaving, even if I couldn't manage to get her to agreeably come along with me.

As I made my way around the side of the barn, I noticed Daddy had allowed the brothers and sisters to set up temporary dwellings in the stables. Warm lights flickered, gentle enough to match the quiet hum of voices from within. As I looked through a gap in the wall, I observed there were clothes hung here and there, as well as bits of bedding laid atop fresh shavings. It seemed the horses had been let out to pasture for the night (and I supposed the night previous). I didn't reckon I had ever considered a place as such to be suitable for the dwelling of nine individuals and their recovered possibles. I figured the floor of the house would have sheltered them more appropriately, but then I remembered the condition of the bunker (which was about the same before the great winds as it was after). I tried to guess which stall had become Sarah Obis' new home, but they all looked the same in the dark; like refugee camps forming a tiny city along a muddied river.

It looked to me as if Sarah Obis wasn't present with the rest, which straightways gave me hope. I reckoned it behooved me to hurry forth and steal away with her before she could rejoin the others, so I made haste along the side of the barn, keeping my eyes peeled for signs of the girl. With all optimism, I hoped I would be able to gather her up privately and be well away before night was too far settled. I mourned the inevitable loss of my parents and the brothers and sisters tearlessly, but there was nothing for the efforts of liberating them from the rack they were bound to. Whether they were mindlessly sold as slaves into the hands of The Prophet or knowingly subject to his violent and destructive whims, there existed no prospect of convincing them to leave Stagwerth's parish after having become so deeply entrenched in that life of servitude. I still had hopes for Sarah Obis, however.

It took me no time at all to notice the shadowed form before me making its way toward the swift darkness of the back pasture. The absence of the bunker fire seemed to dampen the probability that any life ever existed beyond the old barn at all. I crouched at the corner of the fence and allowed my eyes to adjust to the shapes around me. The light weren't the only thing missing with the fire. I longed to stand around its warmth on such a night. The wet cold seemed to ignore my skin and clothes and sink deep into my bone marrow where it pained me with insatiable chills. My nose ran and my eyes had begun to water and sting, despite the moisture in the air. I scanned the dark phantasm as it moved, hoping desperately it was Sarah Obis. I raised my throbbing fingers to shelter my ears the best I could from the gentle winds. The longer I kept my eyes free of tears and on the darkness, the easier it became to see.

I watched quietly as the figure dipped in and out of my vision and finally passed alongside the old barn, making its way in the direction of the trees. My eyes had adjusted suitably enough to tell, it was indeed Sarah Obis.

"Sarah!" I whispered with force. She didn't stop. "Sarah!" I said again, louder. There was no indication at all that she had heard me. Into the trees she went, disappearing as graceful as a ghost toward the Freedom Spring. What was she up to, I searched myself. Surely she knew a bath on such a night would have killed her dead. She would shatter apart at the first subtle movement beneath the frigid waters and would have likely had to crack through a crust of ice to do so.

The night was stiller than ever. The fog had settled all the way down from its place in the heavens to its final rest as a dripping wet sheen upon any and every surface the farm had to offer. The stars were out again for the first time in so long, and the moon had started to empty ever so much. As the glow and hum disappeared behind me, I felt a dense quiet settle in. Even the winds ceased for a time, and all that could be heard were the sounds of some distant patter of hooves and the gentle crunch of the footpath against my boots beneath me. The only movement was my warm breath crystalized upon the black backdrop of the night. It was Christmas Eve, and made all the more beautiful by that crisp, quiet cold.

There was a perversion of motive that took me over in that moment. I followed Sarah Obis, but not with exclusively wholesome intentions of speaking with her. I harbored an overwhelming urge to behold her again and again in whatever private way I could manage. I made my way by memory, apart from the path, to that misplaced and familiar white oak. It was through the trees about twenty yards. The spring was perhaps another ten beyond that. As I drew closer, I asked for God to give me favor with her, should he allow us to speak, and also that I might not tread loudly upon any leaves or twiggery (in case I wished to spy her before then). My hands touched near about every tree I passed. I supposed it was a tick. As I put more and more trees behind me, Sarah Obis' figure began to settle into focus. I looked down and immediately saw the ground surrounding the smooth trunk my hand had just encountered, and noticed it was covered in large, white flakes of bark.

She was standing there at the water's edge, but she had neither disrobed nor touched her feet to the spring, for which I was greatly relieved. She faced away from me. It was an aspect of her figure I had never quite seen before. She was formally less clothed in such a place. I readjusted, careful not to make even the smallest of sounds. It was then becoming evident to me that she aimed to meet someone there, which was why I had decided not to straightways approach her. I kept my eyes on her, all the while feeling more and more exposed beside the tree. At one point, I reckoned that she was perhaps there for me, and all that hiding and sneaking was for nought, but I supposed I was waiting for a sign. I thought perhaps she might speak my name, or maybe a dove would come and light on my shoulder to draw her attention upon me. Instead, I watched her as she changed postures and shook her hair a bit; a preparation for her undisclosed caller.

Then my heart seemed to fly forth from my chest and plunge into the depths of the spring. A tall, dark figure— male in persuasion and gait—had emerged from the path to the right of Sarah Obis. I wasted no time in concealing myself atop the tree. The climb was elementary to me, and I hardly realized I had made it until I was well seated in my regular accommodation. At first, I wondered if it might have been an attacker, perhaps someone from the town who had spied Sarah Obis and formulated less than favorable intentions for her. As I watched, however, I gained that the figure was not only known to her, but quite expected. The two stood facing one another in the frigid stillness. I couldn't hear a word uttered from either, but I reckoned they were talking up a storm by the looks of it.

The cold was blistering. I noticed it more after being removed from the unintelligible dialogue that was taking place before me. The trees broke most of the wind, but the little bit that did get through still managed to cut me in many painful ways and force all sound in the opposite direction. When I was finally able to suppress the way my body felt, I invested the whole of my attention on the two figures still conversing near the spring. They were both standing stone still as ever. I tried my damnedest to tell who the other of them was, and though it was clearly male, he didn't look quite like any of the brothers, which was what still had me a bit worried for Sarah Obis' safety. I supposed it could have been Silas, or maybe Mattie, but that line of thought got me questioning how two people (let alone one) could have gotten away from the barn so unnoticed. There were two more I had considered; one was The Prophet himself, but the frames just didn't quite match up. The other I had in mind didn't make much logical sense, and I didn't even want consider what it would have meant.

They stood for what seemed a witch's eon, unmoved alongside the spring. I partially wondered if they themselves had actually become stuck there, frozen at the joints and unable to move until their hearts had stopped altogether. Then suddenly, just as I had begun to believe they would never budge again, Sarah and the stranger moved closer to one another, barely even enough to notice. I marked that it was uncomfortable to watch, and I began to slowly believe I had come to witness more than just a casual meeting. I became angered. The spring, the trees, that place was nothing more than Sarah Obis' den of transgressions, and my self-appointed chamber seat was that tree. What I reckoned I would witness there in the moments to follow made me sour with regret for any of her seductress ways I had sampled and enjoyed there in times previous. It was liable to take the soul of me, but my eyes remained glued to that impending collision as it poised itself to undoubtedly take place before me.

With the way things were situated, all either of them needed to do was shift a horse's tail hair one way or the other, and I would know who was going to usher in the ruin of Sarah Obis in my mind forever. It was clear a consummation was about to take place, and I knew it was going to have far reaching effects on me for the rest of my days. Furthermore, it was apparent then that Sarah Obis wouldn't have accompanied me away. I didn't reckon there was any way I would have still invited her to either. She was dead inside me before I even knew it; before she had even done a thing, but it wasn't long after that.

It all seemed to happen together. The face of my betrayer came clean as Sarah moved in close to kiss him good (as good as she had always meant to), and he returned it with as much passion as he had always displayed when running from it. The fog from their lungs was locked between them, and their breaths turned too short to make definite plumes. It was still there, but occurred only on the inside. I wanted to hurt myself as bad as I had ever hurt anything before for being so stupid and reckless with my own heart. It was something I should have learned from Aaron before; to never admit to yourself that you want something. That way you are never disappointed when you don't get it. The proof of the infallibility of such an argument was standing before me, then, taking the one thing he never admitted to wanting. The one thing I had always felt safe claiming in my heart as my own. It was certainly the last brand of emotion I expected to encounter upon ever seeing Aaron Cotton again.

There wasn't a single voluntary action left in me. I drowned out the world and remained nothing more than a soul and eyes in my self-sufficient cocoon of a body. Then, in a moment I could only brand as a sign of my own ignorance, a flake of ice appeared on the sleeve of my coverall and woke me from that idle and true nightmare. I first thought a tear had froze against my face and peeled away. Only then did I realize it was something I could only claim as a symbol or an omen. Snow fell amongst the trees; cold ashen drops of snow like the tiniest of white birds, tired with flight and falling listlessly from heaven at different heights, but all in the same pace. I reckoned they could have been falling my whole life, and only then, on that night, at that very second had they finally come down to meet the warm earth of our farm where they should soon melt away and descend into the abyss below.

If any shred of me had survived that kiss, it was well on its way out when the two wandered to the foot of the very tree I had perched. The poetry of life was, at times, astounding to me. They still shared their own latent mixtures of fog and breath even as they laid down beneath me there. I clamped my hand to my mouth and tried not to even breathe, choking back a flood of shock-induced tears as my broken heart barely seemed to beat. I was imprisoned there behind the tightly closed lids of my eyes between bouts of two shared visions: one of partially disrobed and familiar bodies, the other of the trees around me at eye level where nothing else moved save for the falling white flakes. The snow meant more to me then than anything else. Those flakes, which I had never come close to seeing before; which I had hoped to see my entire life, had arrived in as lackluster a fashion as the Christ child upon a manger. Those long-coveted flakes, which then fell on the shivering bare skins of my brother and Sarah Obis and melted quick against their body heats into drops of cold water, meant that nothing was ever perfect, save for what was conceived in the mind.

Warm tears dropped from my face and landed cold on her breast, the same as the snow. Neither of them noticed. Steam rose from their bodies as they joined over and over in that bitter ritual. Sarah Obis whimpered a little at what looked to be painful and pleasureful all at once. Perhaps she reckoned Aaron would only want her then and never after, but I doubted it. Who knew how many times they had consummated before then. Other sounds that broke the night were more by way of satisfaction, and Aaron just kept working, like a machine that never quit. I tried as best I could to keep my eyes on the trees before me; on all that silence. It took everything in me to leave that bark alone and not go on picking as I usually did. The sounds were the worst. I couldn't shut out my ears in a place like that. In that moment, I would have given anything to be someplace else—the ritual ground for all I cared—any place but there. At last they came to the most intimate parts of the ritual, there was no doubt about it. The steam that rose from their bodies then was like a protective barrier, keeping away the cold, and they seemed to forget where they stood, in that frigid, white place.

I fought hard the impulse to take occasional glances in their direction, knowing only the further strife I would incur upon myself by doing so, but it became increasingly difficult not to. When finally I gave in, I was right startled at what I saw. In that instant, I could have sworn to see Sarah Obis turn her head skyward and lay her eyes upon me, like she had done before. Had she seen me in that tree while taking in my brother? Had she learned I was watching and yet still planned to go on in front of me? I started down a bitter and sorrowful road of thought. Perhaps she had orchestrated it that way all along. Maybe she had known I was coming and led me there to destroy me. She had picked that very tree, remembering it was where I sat. She wanted me to see it, not because I should like to, but because she desired to be watched in any and all sinful scenarios.

No. Her attention paid to me scarce even made it that far. I was the last concern upon her delicate mind. She looked into that tree and saw nothing but the black outline of my body against the mass of limbs and stars behind me. Maybe I was a shadow to her; a cloud. Perhaps I was a window in the tree, looking out into a void of stars in space. To her, I was nothing. She had never seen me at all.

When the ritual was over, the two bodies clothed themselves, as Eve had with Adam upon the realization of their nakedness and shame. In textbook fashion, Aaron departed without a word, and made off with haste toward the front of the farm. Sarah Obis went slowly in the opposite direction, still cleaning herself—like a wounded animal—as she went. I stayed still for some time, even after the two had long disappeared into the trees and beyond. I barely moved at all, save for involuntary breaths. I should have liked to remain there forever if I could, in the place where my soul had left me. My eyes had all but dried up, and I was spent in many more ways than just mental or emotional. My very purpose was torn from me and made to stand trial. Perhaps I had never been given a purpose at all. I was a dead shell; like the cicadas that had landed in that tree before me. Some part of me had flown away from there, fleshy and unprotected; some red-eyed, tiny terror had gone off and left my crisp exo-skins there, browned and hollow, latched tight to that barren limb.

It had been a half hour easy since I had left the house. Daddy and Momma would be livid if they found me out of bed, but I knew the chances were against it. I imagined Pastor Obis would be right cross as well, if he discovered what his daughter was sneaking away to do. I wasn't sure how Sarah Obis ever managed to evade her father's sight for more than a few stolen moments at a time, but she had yet to be caught as far as I was aware. I waited a good while, until I was sure she and Aaron had performed whatever delayed aversion methods they deemed necessary for not being seen or seen together. Then I climbed down from the tree and made for the house.

Before I even made it to the old barn, however, I was collared by a silent force from behind. I felt a hand gather around my mouth and another seize my chest and arms, wrenching me backward as I grunted in protest. I fell on top of my host and landed sideways in a bed of sour hay on the hard pallet floor of the overflow stores. Once I had wiggled myself into vain exhaustion and finally realized who my captor was, I was slowly released and allowed to regather my breath and composure. Aaron lay beside me, red-faced and breathing as heavy as me. We delayed another moment before my temper seized me, and I threw myself on top of him with fists full of hay and dirt. I had assaulted him three and four times over before he grabbed me by the shoulders in attempt to restrain me. I reached for his shirt collar and yanked him forth but solicited no response. Instead, he only lay there, holding onto me and keeping me from injuring him badly. His eyes were shut for the cloud of dust and hay I had stirred up.

For the first time, I was winning in a fight against my brother, but I felt not the least bit in control. Before long, my adrenaline failed me, and I collapsed on the ground beside him, choking on tears once again.

"...WHY DID YOU LEAVE?!" I shouted in between bouts of sobbing. Silence. "Why did you go..." I felt his attention paid upon me, like I had felt the night he watched me fake sleeping. He was disturbed by my condition, that much I could tell. Who wouldn't be, I thought. I was, after all, only a shade of my former self, corrupted and tortured by what my eyes had seen and what calamity my heart had known.

Every tear I wiped away seemed to create another muddied stripe across my face. Uncontrolled sounds came from my mouth, and every second we lay there in silence was another second I earned from Aaron's sympathies in the case for my sanity. He had to have gathered by then that I had seen him in the woods. He had watched me come out of the trees, after all. He might have meant to enact upon me some marriage of embarrassment and anger, but I had completely and unexpectedly disarmed him with my desperation. He had no idea what I had been through in the days since he had gone.

"Why are you still here?" he asked me, finally breaking the silence. I snorted once or twice and cleared my throat.

"I'm leaving," I said sharply. "Right now." As I tried to stand, Aaron took hold of my arm and stood beside me.

"Go to the path and wait for me," he commanded, but I wasn't taking orders from him or anyone else. I snatched myself away.

"I'm going away with Miles Beckins." A shocked expression tore across Aaron's face as he seized me again with both hands.

"No!" he near shouted. "You can't! You'll be an accessory!"

"A what?" I said, drying my face.

"The Harbinger's got himself a devilish chore to do before it's all over," he said. "He's your worst chance. You've gotta get clear of the farm!"

"I ain't got to do a damn thing you say!" I replied, yanking free again. The moonlight half shone on Aaron's face as he turned and peered briefly through a gap in the sheet tin on the side of our enclosure.

"Listen," he turned back. "I don't frankly care what you do, so long as it ain't a joyride with Miles Beckins tonight. He ain't what you think. He ain't your salvation. Not tonight."

"Well, I guess lots of people ain't what the seem then," I replied. Aaron stared at me silent. He knew what I meant.

"Look, I don't know what you seen out there—"

"—enough for a lifetime..." I said. Aaron stopped for a second and closed his eyes.

"...She weren't never goin' with you, Moses..." I looked back at him with my mouth closed, breathing normal again through my nose. It wasn't the truth behind the statement that upset me most. The reality of it was always plain to me, I just didn't care to admit it to myself. The bit that stung was the fact that Sarah Obis had spoken on my hopes with my brother. It disgusted me to my core; being conversed on like a child in another room.

I turned away and watched the night beyond the big open door of the storeroom. I could see the hole in the ground that housed the pump. All strewn around it were many shattered crates and crushed phials of water, lit liberally by the moon. Aaron came and stood beside me.

"Solomon made Mattie and Kenzie destroy 'em all," he explained. "The Prophet were right cross with The Samaritan." I looked back at Aaron over my shoulder.

"You know about Daddy then..." I said.

"I've always known," he replied. "Since Daddy first told us the story. It were Stagwerth what surprised me. Damn near shit myself when I first thought I had seen his ghost wandering the tree line one night. When I told Daddy and Momma, they tried to cover it, but I didn't stop my probin'. Like you. That were five years ago."

I turned to face my brother on that cold night as little gusts of wind broke against the storehouse in gentle rattles on its rusted metal outers.

"...Will The Prophet do murder?"

"...Yes, and Beckins will be his hand. I wish I could explain more, but there ain't no time." I contemplated all I knew and felt and weighed it against the confirmations Aaron seemed to make. And though I hated him then, he seemed to know in certainty what was coming, and I trusted that much.

"...What should I do?" I asked.

"Follow me."

Aaron led me in an unorthodox way, through the back paddock, where Dillon (the most vile of creatures on our farm) spent his evenings huffing and puffing and turning up clouds of dust. I was right frightened of the stallion, and seldom went near his dwelling. It was obviously a path familiar to Aaron, however, and his bravery shamed me into finding (or counterfeiting) my own. Next, we wove through piles of shit and shavings so big you could scarce see over them. It was a place I had only visited when accompanied by my brother. We had spied several animal conceptions there where Daddy had never knew our private curiosities. Last, we moved along the backside of the many overgrown horse trailers parked far out in front of the house on the opposite side of the red clay drive.

"Hang on a second," I said, backtracking to retrieve my go duffel from a door we had already passed.

"What's that?" Aaron asked.

"...My stuff," I replied defensively. Aaron bounced his brow once—almost impressed—and bent his body around the corner of the last trailer so as to spy upon the front gate.

"Shit."

"What is it?" I whispered.

"Shit. Shit," he repeated.

"What?!" I demanded again. Aaron bent back around and sat with his back to the trailer.

"They're here," he said simply.

"Who's here? Where?" My eyes grew wide. Aaron nodded in the direction of the gate. I straightways climbed over him and gathered view of a hundred or so firelights which set aglow a hundred more angered faces and farm tools. A strict terror seized me, the way one might experience such surprised fear upon accidentally discovering a nest of angered hornets. I drew back quick and looked Aaron in the face. He was calm, but worried.

"It's alright," he said. "It's alright. We known they were comin', I just didn't reckon it'd be this soon—"

"—You known they were coming?!"

"I tried to stop 'em!" he defended, "but they were hell bent on razin' the place! Them people been kept out too long." he paused. "...And they know who we're hidin'."

"How?!" I asked. Aaron hesitated, and I could tell he was regretful of something substantial.

"...I confirmed it at a town hall." Aaron closed his eyes and wristed his upper lip once. It was close to freezing out and he was sweating still. I stared at Aaron, waiting for him to make eye contact again. "I had to tell 'em. Marlin and some of the other folks got it in their heads that Daddy and Obis were hordin' food and stuffs here and shuttin' the whole town out."

"They are," I said matter-of-factly.

"Well, that's exactly my meanin'," Aaron replied. "They were comin' anyway, but shortly before I left their

325

last meetin', they'd resolved that the brothers and sisters were dabblin' in dark shit and bringin' all this down on everyone's heads. They blame Stagwerth and Daddy and Obis for the plague."

"But the plague's gone!" I announced.

"Gone?"

"Gone!" I repeated. "I counted this mornin'. I mean to say, yesterday mornin'. There ain't no crickets left! Look!" I lifted a tuft of hell grass with my hands and showed my brother the clean soil beneath. Aaron looked direct at me whilst tryin' to discern if it was true, and what to do with such information if so.

"Well, I don't reckon it matters much now," Aaron said. "Even if it is true..."

Just then, we heard a terrible racket, what had to be loud enough to wake the farm, if they weren't awoken already. It was first the sounds of rattled metal against metal, then accompanied by a series of cantankerous crashes, one after another. Aaron and I both looked out upon the gate to see great numbers of enraged townsfolk, full of wrath and ire, casting unified blows upon the gate like some kind of medieval siege tactic. They let forth mobbed shouts and primal roars of bloodlust that frightened me a great deal more than any threat of The Prophet. Our hearts then fell upon what our eyes beheld next. All along that ever-diminishing rail of fence that shared borders with County Road 1, which from time to time fell beneath many layers of trees and foliage and overgrowth, little lights began to spring up or make themselves known. Our land so often seemed infinite to me, black and everlasting even in the moonlight, but those tiny fires, which symbolized the realm of my family's influence, struck hard the boundary of my vision, and I could scarce hope to see beyond the fence or the road for the fires upon them.

"We have to go," Aaron said.

"How do you reckon we get past 'em?" I asked.

"Past 'em?" he shook his head. "Naw, that ain't happenin'." I felt the fear begin to overtake my sense of reason or self-guidance. "C'mon," Aaron said, standing to yank me up.

We made our way in the opposite direction, all the while listening to the sounds against the gate, which was likely to give at any moment. Aaron aimed to backtrack us through the manure piles and Dillon's paddock, but before we could reach the side yard of the barn, I heard a loud and crisp clack, like a gunshot, and a piece of earth exploded at my feet. I looked to the Sentinel tower, but hardly saw a thing before hearing another, and another. Before I knew it, Aaron and I were zigzagging in utter confusion and shielding our eyes from loosed dirt and flying hell grass. My vision was close to nothing until we made it to the stilts of The Sentinel. Aaron had gotten there first and was breathing heavy as he leaned against a pole and cocked his head to see up the ladder. Shots continued to ring out, but none further arrived at our feet.

The gate was too far to see from the ground, but one could reckon that if it was Bill or Silas perched with the rifle, bodies were being laid up quick. Aaron insisted we keep moving, so we did. The manure heaps were darker than the yard (which was illuminated by the great sword of light), so it felt a good bit safer being hidden from The Sentinel's vantage. I thought of the sword's symbolic nature as we wove through the pies. Until that night, I had reckoned it was that single protective omen that had barred

327

any lurker from trespassing successfully. At any moment though, I feared the gate would collapse and the sword of light would come under foot of nearly every living and angered soul in Indian River. I imagined its likeness on the ground being stamped out in shadow, and its blessing, if for only a moment, casting itself upon the heads of those seeking to destroy us. Perhaps it was never there to protect, but only to point in the direction from where our reckoning would come.

Dillon's paddock wasn't half as frightful as the prospect of being burned alive or gored by rusted metal objects. I followed Aaron through the planks of the fence, took nine running steps through the soft sand and was once again flung to the ground on my stomach.

"Stay still," Aaron whispered. I gathered we were nearly spotted by something, and then I confirmed it visually upon seeing Daddy and Momma moving swiftly alongside the old barn in the direction of the back pasture. Looking ahead to the corner, I noticed several other shapes and figures fleeing in the same way. I drew Aaron's attention to them and he verified. "They're goin' to the woods."

"You think they've abandoned the house and barn?" I asked.

"House and barn's already gone," Aaron replied. "Look," he gestured toward the front of the farm with less disruption of spirit than I would have hoped from him. There was a great plume of black smoke rising from where the house sat below the shrub line and adjacent structures. The whole area was aglow with orange and red tones that moved and darkened wildly. The stars were blotted straight out of one half of the night sky, and through the barn, we saw swift-moving silhouettes and flames sent hurled and spinning through the air. "You gotta keep movin'," Aaron spoke solemnly.

"Me? What about you?" I asked in a panic.

"What about me?" he said. "I won't be caught dead in them woods with that psychopath."

"You think I wanna be?!" I replied. "I'm goin' with you!"

"No you're not," he said with an authority he had lost long ago but suddenly regained. "If I don't try and talk these people down, the brothers and sisters are all dead, and there's no way I can do that with you at my side. They'd kill you on the spot."

I saw the logic in Aaron's argument for once in my life.

"...Where do you suggest I go then?" I asked. Aaron stood low and then pulled me up beside him.

"Take the straight path into the woods," he said. "With any luck, you'll pass by the others unseen. And take this." Aaron grabbed the back of my hand and produced from his pocket a phial of that mysterious water. As he closed my fingers around the glass vessel, we stopped together and heard the faint and familiar sound of an engine on the air. The Harbinger had taken flight and was en route to rain doom upon the wretches of Indian River. "Go," he said.

"Aaron...where does it lead?" I asked. "The straight path." I could tell he meant to rush me, but a brief patience came over him then as he attempted to oblige.

"For a while, nowhere. And then..." he stalled there for a minute. I waited for him to finish, with my hand still slightly extended, holding tight to the phial. "...Well, I'll meet you there," he concluded. And with that, he turned and made away in the direction of the barn, and certain confrontation. Before he had gone too far, he turned and cast one final look upon me. I stood there unmoved in his gaze. Even from that short distance away, I thought I must have looked like some veiled and strange creature to him in all that smoke and darkness. A second later, he disappeared into the red night, and I reckoned that was the last time I would ever see Aaron Cotton.

I lingered there another fifteen seconds and watched as a great host of torches marched upon the front pasture toward our farm in loose ranks before I finally turned to make my way through the other side of the paddock. When I had done so, however, I was met by none other than the full on and fast approach of that devilish steed with fire in his eyes. There was nothing for it but to run madly from his path. Had I remained standing there in his way, he would have undoubtedly trampled me into the dust and I would have been lost forever underfoot, eventually engulfed in flame. You couldn't rightly tell in the smoke and dark red pitch of the night, but Dillon was a large breed, tan in color and faster than hell. He had nearly overtaken me just before I dove headlong through the middle planks at the back of the paddock. Well, he had gone and curved away just in time to realize I wasn't brandishing food or anything of further interest, but it didn't change the fact in my heart that I felt he had aimed to kill me dead.

By then, the townsfolk were flooding through the barn and yards in every which way, setting blaze to near about anything they laid eyes upon. There were horrible shouts and loud crashes hailing from all directions, and I scarce knew in which way was safest to move. I reckoned it hardly mattered, in all that chaos, whether I hid amongst the outskirts of the back pasture or blazed right down the center, in-step with the brothers and sisters until I found it opportune to split away in the darkness unseen, but it didn't matter none. By the time I had climbed through the back pins and into the pasture, the rest of everyone had already disappeared down the hillocks and were nowhere to be seen.

I took note of an opportunity to make a dead break across the pasture and seized it, marking that I had not run at such a speed and freedom in a good while. It felt prolific to cover so much ground; not only as a means of evasion, but also as a symbol of recovered progress; something my lifestyle had opposed for so long. It seemed every part of me had become attuned to slow revelation, likened to a baby's steps. A full on run was exactly what I needed, and in no time, I reached the entrance to the straight path with my duffel in tow. The absence of life or surfaces upon it created a void where moon or starlight might have gathered and reflected or given reference to the length of the trail, but instead left it dark and vacant and fully unsearchable, save for the strict edges of its black gulf.

There was a meager collective of things I feared more than the straight path into the woods or what I had dreamt of it in the night, but fortunately enough for me, those things included The Prophet's tongue and a brutal death. Both of which were rounding the corners of my near future if I chose not to embark upon the path my mother had warned me against for the better part of my life. I turned and saw the torchlights hovering about the top of the hillocks in great numbers—hundreds even—and delayed no longer. My fear of that place was turned straightways into a swift comfort as I seemed to feel the very tangibility of my bodily form disappear from sight and disintegrate into oblivion.

Though my body was beyond the vision of any other, and my fate felt somewhat more favorably assured, I could still hear the roars and deep moans of war upon the pasture, as I had the night in which I first audibly witnessed The Prophet's approach. The sounds spurred me on further, and the fear stayed faraway, harbored in my unquenched longing to be free of that place and the threats inherent therein. Soon enough, I was awash in pure darkness, save for a strip of starry night above my head and the bright red glow of siegewerk at my rear. To my left I could hear the clear but distant sounds of many hurried steps upon the woodland floor. Sticks broke and pine leaves crunched underfoot, but there was no accompanied glow of torchlight amidst the ranks of trees, so I assumed it was the brothers and sisters in full retreat from the mob upon the hill.

Our farm was fully and undoubtedly alight with maddened red flames by then. If I ever saw it again, I thought, I was sure it would be as nothing but black and smoldering char, like the treetops above me. I might have forgotten the condition of the woods, had it not been for the properties I could detect. The smell of burnt wilderness was still thick amongst the trees, but I questioned how far the damage really went. I had never gotten the chance to ask Aaron if it was him who set the woods on fire, but I supposed it was likely he would have benefited from trying to off The Prophet and warn us to leave with a singular event. It had done no good, however. In the face of mortal danger, the brothers and sisters, my father and mother, had only one place to go; one guide from whom to seek refuge.

I halted suddenly and slid a short ways along that blanket of pine straws until I could steady myself. I had heard a sound in the trees alongside me that was nearer than any other. I looked back and saw nothing. The torchlights had receded toward the barn, where the townsfolk must have assumed they had cornered us into those flaming pyres and killed us with ease. Into the woods then I peered, in vain, as I was almost certain the thing I had spied had instead spied me first. The next break in the silence was a high-pitched snap that had indeed occurred under pressure. There was a life standing still in the woods before me. I was straightways brought back to my dream, and I shook at the thought of The Prophet appearing with that devilish wheeze. I had no blade of deliverance with me then, however, and I was sure of my fate without some line of defense.

In the silence, a voice called out to me in a volumous and strained whisper.

"Moses!" I couldn't tell from whom the call had come. The tone of the voice had veiled its true identity. I stayed still, hoping that whoever it was had long lost reference to my location. "Moses!" it called out again. I felt it confirmed deep in my chest that I ought to run, but curiosity stayed me. Soon enough, I heard the immodest crunch of footsteps from out of the woods, and I saw the shape of an enemy; not the one I had feared most, but one whose intentions I knew by heart.

"No!" I yelled as I turned and made quick work of the path in the opposite direction. No sooner had I made it three steps, however, than I felt the swift and dull pain of a blunt object visited upon my skull. I then fell limply into the arms of a second captor as I was cradled to the needled floor where I slipped into unconsciousness.

When I came around, or at least started to, it felt as if several days or weeks of my life had passed me by, and there was the worst discomfort pulsing through the synapses of my brain and every diminutive cavity in my skull. My head throbbed along with the intense beating of my heart, as if they were one in the same. Someone was carrying me and moving at a soft and slow pace (by the likes of whose monstrous breast and heavy breath, I assumed to be Mamie). I feared to open my eyes, so I instead tried to assess my surroundings based on my senses secondary to vision. We were moving casually through an untamed landscape; turning past this tree and that, and ducking low frequently. All around was the soft crunch of pine straws underfoot, accompanied by the occasional snap of a twig, but no one spoke. It was more than evident we were with a company of others.

The smell was, for the most part, the same; burned up woodlands and undergrowth, but it had faded significantly. The weather was still bitter cold and right damp, and I felt the confidence of their steps as I was carried deeper and deeper into the woods. We had escaped pursuit and were headed somewhere known, but not to me.

"Mamie," I heard Momma's voice in a whisper clear, quiet as she could bare. We seemed to slow a bit more. "Where'd you find him?" she asked.

"Wanderin' up the easement," Mamie replied. "He tried to run, but hit his head on a tree," She added in a whisper. "Where's Dottie?" Silence came from next to Mamie as Momma stalled.

"...She's safe." She finally said. I felt Mamie turn to Momma, clearly waiting for more.

"Where is she, Maya?" She almost demanded. I felt Mamie stop and reach out for Momma's sleeve. The sounds of the others seemed to fade away into the distance as I continued to feign unconsciousness in the midst of the encounter. "Where is she?" She asked again, even more intently. Momma exhaled once and finally relinquished.

"We put her with the pump." Mamie gasped. "She should be safe there," Momma added.

"In the hole, Maya?!"

"—Oh, you know good and damn well she weren't gonna make it with us!" Momma snapped. "The woman can barely stand from a table, much less flee the farm with fire-wielding townsfolk on her heels!" Mamie was silent. She had overstepped her first allegiance, and it seemed she remembered a time when she would have trusted any and every decision Momma made for the good of the brothers and sisters.

I felt an urgency building as we remained there another moment. At that point, I had become right desperate to open my eyes and began taking cautious glances through the brush of my lashes to gather what intel I could, but it was too dark under the woodland canopy to see anything of note.

I then felt their attentions draw away from one another, and we were soon off again in the former direction. Mamie had given up trying to mitigate the untamed wilderness. Once or twice I felt the keen sting of a thorn braid or splintered branch tread across my face or hand and take with it what felt like ribbons of flesh, leaving cool streaks exposed where I was sure I had lost all my blood. We went on like that for another five or ten minutes until I detected that we had rejoined with the rest of our company and halted quietly in the cold night. We had arrived.

There were calm breaths drawn and whispers exchanged. I dared not try my luck and open my eyes again. It was evident I was surrounded by curious eyes.

"Solomon told us to wait here," I heard Pastor Obis' hushed voice come into range.

"Does he mean for us to cross it in this cold?" asked Mattie with more concern than I had ever heard from him.

"There's nothing beyond the creek..." Daddy answered somberly.

"...What about the Mennonite place, downways?" said Bill. Silence fell across the night. Not even a breath was taken. No one liked the idea of seeking refuge from a murderer like William Justice. The man's title had come from a long tradition of gossip about townsfolk going missing after coming too near his farm. The assumption (which had become perceived truth) was that William had abducted them; killing the men and keeping the women as wives. It was complete hearsay, but none doubted it.

"We can't just stay here," added Silas.

"ARE WE PURSUED?!" Daddy shouted angrily. A collective gasp rose through the trees. Even my eyes opened briefly. "ARE WE?!" Silence fell again as the question was contemplated. Daddy's point was proven in the stillness. "...He'll be here soon" he concluded, attempting to diffuse the tension of revelation that had befallen those gathered there. And with that, the improvised and pseudo-democratic quorum had been adjourned; its members broken apart in quiet defeat.

I was lying then on a soft bit of ground, what seemed to be a bed of compounded soils between the roots of a great, old stream-fed tree. If I listened through the whispers and shuffling of feet, I could hear the gentle sounds of the water, bubbling past small obstacles in the current; rocks, fallen limbs and such. I wanted desperately to open my eyes and witness the creek, given that none of us ever had, save for maybe Daddy. I reasoned with myself that it had come time to feign my awakening and plot my escape as soon as I could manage one.

As I sat up, I felt the almost tangible attentions of the brothers and sisters gravitate towards me and land upon my face. My head truly was pounding, which gave me some bit of dramatic integrity as I opened my eyes and nursed my skull in truth.

"Maya," Daddy said as quick as he had seen me. I could tell he was more keen on Momma coming to my aid than he was of Mamie. Thankfully, my captor hadn't been close enough to realize I had awoken before Momma had seen.

"You alright?" She asked, rubbing my head in the most painful way possible. "You knocked yourself clean out."

"I were tryin' to find you," I lied.

"Then why'd you run from Mamie, son?"

"...I didn't know who she were," I said. "Thought she might've been a townsman." The truth was, Momma knew good and damn well why I would run from Mamie. She had been there when I witnessed the woman squeeze the breath and life from Walter on my very own bed, but what would our little charade of a family have been without keeping up appearances of ignorance.

"Stay here," she said. "I'll fetch you some water." I nodded and continued to probe the contours of that goose egg upon my skull with the tips of my fingers. It was a lucky thing she hadn't seen or mentioned my duffel, which I was then certain I had lost during the struggle between the tree and my captor on the straight path. Momma might have easily linked it with my motive to leave.

I took inventory of everyone at the creek's edge, all the while browsing the scene for my missing duffel. All were accounted for, even Mr. Langford, who was standing ever close to Sarah Obis, doing his best to comfort her, no doubt. Sad enough for both of us, he had been beaten out of the game by Aaron as well, only he didn't know it yet. Beyond the brothers and sisters, I saw the darkened east bank of the creek, whose many turns and bends I had traced with my finger more than once across wilted maps and old cartographer's records of Indian River which I had found in Daddy's dust-covered office drawers. Its shape was confused, for the most part, moving every which direction at least ten or twenty times before ultimately making its way south from the modest body of moving mud water that was our town's namesake, then to Vera Lake and beyond to the Gulf. The only part of it I could see, however, was the moonlit ripples on its onyx black and narrow passage that wove before me through the broad pines and cyprus knees which bent gracefully into the cold shallows below.

The expressions of many amongst the party were of muted concern. None wished to doubt the arrival of The Prophet, but it was the coldest of nights and none of us were certain we would ever reclaim the farm. There was something else there that night, however; some other awareness I wasn't privy to. The brothers and sisters expected something I didn't, and it bothered me more than any lack of collective knowledge ever had. I peered up into the burned and blackened boughs of the tree tops, in search of something, but all my thoughts found were visions of that flesh-eating rabble upon our farm, satiated in their assumptions that we had been burned alive. It didn't much change the urgency of the situation. If The Prophet weren't

to have shown in the following couple of hours, we might
have been helpless for sure in that cold and starved place,
and we would have all wondered from the grave why we
didn't take our chances with William and the Mennonites.

Then, as if on call from my thoughts, a light seemed
to arise from the bank near our side of the creek which
marked the stream's width—only fifteen or twenty yards
across. There on the water's edge, The Prophet appeared, finally, in a glowing white vestment, holding high a kerosene
lantern and faced away from us. His slightly convex and
sagged features became straightways intensified beneath
the light of the flame which danced fiendishly across his
face of patient vacancy. He was a morbid sight there upon
the shoreline; his face hidden away. Perhaps the townsfolk would have mercy on me—I thought—a young boy
of innocence. I could have gone back, rather than follow
the man, whose overwhelming presence had been renewed
afresh in my mind, but I then remembered my original sin;
the one that had gotten us into the whole predicament to
begin with. Though Aaron and I shared the iniquity of the
mole crickets, It would have been me, alone, certain to
receive the full chastisement for our cooperative crime had
I abandoned my family there and retreated to the captivity
of the townsfolk.

As The Prophet remained there, unmoved, I began
to wonder what his plan was. It was more silent than ever.
Even the imagined sounds of angered shouts and unified
coos of bloodlust, which struck chords of fear in our frozen
bones, were too far away to truly hear. We were completely and utterly alone in that cold, blue night. The still fog
upon the water's surface and about the thick tree trunks was
testament to our solitude, and that frightened me a great

deal. The time had come. We looked to The Prophet, and for a moment, felt as if he meant to test our trust in him by remaining still and facing away, but when Momma lifted me hastily to my feet, and we all shoved to the creek's edge, he seemed to move on the gravity of our circumstance.

It was the single most haunted moment of my life, when The Prophet stepped out onto the waters. One that occurred so intimately; so utterly private in the visions of our minds, that we scarce believed we had seen it at all. We looked to each other in shameless disbelief, fully aware that he felt our doubt even as he walked. There were none among us who thought another had witnessed the same. We each looked onward, the way children might have in plain view of something magnificent and puzzled unfolding before their very eyes for the first time. The silence was altogether holy and irreverent. We had openly turned our attention from God, and settled it there upon the misty, blue and moonlit creek where a quiet miracle occurred in our midst. Our mouths remained open, as did our hearts and minds, like thirsty and near-dead travelers whose only function or chore was to drink and drink. We swallowed heartily with our eyes, the visions of Solomon Stagwerth upon the creek, as he tread atop the waters, his feet breaking the gentle currents in twain. Then, a little less than halfway out, he stopped and stood statuesque amidst the black and moonlit flow.

Many of the brothers and sisters had begun to weep without comprehension, for their souls could not grasp or ascertain an understanding of what they had seen there, and their hearts knew no reaction to such things. It was as if they had seen the face of God, but lacked the sanctified eyes required to look upon it properly. We forgot about the life we left behind and watched only that which unfolded before us. I hated him even more for it in my heart, but it wasn't easy to rebuke a man who seemed to have so much of God on his side. After all, would the Lord bless so plainly the career of one who harbored only self-interest or self-worship, I pondered. Or was he just another demon, capable of great and mighty wonders to be beheld by many?

It was then that he beckoned the first of us out onto the water to stand beside him.

He motioned with one hand extended and the other still clasped to the lantern high above, without as much as a glance. Our attentions turned to Peter Langford, who was closest to the water. Surprisingly, he moved without hesitation; faster than any of us might have. He had learned quick not to leave The Prophet in wait. Reality struck our modest congregation. I wasn't quite sure how or in what manner we had expected The Prophet to proceed with us once he arrived, but an exercise in radical and supernatural faith seemed appropriate for the man. The most frightening part then wasn't the risk of freezing to death or drowning in the creek, but the prospect of following in The Prophet's footsteps and somehow managing to successfully deny hard and fast laws of nature and creation, and with Him, walk upon the waters.

Peter's first steps were wet ones, as many or most had expected, but as each step sunk lower into the muddy bed, The Prophet's impatience became straightways palpable under the ghastly white light of his lantern, which was reflected beautifully and full of motion upon the surface of the creek, rendering him twice there in our midst. His rippled likeness was just as formidable as his true self. Peter was thigh deep by then and lacked any promise of rising above the surface. He struggled visibly against the depths the nearer he came to the middle of the creek. Mattie and Kenzie moved to set themselves upon Mr. Langford and bring him back. They were met with restraint, however, from whom I quickly assumed to be Daddy and Pastor Obis, but saw instead to be Bill and Pastor Obis. It was then that I witnessed the acceptance of the situation as it washed over the brothers and sisters like a wave. It was what they had been bred for; that moment, there, and not a single additional muscle was moved in protest following. I realized The Prophet's impatience wasn't due to a lack of faith on the part of the short man, as I previously thought, but rather on his lack of calm and quiet submission to the tides.

The Prophet's shoulders rose and fell calmly. It was as if he had desired that the crossing be utterly silent and without trial. He never even expected any of us to rise above the waters as he had. Then, a powerful rush of wind filled the space unexpectedly, and a great and forceful clap of thunder boomed from The Prophet's chest. It was accompanied by a weight so strong, our knees buckled beneath it and we were pressed to the cold earthen floor. "BE BAPTIZED, MY SON! BURIED AND REBORN TO WHERE THESE WICKED ONES CANNOT FOLLOW!" Mr. Langford fell deep beneath the weight. His chest was almost fully covered then, and there was no hope of him rising again. I felt a great dread pour over me, somewhat opposite from what I had seen upon the others there. It was a sort of enforced trust that I came to witness in their eyes; a dead stare. The Prophet seemed so confident in his words; in his deliverance. It was evident the brothers and sisters were bought by him. I looked to Daddy and Momma to see if they too were willingly readying their lungs to be drowned, but I was unable to spot them amongst the gathered ball of hungered spectators. I watched as the short man worked in vain desperation to push himself up, if only for breath. His hands and legs churned and chomped up great geysers of futility, and I feared more for his reputation in The Prophet's eyes than I did for his fate.

"DO NOT STRUGGLE, PETER! Today, you will join me in my house..." the great voice trailed away, as it did sometimes. The eeriness of which never failed to shake me.

The short man's arms flailed about helplessly as every path in life seemed to culminate there and converge upon us, pushing us further toward the water. I looked upon Peter Langford's face as it bobbed between the cold air above and the even colder depths below. The expression thereon was of such heartbroken sadness and misguided abandonment that I almost felt he would die of pure sorrow before asphyxiation. It was the face of a man who knew he had misplaced his faith; a man who had lived twice, only to die and die. Those last few seconds seemed to pass ever slow, and I felt my turn would come sooner than I would rightly be able to prepare myself for the eternity to follow. The brothers and sisters waited savagely for the current to sweep over the top of Mr. Langford's head and allow him to emerge some place unseen, their feet braced in ready-stances, eager to leap headlong into the frozen flow and please The Prophet, as they had prepared to do their entire lives.

Despite what I perhaps thought, there was no moment of grief or mourning that occurred once the short man had taken his last mortal breath and disappeared, only the quick shuffle of feet as the brothers and sisters maneuvered themselves into a handsome single-file, so ready to greet death. I watched Stagwerth as he patiently beheld the last remnants of bubbling life rise to the surface from Peter Langford's watery grave. He shook his head with such deep-seated shame and disgust that it seemed he could scarce bring Himself to look upon the spot at all. The short man had left the world in a tumult of struggle and doubt; the way some children are birthed in such garish violence, and that disgusted Him.

"O ye of little faith..." he uttered at a normal tone as he seemed to recede down into the water and take his final pulpit.

It was then, as I had almost accepted The Prophet's victory and what was to take place there in the great and willful genocide of my family, that I felt myself yanked backwards and dragged along for some short distance to the tree where I had previously lain. I was sure I had been seized by some citizen who had broken away from the enraged mob and ventured bravely into the deep woods, but in the darkness, I could make out only the faces of Daddy and Momma, crouched low in a shared shadow.

"You've gotta go, Moses!" Daddy said.

"What about you?!" I questioned.

"Don't worry about us," Momma replied as she stood me up, brushed me off and fitted me with my long-lost duffel. "We're subscribed to different fates." I listened with shock. "The Lord's got a separate path for you."

"Come with me, please!" I protested. Daddy grabbed both my shoulders in both his bold hands and spoke.

"Moses, be strong now."

"It ain't your time to pass!" I sobbed. Daddy steadied me, and I paused in that moment of weak and childish abandonment.

"Work's work. And dead's dead," he whispered. "No matter how you use one to get to the other. We all pass at some time, son."

I made the mistake of looking shortly in the direction of the creek where a horrific scene had then begun to unfold.

"Don't look there," Daddy commanded, and I knew why he had said it. Suicide wasn't a sight easily comprehended by human eyes. I believed in Heaven and Hell, I just hadn't previously been of the belief that there were methods beyond war allowed for choosing when to arrive at one over the other. It was always a risky business in my understanding, taking one's own life, but above all my perceived horror surrounding it, there seemed to be a warm and romantic safety in The Prophet's assuredness of what took place beneath the waters, and a great part of me did crave it, in the pit of my heart, if only for fear of what a lifetime of solitude might have had in store.

I asked myself briefly why it mattered to me so much that my fate match that of Daddy and Momma. After all, they were as good as dead at the end of my own planned scenario, given that I would more than likely never see them again anyhow. I had also just recently stood upon the word from the gospels that said, "For this cause shall a man leave his father and mother, and cleave to his wife." That was also when I had expected Sarah Obis to pledge herself to me and not to my brother, Aaron. I suddenly thought of Sarah and felt an overwhelming urgency to look upon her and inform my memory of her passing, but Momma rebuked me with a familiar violence of flesh upon flesh.

"On your way," she said. "Into the creek. Get your legs and swim for the Mennonites'. They'll take care—"

"—He'll murder me!" I protested, given our strict, lifelong prejudice of the folk, but Daddy cupped my mouth with his rough palm.

"You'll do what William says," he commanded. "Trust him like you trust me." The statement didn't speak much to the man's integrity, if I was to measure his honesty against Daddy's.

"Come with me! Please!" I implored them both.

"We can't," Daddy said coldly. "Now, shut up about it."

"You've got your own figuring to do," Momma added. Daddy looked at her as if I was still at a place of immaturity or inconvenience for such details. As if the end of my entire world still wasn't suit enough for the liberties of explanation.

The quiet night took over. No further words were spoken. I had endured a divorce of sorts there; one that I was both relieved and displeased by. As I backed away, I saw Daddy and Momma turn their faces and depart that shared shadow, leaving a measure of space between their bodies where I viewed the ever diminished and quiet march of souls into the ripples of the creek. They resembled nothing more than a bushel of reeds there, all progressively ranked, protruding as silhouettes from the silvery plane. Down and down they went, one by one, without hesitation or struggle or sound, as if simply descending a staircase. The least amongst them was what I assumed to be the top of Sarah Obis' head, neat and still. The water swallowed her up as I had seen it do again and again, only then, there would be no return to the surface with a great gasps in her lungs or cold shivers upon her naked form. I watched the gentle circle enclose over the crown of her head, culminating in one humble peak and drip, accompanied by a single round ripple upon the surface; a fitting symbol of grace and beauty lamented, as it then washed away in the placid flow. And that was the end of her.

I turned from that place with tears welled and overflowing like brackish streams upon the vast flood plane of my face; a cold, wet, red, saturated thing. It was then when I began to run inexplicably. There was an urgency in my heart like none I had ever known before, and all I could manage to do was keep a narrow path with the creek to my side. Whatever fear existed in my heart was straightways washed over with necessity. There was an inherent and instinctual need to flee from something I had forgotten. My duffel bounced rhythmically about the underside of my arm. My movements were loud and unapologetic as I fought the untamed brush and made my way north, savagely.

I thought it was my imagination at first when I heard the plane engine buzz loudly overhead; something having to do with the feeling that had come over me, but it was louder and more clear than I had ever heard. When I looked up, I saw the partial red belly of that familiar craft pass low overhead, carrying what looked to be a great vessel filled with an apocalyptic and volatile solution that sloshed wildly inside its translucent innards. If only it would pass by, I thought. I prayed, and for a moment, it seemed as if it might, but before my eyes could settle and find the path once more, the winged beast let forth a demonic, urinary spew of malignant design, followed by a delayed, reptilian hiss which fell upon my ears painfully.

As I ducked away and quickened my pace, pulling the neck of my coveralls and undershirt up over my nose and mouth, I began to notice the area around me evolve to a darker shade. At first I assumed the great cloud of death above my head had blotted out the light of the moon and stars, but soon I realized I had passed beyond the borders of that ruined landscape and—by the Lord's good graces—had moved into the protection of the untouched, verdant pine canopy. I knew the dense foliage could only for a short while manage to stall the toxic mists which then had begun to fall slowly to the forest floor, but I hoped it would be long enough for me to manage an escape from its pernicious reach. I hoped William's place hadn't been hit yet.

It was then that I heard it; not the harsh and high pitched tones of the plane engine or the fiendish hiss of the liquid release valve, but rather, a sound far worse betrayed. Throughout my childhood, the soft and volumous roar of rain had brought with it a hope of life and restoration (especially in times recent to then). It had even meant deliverance in a season when we would have given anything to have the floodgates of heaven break wide (as they had in my dreams) and wash away the plague that had crippled us so callously. The rain I heard then, however, was accompanied by the return of raw fear; matched finally with the feeling that had set my feet running in the first place. The noise was unmatched and uncontainable, rising higher and higher without end; a quadrillion tiny beads of moisture released as a unified horde of weightless terrors, visited upon the tree tops in a steady fall.

I ran with renewed haste, feeling myself come closer to the creek's edge. I could tell because the woodland was thicker there and more densely untamed. If my memory of Daddy's maps served me proper, I knew I wouldn't have to cross in order to reach William's farm, which suited me just as well, considering I would probably be unconscious before I could get myself dry in a barn or something comparable. Hypothermia was never something I expected to encounter whilst living in the hot, hot Gulf South, and I wasn't in favor of trying it on then.

When first I started to cough, I didn't attribute it to the poisons. It was, in fact, the cold that I thought had overtaken me, but when each breath seemed to further coat my lungs in successive layers of abstract weightiness, I knew something was amiss. The taste was, at first, sugary upon my tongue and nostrils, but soon changed to a bitter, lingered note, like ivory soap. It wasn't long before I was seized by choking spells and moved to buckled postures whilst still running in the direction of the Mennonite place.

All I could seem to gather from memory was that the creek had run along the rear of William's property, but I wasn't able to recall how many bends it took before finally arriving there. As the poisons kept their steady course of penetration into my essential members, I observed the creek, in all its reserved beauty, dip away for moments on end and then return to my side like a faithful friend. Countless times it rose and fell away, gracefully matched to the ever slowing beat of my heart. I could almost hear the audible pounding in my chest. My body was giving out, and I feared the beating I would get from Momma if I saw her in heaven or hell too soon for her liking.

Then, as I had almost come to a complete and utter stop, nearly curled twice upon myself, I cradled my own stomach and wretched loudly before emptying myself upon the straw floor. When at last I looked up, through bloodied eyes, I saw the white peaks of William's silos through the tops of the trees. In the distance, off toward Indian

River, I heard the faint hum of The Harbinger's plane and perhaps the collective moans and wails of a thousand or more townsfolk (but I might have imagined it). It was that sound, and the focal point of those silos that spurred me on to continue taking steps.

I wasn't entirely sure how I came to pass through those remaining ranks of trees to stand amongst the open air, breathing what seemed to be clean breaths. To say I remembered the final stretches of the journey would have only been half right. It seemed I had slipped in and out of competency during that last hundred yards or so, and I would be lying if I said I didn't suspect angels had carried me onward to the outskirts of the Mennonite compound. Though the air seemed pure, I knew it was only a diluted charade. I was still consuming the noxious material, only I couldn't feel it as dynamically. I reckoned any minute then I would pass out and never wake.

I took quick stock of the sights around me. It was true that every last one of William's out buildings were white-washed and pristine. It was also true that the Mennonites seemed to live in a completely self-sustained environment; not unlike our own, but still a great deal more tuned and cared for. There were four silos altogether, which I reckoned were for the storage of harvested milks (we had known from before that William was a cattleman, but I had only speculated it wasn't meat he was raising them for). Beyond the silos (which were closest to me) was the barn and corrals, followed by a simple two-story, white-bricked house. Off in the westernmost corner was a standalone pond, almost fully covered in lily pads and cattails and surrounded by our own woods. I surveyed the area only momentarily and wondered mildly if the well-manicured impression of the place, along with its whitewashed glow perhaps implied that I had come upon the outer streets of heaven instead, and I had indeed passed on. I was soon sadly disproven of such a theory upon being reminded of my condition and the immense pain I was still experiencing in place of total and complete transfiguration and bliss.

I fell to the ground out of involuntary necessity, and began crawling toward the silo closest to me. The short grass was wet with dew or poisons, one, and I didn't posses the bravery to venture a taste or even a smell to prove either. The duffel I carried had begun to come loose of me, and rather than drag it along like Bunyan's burden, I liberated myself of its weight and left it behind, assured that I would return for it if I somehow survived the following half-hour or so. The feeling inside me had turned to rot; like a decayed ichor had coursed through my veins and emptied into the cold pit of my stomach. For the first time ever, I longed to die. Any uncertain journey into eternity (though it filled my heart with dread), must have been less pained than the jagged, twisted knife in my belly, or the bloodied tears that welled in my eyes, or the torturous sensation I was experiencing, like being choked upon wet sand.

I began to call out, to anyone who could hear; any man or beast within earshot.

"HEEEEGRLP..." It felt like a dream. I forced out shouts with all the strength I could muster, but only whispers advocated themselves for me. The sounds that came forth from my mouth were shockingly thin and muted, which straightways frustrated me more, and caused me to strain myself in ways I never thought possible. I felt that if I were to have looked upon myself, then, I might have been undone to the point of turning away, upon seeing the redness of my face or the desperation in my bones. I tried again. The next time was much louder but not in the least bit comprehendible. I was certain that if someone had heard the sound, they would have indeed thought some poor, possessed beast was being birthed upon the lawn in great heaps of blood and other displeasurable circumstance.

It was every last ounce of strength I had left that got me to the silo where I propped myself crookedly upon a single wall of its octagonal structure and spent my last several minutes of consciousness screaming out incoherently and praying to God to save me one way or another. I had just begun to feel the dark circles enclose around my vision when I remembered faintly the last moments I had spent with Aaron in the back paddock. I saw him in front of me then, as clear as I had seen him hours before.

"...Take the straight path," he said. He seemed so real to me then. I could scarce turn my eyes from that plane of spirit that I gazed into. Then he added something I had neglected. Something I had forgotten. "...And take this." he grabbed the back of my hand, as he had before, and placed the phial inside.

"...Where does it lead?" I said aloud, there on the side of that immense structure. I recalled the answer as I stared at him and through him into nothing.

"...To me," he said.

When my focus finally shifted beyond the illusion of Aaron and landed upon my own dire reality, I rediscovered the blue canvas duffel lying there upon the grass halfway between me and the tree line. Inside was my salvation, but I had no strength left to retrieve it. I sat there and stared upon the essentially empty bag. It carried nothing of real consequence, save for one solitary item. So simple a thing;

the phial of water. I had forgotten to carry it along once I let the duffel fall away. What purpose had it served if not for that very moment, I thought, and I had missed it entirely. What a foolishly squandered existence.

I thought on Daddy and Momma; on the brothers and sisters. I thought on Marlin and the townspeople and Don Miguel; on Miles Beckins and Walter. I thought on everything that had transpired from my precautionary game with the caterpillars and the plague, all the way to the disappearance of my family beneath the calm creek waters, and I wondered why God had chose us for such a time as then. All I could fathom was that we, like Noah and his family before us, had been a part of a planned extinction. The barn might have very well been our great ark, but we had abandoned it in search of mirages on dry land. A wicked people, destined for wicked tidings. I swallowed my fate there, and felt foolish for expecting anything less than what our waywardness deserved.

I closed my eyes, rather than let them be closed for me, and ceased my vain screams of desperation. Death's hands began to take and swaddle me in its indescribable comforts. There were promises of warmth in its arms, and I readied myself for where it may take me. It was in that final moment of relinquished will, that I felt my soul begin to pass from me and into some unseen vessel; that I felt my arm fall to my side and brush past a slight and hard-fashioned object of human design which lay seated in the shallow reaches of my pocket.

By then I had nearly forgotten the members of my body or what each of them was for, but the thought of it woke me momentarily from my transit and bid me dip my hand inside my mortal garment and settle one last curiosity before rejoining my fate. My fingers recognized the small glass tube before my consciousness could. When I opened my eyes, however (something I assumed I would never do again), what I saw was that familiar phial, filled with the least bit of clear water; the very one Aaron had given me; the one I was previously most certain was in the duffel halfway across the yard. I had never removed it from my person at all. A renewed hope flooded my spirit as I uncorked the tiny chalice and drank heartily.

The effect wasn't instantaneous, to any degree. Instead, it seemed to grow a great deal worse before it got better. And that's when it happened. A battle was about to be waged for my body and soul, but I wasn't privileged enough to witness any of it with my waking eyes. In fact, the last thing I saw was the plainest set of well-endowed women I had ever laid eyes upon (save for perhaps Mamie) coming toward me with cloths to their faces and haste upon their bosoms. They wore only white, and their heads were covered on top with folded handkerchiefs. They had been in search of me, by the looks of them. They had heard my cries, but it had taken them until then to find me there. Alas, when I could see from the concern upon their faces that they meant to care for me and not kill me, I forfeit my life into their hands and fell away into a deep sleep, comfortably confident I would awake again.

16

When I did indeed open my eyes again, it wasn't to the sight or situation I had perhaps anticipated. I hadn't even slept too terribly long. It was morning; the following morning, and I knew so because I could hear modest songs of Christmas jubilation played upon a clanky upright from somewhere far below me. I was laying in an A-framed room, atop a modest pallet of quilts and pillows, with nothing covering me. Light came into the close and barren quarters from a circular window above my head. All else that existed in the room was a three-legged milking stool and my duffel, which appeared to be untouched.

I thought about how I might escape that ivory tower and make for the place where Aaron awaited me. I knew a firm word and retreat wouldn't do the trick, nor an attempt to exit unseen. Instead I would have to engage in parley with William or his wives or some representative of his folk and negotiate my own release. From the concern displayed by his women, I ventured they had taken pity on me, and would continue to, but I reasoned it was also like a woman to instinctively provide care for a dying child; especially one that had come so close to her home. Perhaps Daddy was wrong though, and William would indeed have no mercy upon me at all. Perhaps he was so deeply entrenched with The Prophet that he would arrest me to that room until I was bones.

A resurrected fear found me then. What if The Prophet was there, I thought. What if the next face through the door were to be that of the man who had laid my family to waste by means of connivery and misguided allegiance? I readied myself for whatever encounter I should have there in that house, but I certainly didn't mean for it to be in a situation where I was cornered. I at least desired the freedom to make a run for it if I should need to. I felt my clothes, then smelled them several times over. They had been taken from me, cleaned and reapplied. Someone in that house had seen me naked, and I didn't wager on it being a woman. I sat up and reached for my duffel. Not even a spell of dizziness or pain reared itself inside my head (which I straightways thought was peculiar). I didn't even bother opening the bag to take inventory of its contents. The weight felt right, and I needed to make time, so I shouldered the thing and stood to my feet without episode.

I moved for the unpainted wooden door, but was frozen in place when my foot impressed a loud creak upon the plank floor. The piano ceased in unison, and a host of bodies, including mine, proceeded to stand eerily still for what seemed ages on end, listening patient and careful for the next telling sign. I stayed in place and felt cold fear rush through my veins in utter silence. Shadows danced through the wide cracks in the floor, and I immediately detected movement. The steps and creaks and brushes upon the stairs and walls were embarrassingly loud. I had never felt as helplessly cornered in my life. There was nothing for it but to stand evenly upon my two feet and face whatever should come through that door.

Seconds later, the door shoved open, swinging towards me, just short of my toes. In its frame stood a simple man in high-waisted brown pants, a tucked, white button shirt and suspenders. He wore black boots and his head was nearly shaven. I always thought it was strange that William went without a flock of facial hairs. It was custom for men of his descent to command a formidable beard, but he did not. He stood there only as a more detailed likeness to the man I had seen in the woods the night the ewe was murdered. I pondered wildly at what the following moments would entail; what revelation, or what end.

"Tell me what happened," he spoke softly. There was a quiet concern in his voice. He stepped forward, partially closing the door behind him and gesturing for me to sit upon the stool rather than continue to stand so awkwardly close. I did. He spoke again as he remained near the door with his hands to his side. "I saw the fires and heard the duster," he said, "but what happened after?" he waited expectantly for me to answer, knowing I would in time. Tears found my eyes familiarly.

"...We went to the creek to wait on The Prophet," I said, noticing William wince mildly at the name. "The townsfolk took our farm and razed it. When The Prophet finally showed, He..." I stalled for fear of the ludicrous words upon my tongue.

"He walked on the water," William finished solemnly. I looked up at him and was straightways stunned by his

composure. "I assume your family and the pastor are dead."
I nodded. Shamefully, my concern was less on the passing
of my family and more on his failure to include Stagwerth
in his assumption.

"Are you with Him?" I asked. William inhaled deeply
and exhaled with contemplation.

"I was, once—"

"—but I seen you the other night," I interrupted.

"Keeping up appearances," he replied. "I've been aware
of the danger of Stagwerth for some time."

"What about your wives—I mean, your family?" William took another deep breath.

"It's only me," he smiled slightly and sideways.

"How do you mean?" I questioned.

"I mean, I'm alone," he said. I stopped. The potential
reality of such a statement had me floored. There was such
a rich lore about William and his family ingrained into my
upbringing. What could it have meant, I wondered.

"What about the women who brought me in last
night?"

"I found you this morning," he answered. I thought
about the image of the women with the covered heads. I
had seen visions before. I supposed delirium could have
induced the imagined rescue. For the moment, I pretended
his word was gospel.

"What about the torches on the pasture? And Mamie?" I asked.

"There have been visitors from time to time," he
replied, looking toward the window. "Travelers I was fortunate enough to intercede with before they had a chance
to meet your family. I suppose the most unforgivable thing,
however, would be my failure to save them."

"Who?" I asked.

"Your family." his face returned to mine as he continued. "Mamie, I could never quite keep away. Her curiosity of the man's power was too fervent."

"How'd she never find you out?"

"Because I knew she would kill me if I ever let her," he replied, drawing my memory to Walter and Mr. Langford. "I kept to myself and convinced her my place was here, protecting the woods."

As difficult as it was to believe, Daddy's claims of William Justice had been shored up against his own testimony, and the unsavory legends about him had been straightways cast out of my mind in favor of the proven man who then stood before me. I trusted him, as Daddy said I would.

"They're not all gone," I mentioned. William cocked his head.

"Well there's no way to know Stagwerth is gone, save for dragging the creek—" he said coldly. "Who else do you mean?"

"...My brother, Aaron. He's alive."

"Where is he?" William asked. Part of me was still reluctant to give Aaron's whereabouts to a stranger, but I knew it might have been the only way of convincing William to let me go to him.

"...Old Pinehelm," I answered.

"Pinehelm," he repeated.

"Yessir. I reckon that's where the straight path leads, and I reckon that's where he is."

"You don't sound sure," he said.

"I'm not sure I'm right," I answered, "but you are." We stared at each other for a good second until he finally spoke.

"Ok." William breathed again. "Let's get you a horse."

"What?" I asked, stunned at the man's kindness of intention.

"Your horse," William replied. "Unless you mean to walk…"

"…But everything's dead and gone."

"Not in these parts," William corrected with his hand on the door. "Miles Beckins may have been a lost soul, intent on fulfilling the evil bidding of a mad man, but darkness wields no victory over living water." With that, my eyes widened, and William Justice disappeared down the staircase, leaving the door wide ajar behind him. I shouldered my duffel and followed.

The rest of William's house was unlike my previous quarters. It was plain as paper, but still looked lived in. We passed through one stairwell, which led to a short hall with two doors. Lastly we passed through a final stairwell which led to the living area. I could manage then to prove with my eyes that he was indeed the only soul living there. All was clean and tidy, but tailored to suit one man's needs and preferences, with things placed in unusually practical places. The clanky upright sat unplayed near the bottom of the stair, and the house was filled with all manner of curious and simplistic items that I greatly wished to study. There was no time to stop and look around, however, as William was out the front door as soon as I had left the last step.

It wasn't until I had gone out on William's lawn in full stride beneath a high and warm sun that I realized I was breathing clean air. I reckoned it was close to 9:00AM, by the looks of things, and the day was still cool, despite the contrasted warmth upon my face. It was easily the clearest day I had seen in a good while. I would have even gone as far to say it was beautiful, if it wasn't for the stench of death carried along with it. Somewhere far out on County Road 1, the toll had undoubtedly risen over night, despite me and Daddy's earlier efforts to preempt it. Just as the homes on that well-traversed path seemed to number more densely as it came closer to town, so I expected the aftermath had raised right alongside it in the wake of The Prophet's plan. Even in my imagination, it was too terrible to dwell on.

"This way," William said as he led me in a quick walk to the side door of his barn. There at the end of a short corridor, I noticed several jugs of water; not the phials from the crates I was used to, but large, translucent vessels gathered together on the dirt floor. "Right here," William interjected, as if to disrupt my observations. I looked to my right and noticed the brown and white painted head of a mild beast who stared back at me with ebon eyes of fidelity, and I knew then, it would be the creature to bear me to my brother. I approached the colt and rubbed its massive jowls with my palm, careful to stay to his side, lest I be pummeled head-on by his titanic skull.

William had gone and returned with a saddle before I could take notice. He was dangerously efficient and never dawdled, eager to do business where business was needed. I took several steps back as the immense creature was walked out of his stall and ground-tied with a bridle.

"What's his name?" I asked.

"He doesn't have one," William replied as he hoisted the saddle into place, atop a layer of blankets, and tightened the belts vigorously beneath.

"Why not?" I asked, shocked that anyone would allow such a beautiful thing to go uncalled for any length of time.

"It's not my custom," he said. "A name incites materialism."

"A name's important," I replied as William held my duffel and gave me a leg up into the first stirrup. "It's all I got now..." William looked up at me as I sat there, and I knew the deep pain he felt for me in his heart. It was written genuinely upon his face as he made his way to the other side.

"...This one," he said, patting my right foot as I sunk it into the other stirrup. He then handed me my duffel, which I hung around the saddle horn. Last, William yoked a set of water jugs onto the back of the saddle and made sure they were even. "In case you get thirsty," he added. I nodded. "There's a trail that starts at the northwest corner of the pond," he said. "It leads right up past the sanctuary and fades away just before your family's tree line. Should be easy enough to follow during the day."

"Yessir," I confirmed.

"Don't linger there, Moses..." he implored gently. I wondered how the man had known my name, but it wasn't much of a stretch to assume he knew me the same way I knew him. "Stick to the tree line, and get to the straight path. There's nothing left for you there..." his instructions were followed by a strict silence that lasted a moment.

"...I'll bring your horse back," I said.

"No need," William replied. "He knows the way." I smiled plainly. "Now go," he said.

I was off then with a gentle nudge, out of the barn and cantering steadily along the yard toward the pond. I turned and looked back at William Justice, standing there in his plain clothes and black boots; my short-lived Samaritan. I hoped in my heart of hearts I would see him again, and I hoped that when I did, we might know each other as friends.

The pond was almost rectangular, flanked on all sides by only a narrow strip of thoroughfare. I might have almost believed it was manmade, if it wasn't for the condition and isolation of the body. As I rode by, I took note of how the surface was covered more in greenery than open water. The grass was so dense, I could scarce make out the edge of the pond, save for when my mount stepped too far to one side. Soon enough, I could make out the path William had spoken of, there in the corner of the surrounding trees. It was well-worn, as if he had used it regularly to cross into our land (which seemed to frighten me briefly). It was more so a footpath than a horse path, but as we traveled further onward, the way seemed to blossom and open up wider, making itself more breathable to ride upon.

I had no desire to make my way slowly through that haunted landscape. It was the place where my family had worshipped and died. The place where a madman had walked and wooed travelers into lifetimes of servitude. A place that had been burned black and played host to dark quorums of ill intent. Even as the morning light cascaded through the withered treetops, its beauty was tainted and turned villainous beneath the cursed deeds of its tenants. I kicked, and was swept up the path with alarming speed. It wasn't long before I realized which of us were in control of the passage. Eventually, I obliged to lower myself into a tightened grip and allow my host to carry me at his own impulses through that forsaken wild.

In no time, we were free of the woodland grasp and had stopped with intent at the foot of the back pasture, where I felt the painted beast beneath me pant voluminously. It was merely a purposed respite, one quarter way through the journey. Though the sight of hillocks and open sky was familiar to me, it felt as if I had not seen it in some years. The place was less burdened by the weight of dead things as I had half expected. I reckoned the boarded horses had all been slain where they stood in their predetermined tombs beneath cover of the barn. Perhaps Daddy had found it more appropriate than letting them die lose upon the pasture in so many great lumps of rot for the birds to carry away. It was a tedious chore for anything but the slow passing of time.

In contrast to the hillocks expressly lacking in death, the edges of the great, round vista was tattered with towers of smoke and billows of smog, struck gray and brown across the cloudless sky. The smell had reached me in the most unwelcome of ways; a polluted scent of smoldering waste and burned refuse. It was undoubtedly the smell of our house and belongings devoured in flames and lingering soullessly in bitter notes upon the air. One pillar of tar-black smoke, however, did distinguish itself against the many shades of plumage about the rim of the trees. It was animated and thin and rose higher than any of the rest; tight and dark where it began, and softly unfurled where it disappeared into a translucent delta a thousand feet up.

In a single impulsive moment, I led the colt to the top of the next hillock to see if I could make out from where the black smoke was rising. It took until I had crested the next three hills before I could begin to gather my thesis. At first, I thought it was the bunker fire, relit with some noxious fuel, but as we crept closer, it was the color of things that began to change my mind. I scanned the perimeter of the back pasture, making sure I wasn't observed or followed by any ghost or set of dead eyes that had returned from the ordeal to wreak awful vengeance upon the last living soul in Indian River. I looked back at the bottom of the pasture; to the straight path, which didn't seem terribly far. I kept it in view as I kicked and felt the colt carry me off toward the fire. I reckoned if I could just manage to keep the tree line accessible, I would be ok venturing from the path as William had petitioned me not to.

Like I said, it was the color of things that drew me along to the base of that incendiary wreckage. My eyes were drunk upon it; the shining red metals, all dislodged at the joints and strewn about the scene in many scooped heaps of black soil. The place smelled of earth and burned fuel, and I read the first words my eyes fell upon. There, half buried in the ground, written on perhaps the largest piece of discernible debris were the words, ST. SIMON'S, and I knew then I was looking into the open grave of a suicidal zealot. The Harbinger must have ditched his plane there the night before, in terrible guilt I reckoned, after visiting his contemptible tidings upon the people of Indian River. I dared not look any closer, lest I see his burned and corrupted body still seated upon that winged steed of doom and never forget it.

It was only then, as I turned the horse south to carry me away from that scene of vile confirmation, that I saw him there with his eyes upon me; not Miles Beckins (or any man I knew by name, for that matter), but one I had only encountered once before. I had met him on a sour cold evening, late after chores, down by the road. He had spied me from the gate and startled me proper. Even there, in daylight, upon the pasture, I was unable to make out the whole of his face, just the same as that night. I had rebuked him then, when he had asked me for bread and water. It was a reflex, as I had felt threatened and was in immediate need of a way to assert myself as one not to be trifled with.

"What says The Boy Beyond the Gate?" he asked with an immediate brand of inquisition I had not expected so frankly. I paused visibly and quaked inside. The man's appearance was enough to shatter me. The oversized hood about his head was from the dark raincoat he wore beneath his olive military issue coat. He wasn't dirty as one might expect of a vagrant, but the yellowed corners of his eyes seemed to emanate with a feline glow that rendered the protective walls of my conscious completely undone.

I choked on words, though I had no idea what I was attempting to say.

"That's ok, boy," he said, gesturing low with his hand. "Best not spoil it with too many words." The vagrant then motioned to the wreckage. "It's all over now." I attempted to interject.

"Beckins were a lost soul—"

"—He were?" the vagrant demanded, then laughed slightly. "And where are the rest of 'em?" I caught myself look to the trees, then turned my head back fast.

"...Burned up in the house," I lied.

"Burned up in the house..." he repeated, looking down and scrubbing his boots against a patch of upturned soil. "Burned up in the house..." The man's voice trailed away and I felt the situation at hand had reached the limits of uneasiness. I feared that at any moment then, the vagrant would snatch me down off my horse and drag me into the trees to have his way on me. If it wasn't for him standing in my direct path, I might have immediately trotted past him and left him to his own suspicions. After all, the house and lands were rightfully his then. He had been the last left alive to claim it, and neither me nor any other soul had the foothold to challenge him.

I aimed to leave before he felt the least bit threatened by my presence. I wanted no part in that piece of ill-wrought acreage. That was all it was to me then; wickedness and folly.

"I'll be on now," I said, skirting the colt to the left of the vagrant. I kept my eyes forward, like a man falsifying his own confidence and comfort. It didn't seem to alert him, however, and though I felt his eyes upon me, I was past him in no time, unchecked and in the direction of the straight path and Pinehelm to see my brother at last. I found it queer that he said nothing to me in parting. Then, as if on cue with my thoughts, the sound of his voice stopped me. My eyes closed shut. Why couldn't I just continue on, I begged of myself. It was the fear of perceived panic what stayed my pace and kept me from kicking that horse into full retreat. I didn't aim to be read as weak or afraid, so I stilled myself. When at first the man spoke, I hoped beyond hope it was a misinterpretation that lingered on the air. Then, with my back turned, I heard it again as it echoed in my mind.

"This land is closed to the wretched." I bit the inside of my cheek until I tasted blood.

Before I could even manage to look back and show him the shame of my face, the painted colt collapsed beneath me. A pitched crack dispersed loudly into all four corners of the pasture and deepened itself as it returned seconds later. The impact of the ground was paltry compared to the sheer dead tonnage which landed upon me, crushing my pelvis to shards and wrenching the bones of my legs into every unholy direction. The blow was followed by an enflamed torment which then bored its way through my abdomen in rhythmic pulsations of indescribable pain and found its way even to the soles of my feet. I stared momentarily at the sun and groaned involuntarily as I felt things occur below my waste that I had not the constitution to dwell upon. With every beat of my heart against that cold ground, I felt rivers of blood empty from me, somewhere beneath that dead beast, and spill away into the dead soils.

The next thing I saw were the boots of the vagrant moving towards me in slow, confident steps. He squatted low, but said nothing. It might have ruined the poetry of it all; the beautiful irony of the encounter. And though he had likely missed his target, he was a more thoughtful man than that, I could tell. I lay as still as possible, as if to appear dead or nearly there. The truth was, I might not have required much more in the way of performance, though it was a comfort to tell myself I only pretended to be on the last strands of life. I forgot to pray then, as I often did in dire times. I thought only of Aaron, and how it was then quite unlikely I would make it to Pinehelm. I thought of how he would never know what became of me, save for him maybe stumbling upon me some day whilst wandering the long-forgotten paths of the farm. Perhaps he would find my cold bones intertwined with those of the horse, and he would wonder who I was.

Time slipped from me then. I closed my eyes for a brief bit of recovery, and when I opened them again, the vagrant was gone. He had unintentionally stumbled upon a scenario that pleased him more than if he were to have actually hit me. I supposed it was the thought of me dying a slow death that suited him better. Maybe he reckoned we were even. Either way, he was an evil sonuvabitch and I didn't feel it was called for. There on my back, I looked into the sky and saw no sign of the smoke in my periphery; only a pale blue ring around a black sun. Momma had told me never to look directly into the sun on a count of it having the power to blind me, but that was what it looked like, for the record, after the tears, of course. I was dying anyhow.

I slipped away again and returned, feeling cold as ice. The black sun hadn't moved but an inch, and I had already forgotten its warmth. Of course there were shivers and cold sweats and all one might imagine in the last few prolonged moments of life, but I had already died once the night previous and it was worse the first time. I completely forgot the pain after my third short sleep and return. Instead, all I felt then was the dull beat of my pulse emanated through my legs and groin, finished off with a subtle burn that faded almost instantaneously. I was numb to the true pain, and I was right thankful for that. I did attempt just a single push against the colt's dead meat, just to say I had, but it was utter vanity. Not even five men the size of Don Miguel could have done it. A tractor might have done the job.

That was the most frightful part; not the pain or the thought of what the lower half of me must have looked like, but the claustrophobic nature of it all. That helpless sensation of inescapable restraint. I had been so close to being rid of it; the secrecy, the sorrow, the indiscernible neglect, and there I was trapped beneath a thousand pounds of my own deliverance. I heard somewhere, like most, that life flashes before one's eyes before they go. That was my last and greatest fear; experiencing it all over again in any fashion, even a quick one. I closed my eyes to see if it was true, but dreamt of nothing. I began to fear in my sleep that I wasn't in fact wounded enough to die from blood loss or a severed vertebrae. Instead, I feared I might be led to perish from starvation or dehydration, days from then. And I waited.

It could have been hours later. It could have been minutes. There was no way to measure the span of ages except for the slow ticking of the sun and the evolutions of different stages of pain. I had already passed into unknown realms of discomfort and become mostly numb, but there were still strange sensations occurring in and around my body, and I assumed it had been ten or twenty minutes since I had experienced something familiar or normal. I became increasingly aware of my lack of knowledge concerning how to go about dying. Not the knowledge to die gracefully, but the procedure behind how to get on with it all. The bottom half of me was in disrepair, and I reckoned there were no signs of rescue until law enforcement from another municipality caught literal wind of the incident in Indian River and came investigating.

I reckoned the best manner in which to speed up the process was to rid myself of residual energy, and perhaps even free myself by some miracle in the process. I raised up with my two arms, which were still good by any definition, and began to negotiate with the lower half of me wedged beneath the horse. Even if my legs were to have been torn completely from me, I figured I would have been in a better scenario for living or dying than I was previously, which was why I straightways pretended not to hear the pops and crunches that accompanied each heave and every ho, and instead went on straining myself into exhaustion. My plan had begun to work, I was sure of it. Less than a minute of the futile repetitions had me collapsed back upon the dirt, no more free than I had expected to be, and utterly spent.

I had never once felt energy evacuated from me in such hurried loads. All I could manage to do was close my eyes and breathe deep, in full expectation that I was ready to pass, and as far as I could tell, I did. I stayed fully conscious behind my eyes, but was then (for lack of a proper word) transported beyond myself and into some place full of visions I couldn't rightly manage to interpret; items and vistas and colors completely unfamiliar and indescribable to me. Suddenly I could no longer recall my name or where I had been before. I was completely alone, save for the feeling that I was accompanied by some invisible host of beings. The sounds were the same as the place from where I had traveled. It was the only thing besides part of my consciousness that had gone with me to that strange new place. There was also the familiar recollection of strict disinformation of the world around me, and I realized that even in death, I was without the luxury of omniscience.

Then, as if I had become too self aware of the dream space I inhabited, I felt myself returning to awake, and I thought it was too soon. Part of me desired to fight off the awareness that was washing over me, and yet another part of me wished to return to familiarity (or what I at least assumed to be familiar). As I opened my eyes and recalled the despondent circumstance beneath which I laid, my heart was straightways warmed in realizing the black sun above me wasn't the sun at all, but rather, the silhouetted shape of my brother looking down upon me. I moved my arms to feel him there, kneeling beside me. His hands had been on my chest, even as I awoke.

"There you are," he said. "Damn."

"Aaron..." I mumbled.

"How could someone be so dumbassed and ignorant," he remarked. I smirked faintly. "I give you simple instructions, real simple, and here I find you, crushed to hell under the Mennonite's horse." Aaron stood and went around the other side of the dead colt, attempting to dislodge me from the most inopportune position possible. He strained once and then breathed. "Where the hell have you been?"

"I think I'm dyin' here," I said.

"Horseshit," Aaron replied abruptly. "I'm gonna get the tractor." He was off then in the direction of the old barn, but before he was too far, I raised my arm high and I slapped and earth violently with a loud thud.

"Aaron!" he stopped with his back to me and his head hung low, fully aware of the vanity in his intention. He knew I was dead no matter what, same as me. My internal organs were crushed and punctured. "Don't leave me again," I said. He observed the situation. We both knew the second the horse was lifted from me would be the second it all fell apart. The weight of the beast upon me was what kept me alive and made it impossible for me to die from anything but depravity.

Aaron then returned slowly to my side, but this time, collapsing into an Indian style posture near my head, intent on awaiting the arrival of what was impending.

"This horse has been shot," he observed plainly.

"...Yeah," I strained to confirm.

"How'd that happen?"

"...Doesn't matter," I grunted. Aaron shuffled around and placed his hand awkwardly on my shoulder, just as an estranged brother might have done for the first time ever. As odd a sensation as it was for both of us, there was a human comfort to it that I wagered was seldom experienced by many in life.

"It's alright," he stuttered, completely unbought by his own words. I noticed my breathing had become shaky.

"Daddy and Momma are—"

"—I know," Aaron interrupted. He breathed once and looked off in any direction but mine. "I seen 'em early this mornin'." In my mind I imagined what Aaron must have witnessed along the banks of the creek; their bodies bloated and blue, tangled amongst the cyprus knees in various clumps where they had been caught by some fallen tree, like cigarette butts on a windy street.

My voice cracked as I offered up a condolence that, for some strange reason, felt fair to me then.

"Sorry about Sarah," I said. Aaron kept his eyes on the distant trees, almost pretending not to have heard me. There was silence for a moment, shortly followed by a loud slurp and violent wiping motion from my brother as he removed his hand from my shoulder and dried his face under cover. I panicked for lack of proper words to offer. "I know she meant a lot...to you."

"It ain't her," Aaron almost gasped (mostly at himself for allowing his emotions to carry him away so quick). His face was flushed and overly dry for its color. I watched him trap every tear in the sleeve of his shirt and realized Aaron Cotton had had a worse time with the loss of Daddy and Momma than even I had. Rightly so. He was closer with them, sharing in some of their more cumbersome secrets from the beginning, and in their allegiance to The Man in the Woods, of course. Aaron had left the farm that night in a rather unfavorable fashion. I reckoned he knew he was struck from Daddy and Momma's good graces for it. That didn't sit right with him. Not only had he neglected them, he had neglected their collective obligation, and I could see he didn't aim to let a repeat occurrence happen with me.

I wondered if Aaron had confirmed the death of The Prophet when he saw the rest of them there in the creek. I meant to ask but straightways felt something foreign occur inside me. My eyes were closing shut, and this time without my help or will. Aaron could tell something was wrong by my stirring. He tried his best to stabilize me with both hands on my shoulders, but it was that unsolicited blackness encircling my vision that frightened me and caused me to recoil. I could feel myself forcing my eyelids wide with every ounce of strength I had left, but the effort was only met with further darkness. I couldn't rightly understand how I had earlier been so accepting of a path accompanied by such savage panic and finality. I didn't want to die then. I didn't want to face the inescapable eternity.

I expected I only had a moment or so left of life, and even less in the way of my senses; one of which had already given out. I could hear Aaron speaking to me, negotiating with me to accept my fate with grace and bravery, though I was unsure if any of it was real. His efforts, however, did succeed somewhat.

"It's ok, Moses! It's ok." I saw his blurred and teary eyes lingering there for a moment; just long enough to hear him make his final peace with me; something he had never taken the courage to do with any soul before (and something he would never know I heard). "I'm sorry, brother. I should have been better," he said. "I'm sorry." It gave me great comfort that he would at least have that. I longed to reassure him of his fixed place in my heart as the only constant friend and kindred spirit I had ever known, but it felt as if I was being swept away at ten times ten thousand miles an hour, and I was helplessly without control of my own impulses.

Man born of woman is of few days and full of trouble. That was the thought which attended me from one life into the next, and it was in such a moment, accompanied by some newly acquired transcendent awareness, that I was led to a stunning revelation. The whole thing; everything recounted of my life in the days, months and years most recent to then—every last bit—had already taken place in a time gone by. The nearest recollection of the events culminating in my death were only a well-informed shade of the time I had lived out before, occurring within that fabled span of moments between life and final death, the possibility of which I had overheard talk of in lofty conversations between men of unfettered minds. That in our final moments of life, we relive its entirety once more. It was surely something to behold for a time, but the revelation passed, as did everything else; replaced by nothing less than grander understandings and divine disclosures, the greatest of which was God's will for me, my brother, my family and our existence on that farm.

THE END

NICK MAY

SELECTIVE SERVICE SYSTEM
NOTICE TO DISREGARD ORDER
FOR INDUCTION

CO: Moses M. Cotton
23 County Road 1
Indian River, FL
32465
March 14, 1966

Dear Mr. Cotton:

I have your letter from March 3, wherein you stated your
brother, Aaron L. Cotton was recently deceased as a
result of the events which occurred in Indian River on
December 24 and 25.

I am writing to inform you that while we are grieved for
your loss and greatly appreciate your offer to serve in
Aaron's absence, we are unable to oblige, given your ineli-
gibility due to unmet age requirements.

I have personally seen to it that Aaron L. Cotton's expi-
ration has been noted in our records. Thank you for your
timely response.

Respectfully,

Norman Barley

Clerk of Local Board No. 1
United States Army

 **Different?**

Off the beaten track?

 **Positively Weird?**

But it's solid art?

Look for it!
Publish it!
at
Eucatastrophe Press
eucatastrophepress.com

More fiction from Energion Publications Imprints

Enzar Empire Press

Tales from Jevlir: Oddballs	Henry E. Neufeld	$9.99

enzarempire.com

Eucatastrophe Press

Megabelt (2nd Edition)	Nick May	$12.99
Minutemen (2nd Edition)	Nick May	$12.99
The Fringe (forthcoming in 2015)	Renee Crosby	$9.99

eucatastrophepress.com

Energion Publications

Allegheny Hideaway	Kimberly Gordon	$16.99
Covenant	Daniel Martin	$17.99
Please Love Me	Kimberly Gordon	$14.99
Prayer Trilogy	Kimberly Gordon	$9.99
The Traveler's Advance	Heath Taws	$14.99
Stories of the Way	Henry E. Neufeld	$9.99

energion.com

Generous Quantity Discounts Available
Dealer Inquiries Welcome
Energion Publications — P.O. Box 841
Gonzalez, FL 32560
Website: energion.com
Phone: (850) 525-3916